A FALL OF PRINCES

VOLUME THREE OF AVARYAN RISING

Tor Books by Judith Tarr

JUDITH TARR

A FALL OF PRINCES

VOLUME THREE OF AVARYAN RISING

TOR

A FALL OF PRINCES

Copyright © 1988 by Judith Tarr

First printing: April 1988

A TOR Book

Published by Tom Doherty Associates, Inc.
49 West 24th Street
New York, NY 10010

ISBN: 0-312-93063-1

Library of Congress Catalog Card Number: 87-51392

Printed in the United States of America

0 9 8 7 6 5 4 3 2 1

To

The Yale Department of Medieval Studies
The Orange Street Gang in all its permutations
And, of course, all the Faithful

But for whom, et cetera.

A Note on Pronunciation

Asanian is a tonal language, written in complex and highly precise characters. My transliteration of Asanian names is therefore, of necessity, enormously simplified, and adapted to the usage of names in the eastern languages, particularly Ianyn and the Gileni speech of Keruvarion's heart. In essence:

•Consonants are essentially as in English. *C* and *G* are always hard, as in *can* and *gold*, never soft as in *cent* and *gem*. *S* is always as in *hiss*, never as in *his*. *Ch* is always hard (*chaos*), never soft (*children*): Asuchirel is pronounced ah-SOO-khee-REL.

•Vowels are somewhat different from the English. *A* as in *father:* Sarevadin is sah-ray-VAH-din; Aranos is ah-RAH-nos. *E* as in Latin *Dei:* Elian is AY-lee-ahn; Han-Gilen is hahn-gee-LAYN. *I* is much as the English *Y:* consider *hymn* and the suffix *-ly,* and the consonantal *yawn:* hence, Ianon is YAH-non; Ziad-Ilarios is zee-AHD-ee-LAH-ree-os; Hirel is hee-REL. *O* as in *owe,* not as in *toss*. *U* as in Latin, comparable to English *oo* (*look, loom*): Uverias is oo-VAIR-ee-ahss.

•*Ei* is pronounced as in *reign:* Geitan is GAY-tahn. *Ai,* except in the archaic and anomalous Mirain (mee-RAYN), is comparable to the English *bye:* Shon'ai is SHOWN-aye. Otherwise, paired vowels are pronounced separately: Asanion is pronounced ah-SAH-nee-on.

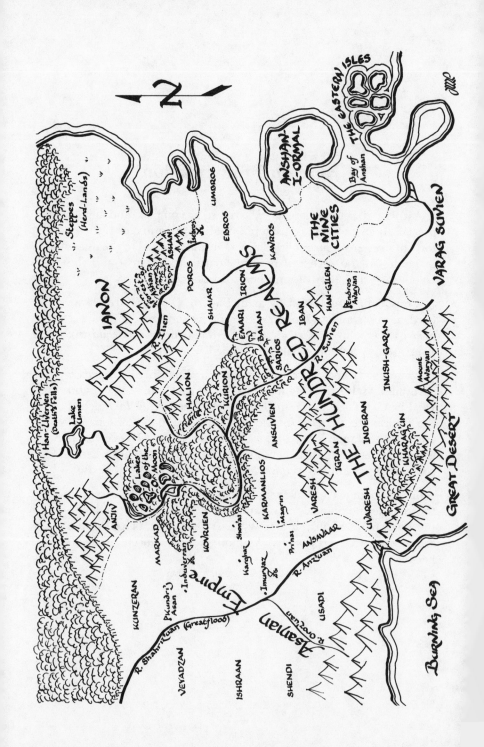

PART ONE

Asuchirel inZiad Uverias

One

THE HOUNDS HAD VEERED AWAY WESTWARD. THEIR BAYING swelled and faded as the wind shifted; the huntsman's horn sounded, faint and deadly.

Hirel flattened himself in his nest of spicefern. His nose was full of the sharp potent scent. His body was on fire. His head was light with running and with terror and with the last of the cursed drug with which they had caught him. Caught him but not held him. And they were gone. Bless that wildbuck for bolting across his path. Bless his brothers' folly for hunting him with half-trained pups.

He crawled from the fernbrake, dragging a body which had turned rebel. Damned body. It was all over blood. Thorns. Fangs—one hound had caught him, the one set on guard by his prison. It was dead. He hurt. Some fool of a child was crying, softly and very near, but this was wild country, border country, and he was alone. It was growing dark.

The dark lowered and spread wide, shifted and changed, took away pain and brought it back edged with sickness. The sky was full of stars. Branches rimmed it; he had not seen them before.

3

The air carried a tang of fire. Hirel blinked, frowned. And burst upward in a flood of memory, a torrent of panic terror.

Those were not cords that bound him, but bandages wrapped firmly where he hurt most. But for them he was naked; even the rag of his underrobe was gone, all else left behind in the elegant cell in which he had learned what betrayal was. He dropped in an agony of modesty, coiling about his center, shaking forward the royal mane—but that was gone, his head scraped bare as a slave's, worst of all shames even under sheltering arms.

The fire snapped a branch in two. The shadow by it was silent. Hirel's pride battered him until he raised his eyes.

The shadow was a man. Barbarian, Hirel judged him at once and utterly. Even sitting on his heels he was tall, trousered like a southerner but bare above like a wild tribesman from the north, and that black-velvet skin was of the north, and that haughty eagle's face, and the beard left free to grow. But he held to a strange fashion: beard and long braided hair were dyed as bright as the copper all his kind were so fond of. Or—

Or he was born to it. His brows were the same, and his lashes; the fire caught glints of it on arms and breast and belly as he rose. He was very tall. For all that Hirel's will could do, his body cowered, making itself as small as it might.

The barbarian lifted something from the ground and approached. His braid had fallen over his shoulder. It ended below his waist. His throat was circled with gold, a torque as thick as two men's fingers, and a white band bound his brows. Priest. Priest of the demon called Avaryan and worshipped as the Sun; initiate of the superstition that had overwhelmed the east of the world. He knelt by Hirel, his face like something carved in stone, and he dared. He touched Hirel.

Hirel flung himself against those blasphemous hands, screaming he cared not what, striking, kicking, clawing with nails which his betrayers had not troubled to rob him of. All his fear and all his grief and all his outrage gathered and battled and hated this stranger who was not even of the empire. Who had found him and tended him and presumed to lay unhallowed hands on him.

Who held him easily and let him flail, only evading the strokes of his nails.

He stopped all at once. His breath ached in his throat; he felt cold and empty. The priest was cool, unruffled, breathing without strain. "Let me go," Hirel said.

The priest obeyed. He stooped, took up what he had held before Hirel sprang on him. It was a coat, clean but not fresh, tainted with the touch of a lowborn body. But it was a covering. Hirel let the barbarian clothe him in it. The man moved lightly, careful not to brush flesh with flesh. A quick learner, that one. But his grip was still a bitter memory.

Hirel sat by the fire. He was coming to himself. "A hood," he said. "Fetch one."

A bright brow went up. It was hard to tell in firelight, but perhaps the priest's lips quirked. "Will a cap satisfy your highness?" The accent was appalling but the words comprehensible, the voice as dark as the face, rich and warm.

"A cap will do," Hirel answered him, choosing to be gracious.

Covered at last, Hirel could sit straight and eat what the priest gave him. Coarse food and common, bread and cheese and fruit, with nothing to wash it down but water from a flask, but Hirel's hunger was far beyond criticism. They had fed him in prison, but then they had purged him; he ached with emptiness.

The priest watched him. He was used to that, but the past days had left scars that throbbed under those calm dark eyes. Bold eyes in truth, not lowering before his own, touched with something very like amusement. They refused to be stared down. Hirel's own slid aside first, and he told himself that he was weary of this foolishness. "What are you called?" he demanded.

"Sarevan." Why was the barbarian so damnably amused? "And you?"

Hirel's head came up in the overlarge cap; he drew himself erect in despite of his griping belly. "Asuchirel inZiad Uverias, High Prince of Asanion and heir to the Golden Throne." He said it with all hauteur, and yet he was painfully aware, all at once, of his smallness beside this long lanky outlander, and of the lightness of his unbroken voice, and of the immensity of the world about their little clearing with its flicker of fire.

The priest shifted minutely, drawing Hirel's eyes. Both of his brows were up now, but not with surprise, and certainly not with awe. "So then, Asuchirel inZiad Uverias, High Prince of Asanion, what brings you to this backward province?"

"*You* should not be here," Hirel shot back. "Your kind are not welcome in the empire."

"Not," said Sarevan, "in this empire. You are somewhat across the border. Did you not know?"

Hirel began to tremble. No wonder the hounds had turned away. And he—he had told this man his name, in this man's own country, where the son of the Emperor of Asanion was a hostage beyond price. "Kill me now," he said. "Kill me quickly. My brothers will reward you, if you have the courage to approach them. Kill me and have done."

"I think not," the barbarian said.

Hirel bolted. A long arm shot out. Once more a lowborn hand closed about him. It was very strong. Hirel sank his teeth into it. A swift blow jarred him loose and all but stunned him.

"You," said Sarevan, "are a lion's cub indeed. Sit down, cubling, and calm your fears. I'm not minded to kill you, and I don't fancy holding you for ransom."

Hirel spat at him.

Sarevan laughed, light and free and beautifully deep. But he did not let Hirel go.

"You defile me," gritted Hirel. "Your hands are a profanation."

"Truly?" Sarevan considered the one that imprisoned Hirel's wrist. "I know it's not obvious, but I'm quite clean."

"I am the high prince!"

"So you are." No, there was no awe in that cursed face. "And it seems that your brothers would contest your title. Fine fierce children they must be."

"They," said Hirel icily, "are the bastards of my father's youth. I am his legitimate son. I was lured into the marches on a pretext of good hunting and fine singing and perhaps a new concubine." The black eyes widened slightly; Hirel disdained to take notice. "And I was to speak with a weapons master in Pri'nai and a philosopher in Karghaz, and show the easterners my face. But my brothers—" He faltered. This was pain. It must not be. It should be anger. "My dearest and most loyal brothers had found themselves a better game. They drugged my wine at the welcoming feast in Pri'nai, corrupted my taster and so captured me. I escaped. I took a senel, but it fell in the rough country and broke its neck. I ran. I did not know that I had run so far."

"Yes." Sarevan released him at last. "You are under your father's rule no longer. The Sunborn is emperor here."

"That bandit. What is he to me?" Hirel stopped. So one always said in Asanion. But this was not the Golden Empire.

The Sun-priest showed no sign of anger. He only said, "Have a care whom you mock here, cubling."

"I will do as I please," said Hirel haughtily.

"Was it doing as you please that brought you to the west of Karmanlios in such unroyal state?" Sarevan did not wait for an answer. "Come, cubling. The night is speeding, and you should sleep."

To his own amazement, Hirel lay down as and where he was told, wrapped in a blanket with only his arm for a pillow. The ground was brutally hard, the blanket thin and rough, the air growing cold with the fickleness of spring. Hirel lay and cursed this insolent oaf he had fallen afoul of, and beat all of his clamoring pains into submission, and slid into sleep as into deep water.

"Well, cubling, what shall we do with you?"

Hirel could barely move, and he had no wish to. He had not known how sorely he was hurt, in how many places. But Sarevan had waked him indecently early, droning hymns as if the sun could not rise of itself but must be coaxed and caterwauled over the horizon, washing noisily and immodestly afterward in the stream that skirted the edge of the clearing, and squatting naked to revive the fire. With the newborn sun on him he looked as if he had bathed in dust of copper. Even the down of his flanks had that improbable, metallic sheen.

He stood over Hirel, shameless as an animal. "What shall we do with you?" he repeated.

Hirel averted his eyes from that proud and careless body, and tried not to think of his own that was still so much a child's. "You may leave me. I do not require your service."

"No?" The creature sat cross-legged, shaking his hair out of its sodden braid, attacking it with a comb he had produced from somewhere. He kept his eyes on Hirel. "What will you do, High Prince of Asanion? Walk back to your brothers? Stay here and live on berries and water? Seek out the nearest village? Which, I bid you consider, is a day's hard walk through wood and field, and where people are somewhat less accommodating than I. Even if they would credit your claim to your title, they have no reason to love your kind. Golden demonspawn they call you, and yellow-eyed tyrants, and scourges of free folk. At the very least they would stone you. More likely they would take you prisoner and see that you died as slowly as ever your enemies could wish."

"They would not dare."

"Cubling." It was a velvet purr. "You are but the child of a thousand years of emperors. He who rules here is the son of a very god. And he can be seen unmasked even upon his throne, and any peasant's child may touch him if she chooses, and he is not defiled. On the contrary. He is the more holy for that his people love him."

"He is an upstart adventurer with a mouthful of lies."

Sarevan laughed, not warmly this time, but clear and cold. His long fingers began the weaving of his braid, flying in and out through the fiery mane. "Cubling, you set a low price on your life. How will you be losing it, then? Back in Asanion or ahead in Keruvarion?"

Hirel's defiance flared and died. Hells take the man, he had a clear eye. One very young prince alone and naked and shaven like a slave—if he could win back to Kundri'j Asan he might have hope, if his father would have him, if the court did not laugh him to his death. But it was a long way to the Golden City, and his brothers stood between. Vuad and Sayel whom he had trusted, whom he had allowed himself to admire and even to love. To whom, after all, he had been no more than he was to anyone: an obstacle before his father's throne.

If it had been Aranos . . .

Aranos would not have failed so far of his vigilance as to let Hirel escape. If Aranos joined in this clever coil of a plot, Aranos who by birth was eldest and by breeding highest save only for Hirel, every road and path and molerun would be watched and guarded. Hirel would never come to his city. And this time he would die.

He would not. He was high prince. He would be emperor.

But first he had to escape this domain of the man called An-Sh'Endor, Son of the Morning, lord of the eastern world in the name of his false god. Whose priest sat close enough to touch, tying off the end of his braid and stretching like a great indolent cat. He rose in one flowing movement, and went without haste to don shirt and trousers and boots, belting on a dagger and a sword. He looked as if he knew how to use them.

Hirel frowned. He did not like what he was thinking. He must return to Kundri'j. He could not return alone. But to ask—to trust—

Did he have a choice?

Sarevan bound his brows with the long white band. Initiate, it meant. A priest new to his torque, sent out upon the seven years' Journey that made him a full master of his order. Four disks of gold glittered on the band: four years done, three yet to wander before he could rest.

"Priest," Hirel said abruptly, "I choose. You will escort me to Kundri'j Asan. I will see that no one harms you; I will reward you when I come to the palace."

Sarevan's head tilted. His eyes glinted. "You do? I shall? You will?"

Hirel clapped his hands. "Fetch my breakfast. I will bathe after."

"No," said the barbarian quite calmly, quite without fear. "I do not fetch. I am not a servant. There is bread in my scrip, and you may have the last of the cheese. As for the other, I have in mind to go westward for a little distance, and I suppose I can suffer your company."

Hirel could not breathe for outrage. Never—never in all his life—

"Be quick, cubling, or I leave you behind."

Hirel ate, though he choked. Bathed himself with his own cold and shaking hands, aware through every instant of the back turned ostentatiously toward him. Pulled on the outsize coat and the ill-fitting cap, and found a cord with the scrip, which perforce did duty as a belt. Almost before it was tied, the scrip was slung from an insolent shoulder, the priest striding long-legged out of the clearing. Hirel raged, but he pressed after.

It was not easy. Hirel's feet were bare and that was royal, but they had never trodden anywhere but on paths smoothed before them; and he had done them no good in his running, and this land, though gentler than the stones and thorns of his flight, was not the polished paving of his palace. And he was wounded with thorn and fang, and still faintly ill from poison and purging, and Sarevan set a pace his shorter legs had to struggle to match. He set his teeth and saved his bitter words and kept his eye on the swing of the coppery plait. Sometimes he fell. He said nothing. His hands stung with new scratches. His knee ached.

He struck something that yielded and turned and loosed an exclamation. The hands were on him again. He spared only a little of his mind for temper, even when they gathered him up. A prince could be carried. If he permitted it. And this barbarian was strong and his stride was smooth, lulling Hirel into a stupor.

Hirel started awake. He was on the ground and he was bare again, and Sarevan had begun to unwrap his bandages. Hirel did not want to see what was under them.

"Clean," said Sarevan, "and healing well. But watch the knee, cubling. You cut it the last time you fell."

"And whose fault was that?"

"Yours," came the swift answer. "Next time you need rest, say so. You can't awe me with your hardihood. You have none. And you'll get none if you kill yourself trying to match me."

Hirel thought of hating him. But hate was for equals. Not for blackfaced redmaned barbarians.

"Up," said this one, having rebound the bandages and restored tunic and hood. "You can walk a bit; your muscles will stiffen else."

Hirel walked. Sarevan let him set the pace. Now and then he was allowed a sip of water. They ate barely enough to blunt the edge of hunger. That must suffice, said the son of stone; they might not reach the town he was aiming for before the sun set. Hirel's fault, that was clear enough. While Hirel struggled and gritted his teeth and was ignored, Sarevan sauntered easily in his boots and his honed strength, unwounded, unpampered, inured to rough living. And why should he not be? He was lowborn.

"I'm a most egregious mongrel," he said as they paused at the top of a grueling slope; and he was not even breathing hard, although he had carried Hirel on his back up the last few lengths, chattering as he went, easy as if he trod a palace floor. "I have Ianyn blood as you can well see, and my mother comes from Han-Gilen, and there's a strong strain of Asanian on both sides. And . . . other things."

Hirel did not ask what they were. Gutter rat surely, and a slave or two, and just enough mountain tribesman to give him arrogance far above his station.

He was up already, prowling as if restless, nosing among the brambles that hedged the hill. In a little while he came back with a handful of springberries, rich and ripe and wondrous sweet.

To Hirel's surprise and well-concealed relief, having eaten his share of fruit and given Hirel the water flask, Sarevan showed no sign of going on. He paced as if he waited for something or someone; he turned his face to the sun he worshipped, and sang to it. Now that Hirel was not trying to sleep, the priest's voice was pleasant to hear. More than pleasant. In fact, rather remarkable. In Asanion he would have been allowed to sing before the Middle Court; with training he might have won entry to the High Court itself.

The sun was warm in its nooning. Hirel yawned. What an oddity they would think this creature: a redheaded northerner, a sweet singer, a priest of the Sun. All the east in a man. He would fetch a great price in the market.

Hirel shivered. He did not want to think of slave markets. His hand found its way under the hood, catching on the brief new stubble. Three days now. And Vuad, Vuad whose mother was an Ormalen slave, had shaken his mud-brown hair and laughed, cheering the barber on. Vuad had never forgiven Hirel his pure blood, or the splendid hot-gold mane that went with it.

"It will grow back." Sarevan's shadow was cool, his voice soft and warm.

Hirel's teeth ground together. "Get," he said thickly. "Get your shadow off me."

It moved. Sarevan stripped off his shirt and rolled it into a bundle and laid it in his bag, apparently oblivious to the offense he had given. He went back to his pacing, tracing precise and intricate patterns like the steps of a dance, humming to himself.

He stilled abruptly, utterly. Hirel heard nothing but breeze and birdsong, saw nothing but shapeless wilderness. Trees, undergrowth, thornbrake; the stones of the slope below him. All the animals they had seen that day were small ones, harmless. None came near them now.

Sarevan made no move toward his weapons. His face in profile was intent but untainted with fear. Hirel was not comforted.

The breeze died. The bird trilled once and fell silent. In the thicket below, a shadow moved. Faded. Grew.

Hirel's mouth was burning dry. A beast of prey. A cat as large as a small senel, the color of shifting shadows, with eyes that opened and caught the sun and turned it to green fire. It poured itself over the stones, so swift and fluid that it seemed slow, advancing with clear and terrible purpose.

It sprang. Hirel threw himself flat. The grey belly arched over him, deceptively soft, touched with a faint, feline musk. He never knew why he did not break and bolt. The beast was on Sarevan, rolling on the hilltop, snarling horribly. And Hirel could not even make a sound.

The battle roared and tumbled to its end. Sarevan rose to his knees with no mark on him; and he was all a stranger, no longer the haughty wanderer but a boy with a wide white grin, arms wrapped about the neck of the monstrous, purring cat. "This," he said, light and glad and almost laughing, "is Ulan, and he says that he is not eating tender young princelings today."

Hirel found his voice at last. "What in the twenty-seven hells—"

"Ulan," repeated the barbarian with purest patience. "My friend and long companion, and a prince of the princes of cats. You owe him your life. He drew off the hounds that haunted you, and gave your hunters a fine grim trail to follow. With a bloody robe at the end of it."

Hirel clutched the earth. It was rocking; or his brain was. "You—it—"

"He," said Sarevan pointedly, "caught wind of you before you crossed the border. I tracked you. Ulan headed off the hunters."

"Why?"

Sarevan shrugged. "It seemed worth doing. Maybe the god had a hand in it. Who knows?"

"There are no gods."

One brow went up. Sarevan ran his hands over the great grey body, stroking, but searching too, as if hunting for a wound. It seemed that he did not find one. A sigh escaped him; he clasped the beast close, burying his face in the thick fur, murmuring something that Hirel could not quite catch. The cat's purr rose to a mutter of thunder.

"They think that I am dead," Hirel said, shrill above the rumbling. "Devoured. By that—"

"By an ul-cat from the fells beyond Lake Umien. That should give your enemies pause."

Hirel managed to stand. The cat blinked at him. He unclenched his fists. "They will not know. They will think of forest lions and of direwolves, and maybe of devils; they are superstitious here. But," he conceded, "it was well done."

Again Sarevan loosed that astonishing grin. "Wasn't it? Come then, cubling. Ulan will carry you, and tonight will find us with a roof over our heads. A better one even than I hoped for."

Hirel swallowed. The cat yawned, baring fangs as long as daggers. And yet, what a mount for a high prince. A prince of cats. Hirel advanced with the valor of the desperate, and the creature waited, docile as any child's pony. Its fur was thick, coarse above, heavenly soft beneath; its back held him not too awkwardly, his knees clasping the sleek sides. Its gaits were smooth, with a supple power no hoofed creature could match. Hirel could even lie down if he was careful, pillowed on the broad summit of the head between the soft ears.

Quiet, almost comfortable, he let his eyes rest on nothing in particular. Trees. Shafts of sunlight. Now and then a stream; once Ulan drank, once Sarevan filled the flask. The priest looked content, as if this quickened pace suited him, and sometimes he let his hand rest on the cat, but never on Hirel.

The sun sank. The trees thinned, open country visible beyond, hills, a ribbon of red that was a road. On a low but steep-sided hill stood a wall and in it a town. A poor enough place: a garrison, a huddle of huts and houses, a tiny market and a smithy and a wineshop, and in the center of it a small but inevitable temple.

They were seen long before they came to the gate. A child herding a flock of woolbeasts along the road glanced back, and his eyes went wide, and he flung up both his arms, waving madly. "Sa'van!" he shrilled. "Sa'van lo'ndros!"

The cry ran ahead of him, borne by children who seemed to spring from the earth. They poured out of the gate, surrounded the travelers, danced about them; and several hung themselves about Sarevan, and a few even overwhelmed Ulan. Hirel they stared at and tried to babble at, but when he did not answer, they ignored him.

Their elders came close behind, slightly more dignified but no less delighted, chattering in their barbaric tongue. Sarevan chattered back, smiling and even laughing, with a child on each shoulder and half a dozen tugging at him from below. Obviously he was known here.

Hirel sat still on Ulan's back. He was tired and he ached, and no one took the least notice of him. They were all swarming about the priest. Not a civilized man in the lot; not even the armored guards, who made no effort to disperse the crowd. Quite the opposite. Those few who did not join it looked on with indulgence.

For all the press of people, Sarevan moved freely enough, and Ulan somewhat behind carrying Hirel and a bold infant or two. One tiny brown girlchild, naked and slippery as a fish, had chosen Hirel as a prop, nor did his stiffness deter her. She was not clean. From the evidence, she had been rolling in mud with the dogs. But she clung like a leech and never knew what she clung to, and he was too taut with mortal outrage to hurl her off.

The tide cast them up at last in front of the temple. Small as it was, it boasted a full priestess. A pair of novices attended her, large-eyed solemn children in voluminous brown who might have been of either sex; but perhaps the taller, with the full and lovely mouth, was a girl. They were both staring at Sarevan as if he had been a god come to earth. But the priestess, small and round and golden-fair as an Asanian lady, met him with a smile and a word or two, and he bowed with all proper respect. Her hand rested a moment on his bright head, blessing it. Yes, she was highborn; she had the manner, and she had it as one bred to it.

Half of his own will, half of his body's weariness, Hirel slid from Ulan's back and leaned against the warm solid shoulder. The child, robbed of her prop, kept her seat easily enough, but her wail of outrage drew a multitude of eyes. Hirel drew himself up before them. Dark eyes in brown faces, and Sarevan's darkest of all, and the priestess' the golden amber of the old pure blood. Of his own. She saw what he was. She must.

Sarevan spoke, and the eyes flicked back to him, abruptly, completely. He did not speak long. He turned to Hirel. "Come," he said in Asanian. And when Hirel gathered to resist: "You may stay if you please, and no one will harm you. But I intend to rest and to eat."

Hirel drew a sharp breath. "Very well. Lead me."

The crowding commoners did not try to pass the gate, although several of the children protested loudly the loss of their mounts. Sarevan paused to tease them into smiles. When the gate closed upon them, he was smiling himself.

"Ah, lad," the priestess said in Asanian considerably better than his, "you do have a way with them."

Sarevan shrugged, laughed a little. "They have a way with me." He laid his hand on Ulan's head and not quite on Hirel's shoulder. "I have two who need feeding, and one has hurts which you should see."

Hirel could suffer her touch, the better for that Sarevan left them in a chamber of the inner temple and went away with the novices. She did not strip him unceremoniously, but undressed him properly and modestly, with his back to her, and she bathed him so with sponge and scented water, and offered a wrapping for his loins. After the barbarities he had endured, that simple decency brought him close to tears. He fought them, fumbling with the strip of cloth until he could turn and face her.

She inspected his hurts with care and without questions. "They are clean," she said at length, as Sarevan had. She wrapped the worst in fresh new bandages, left the rest to the air, and set a light soft robe upon him. As she settled the folds of it, the bare plain room in which they stood seemed to fill with light.

It was only Sarevan. He had bathed: his hair was loose, curling with damp, his beard combed into tameness, and he had found a robe much like Hirel's. He was rebinding the band of his Journey as he came; his quick eyes glanced from the priestess to Hirel and back again.

"You have done all that you should," she said, "and done it well." With a gesture she brought them both out of the antechamber into the inner temple, the little courtyard with its garden, and the narrow chamber beyond, open wide to the air and the evening, where waited the novices with the daymeal. A poor feast as Hirel the prince might have reckoned it, plain fare served with little grace, but tonight it seemed as splendid as any high banquet in Kundri'j Asan. No matter that Hirel must share it with a barbarian and a woman; he had a royal hunger and for once a complaisant stomach, and the priestess was excellent company.

Her name was Orozia; she came of an old family, the
Vinicharyas of eastern Markad. "Little though they would rejoice
to hear me confess it," she said, sipping the surprisingly good wine
and nibbling a bit of cheese. "It is not proper for the daughter of a
high house to cleave to the eastern superstition. And to vow herself
to the priesthood . . . appalling." She laughed with the merest
edge of bitterness. "My poor father! When I came to him with my
braid and my torque, dressed for my Journey, I thought that I had
slain him. How could he ever explain this to his equals? How would
he dare to hold up his head at court?"

"He was a coward," Hirel said.

She bowed her head, suddenly grave. "No. He was not that. He
was a lord of the Middle Court whose fathers had stood higher,
and he had the honor of the house to consider. Whereas I was
young and cruel, burning with love for my god, whom he had
scoffed at as a lie and a dream. He was a fool and I was a worse one,
and we did not part friends. Within the year he was dead."

Hirel bent his eyes upon his cup. It was plain wood like the
others, unadorned. The cap, Sarevan's coarse awkward commoner's cap, slipped down, half blinding him. With a fierce gesture he
flung it away. The air was cold on his naked head. "Within the year
my brothers will not be dead. They will be shorn and branded and
gelded as they would have done to me, and sold as slaves into the
south." He looked up. The novices had withdrawn. Priest and
priestess regarded him steadily, black eyes and amber, unreadable
both. He wanted to scream at them. He addressed them with tight
control. "I have no god to make me wise. No dream. No lies. Only
revenge. I will have it, priests. I will have it or die."

"They would have been wiser to kill you," Sarevan said.

Hirel looked at him with something like respect. "So they would.
But they were both craven and cruel. Neither of them wanted my
blood on his hands; and even if I were found and recognized, what
could I do? A eunuch cannot sit the Golden Throne. Their
misfortune that they listened to the barber who was to geld me. I
must be purged, he said, and left unfed for a day at least, or surely I
would die under the knife. That night I found a window with a
broken catch, and made use of it. Fools. They called me Goldi-
locks, and Father's spoiled darling, and plaything of the harem.
They never thought that I would have the wits to run."

"No one ever credits beauty with brains." Sarevan sat back in his chair, gloriously insolent, and said, "Tell me, Orozia. Shall I take this cubling back to his father? Or shall I take him to mine and see what comes of it?"

Hirel sat still as he had learned to do in the High Court of Asanion, toying with a half-eaten fruit and veiling his burning eyes. Treachery. Of course. Haled off to some northern hill fort, given to a kilted savage, set to cleaning stables for his meager bread. And he was trapped here with a woman who had abandoned all her honor to take the demon's torque, and with a man who had never known what honor was.

"You know what you will do," said the priestess, eyes level upon Sarevan, and she spoke to him with an inflection that raised Hirel's hackles. Not as to the inferior he was, or as to the equal her graciousness might have allowed, but as to one set high above her. "But if I am to be consulted, I advise the latter. His highness is in great danger in the west, and you would be in no less. Avaryan is not welcome in Asanion. In any of his forms."

"Still," said Sarevan, "the boy wishes it."

"When did that ever sway you, Sarevan Is'kelion?"

The barbarian grinned, unabashed. "I should like to see the fabled empire. And he needs a keeper. Demands one, in fact."

"I need a guard," snapped Hirel. "You do not suit. You are insolent, and you try my patience." He turned his shoulder to the mongrel and faced Orozia. "Madam, I shall require clothing and a mount, and provisions for several days' journey, and an escort with some sense of respect."

She did not glance at him. Her eyes fixed on Sarevan. She had changed. There was no lightness in her now, nor in the one she spoke to. "Have you considered what your death would mean? They are killing priests in Asanion. And if they learn what you are . . ."

"What I am," Sarevan said softly, "yes. You forget the extent of it. I will venture this."

Her voice shook slightly. "Why?"

He touched her hand. "Dear lady. It is no whim. I must go. I have dreamed it; the dream binds me."

Her eyes widened. She had paled.

"Yes," he said, as cool as he had ever been. "It begins."

"And you submit?"

"I wait upon the god. That he has given me this of all companions—that is his will and his choice, and he will reveal his reasons when he chooses."

Her head bowed as if beneath a bitter weight; but it came up again, with spirit in it. "You are mad, and you were born mad, of a line of madmen. Avaryan help you; I will do what I can." She rose, sketched a blessing. "It were best that I begin now. Rest well, children."

Two

HIREL KNOTTED HIS HANDS INTO FISTS AND BURIED THEM IN the hollows of his arms. "I will not!"

They had cajoled him into the rough garb of a commoner, and given him a cap that fit him properly, and begun to persuade him that he could pretend to be lowborn. If he must. But when the smaller and plainer novice came toward him with a short sharp knife, he erupted into rebellion. "I will not make my hands like a slave's. I will *not!*"

Orozia's patience strained somewhat at the edges, but her words were quiet. "Highness, you must. Would you betray yourself for merest vanity? A commoner cannot make his hands beautiful; it is banned."

Hirel backed to the wall. He was beyond reason. The cap bound his throbbing brows; the harsh homespun garments grated on his skin. The long nails, touched still with fugitive glimmers of gilt, drew blood from his palms. But they were all he had left. The only remnant of his royalty.

Firm hands seized his shoulders, lifted him, set him down again with gentle force. "Look," Sarevan commanded him.

He struck the mirror with all his strength. It rang silver-bright but did not bend or break. In it trembled and raged a peasant's child.

"Look," said the barbarian behind him. Forcing him, gripping his head when he struggled to spin away.

Compelled, he looked. Lowborn. Drab-clad, bare-skulled, wealthless and kinless. But the skull was elegant, pale as ivory, sheened with royal gold; and the face was fine, gold-browed, the wide eyes all burning gold, the thin nostrils pinched white with anger. A peasant with the look of a thoroughbred and the bearing of an emperor— "Who will ever believe the lie?"

"Anyone," answered Sarevan, "who sees the clothing. If you have the hands to prove it."

"Not the face?"

"Faces are the god's gift. Hands are made, and the law limits them." Sarevan raised one of Hirel's easily despite resistance. "Keri."

Woman's name, stolid all-but-sexless face. And the other, sweet-mouthed, had proven to be male; he waited to pounce if his fellow novice had need. Hirel thrust out his stiff hands. "Do it then, damn you. Make me all hideous."

They laughed behind their eyes. Hirel the Beautiful, shorn and clipped, was still a pretty creature, a plaything for a lady's chamber. He spat in the reflected face, blurring it into namelessness.

"You have blessings to count," Sarevan said, cool and amused. "Two, to be precise."

Hirel's voice cracked with bitter mockery. "What! Will you not take them, too?"

"We take nothing which cannot be restored." The priest leaned against the wall, arms folded. "Think of it as a game. A splendid gamble, the seeds of a song."

"Certainly. A satire on the fall of princes."

Sarevan only laughed and flashed his bold black eyes at the priestess, who blushed like a girl. Yet for all of that, when she spoke to him she was grave and almost stern. "Be gentle with him, Sarevan. He is neither as weak as he looks nor as strong as he pretends, and he was not raised as you were."

"I should hope not," snapped Hirel.

They were not listening. They seldom were. The priestess' eyes

said a multitude of things, and the priest answered with a level
stare. She beseeched. He refused. He had a look about him, not
hard, not cold, but somehow implacable. At last he said, and he
said it in Asanian which he need not have done, "This is a suckling
infant who fancies himself a man. He is haughty, intolerant, and
ruinously spoiled. Would you have me cater to his every whim?"

"Haughty," she repeated. "Intolerant. Ruinously spoiled. And
are you perfection itself, Sarevan Is'kelion?"

"Ulan likes him," Sarevan said. "I'll be as gentle as I can bear to
be. Will that content you?"

She sighed deeply. "I think you are mad. I know he will find no
one he can trust more implicitly. Curse your honor, Sarevan, and
curse the compassion which you will not confess; and be warned. I
have sent word of this to your father."

That had the air of a threat, but Sarevan smiled. "He knows,"
he said. "I sent him a message of my own. I'm a dutiful son,
madam."

"He has given you leave?"

Sarevan's smile gained an edge. "He's made no serious effort to
stop me."

Her head came up. Her brows met. "Sarevan—"

He met her eyes in silence, his own level, glittering. After a
stretching moment, Orozia's head bowed. Her sigh was deep.
"Very well. There will be a price for this; pray Avaryan it is no
higher than it must be."

"I will pay as I must pay," said Sarevan.

She did not look up, as if she could not. "Go, then," she said.
Hirel could barely hear her. "And may the god protect you."

The road into Asanion stretched long under Hirel's protesting
feet. Mounts they had none and were not to get, and Ulan was not
precisely a tame cat. He came and went at will, hunted for them
when it pleased him, vanished sometimes for an hour or a morning
or a day. He was only rarely amenable to carrying a footsore
prince.

But Hirel did not press him. *Spoiled,* Sarevan had said. It rankled
like an old wound. Worse than Hirel's own hurts, which healed
well and quickly, and left scars he did not look at. *Spoiled to ruin.*
His brothers had said much the same. It had not hurt as much

then, perhaps because they had weakened and paled it with envy and slain it with treason.

Sarevan had only said it once. It was enough. Hirel would show him. Did show him. Walked without a word of protest, though the sun beat down, though the rain lashed his ill-protected head. Climbed when he must, stumbled only rarely, and slowly hardened. At night he tumbled headlong into sleep.

It was a drug of sorts. It helped him to forget. But he had dreams of barbers and of knives, and of his brothers laughing; and sometimes he woke shaking, awash in tears, biting back a howl of rage and loss and sheer homesickness.

Slowly they worked their way westward. They did not strike straight into Pri'nai; they angled north, keeping for an unconscionable while to the marches of Keruvarion. Rough country, hill and crag and bleak stony uplands all but empty of folk, and those few and suspicious, hunters and herdsmen. Sarevan's torque was his passport there, that and the brilliance which he could unleash at will. He could charm a stone, that one.

He tried his utmost to charm Hirel. He told tales as they walked. He sang. He simply talked, easily and freely, unperturbed by silence or shortness or outright rejection. His voice was like the rhythm of walking, like the wind and the rain and the open sky: steady, lulling, even comforting. Then he would fall silent, and that in turn would bring its comfort, a companionship which demanded nothing beyond itself.

"Your hair is growing," he said once after a full morning of such silence.

Hirel had lost count of the days, but the land seemed a little gentler, the air frankly warm. Sarevan had stripped down to his boots and his swordbelt and his scrip, and nothing else. Even Hirel had put aside his cap and unbuttoned his coat, and he could feel the light touch of wind on his hair. His hand, searching, found a tight cap of curls.

Sarevan laughed at his expression. "You're going brown, do you know that? Take off your coat at least and let Avaryan paint the rest of you."

He could say that. Splendid naked animal, he did not burn and slough and darken like a field slave. But the sun was warm and Hirel's skin raw with heat, and Sarevan knew no more of modesty

than of honor or of courtliness. With hammering heart Hirel
undid the last button, dropped the coat and the shirt beneath,
breathed free. And flung the trousers after them with reckless
abandon.

He had done it. He had widened those so-wise eyes. He knotted
his hands behind him to keep them from clutching his shame, and
bared his teeth in a grin, and fought a blush.

Sarevan grinned back. "They'd have my hide in the Nine
Cities," he said, "for corrupting the youth."

"What are you, then? Ancient?"

"Twenty-one on Autumn Firstday, infant."

Hirel blinked. "That is *my* birthday!"

"I'd cry your loftiness' pardon for usurping it; but I had it first."

Hirel found his dignity somewhere and put it on, which was not
easy when he stood bare to the sky. "I shall be fifteen. My father
will confirm all my titles, and give me ruling right in Veyadzan
which is the most royal of the royal satrapies."

Sarevan's head tilted. "When I turned fifteen I became
Avaryan's novice and began to win my torque." He touched it, a
quick brush of the finger, rather like a caress. "My father took me
to the temple in Han-Gilen and gave me to the priests. It was my
free choice, and I was determined to embrace it like a man, but
when other and older novices led me away, I almost broke down
and wept. I would have given anything to be a child again."

"A prince stops being a child when he is born," Hirel said.

"What, did you never play at children's games?"

That was shock in Sarevan's eyes, and pity, and more that Hirel
did not want to see. "Royalty does not play," he said frigidly.

"Alas for royalty."

"I was free," snapped Hirel. "I was learning, doing things that
mattered."

"Did they?" Sarevan turned and began to pick his way down
from the sunstruck height. Even his braid was insolent, and the
flex of his bare flat buttocks, and the lightness of his tread upon
the stones.

Hirel gathered his garments together. He did not put them on.
Carefully he folded them into the bag Orozia had given him, in
which he carried a second shirt and a roll of bandages and a packet
or two of journey-bread. He slung the bag baldric-fashion and

shouldered the rough woolen roll of his blanket. Sarevan was well away now, not looking back. Hirel lifted a stone, weighed it in his hand, let it fall. Too paltry a vengeance, and too crude. Carefully, but not slowly, he set his foot on the path which Sarevan had taken.

Hirel paid for his recklessness. He burned scarlet in places too tender for words; and he had to suffer Sarevan's hands with a balm the priest made of herbs and a little oil. But having burned away his fairness, he browned. "Goldened," Sarevan said, admiring unabashed, as he did everything.

"There is no such word."

"Now there is." Sarevan pillowed himself on Ulan's flank, face to the splendor of stars and moons, a creature all of fire and shadow.

It struck Hirel like a blow, startling, not quite unpleasant. Sarevan was beautiful. His alienness had obscured it, and Hirel's eye trained to see beauty in a fair skin and a sleek full-fleshed body and a smooth oval straight-nosed face. But Sarevan, who by all the tenets of artist and poet should have been hideous, was as splendid as the ul-cat that drowsed and purred beside him.

Hirel did not like him the better for it. And he, damn him, cared not at all. "Tomorrow," he said, half asleep already, "we cross into Asanion."

For all the warmth of air and blanket, Hirel shivered. *So soon?* part of him cried. Too large a part by far, for his mind's peace. But the rest had risen up in exultation.

There was no visible border, no wall or boundary of stone. Yet the land changed. Softened. Rolled into the green plains of Kovruen, ripening into summer, rich with its herds and its fields of grain, hatched with the broad paved roads of the emperors and dotted with shrines to various of the thousand gods.

Sarevan conceded to civilization. He bound his loins with a bit of cloth. Hirel put on his trousers and the lighter of his shirts, and hated himself for hating the touch of them against his skin. But he gained something: he could walk barefoot on the road, his boots banished to his bag. It would have been more of a pleasure if Sarevan had not strode bootless beside him, near naked and gloriously comfortable.

People stared at the barbarian. For there were people here, workers in the fields, walkers on the road. There was nothing like him in that land, or likely in the world. No one would speak to him; those whom he approached, ducked their heads and fled.

"Are they so modest?" he asked Hirel, standing in the road with his braid like a tail of fire and the sun swooning on his dusky hide.

"They take you for a devil," Hirel said. "Or perhaps a god. One of the Thousand might choose to look like you, if it suited his whim."

Sarevan tilted his head as if he would contest the point, but he said nothing. He did not make any move to cover himself. No garment in the world could make him smaller or paler or his mane less beacon-bright.

Hirel frowned. "You might be wise to take off your torque."

"I may not." It was flat, final, and unwearied with repetition.

"I can call it a badge of slavery. Perhaps people will believe me."

"Perhaps your father will swear fealty to the Sunborn." Sarevan settled his scrip over his shoulder and began to walk. "I'll not rely on deceptions, but trust to the god."

"To a superstitious lie."

Sarevan stopped, turned lithely on his heel. "You believe that?"

"I know it. There are no gods. They are but dreams, wishes and fears given names and faces. Every wise man knows as much, and many a priest. There is great profit in gods, when the common crowd knows no better than to worship them."

"You believe that," Sarevan repeated. He sounded incredulous. "You poor child, trapped in a world so drab. So logical. So very blind."

Hirel's lip curled. "At least I do not spend my every waking hour in dread lest I give offense to some divinity."

"How can you, a mere mortal, offend a god? But then," Sarevan said, "you don't know Avaryan."

"I know all that I need to. He is the sun. He insists that he be worshipped as sole god. His priests must never touch women, and his priestesses cannot know men, or they die in fire. And if that is not punishment for offending the god, what do you call it?"

"We worship him as the sun, because its light is the closest this world may come to his true face. He is worshipped alone because he is alone, high lord of all that walks in the light, as his sister is queen of all darkness. Our vows before him are a mystery and a sacrifice, and their breaking is weakness and unworthiness and betrayal of faith. The god keeps his word; we can at least try to follow his example."

"Are you a virgin, then?"

"Ah," said Sarevan, undismayed. "You want to know if I'm a proper man. Can't you tell by looking at me?"

"You are." A virgin, Hirel meant. He looked at Sarevan and tried to imagine a man grown who had never, even once, practiced the highest and most pleasant of the arts. It was shocking. It was appalling. It was utterly against nature.

Hirel eased, a little. "Ah. I see. You are speaking of women. It is boys you love, then."

"If it were, cubling, you'd know it by now."

Bold eyes, those. Laughing. Knowing no shame. He was proud to be as he was. He was all alien. Hirel's gorge rose at the sight and the thought of him.

"I serve my god," he said, light and proud and oblivious. "I have walked in his presence. I have known his son."

"Avaryan's son." It was bitter in Hirel's throat, but less bitter than what had come before it. "The mighty king. The conqueror with the clever tale. He is a mage, they say, a great master of illusion."

"Not great enough to have begotten himself."

"Ah," said Hirel, "everyone knows the truth of that. The Prince of Han-Gilen sired him on the Ianyn priestess, and arranged his mating to the princess his half-sister, and so built an empire to rule from the shadows behind its throne."

"By your account, the Emperor of Asanion has that in common with the Sunborn: he wedded his sister. But he at least rules his own empire. However diminished by the encroachments of the Red Prince's puppet." Sarevan's mockery was burning cold. "Child, you know many words and many tales, but the truth is far beyond your grasp. When you have seen the Lord An-Sh'Endor, when you have looked on my god, then and only then may you speak with honest certainty."

"It angers you. That I will not accept your lies. That I will not bow to your god."

"That you cannot see what stares you in the face." Sarevan spun about, braid whipping his flanks.

Hirel wanted to savor the victory, that insufferable mask torn aside at last. But fear had slain all gladness. That he had driven the barbarian away: this alien, this mocker of nature, whose face at least he knew. Whom alone he could dream of trusting, here where he was alone, unarmed, and every stone might harbor an enemy. He ran after the swiftly striding figure.

Sarevan slowed after a furlong or two, but he did not speak, nor would he glance at Hirel. His face was grim and wild. Oddly, he looked the younger for it, but no less panther-dangerous.

"Perhaps," Hirel said in a time and a time, "your Avaryan could be a truth. A way of understanding the First Cause of the philosophers."

It was as close to an apology as Hirel had ever come. It fell on deaf ears. Damned arrogant barbarian. It must be all or nothing. Avaryan with his disk and his rays and his burning heat, and how he had ever begotten a son on a woman without scorching her to a cinder was not for mere men to know. Hirel threw up his hands in disgust. Perhaps that tissue of lies and legends was enough for a simple man, a partbred tribesman. Hirel was a prince and a scholar. And he did not grovel. He let Sarevan stalk ahead, walking himself at a pace which suited him, letting the road draw him westward.

They were coming to a city as it would be reckoned in these distant provinces, a town of respectable size even for the inner realms of the empire. The shrines came closer together now, and many were shrines to the dead, stark white tombs and cenotaphs, hung with offerings. It was easy to mark the newest or the richest: the birds were thick about them, and the flies, and now and then the jeweled brilliance of a dragonel. In the dust-hazed distance Hirel could discern a wall with houses clustered about it.

"Shon'ai," Sarevan said.

At first Hirel tried to make it a word in a tongue he knew. Then he grimaced at himself. It was only the name of the town. People were thickening on and about the road, moving toward the gate, some laden with baskets or bales, or drawing handcarts, or leading burdened beasts. Hirel saw the haughty figure of a man in a chariot, and a large woman on a very small pony, and a personage carried in a litter.

Swiftly as Sarevan moved, in a very little while they were in the midst of the stream. Hirel kept close to the priest. He had seen no one at all for so long, and then had walked so far apart, and after days of Sarevan's black eagle-mask these round golden faces were strange.

Of course they stared. Children ran after Sarevan, once or twice even dared to throw stones at him. The stones flew wide. The priest glanced neither right nor left. He walked as a prince was trained to walk, as a panther was born to. He towered over everyone who came near him.

The gate of the town was open wide, the guards making no effort to stem the tide of people. It was no mere market day but the festival of a god. Which meant a market indeed and a great deal of profit, but processions with it, and sacrifices, and much feasting and drinking and roistering. There were garlands of flowers everywhere within the walls, on all the houses and the several temples, and on every neck and brow and wrist.

Hirel clung to a dangling end of Sarevan's loincloth and let himself be towed through the crowds. Very soon now he was going to disgrace himself. It was different for a prince. Where he went, the way was always clear, the throngs held at bay. Not pressing in, breathing foul in his face, bellowing in his ear. He could not see. He could not think. He could not—

A strong arm swept him up. Hoofs and horns and seneldi bellings ramped where he had been, clove a path through the press, and vanished. Hirel's arms had locked about Sarevan's neck. His breath came in quick hard gasps. "Take," he forced out. "Take me—"

Sarevan wasted no words. He breasted the crowd, and no one touched him; and in a blessed while the crowd was gone. Hirel raised his head, blinking. It was dark. Sarevan was speaking. "A room, a bath, and wine. Silver for you if you are quick, gold if you fly."

Slowly Hirel focused. They were in a wide room, surrounded by carpets, cushions, tables, an effluvium of ale. An inn. Eyes glittered out of the gloom, many eyes, every patron struck dumb it seemed by the spectacle at the door. One man stood close: a round buttery

creature with an astonishingly sour face. "Show me your silver,"
he said.

Sarevan's grip shifted on Hirel, and Hirel thought he saw a glint
of gold. Certainly the innkeeper saw something that satisfied him.
"Come," he said.

The room was tiny, no more than a crevice in the roof; Sarevan
could stand erect only in the center. But it was clean, it had a
window which opened after a blow or two of the barbarian's fist,
and its bed-cushions were deep enough to drown in. The bath
when it came was hot and capacious, the wine cool and sweet, and
cakes came with it, and dumplings filled to bursting with meat and
grain and fruit, and a dish of soft herbed cheese.

"No," Sarevan was saying, "it's not catching. He's always been
delicate, and the excitement of the festival . . . you understand.
With these thoroughbreds, one has to take such care, but the
beauty is worth much; and he serves me well, in his way."

Hirel fought his way back to full awareness in time to see the
innkeeper's leer, and the closing of the door upon it. He lay in the
deep soft nest of the bed, and he was wrapped in a drying-cloth,
damp still from a bath he could hardly remember, with the taste of
wine on his tongue. The innkeeper had been ogling him. The
mongrel had said— "How dare you call me your slave?"

"Would you rather I called you my catamite?" Sarevan inquired.

"You did just that!"

"Hush," Sarevan said as to a fretful child.

Hirel raised his voice in earnest. "May all the gods damn you
to—"

A hand clapped over his mouth. "The gods do not exist," the
priest reminded him with poisonous sweetness.

He choked and gasped and twisted, and found the edge of that
quelling hand, and bit hard.

He won all he could have wished for. Sarevan's breath left him in
a rush; his hand snapped back. Hirel stared. The priest's skin was
not opaque at all. It was like black glass; and a corpse-light burned
ghastly beneath. His lips were grey as ash.

But Hirel had not even drawn blood.

Sarevan withdrew as far as he might, which was only a step or
two. His hand trembled; he thrust it behind him. It was his right
hand. Hirel committed that to memory. This man of limitless

strength and overweening arrogance had a weakness, and it was enormous and it was utterly inexplicable, and it was worth bearing in mind. It evened the score, somewhat.

"Cubling," Sarevan said, and his voice did not come easily, "did your teachers never instruct you in proper and honorable combat?"

"With proper and honorable opponents," Hirel answered, "yes."

Sarevan tilted his head. Considered. Bared his white teeth and saluted left-handed, as a swordsman would concede a match.

"And I am not your servant," Hirel said.

"So then, you are my catamite."

Hirel hissed at him. He shook out his hair, laughing almost freely, and availed himself of the cooling bath.

Three

HIREL SLEPT A LITTLE. WHEN HE WOKE, SAREVAN WAS GONE. He knew a moment's panic; then he saw the worn leather of the priest's scrip hanging from a peg by the bed. Everything was in it, even the small but surprisingly heavy purse. He had not gone far. Hirel relieved himself, nibbled the remains of a seedcake, poured a cupful of wine and peered out of the window. Nothing below but an alleyway. He wandered back to his cushions, sipping the sweet strong vintage. It was not one he knew; not nearly fine enough for a high prince in his palace. But in this place it was pleasant.

He settled more comfortably. The room was warm but not unbearable. One of his scars itched within where he could not scratch it: one of the deep furrows in his hip and thigh. The guardhound had caught him there, terrifying him for his manhood; he had found strength he had never known he had, and broken the beast's neck. The hound had paid the proper price, but Hirel would bear the marks until he died, livid and unlovely against his skin.

He was changing. He was thinner, with ribs to count. His child-softness was sharpening into planes and angles. A fleece of down was coming between his legs, and he was not the same beneath it. He was becoming a man.

Perhaps he would call for a woman. That would wipe the leer from the innkeeper's face. Sarevan, poor maiden priest, would wilt with envy.

Hirel frowned. He could not imagine Sarevan wilting. More likely the creature would stand by the door and fold his arms and smile his most supercilious smile, and make of manly virtue a creeping shame.

"Damn him," Hirel said. His voice lacked conviction. "I will go. I will go now and find my own way home. My brothers will fall down in terror when they see me; and I will have my vengeance."

He clasped his knees and rocked. His eyes blurred; he could not stop them. Alone, all alone, with only a demon-worshipping madman to defend him. No one in the empire even knew he lived; and those who cared could care only that he was not safely dead. His mother who had loved him, and yes, spoiled him shamefully, his mother was two years dead by her own hand, and his father was a golden mask upon a golden throne, and his brothers would have sold him a eunuch into the south. And he was going home. Home to hate and fear and at best indifference; to the nets of courtiers and the chains of royalty, and never a moment without the dread of another betrayal.

A shudder racked him. He must go back. What else was left to him?

He knew what he must do. Dress. Gather the last of the food. Take a handful of silver from Sarevan's purse. Just enough to buy a mount and to keep him fed until he came to Kundri'j Asan. When he was done, he would repay the lending a hundred times over: send a bag of gold to Orozia in the town the name of which he had never troubled to learn, and instruct her to give it to the priest.

He went as far as to rise, to turn toward his clothes. They were wet. He was close to tears again.

The door opened. Sarevan had to stoop to pass it. Lean though he was, his shoulders were broad; he filled the cramped space. His face was set in stone. His eyes were burning.

The wall was rough and cool against Hirel's back. He did not even remember retreating to it. Somehow the priest had divined what he would do. Theft; flight.

No. Only true mages walked in minds, and there were no true
mages, only charlatans. Sarevan turned blindly about, hands
clenching and unclenching. One, the bitten right, rose to his
torque and fell again. "They burned it," he said low in his throat.
"They burned it to the ground."

"What?" Hirel snapped, sharp with guilt and startlement.

At first he did not know if Sarevan heard. The eyes never turned
to him. But at length the voice answered, still low, almost rough.
"Avaryan's temple. They burned it. They burned it over the heads
of the priests, and sowed the ashes with salt, and set up a
demon-stone in the midst of it, cursing Avaryan and his priesthood
unto the thousandth generation. But why? Why so immeasurable a
hate?"

It was a cry of anguish. Hirel's throat ached with the power of it;
his own words came hard, half strangled. "Avaryan is the enemy
here, the symbol of the conqueror, of the empire that has dared to
rise and challenge us. His priests are suspected as spies, and some
have been caught at it. But hatred of that magnitude . . . I do not
know."

Sarevan's laughter was frightening. "*I* know. It is politics, cold
politics. A game of kings-and-cities, with living folk for pawns.
Burn a temple, open the way to the destruction of its patron's
empire. They died in torment, my brothers and sisters. They died
like sea-spiders in a cauldron."

"Perhaps," said Hirel, "they offended someone in power. No
great conspiracy; a personal vendetta. But whatever is the truth of
it, you are not safe here, and you should not linger. By now all
Shon'ai will have seen your torque."

"Oh, yes, they have seen it. They have all seen me, the mongrel,
the monster, the demon's minion. I cast down the cursed stone and
laid a curse of my own upon it, and sang the god's praises over it."

"You are stark mad."

"What! You did not know?"

"They must be hunting you now." Hirel's heart raced, but his
brain was clear. "We can run. The crowds will hide us. You can
stoop, and cover your body and your hair, and feign a limp,
perhaps."

"No," Sarevan said. "One at least of my torque-kin remains
alive, although the prison is hidden from me. But I will find it.

Before Avaryan I will find it." He spoke as if the prison's hiding were an impossible thing, a deep and personal insult. Yet when he looked at Hirel he seemed utterly sane, cool and quiet, reasonable. "You will go. Ulan will come to you when you have passed the gates; he will guard you and guide you and bring you safe to your father. No one will molest you while you travel in his company."

True, all true, and very wise. Hirel had intended to do much the same.

But.

"I will not abandon you," he said stiffly.

"Cubling," said Sarevan, "you cannot help me, you are certain to hinder me, and it is altogether likely that I will get my death in this venture. It was a mage who laid the curse on the temple; he is strong, and he will not be merciful."

Hirel sneered. "A mage. I tremble where I stand."

"You should, child. He's no trumpery trickster. He has power, and it is real, and it tastes of darkness."

"Superstition. I know better. I have seen the mages in Kundri'j Asan. Powders and stinks and spells and cantrips, and a great deal of mystical posturing. It deceives the masses. It enriches the mages. It amuses my father to retain a few of the more presentable in his court. They can do him no harm, he says, and one day they might prove useful."

"That day has come, and the lord of this province has seized upon it. I am going to do battle with the sorcerer."

"You dare it?" Hirel asked, meaning to mock him.

"I dare it. You see, cubling," Sarevan said, "I am one myself."

Hirel blinked at him. He did not sprout horns, or cloak himself in stars, or spawn flights of dragonels from his cupped hands. He was only Sarevan, too large for that cupboard of a room, and rather in need of a bath. The reek of smoke and anger lay heavy upon him.

He gathered Hirel's garments and dropped them on the bed. "Dress yourself. You must be away from here before they close the gates for the night."

Slowly Hirel obeyed. He would be well rid of this lunatic. Mage, indeed. Gods, indeed. A little longer and the barbarian would have had Hirel believing it.

Sarevan saw to Hirel's bag, packed the seedcakes and a napkinful of dumplings, added his own waterskin, and rummaging in his scrip, brought out the purse. Without a word or a glance, he laid it in the bag.

Hirel's throat closed. Sarevan held out the bag; Hirel clutched it to his chest. "Come," the priest said.

Hirel tried to swallow. Time was running on. And he could not move.

Sarevan snatched him up; and he left the inn as he had entered it, carried like an ailing child. The streets were as crowded as ever, the shadows growing long with evening. Hirel began to struggle. Sarevan ignored him. There was a new tension in the priest's body, a tautness like fear, but the press was too tight, the current too strong; he could breast it, but he could not advance above a walk, with many turns and weavings and impasses. It was like a spell, a curse of endless frustration.

At last he could not move at all, and from his shoulder's height the inn was still visible, its sign of the sunbird mocking Hirel's glare. "I will do it," Sarevan muttered. "I must."

"What—"

Sarevan stood erect and breathed deep, and Hirel felt— something. Like a spark. Like a flare of heat too brief to be sure of. Like a note of music on the very edge of hearing. All the small hairs of his body shivered and rose.

"There!" Sun flashed on helmets; a senel tossed its horns and half reared, its rider calling out, sweeping his arm toward the priest. Sarevan plunged into the crowd. It parted before him. But against the company behind came a second, barring the broad way, and the throng milled and tangled itself, and no escape but straight into the air. And Sarevan seized it. He launched himself upward.

For a soaring, terrifying moment he flew, and Hirel with him, and people cried out to see it. Then darkness filled the sky. Something like an eagle stooped above them, but an eagle with wings that spread from horizon to horizon. With a sharp fierce cry Sarevan reared back, gripping Hirel one-handed, hurling lightnings.

Hirel saw the arrow come. He tried to speak, even to shape a thought. The dart sang past his cheek and plunged deep into the undefended shoulder. Sarevan cried out again, sharper and fiercer still, and dropped like a stone.

"Fascinating," said the Lord of Baryas and Shon'ai when he had heard his captain's account, inspecting the prisoners bound and haughty before him. Hirel had only a set of manacles, which was an insult. Sarevan was wrapped in chains, his shoulder bound with a bandage, and his face was grey with pain. But he met the lord's stare with perfect insolence.

The lord smiled. He was tall for an Asanian, a bare head shorter than Sarevan, and slender, and exquisitely attired. His slaves were skillful: one had to peer close to see that he was not young, that his hair was not as thick as it feigned to be. But his eyes were not the eyes of a fool. "Fascinating," he repeated, circling Sarevan, lifting the loosened braid and letting it fall. "High sorcery in my own city before the faces of my people, and the sorcerer . . . What is your name, priest of Avaryan?"

"You know it as well as I," said Sarevan with perfect calm.

"Do I?" the lord inquired. He raised a hand. "Unbind him."

Soldiers and servants slanted their eyes and muttered, but under their lord's eye they obeyed, retreating quickly as if the sorcerer might blast them where they stood. He barely moved except to flex his good shoulder and to draw a breath. "Ah then, perhaps I've changed a little; I was somewhat younger when we met. I remember you, Ebraz y Baryas ul Shon'ai."

"And I you," the lord admitted, "Sarevan Is'kelion y Endros. I confess I never expected to see you here in such state, with such attendance."

"What, my boy?" Sarevan grinned and ruffled Hirel's hair. "Do you like him? I found him in a hedgerow; I'm making a man of him, though it's hard going. His old master didn't use him well, and he's not quite sane. Fancies himself a prince of your empire, if you can believe it."

Ebraz barely glanced at Hirel, whose rage bade fair to burst him asunder. "He has the look, true enough. They breed for it in slave-stables here and there; it fetches a high price."

"I had him for a song. The strain is flawed, it seems. It produces incorrigibles. But I've not given up hope yet."

"What will you do with him when you have tamed him?"

"Set him free, of course."

Ebraz laughed, a high well-bred whinny. "Of course!" He sobered. "Meanwhile, my lord, you have presented me with rather a dilemma. By command of my overlord, all priests of Avaryan are outlawed in Kovruen; and you have not only stood forth publicly as a bearer of the torque, you have also wielded magecraft without the sanction of the guild."

"Guild?" Sarevan asked.

"Guild," Ebraz answered. "Surely you know that your kind are licensed and taxed in the Golden Empire." He spread his narrow elegant hands. "So you see, my lord, between emperor and overlord I am compelled to hold you prisoner. I regret the necessity, and I regret still more deeply the circumstances which led to your wounding. You can be sure that I will send to my lord with a full explanation. And to your father, of course, with profoundest apologies."

Sarevan flinched, although he tried to make light of it. "You needn't trouble my father with my foolishness."

"But, my lord, if he discovers for himself—"

"We can take care that he does not. Imprison me if you must, I've earned it, but spare me my father's wrath for yet a while."

The lord smiled in understanding. "I can be slow to send a message. But Prince Zorayan must know; your freedom lies in his hands."

"That will suffice," said Sarevan. He swayed; his lips were ashen. "If you will pardon me—"

"That would not be wise, my lord."

Hirel started. A man had come out of nowhere, a man who looked much less a mage than Sarevan, small, dark-robed, quiet. "My lord," he said, "this weakness is a lie. He plots to deceive you, to cozen you into giving him a gentle imprisonment, and thence to escape by his arts. See, such a fine fierce glare. He knows that his power is no match for mine."

"No?" asked Sarevan, eyes glittering. He no longer looked as if he were about to faint. "I would have had you, journeyman, but for an archer's good fortune. You are but a spellcaster, a slave to your grimoires; I am mageborn."

"Mageborn, but young, and arrogant with it. Arrogant far beyond your skill or your strength."

"Do you care to test me, conjurer? Here and now, with no book and no charmed circle. Come, summon your familiar; invoke your devils. I will be generous. I will hold them back if they seek to turn on you."

"I have your blood, Sunchild," the mage said calmly. "That is book and circle enough."

Sarevan's breath caught. His defiance had an air of desperation. Feigned, perhaps. Perhaps not. "You cannot touch me."

"Enough," said Ebraz quietly, but they heard him. "I cannot afford an escape, my lord. Surely you understand. Your word would suffice, but . . . Prince Zorayan is not an easy man, and he is not altogether certain that he trusts me. I must be strict. For appearance's sake. I will be no more rigorous than I must."

"I will remember," Sarevan said. Warning, promising.

"Remember, my lord, but forgive." Ebraz signaled to his men. "The lower prison. Minimal restraint but constant guard. Within reason, let him have whatever he asks for."

It was dark. It was damp. It stank. It was a dungeon, and it was vile, and Sarevan smiled at it. "Spacious," he said to the guard who stood nearest, "and well lit; and the straw is clean, I see. Rats? Yes? Ah well, what would a dungeon be without rats?"

They had taken off Hirel's chain. He bolted for the door. A guard caught him with contemptuous ease, and took his time letting go, groping down Hirel's trousers. Hirel laid him flat.

Sarevan laughed. "Isn't he a wonder? Protects his virtue better than any maid. But with a little persuasion . . ."

The guards were grinning. Hirel's victim got up painfully, but the murder had retreated from his eyes. He did not try to touch Hirel again.

They left the dim lamp high in its niche, where it bred more shadows than it vanquished. The door thudded shut; bolts rattled across it. Hirel turned on Sarevan. "You unspeakable—"

"Yes, I held your tongue for you, and it was well for you I did. If my elegant lord had taken any notice of you, he would have kept you. He likes a pretty boy now and then. But he likes them docile and he likes them devoted, and I made sure that he thought I might have tainted you with my sorceries. Why, your very face could have been a trap."

"What do you think you have led me into? I could have been free. I could have proven my rank and had an escort to my father."

"You could have been held hostage well apart from me, with no hope of escape."

"What hope is there now?"

"More than none." Before Hirel could muster a riposte, Sarevan had withdrawn, turning his eyes toward the deepest of deep shadows. His breath hissed. He swooped upon something.

Hirel's eyes were sharpening to the gloom. He saw what Sarevan knelt beside. A bundle of rags. A tangle of—

Hair like black water flecked with white. The tatters of a robe such as all priests wore by law in Asanion, torn most upon the breast where the badge of the god should be. The prisoner had on something beneath, something dark and indistinct, but glinting on the edge of vision.

Hirel's stomach heaved. It was no garment at all, but flesh flayed to the bone. And the face—the face—

It had been a woman once. It could still speak with a clarity horrible amid the ruin, and the voice was sweet. It was a young voice, light and pure despite the greying hair. *"Avar'charin?"* It shifted to accented Asanian. "Brother. Brother my lord, *Avar'charin.* I see you in the darkness. How bright is the light of you!"

Sarevan stroked the beautiful hair. His face was deadly still. "Hush," he murmured. "Hush."

She stirred. Though it must have roused her to agony, she touched his hand. His fingers closed over hers, gently, infinitely gently, for they were little more than blood and broken bone. "My lord," she cried with sudden urgency, "you should not be here! This land is death for you."

"It has been worse for you." His voice was as still as his face.

"I am no one. My pain belongs to the god; it is nearly done. But you—Endros iVaryan, you were mad to pass your father's borders."

"The god is leading me. He brought me to you. Give me your pain, sister. Give me your suffering, that I may heal it."

"No. No, you must not."

"I must."

She clutched him, although she gasped, although her broken body writhed with the effort and the anguish of it. "No. Oh, no. They left me alive for this. They left lips and tongue. They knew—they wanted—"

Sarevan's face was set, closed, implacable. He laid his hands on that head with its bitter paradox of beauty and ruin. The air sang; Hirel's flesh prickled. Almost he could see. Almost he could hear. Almost *know*. Power like wind and fire, solid as a sword, ghostly as a dream, terrible as the lightning. Gathering, waxing, focusing. Reaching within the shattered body, willing it to live, to mend, to be whole.

"No!" cried the priestess, high and despairing.

The bait was taken, the trap was sprung. The hunter came in wind and fire, but his fire was black and his wind bore the stink of darkness.

The healing frayed and chilled and broke. Sarevan reared up, and the masks were gone, torn away from purest, reddest rage. He roared, and it was no man who sprang, but a great cat the color of night, with eyes of fire.

Hirel had no pride in the face of a world gone mad. He cowered in the farthest corner. Perhaps he whimpered. He scrabbled at the wall, hoping hopelessly that it would give way and free him from this horror.

As far from him as the cell's walls permitted, and much too hideously close, there was nothing to see, and there was everything. A cat crouched over a shapeless thing that had been a woman. A cat that was also a redheaded northerner, locked in combat with something that was now Lord Ebraz' tame sorcerer and now a direwolf with bloody jaws.

The cat's fangs closed upon the wolf's throat. It howled; it fought. The cat grunted, perhaps with effort, perhaps with the laughter of the prey turned hunter and slayer. The wolf slashed helplessly at air. Cruel claws rent its body. Its blood bubbled and flamed like the blood of mountains.

With a last vicious stroke, the cat flung down his enemy. A man all broken and bleeding, and his blood had still that fiery, sorcerous strangeness. Power, Hirel knew without knowing how.

The mage bled his magic at Sarevan's feet. "Thus," said the priest, cold and proud, "do you learn the law. A journeyman does not challenge a master. Go now; reap the reward your folly has won you. Live without power and without magic, and know that Avaryan's line cannot be cast down by any mortal man."

The enemy vanished. Sarevan began to sink down beside the body of the priestess.

Wind swept over him, with fire in its jaws. It caught him unawares. He reeled and fell. Hirel's wandering wits observed the priest's braid, how bright it was as he toppled, bright as new copper, clashing with the blood upon his bandages.

He twisted in the air, supple, impossible, feline. His form blurred and steadied, human shape grappling with living shadow. There were eyes in the shapeless darkness. Terrible eyes: golden, luminous, and infinitely sad. *I must,* they said, as the sky speaks of rain. *You threaten us all. I cannot grant you mercy.*

"Mercy?" Sarevan's wrath had gone quiet. "Was it mercy you granted my torque-sister? Share it, then. Share it in its fullness."

They closed, darkness and darkness, flesh and shadow. The shadow—Hirel giggled, quite contentedly mad. The shadow had the voice of a woman and the suggestion of a woman's shape: a soft curve of cheek, a swell of breasts, a slimness of waist. So close and so fiercely did they do battle that they looked to be locked in an embrace less of war than of love. Hirel's manhood rose in fancied sympathy. His breathing quickened. It was a woman, that shadow, and such a woman, ineffably beautiful, ineffably sad. All Asanion dwelt in her body and in her great grieving eyes.

Sarevan destroyed them. Hirel howled. Now that he must move, he could not. He raged and he wept. He forsook the last rags of his sanity. Yet through it all, his eyes saw with perfect and hideous clarity.

As Sarevan had broken the wolf, so he broke the lady of the empire and cast her down. But she clung to consciousness. She smiled as he set his foot on her. Her smile was beautiful, and yet it was horrible; for it was a smile of triumph. "The battle," she said, "is yours, O slave of the burning god. But the war is mine." She grasped his foot with her last desperate strength, and thrust it up and back. Lightnings leaped from her hands. She laughed, high

and sweet and taunting. It was laughter made to madden a man, if
he were young and proud and filled with the wrath of his god. It
pricked, it stung. It drove Sarevan back; it roused his power anew.
He wielded the lightning like a sword. He swooped upon his
tormentor and smote her where she lay.

Four

THE SILENCE WAS ABRUPT AND ABSOLUTE. SAREVAN STOOD empty-handed. His face was grey, his bandage all scarlet. Slowly, stiffly, he knelt. He touched the body of the sorceress. It lay whole and unmarred, as if it slept; but no breath stirred.

Sarevan sat on his heels. "'Varyan," he whispered. "O Avaryan."

Hirel, having tasted the warmth of madness, found sanity grim and cold. He stood over the priest and the sorceress. The priestess was gone, if she had ever been aught but illusion.

Sarevan raised his head. His eyes were dull. Even his hair seemed dim, faded, all the brightness gone from it. He scraped it out of his eyes. "I killed her," he said calmly.

"So I see," responded Hirel.

"Do you? Can you?" Sarevan laughed. It was not comfortable to hear. "That was the trap. To make me kill her. To make—me—" His voice cracked like a boy's. He leaped to his feet, staggered, caught himself. "Quick now. Walk."

"Where?"

Sarevan swayed again. He looked about, peering as if he could

43

not see; he drew a breath that caught in his throat. "Walk," he gritted. "Walk, damn you."

They walked. The door melted away before them. No one saw them, and they saw no one. Perhaps they did not walk in the world at all. They came up out of the dungeon, and they walked through a high house richly furnished, part of which Hirel thought he could remember; but not even an insect stirred. And the gate opened not upon the city of Shon'ai but upon greenness and sunlight and a whisper of water.

Sarevan stumbled and fell to his knees. Hirel snatched at him; he pushed the hands away. His head tossed from side to side. His eyes were wide and blind. "It's gone," he said. "All of it. All gone." A sound escaped him, half laughter, half sob. "I gave her the death she longed for. She—she gave me worse. Infinitely worse."

"What—" Hirel began.

Sarevan's eyes rolled up. Slowly, bonelessly, he toppled.

Hirel caught too late, managed only to drag himself down under a surprising weight. It ended across his lap, leaden heavy, barely breathing. Trapping him, pinning him to the ground. He struggled briefly and wildly.

Abruptly he stilled. Willing himself to be calm, to think. It was the fiercest battle he had ever known, and the greatest victory.

Hirel regarded the face upturned in his lap. It was much the same as ever, dark, high-nosed, haughty; even unconscious it bore the hollows of exhaustion.

Hirel shivered in the sun's warmth. This creature had called upon a power that could not, should not exist. Had flown without wings, and wielded the lightning, and destroyed two mages who had come against him. Sarevan who had found an Asanian prince in a fernbrake and condescended to be his guard; who never wore more than he must, who was conspicuously vain of his body, who ate and drank and slept and sometimes had bad dreams. He sweated when the sun was hot and shivered when the night was cold, and bathed when he needed it, which was often enough, and relieved himself exactly as every other man must. No showers of enchanted gold.

Hirel bit his lips until they bled. There were mages, and Sarevan was one, and if mages could be, then what of gods?

Perhaps it had been a dream.

The earth was solid beneath him, cool, a little damp. The air bore a scent of sunlight and of wilderness. The weight across his thighs was considerable, and inescapable.

Sarevan. Sarevan Is'kelion, Sarevan Stormborn, Sa'van lo'ndros who could not be what he could not but be. Sa'van lo'ndros, Sarevadin li Endros in the high Gileni tongue that Hirel's father had commanded he learn: Sarevadin the prince.

Hirel had some excuse for idiocy. When a high prince of Asanion was born, all menchildren born that day and for a Greatmoon-cycle round about were given his name. It confused the demons, people said, and spread the gods' blessing abroad upon the empire. And some of the Sunborn's Ianyn savages had taken wives among the women of the Hundred Realms, and many more had not troubled with such niceties, with mongrels enough to show for it. And surely the heir of a very god would not be walking the highroad of his own free will with all his worldly goods in a battered bag.

Sarevadin the prince, son of the Sunborn.

What a hostage.

What an irony.

But there was one wild tale at least—

Hirel lifted one long limp hand. The right, that one which had shown itself to be Sarevan's great weakness. A shaft of sun caught in its palm and flamed. *Ilu'Kasar*, the brand of the god, that he had from his father.

Suddenly Hirel was whitely, gloriously angry. Sarevan had said no word, not even one; had taken a wicked delight in Hirel's stupidity. Letting Hirel look on him as lowborn, driving Hirel wild with his arrogance, laughing all the while at the blind and witless child. Hoping very likely to play the game clear to Kundri'j Asan, and melt away unknown, and rise up in Keruvarion and tell the tale to all who would hear. How the High Prince of Keruvarion saved the life of the High Prince of Asanion, and took him back to his safe nest and his doting father, and won scarcely a civil word in return. "Why," Sarevan would say as he quaffed ale with his father's bearded chieftains, "the poor infant could hardly recall his own name, let alone mine, he was so prostrated by the shock of having to do up his own trousers."

Hirel bit down on the back of his hand. He was going to howl.

With rage, with laughter, what matter? He had been a prisoner in the dungeon of one of his own lords, with a sorcery on his tongue whenever he tried to speak his name, and the son of An-Sh'Endor had set him free. Casting them both here, wherever here might be, in a welter of magic and a flood of words that, uncomprehended, roused nothing but dread.

Hirel's eyes flinched from the dazzle of the *Kasar*. It was true gold, bright metal in the shape of the sun's disk, many-rayed, born there, bred in the flesh by a god's power. It burned, the tales said, like living fire. Small wonder that Sarevan had nearly fainted when Hirel sank his teeth into it.

Hirel laid the hand on Sarevan's breast. "Consider," he said to it, "what I know and what I surmise. Your god is being driven from Asanion as quietly as may be, and as completely. The Order of Mages has withdrawn from the Nine Cities and reappeared in Kundri'j Asan under the open protection of the Charlatans' Guild and the secret sanction of the emperor my father. He wields them as he wields every weapon, as a counter to the power of the emperor your father.

"And here we lie, you and I, only your god knows where. Is that the heart of your plot, High Prince of Keruvarion? To bewitch and abduct the High Prince of Asanion?"

Sarevan did not move.

"Sarevadin Halenan Kurelian Miranion iVaryan. See, I know you. I have you wholly in my power. Shall I slay you while you lie helpless? Shall I bear you away to be my slave in Kundri'j?"

Not a sound, not a flicker. Sarevan was alive, but little more; somehow he had thwarted the surgeon's close stitching, and he was ghastly grey, and perhaps there was more amiss that Hirel could not understand. Something uncanny, something sorcerous. And they were alone, foodless and waterless, without weapon or baggage; and a pair of trousers for each, neither excessively clean, and a single torn shirt. And a torque of gold, for what that was worth.

Much, even if it were no more than gilded lead. Hirel had only to unclasp it and run, and hide, and twist it out of recognition and hammer it with a stone and sell a bit of it in the next town he came to. If there was a town. If it was close enough to find before he starved.

What a blow to Keruvarion his empire's enemy, if he left its high prince to die in a nameless wood. No matter if he died himself; he would only make truth of Sarevan's deception, and his father had a surfeit of sons. He might even win free to tell the tale. Magics and sorceries and all.

Carefully, patiently, Hirel extricated himself from beneath the limp body. It was not difficult, now that he was calm. He stood over Sarevan. The Varyani prince sprawled gracelessly in the leafmold that had so bound Hirel, and truly, if he had not died yet, he would die soon.

With a small hoarse sound, Hirel bent over him. The torque gleamed no more brightly than the Sun in the branded hand. Hirel caught the wrist, drew the slack arm around his neck, set his teeth and heaved. Sarevan came up by degrees, so slowly that Hirel shook with the strain, so awkwardly that he almost despaired. Half carrying, half dragging the long body behind him, he lurched and stumbled toward the whisper of water.

Light burst upon him, and treelessness: a broad stretch of lake girdled with trees and sharp stones, ringed with the white teeth of mountains. He lowered Sarevan to the sand that lapped to the forest's edge, and tried to stand erect, gasping, as his sight swelled and faded and settled to a dark-edged blur. Through it he dipped water in his hands, drank what he might, and poured a pitiful few drops into Sarevan.

Hirel lay on the sun-warmed sand. Only for a moment. Only until he had his breath back. Sarevan lay deathly still beside him. He surged up in dread; the bandaged breast lifted, fell again. Clumsily, swallowing bile, he loosened the bloodied wrappings.

The bleeding had ebbed. Whether that was good or ill, Hirel did not know. But the small tidy wound had grown to an ugly gaping mouth. Hirel tore at his shirt, shaking, wanting desperately to cry. He had no skill in this. He had no skill in anything that mattered. The Dance of the Sunbird, the seventeen inflections of the imperial salutation, the precise degree of the bow accorded by a lord of the ninth rank of the Middle Court to a prince of the blood . . .

His hands made a bandage, of sorts. It was not pretty. Perhaps it was too tight. He tied it off with a bowman's knot, which skill at least he had, and sat on his heels, spent. The sun's heat stroked his

aching shoulders. He turned his face to it, eyes slitted against its
brightness. "What now?" he demanded, as if it could answer; as if it
were truly a god and not merely the closest of the stars. "What can
I do? I am but a pampered prince. I know nothing but courts and
palaces. What use am I here?"

The sun shone on oblivious. A small wind played across the
water. Far out, a fish leaped. Hirel's entrails knotted with hunger.

He grasped Sarevan by the unwounded shoulder and began to
shake him. "Wake," he said over and over. "Wake, damn you."
Cursed barbarian. Son of a fatherless man. Pitiful excuse for a
sorcerer, he, who swooned like a maid after the merest wizardly
skirmish. Would he die, then, and give Asanion a victory to rejoice
in? Hirel reared back and struck him, and struck again, ringing
broadhanded slaps that rocked the head upon the lifeless neck.

It rocked of its own accord. Sarevan's body twitched, shuddered.
Hirel smote it with all his strength. The long limbs thrashed.
Convulsed. Surely Hirel had killed him.

Sarevan sat bolt upright, eyes stretched wide, white-rimmed, lips
drawn back from white sharp teeth. Before Hirel could move, the
Varyani prince had him, and the strength of those hands was
terrible. But it did not hold. Hirel braced Sarevan before he could
fall; he said half in a gasp, "I can't—my power—I have no—" He
drew a sharp breath, and spoke more faintly but also more clearly.
"I have no power to help either of us. When I slew the sorceress, I
slew it. That is the law which constrains all mages."

"You never used wizardry to feed us, that I knew of."

"I walked into my enemies' hands. I let my temper master me. I
let it destroy me." There was a silence. Hirel did not fill it. Sarevan
closed his eyes as if in pain, but he spoke with some semblance of
sanity. "What do we have with us?"

"Nothing," Hirel answered flatly.

"Nothing at all?" Sarevan looked about, and his eyes closed
again. "I don't remember this place."

For a long moment Hirel could find no words to speak. When
they came, they were as faint and foolish as Sarevan's own. "You
cannot remember? But you brought us here!"

A spasm crossed Sarevan's face. His hand went to his brow. "My
head," he said. "It's an anvil, and Vihayel Smith's own hammer
beating down on it. I can't think. I can hardly—"

"We were in prison in Shon'ai," Hirel said, shaping the words with desperate care. The priest's face was appalling, struggling so hard to remember, and in such pain, that Hirel could not bear to look at it. "You fought a sorcerer, then a sorceress. We left, and we came here, and you fell. You slept."

Sarevan touched his bandaged shoulder. His eyes were open, and they had cleared a little; they were no longer quite so bewildered. "This—this I remember. I've served you ill, cubling; I think we're even farther from your city than we were before. This place has a feel of Keruvarion."

"Not of the Eastern Isles? Or the lands beyond the desert? Or the uttermost west?"

"We're not dead quite yet, cubling," Sarevan said dryly; "and even with my well of power gone dry, I know my own country. Somewhere among the Lakes of the Moon, I would guess; though which of them this is, I can't tell you. My power brought us as far eastward as it could before it failed." His brows knit. "Us . . . The priestess. I couldn't heal her. I left her—I forgot—"

Hirel cut across his dismay. "She died before your battle began. She is safe, if death is safety."

Sarevan turned onto his good side, drawing up his knees. Sweat sheened his brow and his breast and trickled down his back. Sand clung to him, dimming the brightness of his beard; his hair was knotted with it. He would have been pathetic but for the sudden fierceness of his eyes. "She's free. I gave her that much. The god will grant her healing."

"Add a prayer for yourself," Hirel said sharply. "You are alive to make use of it. Are these Lakes of the Moon a wilderness, or do people dwell here?"

"There are people, offshoots of the northern tribes. They wander with the beasts they hunt, and breed seneldi, and worship Avaryan in the free places far from temples."

"Very well," said Hirel. "We look for them. Lie here and be quiet while I search out a way to carry you."

"I'm not an invalid. I can walk." Sarevan proved it. He rose. His lips were nearly white. Stepping with care, as if he walked on glass and not on white sand, he approached the water and waded in.

Hirel was there when the fool's knees gave way. The water lightened him, and he was clinging grimly to his senses; Hirel dragged him out of the lake and into the shade of a tree, propping him against the bole. Wet though he was, he trembled not with cold but with exhaustion. "Power," he gasped. "Power's price is deadly high."

He slept thereafter, or slid into unconsciousness. Hirel looked at him and thought of despair. He would not be walking while this day lasted. Nor could Hirel carry him alone. He was too awkward a burden.

Hirel rose and wandered beside the water. Saplings or long branches; something to bind them with—he could sacrifice his trousers if he must.

He stopped short. He was going to make himself a beast of burden. And he had not even thought of it before he had the first straight weatherworn bough, testing its soundness, snapping the twigs that bristled from it. He was becoming what he seemed. Commoner, servant. Degrading himself for the sake of a greater rival than any of his brothers, the son of the man who had sworn to bring east and west together under his rule: to cast down Asanion and consecrate all the world to his burning god.

"No," he said aloud in the green silence. It was power, of a sort. Revenge of properly royal subtlety. Debt for debt and life for life. A weapon in his hands that hitherto had had none.

In the end he found half a dozen branches that would do. He dragged them back to the place where Sarevan lay, where the shadow was lengthening from noon, and took off his trousers. The sand was warm under him as he sat and began to make a litter.

Sarevan murmured and twitched. When Hirel touched him he was fire-hot, yet sodden as if he had bathed in the lake. He would not swallow the water Hirel brought him. As Hirel dragged and lifted and prodded him onto the makeshift litter, he gasped and cried out and tried feebly to resist.

Girded with the last ragged strips of his clothing, bare of aught else, Hirel fitted himself between the bars of the travois and set out along the lake's shore. Undergrowth hindered him; hollows opened before him; fallen trees barred his way. Slowly but inexorably the earth bent him away from the water, toward the trackless wilderness. The lashings of the litter wavered and threatened to work free; the ferns and the leaved branches with which he had cushioned it thinned and scattered. His feet bruised, his hands blistered and bled. Thirst rose up to haunt him. Grimly he pressed on.

The land grew rough and stony. Hirel's breath caught in a sob. He was too small. He was too weak. He could not repay this debt which Sarevan had laid on him.

No more could he leave the madman to die. Not now, after so much pain. He shifted the bars in his throbbing hands. Sarevan babbled delirious, sometimes in words Hirel knew, more often in tongues he had never heard.

The slope steepened, leveled for a bit, dipped and began to rise again. Hirel's heart was like to burst in his breast. His sight narrowed to a lone bright circle directly before him, dimming as the sun sank.

The litter caught. Hirel tugged. It held. Too weary even to curse, he turned. Wild green eyes met his glare, and a great grey body weighted the foot of the travois. "Ulan," Hirel whispered in relief too deep even for wonder. "Ulan!"

The cat growled softly, nosing Sarevan, touching his brow with the tip of a broad pink tongue. The growl deepened. Ulan's jaws opened, closed with utmost gentleness about Sarevan's wrist and tugged.

Hirel cried out. "No!" Ulan paused, as if he could understand. "No, Ulan. He is ill. You must not."

Ulan crouched like a pup in a tug-of-war, and backed slowly. Sarevan's body slid from litter to leafmold. When Hirel would have leaped, the slash of Ulan's claws drove him scrambling back. The ul-cat shifted, twisted; and Sarevan lay on the long grey back, face down, and the cat's glance was a command. Cautiously Hirel came to his side, set a steadying hand on his burden. They began to walk.

There were gods. Almost Hirel could believe that there were gods.

Or demons. Ulan led Hirel round a deep cleft in the earth, dark already with night, and down a long hill, and as the land leveled, a hound bayed perilously close. Hirel froze. His scars throbbed. A shriek welled from the very heart of him.

From a deep covert burst a beast of hell: black hide, white fangs, red maw gaping wide. Hirel's scream died behind his teeth.

Ulan raised his head and roared. The hound stopped as if struck. Its pack, bursting from the thicket, tangled in confusion. Hunters scattered them, bright barbaric creatures aclash with copper, resplendent in paint and feathers and embroidered leather. They were as dark as Sarevan, with here and there a tinge of brown or bronze; their hair was braided about their heads and down their backs, and their beards were braided on their chests. Copper gleamed on saddles, on bridles, on the horns of the stallions; one black giant on a black charger blazed with plates and chains and circlets of gold.

They drew in in a running circle, slowing, stilling, staring at the cat and the two princes. Hirel raised his chin and then his voice, sharp and clear above the blowing of hard-ridden seneldi. "Draw back, I say. Draw back! Would you slay your prince?"

The riders murmured. The gold-laden chieftain looked long at the man on the ul-cat's back. Suddenly he sprang down. He seized Sarevan's dangling hand, turning it, baring the *Kasar*. Breaths caught all about him. The giant spoke at some length and with no little intensity; his followers listened, eyes flicking from him to Sarevan.

The chieftain faced Hirel. "We are friends," he said in trader's argot rough with the burr of the tribes. "We follow Avaryan. He sent us to find you."

Hirel wavered, tensed against treachery. The giant's eyes were steady. Hirel shrugged very slightly. Why not, amid all the rest? Why not a tribe of savages running errands for a god? The chieftain raised Sarevan as if the prince had been a child, and mounted again in a graceful leap, a feat that loosened Hirel's jaw. But when a grinning savage swung his stallion toward Hirel, hand outstretched, Hirel vaulted onto Ulan's back. The tribesman laughed and veered away.

They were savages indeed, these folk who called themselves Zhil'ari, the People of the White Stallion. Their tents stood in a scattered circle near a jewel of a lake, and their bold bare-breasted women sang as the hunters returned, a fierce high song that shifted to a wail like the crying of wolves. Hounds and children joined in it, and the deeper voices of the men who had stayed behind, and above it all the belling of stallions.

They took Sarevan away. When Hirel moved to follow, no path opened for him, only a wall of alien faces limned in firelight. Even the children stood as tall as he, or taller. Giant as he had thought Sarevan, here the Varyani prince would be the merest stripling. Again Hirel raised his chin and his voice. "Let me pass."

His tone was clear, if not the words. White teeth gleamed. Someone laughed as one laughs at the cleverness of a child or an animal. Hirel walked forward.

They yielded willingly enough, although some ventured to touch, a brushing of fingers over Hirel's hair and down his back. His skin quivered, but he did not falter. He thought of Sarevan in Shon'ai, and stood a little straighter for it, and turned where he had last seen the priest. The chieftain's stallion grazed before a tent like all the others, a dome of painted hides. Hirel lifted the flap and stepped as if from world to world.

He stood in darkness after the glow of firelight. The air was full of chanting, thick with some sweet potent smoke. It dizzied him, and yet it cleared his brain.

Little by little his eyes focused. He saw the stream of fire that was Sarevan's hair, and the chieftain in his gold and his finery, and Ulan a shadow by the wall; and last of all a woman. She was old, her breasts dry and slack, her swollen belly propped on stick-thin legs. It was she who chanted in a startling, sweet voice; she who fed the fist-small brazier which begot the smoke and the feeble glimmer of light. She did not pause or turn for Hirel's entering, although the chieftain glanced at him.

Hirel moved slowly toward the bed. In this little time someone had combed out that wild fiery mane, and smoothed the tangled beard, and taken off the makeshift bandage. Had Sarevan looked so skull-ghastly under the sky?

Hirel bent close. The wound of the arrow was closing, a raw red scar on the dusky shoulder. The fever—

"He cools," said the chieftain. "The god has spoken. Our lord is not to die."

"I do not understand this sorcery. How he could die from it."

"It is sorcery. It is for sorcerers to understand."

Hirel opened his mouth to upbraid the man's insolence, and closed it again. The smoke, the keening chant, grated on his senses. He fled them for the clean quiet night.

Hirel sat by the water and tried not to be ill. Brightmoon fled westward, pursued by the great pale orb of Greatmoon, and the light they shed together was coolly brilliant. Bright enough to read by, Hirel's tutor would have said. Young girls as tall as tall men, trying to be solemn, had brought him food, drink, salve for his blistered hands, and with ill-suppressed giggles, a garment. His gorge rose at the sight and scent of the meat, the fruit, the strong salty cheese; but his stomach cried out for mercy. Slowly at first, then with ravenous hunger, he emptied the plates and bowls. The cup was full of pale liquid; he tasted it and gagged on its potency, and settled on water from the lake. As the salve worked its cooling magic on his palms, he deciphered the long strip of leather tanned as supple as cloth, wrapping it about his middle. He had not even remembered his nakedness until he was clad, and then he blushed scarlet, here where no one could see.

A sound brought him about. Another long lithe maiden, but this one's eyes were downcast, her gift aglow upon her lifted palms. "Take," she said in halting tradespeech. "Take, see."

It was gold, a crescent of the beaten metal, and from its center hung a claw of golden wire clasping a great teardrop of amber, all frosted under the moons. Hirel took the necklet, held it up. The girl smiled. Her finger touched the pendant and set it swinging, and brushed the lid that shielded his amber eye. "Take," she said, and more in her own tongue, a swift bright stream. When he hesitated, she lifted the jewel lightly from his hands and leaned forward. Her breasts swayed close; gold clasped his neck, rested cool upon his chest. She was very lovely, even with her paint and her braids, her height and her slimness and her tarry skin. Her ornaments were gold and amber. Perhaps she was a princess.

Hirel had thought that he could only sit and stare and drown in nightmare. But she smiled. He smiled in return, shakily. She touched his hair. He touched one of her gold-woven plaits, and her cheek that was richest velvet, and her sweet young breast. She murmured a word. He drew her down to the grass.

"I must go," Sarevan said. Two days in deepest dream, with the shaman chanting and raising her smokes over him, and no sooner had he waked than he tried to leap up. "I must go. I must speak to my father."

Weak as he was, even Hirel could hold him down with one hand. But he would not surrender. "We must ride to Endros. The storm is coming. I must be with my father before it breaks."

"If you ride now, it is you who will break." The wisewoman cradled his head and held a cup to his lips. "Drink."

Sarevan drank with perfect obedience, hideous though the concoction was, herbs and honey boiled in mares' milk. He hardly even choked on it. But as soon as the last of it was gone, he began again. "The day I'm too feeble to sit a senel, that day you can lay me on my pyre. Now let me up; I have bargains to strike with the one who rules here."

"Rise, and you strike bargains with none but death."

"Will you deny a dreamer his dream?"

The wisewoman's lips tightened. Hirel knew that look. His physicians had always had it when he was young and sickly, when he would not lie abed like a mindless receptacle for their potions. Driven by the memory, he slipped out of the tent. Even from outside it he heard her voice raised in expostulation.

Azhuran the chieftain sat in his open tent hearing a dispute, while his wives made him hideous with scarlet paint. When he saw Hirel he rose, scattering wives and warriors. His great arms swept Hirel from his feet. "Little stallion!" he roared. "Little goldenhead, you like my daughter, eh? Woman, be gracious, fetch a cup for Zhiani's man."

Between training and plain shock, Hirel took the massive golden cup. It reeked of mares' milk. He steeled himself to sip, set the thing aside with as much grace as he could muster, faced Azhuran. Seated on the ground, the giant was still taller than he. He knew his cheeks were scarlet. Surely, though he dared not look down to be certain, he was blushing from crown to kilt.

"She likes you," declared Azhuran, loud enough for the whole tribe to hear. "You have arts, she says. You're a lion. A bull. A stallion. A beardless, braidless, girl-voiced lad—miraculous! Are they all like you in your country?"

That Hirel did not die then, he ascribed to the malice of the nonexistent gods. The Zhil'ari were all gaping, and the women were leaning forward with hungry eyes. Traitorous Zhiani was not among them. Serpent-supple, serpent-tongued Zhiani. She had dallied nightlong by the lake, and left him at sunrise with many kisses, only to bring back half a dozen maids nearly as lovely as herself, who fed him and adorned him and made much of him. And again at night they had played together, he and she, in the grass under moons and stars. She was insatiable. She was honey-sweet. She was born to the high arts. And she was treacherous. She had trumpeted his prowess to any who could hear. If he left this tent alive, he would kill her.

Her father laughed and prodded Hirel in the most vulgar of places. "*Sa, sa,* little stallion! Did you leave your tongue in your bower by the water? Tell me what brings you here. Would you like gold? Seneldi? Another woman to teach your western dances to? Though that might not be so simple; my daughter has sharp claws, and she's using them on any who even hints at taking a try at you."

Hirel's voice astounded him; it was utterly steady. "Sarevan," he said. "Sarevan would speak with you."

Hirel had conjured rightly. Azhuran was up again at once without question or protest, shortening his stride a little so that Hirel needed only to trot to keep pace, seeking Sarevan's tent amid a straggle of curious folk.

Sarevan sat up in his bed, and the old woman stood well apart from him, and the air between them quivered with tension. Hirel thrust himself into it. "The chieftain is here," he said to Sarevan. "Strike your bargains as you can, but be quick about it. You have need of rest."

He was certain that the witch would cast a curse on them all. But she stood back, arms folded, and glowered in silence. Azhuran bent over the Varyani prince, speaking in a rumble in his own tongue.

The bargaining went on for a very long while. Ulan came in the heat of it, when the old woman had added her own voice to the rest. The cat lay down unperturbed, drowsing with one ear cocked. Hirel settled against the warm solid body and tried to make sense

of the words that flew back and forth above his head. It kept him
from remembering shame; from resorting to murder.

"Swift seneldi," Sarevan said when the chieftain had gone back to
his judging and the wisewoman departed in disgust, "and provisions, and clothing for us both." He had barely voice left to speak,
but he looked eminently satisfied.

"At what price?" asked Hirel.

"A concession or two from my father, concerning mainly the
freedom of the tribe to hunt on royal lands, and employment in my
service for certain of Azhuran's young men."

"I did not mean that. He could ask nothing which your father
would not happily pay. At what price to you?"

"None," answered Sarevan. "We ride tomorrow."

Hirel sucked in his breath. He had meant to put an end to the
old woman's railings. Not to begin a new madness. "I see that I
erred," he said with a twist of scorn. "I credited you with a
modicum of sense."

"I have to go," Sarevan said.

"Send Azhuran's young savages in your place, and follow when
you are stronger. Surely one of them can be trusted to carry your
message."

"Not this." Sarevan sighed and closed his eyes. "Let be, cubling.
I do what I must."

"You are a howling madman."

Sarevan smiled thinly. He let the silence stretch; Hirel chose not
to break it. It seemed that Sarevan had slid into sleep, until he said,
"I've included you in the bargain. We'll go to Endros together."

Hirel went rigid. "We will not. I too can strike bargains; I will
find my way to Kundri'j. I am free of you now, as you are free of
me."

Sarevan's eyes opened. They were deep and quiet, and there was
regret in them, but iron also. "I'm sorry, cubling. I wanted to take
you home and have done with it. But now you know who I am, and
you guess what I must say to my father. I can't chance your
reaching Kundri'j Asan before I come to Endros."

"And what," asked Hirel softly, as a prince must, and above all a
prince betrayed, "gives you either right or power to constrain me?"

"Necessity," said Sarevan. "And the Zhil'ari."

"Potent powers," Hirel said, soft still, but never in submission. "But of right, you speak no word, as of honor you know nothing: you who so long deceived me, and cozened me, and reveled in your lies."

Sarevan sighed with all the weariness in the world. "Maybe I did take too much pleasure in it. It's past; I've paid. Now need drives me, and you must come perforce, because you are what you are. You won't suffer for riding with me. You'll be treated with all honor; I'll see that you have occasion to speak for your empire."

"My father will come with an army to free me."

"More likely he'll treat with us for your safe return."

"It comes down to that, does it not? You but played with me while you spied in Asanion. Now you tell the truth. You always meant me to be your hostage. Gods, that I had killed you when I had the chance!"

Sarevan raised himself on an arm that trembled but held. "I swear to you, Hirel Uverias, this is no betrayal. You will see your home and your people again; you will stand again in Kundri'j Asan. But first I must carry this message to my father."

"Must," Hirel echoed him. "Always *must*. And what compels you? You were not your father's only spy. Surely one at least will not be caught as you were caught."

That stung: Sarevan tensed and nearly fell. But he said as calmly as ever, "None of them has dreamed as I have dreamed. None of them is my father's son."

"Speak to him from afar. Wield the magic you are so proud of."

"I have none." Sarevan's elbow buckled; he fell back, with a gasp at the jarring of his shoulder. "I told you, it is gone. You will ride with me. You need not try to escape. Azhuran's warriors are instructed to guard you."

Not ostentatiously. But wherever Hirel went, there were a few hulking tribesmen about, loitering, gaming, blocking every path of escape. When he swam in the lake, half the Zhil'ari came to join him, men and women alike, flaunting their nakedness. One slipped up behind him and tugged wickedly; he yelped more in startlement than in pain. Zhiani's merriment rippled in his ear. She wanted to play, there, in front of everyone. He remembered that he was going to kill her. After he had killed Sarevan.

Her fingers did something exquisite. He groaned aloud, and no one even heard. Close by, between himself and the shore, two men locked in passion, a great grizzle-bearded man and a downy-cheeked boy; little children gamboled over and about them. It was unspeakable. And it held him as firmly as any bars, and Zhiani's hands and mouth were chains, and the world itself his prison.

They were not like his brothers and their accomplices in Pri'nai. No one was careless here, or underrated Hirel for his youth and his prettiness and his sheltered innocence. When morning came, he was still in the camp, and Zhiani made much of his leaving, sighing and kissing him and heaping him with gifts. He had decided to let her live. She was only a savage; she could not know what she had done to him.

Perhaps he might take her with him. She was no fit wife for a high prince; yet she made a remarkable concubine. No one in Kundri'j had anything like her.

If he ever saw Kundri'j again. But he would take her. For comfort. For company. She bathed him, kissing him wherever the fancy took her, nibbling here and there, but when desire rose and he reached for her, she eeled away. "No more," she said in deep regret. She dressed him with a little less playful wantonness, and clearly she did not approve of the breeches which he had insisted on. "Woman," she muttered. "Woman-weak." But she helped him into them, skin-snug as they were, and fastened the codpiece with rather more pleasure, and the heavy plated belt; and settled the embroidered coat, leaving it open so that the gold of her first gift shone clear on his chest. Last of all she brought out the high soft boots, and in her mind they seemed to make up for the effeminacy of the breeches. Small feet were much prized among these broad-footed savages; his, narrow and fine and only lightly cal-loused, the scars of his wandering beginning to fade, delighted her almost as much as the golden brightness of his hair.

When she was done, he looked like a prince again, cropped head and all. He saw it in her eyes. She brushed his eyelids with royal gold, caressing as she did it; her finger traced a curve upon his cheek. Asking with silent eloquence. Offering paints: gold, scarlet, green. Almost he yielded, but he had a little sense left. "No," he said firmly. "No more."

She sighed, but she withdrew, holding back the flap of her tent. The others were waiting. Nine painted, jangling, kilted giants

holding the bridles of their tall seneldi; and Sarevan. Sarevan on
his own feet, painted and jangling and kilted like any Zhil'ari buck,
with his hair in two narrow braids flanking his face and a long tail
behind, and a red-eyed, redmaned demon of a stallion goring the
air beside him. He turned toward Hirel; his face was a terror,
painted in barbaric slashes of white and yellow, his beard braided
with threads of gold. But his arrogance was the same, and the
white flash of his teeth. "You took your time, cubling," he said.

"I had help." Hirel looked about. "Am I permitted to ride? Or
must I be bundled upon a packbeast?"

"You ride," Sarevan said. He gestured; a boy led forward a
tiger-striped mare. She was not as tall as the others, though still no
pony, and she was no great beauty. Her like would never have been
suffered in Hirel's stables in Kundri'j. But she moved well, and she
had a bright wicked eye in her narrow head, and when Hirel took
the bridle she snorted and stamped and threatened him with her
teeth. He laughed. He liked a senel with a temper.

He vaulted into the odd high saddle with its softening of fleeces,
its festoons of straps and rings and bags. But there was a senel
under it all, lightly bitted and gathering to test him, and if there
was anything he could do, it was ride. Shorn, captive, and thrice
betrayed, in this at least he had come home.

The others were mounting. Azhuran had come while Hirel was
absorbed in his mount, and Zhiani was close by her father,
watching him speak to Sarevan. Hirel nudged the mare toward
them. Sarevan ended his colloquy and mounted lightly, favoring
his wounded shoulder only a little.

Azhuran saluted Hirel. "Good morning, little stallion," he said.

Hirel inclined his head. "You have been most generous. I thank
you; if ever I can repay you—"

"It was nothing," Azhuran said. "We did it for the prince. If
anything, we're in your debt. My daughter asks me to thank you
with all her heart. You've taught her more than she could ever
have hoped for, even from a yellow dwarf."

Hirel would ignore the insults. He would remember who and
what these people were. He would—

The chieftain's grin was abominably lewd. "Yes, you're the best
teacher she's ever had. Come Fall Gathering, when she spreads her

girdle in front of the tent, she'll win a high chief's son; and he'll
give a whole herd to lie in her bed."

Zhiani stood beside her father, and she was smiling luminously,
not a tear to be seen. Hirel's teeth locked upon the words he would
have said. That he was more than a high chief's son. That she
could be a queen; or as close to it as her barbarian kindred might
ever come. She had never loved him, only the arts which he could
teach her, which every Asanian nobleman learned from his early
youth. He was nothing to her but the passport to a rich husband.

"May you wed as you wish," he said to her in his court voice, that
could mask anything. Anger. Hurt. Reluctant relief. "May your
husband give you many sons."

The mare fretted. Hirel let her dance about, away from Zhiani's
heartless smile, toward his captivity.

It would, he vowed, be brief. As brief as wits and will could make
it.

He did not look back. The company sprang whooping into a
gallop; he kicked the mare after them. She bucked, squealed, and
set herself to outpace the wind.

Five

H E KILLS HIMSELF," SAID THE SMALLEST OF THE NINE ZHIL'ARI, who stood hardly taller than Sarevan.

They were camped by the southernmost of the Lakes of the Moon. Hirel eyed it longingly. If only this great lanky creature would go away, he could bathe and swim and loosen his travel-wearied muscles. But Zha'dan had caught him alone, and was not inclined to sacrifice the opportunity.

Hirel took off his coat and hung it tidily from a branch. With equal care he said, "Sarevan looks well enough to me. He rides without falling. He eats well. He—"

"He keeps the saddle because he refuses to fall. He pretends to eat, but the demon cat eats for him. He paints himself not for beauty as is proper: he hides what the riding does to him."

Hirel loosened his belt. The savage watched with interest. Hirel let his hands fall. He was not ready to strip in front of this glittering meddler; no matter that the whole tribe had seen all of him there was to see. There was no logic in modesty.

Nor in Sarevan's weakness, if it came to that. "His wound is healing. It was healing before we left the village. His wizardry— how can he be dying of that?"

Zha'dan regarded him as one would regard an idiot. Hirel watched tolerance dawn behind the paint. *Ah,* it said. *Foreigner.* Zha'dan took care with his words, stumbling a little with the roughness of tradespeech. "Mages are very great, like gods. But they are not gods. They are men. They pay for their magics. Small magics, small prices. Great magics, prices sometimes too great to pay. The body pays, always. And the power itself pays more. The great one—he fought great mages, and he won, but he killed one. A stone, you throw it, it strikes down the *kimouri,* but maybe it comes back. It strikes you too. It puts out your eye. So with power, and mages who use it to kill. Death's price is power's death."

"And the body's?"

"The power is the body," said Zha'dan. "If the great magics were all mine to use, and I lost them because I let myself fall into a trap, I would want to die."

"What are you asking of me?" demanded Hirel. "I have no power to wring sanity from that madman."

"He is no god to you. You can make him act like a man of sense."

"Sense? In Sarevan Is'kelion?" Hirel laughed almost freely. "Tribesman, you seek a miracle. Pray to your god. Perhaps he will hear you."

Hirel retrieved his coat, with a sigh for his lost bath. While Zha'dan stood in silence, eyes wide and hurt like the eyes of a wounded *kimouri,* Hirel stepped around him and walked away.

The nine Zhil'ari were becoming people, if slowly. There was Zha'dan, who hovered and worried; who painted concentric circles in scarlet on his brow and on his breast, and who liked to sing in a loud unmusical voice. There was Gazhin his brother, who always bellowed him into silence, and who was as burly as Zha'dan was slender. Unlike the others, whose beards were still uncertain of their welcome, he had thick copper-wound braids that brushed his breastbone. There were the twins, Rokan and Kodan, as like as two pups of the same litter, but Rokan painted himself with crimson, Kodan with blue. Sometimes Hirel amused himself in trying to find the faces behind the thickets of hair, and in wondering how their women could possibly endure to kiss those bristling cheeks. Small wonder that Zhiani had taken such delight in learning the arts of love from a beardless Asanian boy.

They had made camp boisterously, as seemed to be their wont, and amid apparent chaos, but it was very well made: a firepit dug, the daymeal set to cook, a guard sent off into the trees. The rest tended seneldi or swam in the lake. Two coupled in the open like animals; Hirel did not think they were the same two whose thrashings had kept him awake all last night.

The one on top saw him staring and grinned, never missing a stroke. He tore his eyes away. This was an art. It had its times, its private places, its rites and its cadences. And always it was to be regarded with reverence as the highest of earthly pleasures. These great hulking shaggy men, with their noise and their contortions —they made of it a mockery.

"This is play. With women, it's as sacred a rite as ever you could wish for." Sarevan stood beside him, perfectly steady, garish in his paint. Hirel saw no black bird of death perched on his shoulder.

"Sacred." Hirel snorted his contempt for the very word. "Sacred enough to buy with gold and amber and to trumpet from the mountaintops."

"No priest enters his rite unrehearsed," said Sarevan. He looked Hirel up and down. "I confess, I didn't believe you were capable. Even after all the tales I'd heard. Is it true that the training begins in the cradle?"

"I am not an infant!" Hirel's voice cracked upon the words.

Sarevan laughed. "Of course not, cubling. But does it?"

"Yes." Hirel's eyes would not lift from the ground. "It is an art. Like dancing, like weaponry, like courtcraft. The sooner begun, the greater the skill."

"Even with that?" At last Hirel could look up. Sarevan looked bemused, and amused, and insufferable. "I suppose I should envy you. I merely learned dancing and weaponry and courtcraft, and the rest was for whispering in corners. For a while I committed a dreadful sin. I went into the minds of people who were loving. Women, even. One day my mother caught me at it. I was mortified, and I knew that I was about to be flayed alive."

"Were you?" Hirel asked in spite of himself.

"Oh, yes. With words so keen, the air bled where they passed. And then I had to serve my penance. I'd been trying to see if I could will a child out of the coupling, and it turned out I had. I lived in the woman's mind throughout her pregnancy, and it was far from an easy one, even in our nest of mages: it was her first, and she was old for it, one of my mother's warrior women who'd never taken time for childbearing until I tampered with her protections. She forgave me. Eventually. After we'd birthed her daughter together."

"But how—"

"I lived in two bodies, and my own was often asleep. My tutors were much concerned. If they had known . . . It was hard sometimes, to know I was a boy of twelve summers, strong and quite disgustingly healthy, but to feel like a woman of thirty with a child growing in her belly. Toward the end I had to watch every moment, or I'd even walk like her. And that was painful, stretching a boy's bones to move as a woman's. But never as painful as hers, that stretched to carry the child."

"Preposterous," said Hirel.

"Utterly." Sarevan lay near the fire, and Ulan came to be his bolster. "When we come to Endros, you must meet Merian. My mother is fostering her, and I when I can be near her. She's a very charming impossibility."

"*You* are impossible." Hirel sat on his heels. Sarevan had closed his eyes. The lids were painted, following the tiger-patterning of the rest, so that his features seemed to blur and shift, eluding the steadiest stare. But if Hirel narrowed his eyes and glanced side-long, he could see the bones thrusting high beneath the thin-stretched skin. And that was not paint which paled Sarevan's lips, nor dew which gleamed on his brow. For all his seeming ease, his body was taut, its trembling not quite invisible.

Hirel blinked and found himself meeting Ulan's eyes. The cat yawned. His tail twitched and raised and came to rest over Sarevan, protecting, guarding. Sarevan seemed to have slid into a doze.

Hirel went away in silence, found what he needed, came back. As he touched sponge to the damp brow, Sarevan's eyes snapped open. Hirel considered modes of unarmed combat. But Sarevan lay still. With oil and salve, then water with cleanroot rubbed in, Hirel washed away the paint. And having done that, for thorough-ness he bathed the rest, as if he were a servant; and Sarevan never said a word. Except, at the end: "You have light hands."

"Training," said Hirel with a touch of irony. It helped to hide dismay. If he had looked on a dying man before the Zhil'ari found them, now he saw one all but dead.

And yet Sarevan rode so well—pretended so well. How could he do that?

"Because," answered Sarevan when it burst out of Hirel, "I must." He smiled, alarming as the grin of a skull. "I won't die. When I come to Endros, my father will heal me. I'm certain of it."

It was well for him that he could be. Hirel lidded jars, wrung out sponges, emptied the basin into the roots of a tree. The sun had gone down at last; the stars were coming out, and Greatmoon waxing to the full, broad as a shield in the darkening sky. Savory scents hung over the camp where the Zhil'ari gathered and babbled and waited to be fed. The lovers were done, sitting by one another; the green-painted one oiled and braided the other's hair.

The lake was all silver and black, glowing with the last of the light. A flock of water birds drifted and murmured, black-waked black shapes on the sheet of silver. Hirel dropped his garments and waded into the water's sudden chill, drew a breath, plunged.

Midway between the shore and the gathering of birds, he floated on his back. The air was cold on his wet face, the water warm about the rest of him. One lone splendid star stared down into his blurred eyes.

Tonight he could do it. Take the striped mare and a sackful of food and run. Last night he had wandered, testing, and the sentry had only grinned and saluted him, taking no particular notice of his rovings. None of them seemed to know who Hirel was, or to care; nor did any keep watch. Feckless boys, all of them. And Sarevan was too ill and too urgent to give chase for any great while. If Hirel slipped away as soon as everyone slept, and rode uncaught until morning, he would be safe thereafter.

He turned onto his face and swam slowly to shore. In camp they were eating, and being uproarious about it. Hirel dried himself, pulled on his breeches, slung coat and cloth over his shoulder.

There was meat on a spit still. Hirel slid round a savage who was not inclined to move. Laughter rumbled; Hirel spun, startled.

The man looked down at him. Very far down. The eyes were very dark in the gaudy face, taking Hirel in at leisure and with unmistakable intent. Hirel bared his teeth, which were very sharp, and let the hulking lout choose whether to call it a grin or a snarl.

The eyes began to glitter. A hand closed about Hirel's privates. With all his strength he held himself still, although his teeth set. "Let me go," he said.

The savage let go, not without a bit of fondling. He said something; the others laughed. Hirel's fingers clawed. The man grinned all over his harlequin face, and went to fill it with roast wildbuck.

"He said," said Sarevan, "that for some things a dagger is more effective than a broadsword."

"Would he know?" Hirel retrieved the spit and addressed himself to its savory burden. Azhuran's hellions drank and copulated and caterwauled themselves toward sleep. Sarevan, having eaten—yes, Ulan was getting most of it, even under Zha'dan's reproachful eye—rolled himself in his blanket and closed his eyes.

Hirel lay down as if at random some little distance from the fire's light, and pretended to sleep. One by one the others succumbed.

Hirel waited. Sleep crept up on him; he beat it back with a litany. Asanion. Asanion and the Golden Palace, and all his royalty restored.

With infinite slowness the fire died. The last rowdy youth dropped like a stone, cup rolling from his hand. Hirel counted, and almost crowed. Their sentry had come back to eat, and had tarried to finish the last of the mares'-milk wine, and they had forgotten to post another. They were all asleep in a tangle by the embers.

Hirel drew a breath. No one stirred. Inch by inch he drew his blanket over his head. Waited. No sound but snoring. Darkswathed, veiled in night, Hirel crept away from the sleepers. The seneldi grazed near the lake, loose as these tribesmen liked to leave them, trusting to the training that kept each beast within sight of its master.

The saddle was still in the brush where Hirel had hidden it, and the bridle, and the waterskin and the laden saddlebags. He rolled his blanket and bound it to the saddle, and, taking a bit of fruit, went to find the mare.

Darkness surged out of the earth, rolled over him, threw him down upon the cruel hardness of defeat.

"I thought you'd try it tonight," Sarevan said, dropping to one knee beside the massive shadow that was Ulan. Greatmoon made his face a featureless darkness; his eyes gleamed in it like an animal's, his teeth flashing white as he spoke. He seemed more amused than not. "A brave effort, cubling, but alas, perfectly predictable. Ulan, let him up."

Hirel rose slowly, judging distances. One of the stallions was close enough to—

"Don't even think of it," Sarevan said softly.

"So that was a lie," Hirel said. "You still have your magic. You can read my mind."

"I can read your eyes. And your face. And your body. I fear I'll have to bind you, for a little while. Until we've gone too far to make escape worth the trouble."

"Then you will have to drag me in chains all the way to Endros Avaryan."

"I brought no chains. Leather thongs will have to do." Sarevan bound Hirel's hands in front of him, firmly though not cruelly, and led him back to the fire. No one woke to see. No one needed to. Even the bonds were not entirely necessary: Ulan set himself by Hirel, and Hirel raged and wept behind his frozen face, but he did not fancy bolting for it with the cat on his heels.

Sarevan laid his head on Ulan's flank and went to sleep. Hirel sat wide-eyed, motionless, and watched the sky wheel into dawn. Long before then, he was certain. Sarevan had plotted this. To test Hirel. To seal his captivity.

And Hirel had been within a whisper's span of pitying him, racked with sickness as he was, bereft of all his bright magic.

Sarevan did not make good his threat. In the grey morning he loosed Hirel's bonds and said, "If you will give me your word, I will let you ride free."

Hirel flexed his stiff shoulders, eyes burning upon that hated, mongrel face. It waited without expression. Would wait until the sun fell, in perfect patience. Hirel's gaze dropped. "Yes," he muttered. "I give it."

"It is accepted."

And Hirel was forgotten, left to gather his belongings and tend his mount and fall into the line of riders. Sarevan led, as always; Ulan kept pace with him. The others rode in no perceptible order, except that Hirel took care to hold the rear. They left the lake, winding up a steep wooded ridge, and wound down into a long valley. Trees closed in, but the valley's center was clear, like the last gasp of a road: grass and stones and stretches of barren earth.

Toward midday the vale bent westward, rising into a long gentle slope lightly furred with trees. Stones crowned the hill, a rough circle that held a suggestion of men's hands, but hands long fallen to dust. Hirel slowed his mare as if to stare. No one noticed. He let the gap widen. Sarevan was far ahead, striking for the eastward ridge, and Ulan loped before him.

Hirel clapped heels to his mare's sides, bending over her neck. She bolted toward the hill.

Behind them, a shout went up. Hirel lashed the mare with the rein-ends; she shifted from flat gallop to full flight.

They were far behind, all his jailers. Hirel grinned into the teeth of the wind.

His jubilation shuddered and died. A grey shadow flowed over the ground, and its eyes were green fire, and it was closing. It was angling. It was moving to cut him off.

"No," he said, not loudly. He bent lower still, singing into the flattened ear, praising, cursing, willing the mare onward. Up the hill. *Up.*

She stumbled. He caught her, bearing her up by main force, driving her forward. Ulan filled the corner of his eye. The great jaws gaped; the white fangs gleamed. The stones. If Hirel could only come to the stones, he could defend himself. Before he fell. As he must. Damn that unnatural cat to the hell that had spawned it.

The circle floated before him. Avaryan sat above the tallest stone and laughed, a great booming roar, filling Hirel's brain. Even in his desperation he could reflect that he was at a sore disadvantage: he had no god to set against this flaming monstrosity. Logic was a very poor defense; philosophy crumbled like a tower of sand. And all Asanion's thousand gods were but a tale to frighten children.

The mare veered. Ulan's jaws clashed shut where her throat had been. Hirel fought with rein and leg, beating her back toward the west. She struggled, stiff-legged, throwing up her head. Ulan snarled. She went utterly mad.

Slowly, leisurely, Hirel wheeled through the air. The earth was a bitter shock. Sharp cloven hoofs flailed about him. He could only lie and gasp and wait to die.

A blur of fire and shadow became Sarevan's face. Hirel sucked in blessed air. Sarevan's expression, a cool corner of his mind observed, did not bode well for him. He had seen it once ablaze with temper, and that had been frightening. But this cold stillness was more deadly by far.

Little by little his lungs remembered their office. The rest of him was bruised but unbroken. He sat up shakily; no hand came to his aid. They were all mounted, staring, save for Sarevan on one knee beside him. Sarevan watched with eyes that granted him nothing. Not mercy, not fury, not even contempt.

Hirel rose dizzily, swallowing bile. He was eye to eye with Sarevan. In spite of themselves, his fists had clenched.

At last the Varyani prince spoke, soft and cold. "You gave me your word."

Hirel laughed, though it made his head throb. "I do not waste honor on animals."

This silence stretched longer even than the one before. Longer, colder, and more terrible. Sarevan stood. He towered like the standing stones, like the god enthroned upon them. He raised a hand.

The Zhil'ari who came at the signal had no illusions of gentleness. He bound Hirel's hands behind him, a tightness just short of pain, and set him in the saddle of the lathered and trembling mare, and bound his feet together beneath her belly. Taking the reins, he mounted his own tall stallion. Sarevan was astride, waiting. They turned again toward the east.

Six

I T WAS NOT HURTING IN THE PROPER PLACES.

Hirel steeled himself to endure his bonds. He had earned them; he bore them as brands of pride, that he was neither coward nor traitor to ride tamely into his enemy's stronghold. After the first grueling hours his captors relented, securing him by his hands only, and those in front of him.

He could suffer the constant watch by day and by night. He could face his guards without rancor, the more for that they bore him none of their own. Indeed, they looked on him with something close to respect. They saw that he was fed, that he was clean, that his needs were looked after. "You tried," Zha'dan said once. "That's the act of a man."

No, it was not his captivity that hurt. It was the chief of his captors. Only Sarevan never spoke to him, or went near him, or deigned to take notice of him. The others would be enemies if war compelled it, but they bore Hirel himself no ill-will. Sarevan did not merely hate Hirel; he despised him.

And what had Hirel done, that Sarevan himself had not equaled or surpassed? He was a fool and a child to be so outraged; and Hirel was mad to be so troubled by it. It should not matter. They had been born to be enemies, the sons of two emperors in a world wide enough only for one. Their meeting and their companion-

71

ship had been scarred with contention. They would come together inevitably in war, that last battle which would raise one throne where now were two.

Yet it did matter. Hirel did not like Sarevan, had never liked him. Nothing so harmless or so simple. This estrangement, this cold distance, with Sarevan riding always ahead, growing thinner and frailer, fighting harder with each hour to remain erect and astride—Hirel wanted to burst his damnable bonds and kick his mare to the red stallion's side and rail at the fool until he smiled his white smile, and bowed his haughty head, and let himself be carried. Or at least until he acknowledged Hirel's existence. And let someone, anyone, bolster his waning strength.

Sarevan entered the Hundred Realms like a shadow of death, but he entered them alive and breathing and guiding his own senel. In one thing only he had yielded to necessity: he had bidden his Zhil'ari to tie him to the saddle. They did not like it, but they obeyed. They understood that kind of pride.

Hirel had it. It had held him aloof and silent, royalty imprisoned but never diminished. It brought him at last to a crux. If he must go in bonds to Endros Avaryan, he would not go with Sarevan's contempt upon his head. Fool or madman or no, Sarevan was a prince. That much, Hirel would grant him. And princes could be enemies, could hate one another with just and proper passion, but scorn diminished them both.

Greatmoon, waning, still filled the sky. Although this was a richly peopled country, the company had camped at a distance from the last town. Sarevan had no wish to be slowed by the duties of a prince. He wore again his paints and his finery, and such a welter of gauds in his hair and beard that their color was scarcely distinguishable. Riding in the midst of his savages, with Ulan wandering where he would, even on the highroad the prince was scarcely remarked. Hirel won far more stares, with his High Asanian face and his Zhil'ari fripperies and his bound hands. People ogled the wild barbarians; they spat on the yellow spy. Sarevan they did not know at all.

Even so, he did not test his disguise in inn or hall. This night they had fish from the swift icy stream, and bread which they had had of a farmwife going to market; and Zha'dan made a broth of herbs and grain and the long-eared *kimouri* which Ulan brought from his hunting, and coaxed it into Sarevan. Hirel watched from across the firepit. Sarevan could not feed himself; he could barely swallow. He was no more than skin stretched over bone. As he lay propped against his saddle, only his eyes seemed alive; and those were dim, clouded. He was not fighting his nursemaid. He had no strength for it.

Hirel stood. Rokan was his guardhound tonight, he of the crimson paint; the Zhil'ari watched but did not hinder as Hirel skirted the fire.

Sarevan did not see him. Would not. He sank down beside the prince, letting his bound hands rest on his knee. Zha'dan acknowledged him with a glance. Sarevan was as still as before, but the air about him had chilled.

Zha'dan lowered the bowl. It was scarcely touched. His finger brushed the bandage on Sarevan's shoulder. It was new, clean, startlingly white. "It's festering," he said, not trying to be quiet. "He's been hiding it. Keeping anyone from looking, till I noticed that the wrappings hadn't been changed in days. It needs cautery; he won't let me. He'd rather lose his arm than chance a little pain. Maybe he figures to die first."

"Only cautery?" Hirel asked, reckoning days, and the little he knew of such wounds, from when a slave had pierced himself with an awl in the stable. The man's arm had swelled, and streaked red and then black, and begun to stink; he had lost the arm, but he had died. The surgeon had waited too long to cut.

One could not see the poison's spreading on skin the color of nightwings. But one might be able to feel the heat of it. Bound, Hirel was awkward. He did not try to unwrap the bandage. His fingers searched round about it. The skin was dry, taut, fever-hot, but fevered everywhere the same. It did not flinch away from him.

"If it has spread," Hirel said to Zha'dan, "it has not spread far."

"Must you discuss me as if I were already dead?"

Hirel was careful not to start, or stare, or blurt out something unwise. He favored Sarevan with a cool regard, and rebuked his heart for singing. "Would you rather we went away and whispered?"

The dark eyes were clear and perhaps not utterly unyielding. "I do not fancy hot iron in my shoulder. My father will heal it more gently and much more completely."

"Your father will heal everything, it seems. If you get so far."

"I mean to," said Sarevan.

"He will fulfill your expectations, or he will answer to me."

The eyes widened. "What right have you—"

Hirel held that burning stare and made it fall. "There is," he said levelly, "a debt or two. And the issue of . . . comradeship."

"Great value that you lay on it," said the cool bitter voice.

"What would you have done in my place?"

Sarevan pondered that, which was a victory in itself. At last he sighed. "I would have found a way to avoid giving my word."

"You demanded my word. You did not stipulate that it embody my honor."

Sarevan stared. Suddenly he laughed, hardly more than a cough. "Asanian oathtaking! Cubling, when I told Baron Ebraz that you were incorrigible, I never knew how right I was. Will you swear again, now that we're so close to Endros? This time," he added, "with honor in it."

Hirel's silence was long enough to trouble even Sarevan's complacency. But his pride had had enough of trying to force nature's relief while a painted barbarian looked on and smirked. He held out his hands and said, "I give you my true word of honor, as high prince to high prince, that I will not attempt to escape until I stand before your father in Endros Avaryan."

"And I give you mine," said Sarevan, "that we will accord you all honor, and return you to Kundri'j Asan as soon as we may." He raised a spider-thin hand. "Cut the cords, Zha'dan."

He did it quickly, with a swift smile. Hirel leaped up and stretched wide, exultant. Sarevan's grin was a white flash in the firelight. Hirel answered it before he could help himself. "Now," he said, dropping down again, "what is this I hear of your dainty stomach? Here, eat. I command you."

Rather to his surprise, and much to everyone else's, Sarevan obeyed. But of course; it took a prince to compel a prince.

When the Zhil'ari in council reckoned that they were two days' ride from Endros, Hirel left his mare to run with the rest, and swung onto Sarevan's crupper. Sarevan cursed him in a hiss, but he took no notice. The body that so brief a time past had seemed so heavy was as light as a bundle of sticks. He was in the saddle behind it, unbinding the lashings, before anyone could move; and Zha'dan came when he called, and took the Varyani prince in his arms. Thereafter the Zhil'ari took turn and turn. "Consider it my revenge," he said to the smoldering eyes. By then he was back on his mare again: she did not take kindly to infidelity.

That night there was a battle. The Zhil'ari would have them lodge in a town called Elei; they were curious, and they had discovered a great liking for southland wine. But Sarevan would not have it. "The temple will know," he said in the whisper that was all the voice he had. "They will come for me. They will drug me to keep me quiet. They will try to heal me themselves before they send me to my father." He struggled feebly in Gazhin's arms. "Let me up, damn you. Let me ride. I can come to Endros sooner by myself."

"But—" Gazhin began.

"No." They all stared at Hirel, except Sarevan, whose effort had robbed him of his last strength. "Better that he rest tonight and ride another day, and gain the tending he needs."

It was not so simple, and at times it was acrimonious, but in the end they rode through Elei without stopping. Beyond the town the land rose in a long ridge like a breaking wave. Trees clothed the ridge and crowded into its hollows, yet high up, almost to the summit, they found a haven: a green meadow, golden with the last long rays of Avaryan, starred with flowers. From a rock near its eastern edge bubbled a spring.

It was early yet. Ulan had come as he always did, bringing a gift for the pot; he dropped it by the half-dug firepit and sought his lord. Sarevan, lost in a dim dream, knew nothing and no one. The cat nosed him from head to foot, growling on the edge of hearing. Sarevan stirred, but at random, unconscious.

"Tomorrow, Ulan," said Hirel through the tightness in his throat. He was not certain, but he thought that he had found a long tongue of greater heat on arm and side beyond the bandage, and the flesh was taut, swollen, unpleasant to the touch. "Tomorrow the Sunborn will work a miracle." He turned away too quickly, striding he cared not where.

The clamor of the camp faded behind him. The way was steep and stony, yet trees clung there, gripping the rock with clawed fingers. He welcomed the pain, the breath beaten out of him, the earth that, though strong, still yielded before him. He was dwarfed here but only as all men were made small by the immensity of the world.

A shadow sprang past him. He cried aloud in the anger of despair. But Ulan had not come to herd him back to his captivity. The cat climbed ahead of him, sometimes outstripping him, sometimes circling back, bearing him company. Yes, they were in the same straits, they two. Did Ulan's anger match his own, that he could care so much, and come so close to grief, for a redheaded madam.

The summit was a triumph and a disappointment. Hirel had conquered the Wall of Han-Gilen, but he had gained no sight of the fabled City of the Sun. A broad plain stretched away below him, the plain of Han-Gilen watered by the flood of Suvien, but although the sky was clear above and behind him, all before lay under a pall of storm. Clouds boiled; lightning cracked. Rain cloaked the heart of the Sun's empire.

The wind blew fierce in Hirel's face. Challenging him, son of the Golden Throne, trespasser in the land of his enemies. He flung up his arms, defying it. It buffeted him upon his precarious perch. He stood firm; with infinite reluctance it surrendered. With a snap of laughter, he turned away.

He followed Ulan down, slipping and slithering, catching himself on treetrunks. The sun had sunk with alarming rapidity; already it was growing dim among the trees. Ulan descended more slowly, and Hirel caught the thick fur of the cat's neck, bracing himself against a sudden sharp incline.

He did not discover the hollow so much as he fell into it. It was like the one in which they had camped, like many another along this crannied wall of a mountain: an oval of grass hemmed in with trees and watered by a spring. But here the trees crowded close, and a bastion of stone reared up above the meadow, slanting inward into darkness. It was a comely enough place, but Hirel did not like it; and not only because Ulan surveyed it with raised hackles. The cavemouth gaped like a lair of dragons.

Because his body bristled and his heart thudded, Hirel forced himself forward. It was only a clearing growing dim with evening. If anything lived in the cave, surely it was no match for the ul-cat that stalked stiff-legged by his side.

The spring bubbled and sang into a basin of stone. Hirel bent to drink, and froze. Something lay in the water. Something white and shapely, a work of fine craftsmanship, shaped very like a skull. The skull of a child or a small woman, delicate as it was, contemplating the sky with golden jewel-eyes.

Hirel's throat burned with thirst, but he backed away from the water. Ulan crouched before the cave, snarling. Hirel came to his side, moving slowly, helpless to hold back.

If this was a guide, the skull in the spring had belonged to a child. This one had been a boy, one of the red-bronze people of this country, finer-featured than most, his hair the color of tarnished copper. He had not died swiftly, and he had not died easily. In the emptied sockets of his eyes, twin topazes glinted, staring up at Hirel in a horrible parody of awareness.

Hirel had known when he saw the skull, and had not credited what he knew. The darkside rites of Uvarra Goldeneyes were not uncommon in Asanion even in these enlightened days. But he had never thought to come upon them so far east, so deep into Avaryan's country, within sight of Endros itself. The Thousand Gods belonged to the west, and this one most of all, queen of light, lord of the flaming darkness, goddess and god, redeemer and destroyer. Hirel bore her name of the light; his name of the dark had been bestowed upon a lion's cub and the beast sacrificed to Uvarra, that Asanion's heir be proof against all powers of the night.

Superstition, he had always called it. He had better night eyes than most, and he had never been afraid of the dark, but that had nothing to do with gods or demons. Uvarra was naught but that figment of man's mind which, borne eastward, had become Avaryan, and grown from deity of birth and death into sole true god. How like the east to call the bright face male, and to name the dark a goddess, and hate her and fear her and ban all her worship. In Asanion they looked on it as a necessity, however grim, like death itself that was the Dark One's servant.

This was not a sacrifice to distorted and tongue-twisted Uveryen. She did not make use of Eyes of Power. And carved on the boy's breast above the empty cavern of his belly were words in fine curving script, the holy writing of Asanion in one of the older tongues, addressing the one whom Hirel, Lightchild and night's protected, was not supposed to name.

He had done it before, often. He did not do it now. He could not. He was remembering his logic. If there were mages . . .

Ulan moaned deep in his throat. The same keening sound escaped Hirel before he could strangle it. He pulled himself onto the warm comforting back and kicked the long sides as if the cat had been a senel. Ulan snarled at Hirel's presumption, but he wheeled about and bore the prince away.

* * *

Hirel saddled his mare with many pauses. She stood quietly for once, as if she knew that he had been sick all night. Blackly, stomach-wrenchingly, helplessly sick. It was not only the hideousness of the sacrifice. All the horrors of the world had come crashing upon his head, all at once, without mercy. And there was no one here who cared enough to minister to him.

Now, in the hour before sunrise, his emptied stomach lay quiet. He was weak, but he felt light, purged, even the sourness in his mouth put to flight by the herb that sweetened the mare's breath. He ran his hand over the black-and-dun silk of her neck. She nibbled his hair. He laughed a little, for no reason, unless that the night was over and the day was coming and he had emptied himself for a brief while of the horror in the clearing.

The mare tensed to shy, but held her ground. Ulan ignored her with lordly disdain. He dropped something at Hirel's feet, turned away.

All the sickness flooded back. Hirel doubled up with it. An eternity, and it passed, and still the hideous beautiful thing gleamed out of the grass. An orb of topaz the precise size and shape of a child's eye. It did not blast Hirel's trembling fingers, and yet he shuddered at the touch of it. He thrust it into the pouch at his belt, where it burned until his mind schooled itself—almost— to forget. Until he must remember.

They rode hard, unsparing of mounts or selves. Sarevan had fallen into unconsciousness like death, passed like baggage from hand to hand, unmoving, oblivious. They scaled the Wall, riding far from the place of sacrifice, and there at last with its veil of storms cast aside was the city they sought: Endros Avaryan, Throne of the Sun, white walls and towers of gold, and the crag above the river, and the magewrought tower a black fang upon the summit. Darkness and light face to face across the rush of Suvien, but both begotten of the mind and the hand of the Sunborn.

They spurred toward it. The mountain shrugged them off; the plain unrolled itself before them, broad green-golden level scattered with villages. They were marked, a wild riding of lakeland savages with a western prince, and one who seemed a savage borne lifeless on a saddlebow. They were not challenged. They were a strong company, and this was the heart of an empire at peace.

Hirel, exalted with emptiness and with the aftermath of illness, gazed steadily upon the walls of Endros. They mocked it in

Kundri'j, called it a whitewashed village, an encampment of stone, a rude mockery of the Golden City itself. It was all raw, they said, all harsh stone and bare stripped earth, its white and gold too stark for beauty: the hubris of a barbarian veneered with southern gentility, proclaiming for all to hear: *See, I too can make an empire, and raise up a city, and dare to ordain that it will endure a thousand years.*

And yet, the nearer it came, the lovelier it seemed. Stark, yes, but wrought in a harmony of curve and plane and angle. It looked clean and young, like snow new-fallen in the morning, but not raw; it seemed to grow out of the earth as a mountain does, sudden and splendid and inevitable.

Not that it failed of reality. People lived in it, traveled to and from it, ate and chattered and sang, labored and idled, bought and sold and traded, had need of cesspits and middens and graves. They were a varied people, mannered according to their breeding. Hirel saw black giants, painted and unpainted, bearded and shaven smooth, the women bare to the waist or veiled to the eyes, striding as if they owned the world; almond-eyed folk of the plains, red or bronze or brown, who stared openly and speculated audibly and never knew what the outlanders carried into their city; here and there a white oddity from the Eastern Isles, walking aloof; and many a figure painful in its familiarity, small among the rest, sleek and full-fleshed, with skin in every shade of gold from dun to old ivory, and curling fair hair, and great-irised tawny eyes. Though none had skin as pale as Hirel's had been, or hair so pure a gold, or eyes that often seemed all amber. *They* had courtesy; they did not stare, and they kept their thoughts to themselves, going smoothly about their business.

Ulan was gone again. He shunned cities; even this one, it seemed. Well enough: if he were known, so might Sarevan be, and then would be pandemonium.

But anonymity had its troubles. Hirel, bred in palaces, knew of guards and their office. It had not occurred to him that his companions might come within its sphere. To all appearances they were a ragtag company, a pack of savages from the gods knew where, and Sarevan's name was insufficient passport to the inner reaches of the palace. The outer reaches were splendid enough, to be sure, and quite royally bewildering in their complexity; many persons offered guidance, for a fee, and many more shied away from the redolent corpse in Rokan's arms. Somewhere among the

courts, a number of armed men persuaded the Zhil'ari to leave
their mounts and their weapons behind, not without a broken
head or three.

They would have been ejected then, but for Zha'dan's swift hard
words. Hirel had caught a glancing blow meant for someone else;
he could not fit his mind properly around any tongue. He heard
only the name of Avaryan and the overtones of menace. The
guards let them by, afoot and unarmed and drawing close together, with Sarevan shifted to the care of Gazhin who was largest and
strongest.

They wandered for an age, to no purpose. "We would see the
emperor," Zha'dan kept saying in passable Gileni. He was laughed
at, or sneered at, or ignored. "We have your *prince,* damn you. We
have the emperor's son!" The laughter sharpened. That? men
mocked. That had been a stripling savage before it began to rot,
and tricks did not succeed here, and his imperial majesty did not
stoop to the raising of outland dead.

It was a brown man who said that, a plump jeweled creature
whose every pore breathed forth the air of a petty functionary.
Someone else, moved by their desperation if not by the name of
their charge, had directed them to him. He sat in his gilded cranny
and despised them, and his mind was set in stone. He did not know
their painted skeleton. Both its fists were knotted in rictus and
would not unclench for proof; and in any case it was well known
that the Prince Sarevadin journeyed among his loyal subjects in
the west. They were lying in order to get at the emperor, he heard
such lies all too often, the whole world would sell itself into the hell
of falsehood to gain a moment of the Sunborn's notice. Or of his
favor. Or of his fabled magic.

They left him still expounding upon the necessity of protecting
the emperor from his importunate people. Most of the Zhil'ari
were for storming the inner gates. Gazhin curled his lip at them.
"You are perfect idiots. You'll end in chains, and all for nothing. I
say we go to the temple. They'll know my lord, and they can bring
his father to him. We should have gone there first."

Hirel scowled at the tiled pavement. That was his fault. He had
argued for the straight path to the emperor, and the Zhil'ari,
ignorant of palaces, had let him have his way. But they had learned
quickly enough.

For all their urgency, they paused in the quiet courtyard to which their contention had taken them. A fountain played in it; they bathed their heated faces, and the wounded laved their bruises, and Zha'dan sponged Sarevan's body. Hirel drank a little, found that he could keep it down if he tried, wandered away from them.

In truth this was more garden than court. Tiles rimmed it and circled the fountain; the rest was all grass and flowers and one slender young tree guarding a gate. It opened to Hirel's touch.

Grass again, level, shaved smooth. A groom rode a senel there, a black stallion of very great beauty. It could not but be of the Ianyn breed, that was reckoned the best in the world; although its horns curved in the scimitars of age, it moved like a youngling. Leap, curvet, caracole; sedate sidewise canter and sudden fiery plunge, with always the perfect control of the dancer or the warrior. And yet it wore no bridle, its rider motionless in the light flat saddle, hands upon his thighs.

Hirel's eyes drew him across the grass. He had never seen such riding. He wanted to learn it. Now. Utterly.

He was not seen. The stallion fixed inward upon his art. The man rode as in a trance. A young man, all night-dark, one of the smooth-shaven northerners. He was a priest of Avaryan. Very like Sarevan, in truth, if Sarevan had not had that fiery mane: his heavy braid swinging to his senel's rump, and his kilt threadbare above bare feet, and his chest bare and his torque bright beneath the keen eagle-face. He was not outrageously handsome as Sarevan was, but neither was he ugly; he was simply himself.

The senel gathered himself from a flying gallop into a dance in place, cadenced like a drumbeat, stilling to stone. Hirel's numbed brain struggled. They were stone. Black man on black stallion, with gold about the man's neck and glinting in his ear, and dun-drab paint fading on the sculpted kilt, and rubies feigning seneldi eyes.

The carven rider left the carven saddle, and Hirel stared. For all his northern face and his northern garb, this stranger was no giant; he was merely a tall man. Asanian-tall, middling in the south, small as a child among the tribes. For the first time since he woke beside Sarevan's fire, Hirel felt the world shrink to its wonted size. He was a well-grown stripling, tall for his age, like to overtop his father who was not reckoned a small man; and he could look this man in the eye without strain. "You cannot guess," he said, "how blessed it is to stand straight and look into a face, and not into a breast or a belt or worse."

The rider smiled, and his smile was splendid; it made him look even younger, little more than a boy. "That is quite the most pleasant thing anyone has ever said about my size." He had a marvel of a voice, deep yet clear. Like Sarevan's. Incredibly like.

Hirel was never an idiot twice running. And he had seen enough of magic to credit a stroke of sheerest, blindest luck. But he was all fuddled, and it did not come out properly. "This," he said. "Is this the Mad One?"

"Indeed," said the rider in rags and gold, as the stallion suffered Hirel to stroke his neck. He was hardly warm, for all his dancing. He blew into Hirel's hand, feigned to nip, rolled his wild eye when Hirel smiled. Hirel turned with a hand on the black mane. The man watched him, amused and, it seemed, intrigued. "You've just joined a rare fraternity, stranger: the chosen few who can lay hands on the battle charger of the Sunborn."

Hirel did not bow. If he did, he knew that he would fall; and a high prince did not perform the prostration. "We have brought your son to you, lord emperor. But no one will believe us, and we are turned away wherever we go, and I fear—"

He never finished. The Lord of Keruvarion had vanished. Hirel was alone with the Mad One, who held him up. "But," he said, "the Sunborn is *old*. Older than my father."

He unwound his fingers from the long mane. He had to follow the emperor. The Zhil'ari would not be likely to recognize their lord, ragged as he was. That would be a bitter turnabout; and Sarevan on the very brink of death, if not past it.

Hirel burst through the gate, stopped short. The Sunborn stood in the center of a circle. All the Zhil'ari had fallen back with awe in their eyes. They knew their master, perhaps as beasts might, by instinct. Only Gazhin, burdened with Sarevan, had not moved from his seat on the fountain's rim. His face was blank, blinded.

The emperor looked down at the shape in Gazhin's arms. He wore no expression at all. But he looked young no longer. He was grim, old; worn to the bone by the long hard years.

He took up the lifeless body. With utmost gentleness he cradled it. He did not speak. Perhaps he could not. He turned in silence, and walked through the sudden throng as if it had been empty air, and was gone.

Seven

HIREL HAD WON ENTRY FOR ALL OF THEM INTO THE INNER palace, and they were accorded some semblance of honor. The poor savages from the Lakes of the Moon, bereft of a battle, were utterly at a loss. They shrank from the hampering walls, and eyed the ceilings uneasily, and jumped like deer when doors shut behind them. The smooth laconic servants terrified them as no armed warrior could; they huddled together, a draggled flock of sunbirds with wary darting eyes.

They fastened upon Hirel as the only familiar creature in an alien world. He saw them through a feeding, which he did not share, and through a bath, which was rather simpler. They were clean people, cleaner in strict truth than most Asanians. The great ever-running stream of water, heated in furnaces, fascinated them; they played in it like children, forgetting at last to be afraid of the men who tried valiantly to serve them. Hirel, who had never seen them without their paint and their braids, was rather pleasantly surprised. They looked almost human with their faces bared under the water-sleeked beards.

Then a man came at them with a razor. Offering, not compel-

ling, but they bellowed like bulls. He retreated rapidly. Gazhin
lunged after him, blind with outrage.

Hirel shouted. His voice cracked hideously. Gazhin veered,
shocked, beginning to come to himself. The servant escaped
forgotten.

Hirel dragged himself out of the water, in which he yearned to
lie until it washed away all his troubles. He found the man who
seemed to command the servants; who bowed respectfully enough,
but not as to a prince. "Let them be," Hirel said, "and quarter
them with me. They belong to the Prince Sarevadin; if—when he
is able, he will dispose of them as he sees fit."

The man bowed again. Hirel would approve of him, when this
creeping exhaustion passed. And still so much to do. He did not
know where Sarevan was. No one would tell him. He did not even
know if the emperor had come in time: if Sarevan lived, or if he
was dead.

With tradespeech and with plain force, Hirel persuaded his
unwelcome entourage to remain in the rooms they had been
given. A small suite in Hirel's estimation, appropriate for a very
minor nobleman, but endurable. The garments given him
matched his lodgings, and those would not do at all; he returned to
his travelworn Zhil'ari finery and put on a fair sampling of Zhiani's
golden gifts. When he left, the tribesmen were restoring one
another's paint, and exploring the rooms with affected noncha-
lance, and taking liberal advantage of the wine which the servants
had brought them.

Sarevan would have said that the god guided Hirel. Hirel called
it luck, the second such stroke since he came to Endros. He chose a
passage at random, and it led him through a court and along a wall
and up a stair. One or two servants passed him, preoccupied.
There were no guards. It seemed a servants' way, narrow,
unadorned, and leading past occasional unassuming doors. The
one at the end led to a more public corridor, broad, high, and
hung with tapestries which Hirel's wavering eyes did not try to
examine.

There were doors, but only one was guarded, and that by two
who were high and most haughty, liveried in scarlet and gold. For
an astounded instant Hirel thought that the shorter of the two was
Sarevan. But this was more boy still than man; his bright hair made

his skin seem doubly dark, but it was shades fairer than Sarevan's, like old bronze, and his features were blunter though still very fine, the nose straight, the long mouth apt to laughter. But at the moment it was set hard, the dark eyes glittering with unshed tears.

It was he who leveled his spear on Hirel and spoke the challenge. "Who trespasses in the domains of the emperor?"

Hirel eyed the spearpoint that hovered a handspan from his throat. It was exceedingly sharp, though not as sharp as the voice of its bearer.

He glanced at the second guard, an enormously tall and long-limbed creature who was, for all of that, quite definitely a woman. She reminded him inevitably and a little painfully of Zhiani, even to the look in her eye, the frank appreciation of an attractive young male. She was not as beautiful as Zhiani. Too lean, too firm of feature. Yet as his hope of escape, she was lovely beyond compare.

He addressed her carefully, in the Gileni the other had used. "I would look on the high prince. I mean him no harm."

The spear touched his throat. "Sure you don't," growled the Gileni princeling. "They're getting bold, these cockerels, sending their spies into the Sunborn's own bedchamber."

Hirel swallowed. Metal pricked. He retreated a hair's width. "I was one of those who brought Prince Sarevadin here. We have been companions. I would see him."

"So would all the rest of the world." The woman spoke without gentleness, but also without hostility. "Apologies, stranger, but no one passes. Emperor's orders."

"I would pass. I must see him. I must tell him—"

The Gileni cut him off. "No one will be telling him anything for a long time. Maybe never. Thanks to your kind, Yellow-eyes." He wept openly, without shame, his words spat out in a fire of hate. But the spear had wavered. Hirel slid inside it.

Firm hands caught him, thrust him back, left him where he had stood before, in utter ignominy. "Don't try that again," the Ianyn woman warned him, not without amusement. "You're the western-er he came with, I'll credit that, but no one sees him now. The emperor is working a great magic over him. No one can pass the wards until the working is done."

"He lives," said Hirel. He did not know what he should be thinking. He knew that he should not be as glad as this.

"He may live," the woman said. "He may die. He walks in the shadows; he may not want to come back. Or he may not be able to."

Hirel's heart contracted. "He must not do that. I do not wish it."

They stared at him. The Gileni's scorn was a lash across his skin. He was past caring for it: or for reason or logic or princely policy, or for anything but his own will. "I do not wish it," he said again.

"Are you a mage, then?" the Gileni mocked him. "Can you master even the Sunborn with your power?"

Hirel looked at him, but did not see him. The Eye of Power burned at his belt, burned and sang. "I am high prince. I am his equal. He will not die while I have will to hold him."

Perhaps they spoke again. He did not heed them. He turned away from them, the red Gileni who hated him, the black Ianyn who laughed at him. Barbarians. This alien country, these alien faces, they crowded upon him. They bore him down.

He found a door without guards, that opened on an empty room that opened on light and greenness. A shadow glided from amid the green. Even Ulan languished in exile from his prince. He did not precisely come to Hirel for comfort, but when Hirel's knees, weakening, cast him upon the carpet, Ulan was there to cling to.

Hirel buried his face in the musky fur. He would not be sick again. He would not. He wept instead. Because he was alone, and forsaken, and betrayed. Because his only anchor to this unlovely world was dying or dead, in a welter of magic.

Ulan was patient. He did not upbraid Hirel, or remind him with elaborate tact that a high prince did not cry. A high prince did nothing but bear the deadly burden of his robes, standing like a carven image for an empire to worship, enduring until he should be set upon the Golden Throne in the mantle of gold, with his face forever hidden behind the golden mask.

That was the dream, the nightmare which had haunted Hirel since he was a young child. In it the world was all gold, harsh, yellow, heavier than lead; and he was borne on it, shrouded in it, chained with it, and above him loomed a mask of gold. It lowered slowly, infinitely slowly. It was the precise shape of his face, but it

opened nowhere, blind, nostrilless, its mouth but a sculpted
curve. Twist, struggle, cry out though he would, he could not
escape it.

Sometimes it came close enough to rob him of sight and breath
and voice. But always he woke before it touched his skin. If ever it
came so far, he knew surely, he would wake and it would truly lie
upon him. And his face forever after would be not his own, but the
beautiful inhuman mask of the emperor.

Hirel lay coiled with the ul-cat, his tears drying slowly on face
and fur. He had not had the dream since he fled from Pri'nai.
That much he owed to the kindness of his brothers.

Very softly Ulan began to purr. Hirel let it lull him into a sleep
blessedly free of dreams.

When Hirel woke, miraculously hungry, all nine Zhil'ari were
there in their paint and their finery. Whatever this room was, they
seemed to have laid claim to it and its garden. There were servants
about, distraught, but none braved Ulan's claws to eject the
invaders. Hirel sent one for food and drink.

The garden had a pool of some size, which one or two of the
Zhil'ari were playing in. Hirel bathed lightly, considered, sent
another of the hovering servants for garments proper to a
gentleman. Those which came were adequate, cut of good plain
cloth in the southern fashion; they fit well enough.

Ulan growled. A voice babbled. The growl rose to a roar. Hirel,
emerging from the garden, found that the cat had cornered a
stranger. Save that he had a strong tinge of Asanian gold in his
plump cheeks, he was the image of the creature who had barred
them from the emperor. "Please," the man said faintly. "Please,
sir . . ."

Hirel laid a hand on Ulan's head. The ul-cat subsided to a
crouch, but his lips wrinkled still, baring his formidable fangs.
Hirel looked his victim up and down. "You have a purpose here?"

The man gathered himself together with an effort that shook his
body. "Sir, you cannot— This is one of the empress' private
chambers. It is not suited for . . . guests."

Hirel looked about. "True. It needs a bed or two. And a canopy
would not be amiss, should it rain when we would bathe."

The servant bridled at Hirel's princely hauteur, all fear forgotten. "You are trespassing in the personal quarters of her imperial majesty. If you do not leave of your own accord, I shall see to it that you are escorted out."

"I think not," said Hirel coolly. "The beds. Fetch them. And wine. The canopy can wait if it must, but cleansing-foam and cloths cannot."

A poor servant, this one, to have risen so high. He lost his temper much too easily, and with it his lordly accent. "This is not a barbarian pigsty!"

"Unless," Hirel mused, "you can provide me with a suite of rooms close by the Prince Sarevadin. Very close. And with service appropriate to my station."

"You'll get service. Direct to the slave-chain that let you loose."

"You are no good to me, I see. Go away, I tire of you." Hirel loosed Ulan. With a joyous leap, the cat drove the fool from the room.

Having tried servants of varying ranks, they resorted to guards, who could not pass a door filled with Ulan and who dared not empty it with bronze. Idiots; they never considered a raid through the garden, for what good that would do, with all the Zhil'ari prowling there, armed to the teeth. Hirel did not ask where the weapons had come from. Savages had ways, and theft was not a sin they knew the name of.

The guards withdrew. Of the services Hirel had required, only the wine came, and food later, when he demanded it again and peremptorily. The Zhil'ari were sparing with the largesse. A game was no pleasure if one were too far gone in meat and wine to play.

Hirel was no longer hungry. He drank a little, for the taste, and played with a fruit. He wandered restlessly, returned to the pool, prowled the room. No word came from the corridor's end. No sound, no scent of wizardry. The guards changed twice. Their faces were somber. They never opened the door, that he could see, nor did anyone pass them. They might have been warding an empty room.

Night loomed and fell. Hirel slept fitfully. A dream found him. He fought it, but it was strong. It seized him and pulled him down.

He walked in a dim country, under cold stars. A shadow walked beside him. They were comfortable, walking, two shadow princes in the shadowlands. Even here, Sarevan's mane was as bright as a beacon.

Something in Hirel was trying to brand it a nightmare: the dim strange hills, the icy stars, the air that was like no air of living earth. But Sarevan was there, and he was as he always was, striding lightly, wrapped in one of his silences. Once or twice he glanced at Hirel and smiled. It was a warm smile, with a touch of wickedness. *We belong together,* it said, *you and I: high prince and high prince.*

Hirel bowed his head, accepting. In this place, one did not deny truth.

The air was full of thunder. Hirel became aware of it by slow degrees. It was strangely like voices calling in chorus. Naming a name. *Sarevadin. Sarevadin!*

Sarevan barely paused in his striding. Hirel looked back. Far away on the edge of sight, light glimmered. He frowned. "They are calling you," he said.

His voice fell soft in the dimness. Sarevan glanced aside, shrugged minutely. It was no matter of his.

"But," said Hirel, "it is. Come, listen. They are calling you to the light."

The darkness beckoned, sweet and deep.

Hirel caught at Sarevan's body. It strained away from him; he tightened the circle of his arms. Sarevan twisted about within them, tensed for battle, but pausing, snared by surprise. "Listen," Hirel said. "For me."

"And what," asked Sarevan, "are you?"

"The other half of you," Hirel answered him.

Sarevan's brows met. Not, Hirel thought, in resistance. As if Hirel had given him something to ponder.

"Listen," Hirel bade him. "Listen."

Hirel snapped erect. It was deep night, but not the night of the shadowlands. The air of the empress' garden was cool and sweet; only the snoring of his companions broke the silence. He lay down again in Ulan's warmth and tried to still his trembling. The dream was gone. Nor was there any doubt in him that it had been a dream; but it haunted him.

*   *   *

Morning dawned cool for all the brilliance of the rising sun; the
water of the pool was cold. Hirel plunged into it, to wash the night
away, to force his mind into wakefulness. He was there when the
servants brought food that the Zhil'ari fell upon with delight. He
was still there when the tall man came.

Another of these damnable giants, Hirel thought as he looked
up and up at the figure on the pool's rim. Not a young one, this; his
beard was white, his hair iron grey. But he stood as a young man
stands, light and alert, and he fixed Hirel with a singularly
disconcerting stare. As if he could see through the other's eyes into
the thoughts behind, and what he saw made him want to laugh and
rage in equal measure. Ulan sat by him. Leaning against him.
Purring thunderously. "So," he said in Gileni with a lilt that spoke
of Ianon, "you're the invader who's setting the palace on its ear. I
don't suppose you've thought to *ask* for what you want?"

Hirel was abashed, and despised himself for it; it made his words
rough and haughty. "I asked. I was not given. Therefore I took."

"You demanded the impossible. You took what your temper
could encompass." The northerner held out a hand. "Come out of
the water, princeling."

Hirel came. He did not accept the hand. He did not blush that
he was naked, or that he must dry himself, shivering until his teeth
rattled, and dress under that bold stare. Ulan he would not
acknowledge at all. The cat was a traitor, precisely like the rest.

The Zhil'ari circled warily. The northerner flashed them a
blindingly brilliant smile, and addressed them in their own tongue.
They listened; their eyes widened, their jaws fell; they flung
themselves at his feet, kissed them fervently, and bolted.

Hirel stood alone, abandoned, and blue with cold, too bitter
even to be angry. The tall man's smile shone in vain upon his
despair; the warm deep voice was but a grating in his ears. "I told
them that they could look in on their seneldi and claim their own
weapons, and if they would be so kind, the owners of those they
carried would like them back again; and when they were done with
all of that, the captain of the high prince's guard would speak with
them."

"That is not all you told them."

"Maybe not." Since Hirel was not inclined to move, the northerner sat cross-legged on the grass. A kilt, Hirel reflected coldly,

was an utterly immodest garment. The barbarian did not care. Although he was nothing royal, he could not be, he was quite as supercilious as Sarevan. He raised a knee and clasped it. He was much scarred and not the least ashamed of it, and yet he was good to look on as all these northerners were, with his carven features and his lean long-muscled body and his own, peculiar, gangling grace.

"I thank you for that," he said.

"You are a mage," Hirel said flatly.

One shoulder lifted in a shrug. "After a fashion. I wasn't born to it; I'm no good at all with spells. I've grown into a trick or two, no more."

"You know who I am."

"It's obvious enough. I've met your father; and you're his image. I bring you my emperor's apologies. At first he didn't know you, and then he had Sarevan to think of."

Hirel snatched at what mattered. "Sarevan—is he—"

"He lives."

"He lives," Hirel repeated. He could not even name the force that dimmed his eyes, that set his heart to beating in a swift painful rhythm. "And his—his—"

"His father is recovering. And his mother. It was a hard battle. For a while—for a very long while I thought we'd lost them all."

Hirel regarded the face gone grim with memory, and knew what the mage was not saying. "You were with them."

"We all were, in power if not in body. Even Prince Orsan, all the way from Han-Gilen, and that whole redheaded tribe of his, and every priest in the city. That's how dire it was, and how much we owe you for keeping the young idiot alive for as long as you did."

"I am sure that it delights you to owe such a debt to a yellow barbarian."

The northerner's eyes glinted. "We can survive it. What's driving us wild is that you insist on camping here when there's a whole suite of honor waiting for you. Be kind; take it."

"First I must see Sarevan."

"Of course. He's been asking for you." The man rose, making no attempt to suppress his mirth at Hirel's expression, and beckoned. "Come."

* * *

They had moved the prince, taken him to his own rooms in a high tower of the palace. Hirel entered the topmost chamber slowly, telling himself that he was only cautious. It was a very pleasant place, all light and air, with more in it of taste than of opulence.

The bed was almost demeaningly small, hardly more than a cot set in an alcove. No hordes of attendants fluttered about it, only one quiet person in a torque, who made herself one with the shadows as Hirel crossed the tiled floor. Ulan reached the bed in a bound, all but overwhelming the figure in it, who laughed breathlessly and clasped him close.

This was not Sarevan. This was a boy, gaunt to transparency, with such a light shining out of him as the poets spoke of, that shone in saints or in the dying. His braid lay on his white-clad shoulder and snaked along his side, and the shaft of sunlight on it turned it to red-gold fire, but he had no beard. Even bone-thin as he was, his face was very young and very fine, and almost as pretty as a girl's.

Then he saw Hirel, and his eyes were Sarevan's, bright, arrogant, and thoroughly insouciant. Likewise the voice he raised in greeting, although it was as thin as his body. "Cubling! What took you so long?"

"Inefficiency," Hirel's guide answered for him. "Don't overdo it, children. I'll come back when your time's up."

Sarevan watched him go, smiling with deep affection. "You should be honored, cubling. The Lord of the Northern Realms doesn't often stoop to run errands."

Hirel stared at the closing door. "The Lord of the Northern Realms?"

"Vadin alVadin himself, Baron Geitan, sworn brother to the Sunborn, whom men call the Reborn, and the Chosen of Avaryan, and the Regent of Ianon and the kingdoms of the north." Sarevan's eyes danced. "What, cubling! Is that awe I see in your face? Can there actually be a hero alive whom your loftiness will condescend to worship?"

Hirel schooled his traitor face to stillness. "He is very famous. Notorious, in truth. When nurses need a name with which to subdue their charges, and the Sunborn's has lost its potency, they invoke the horror of Vadin Uthanyas, Vadin who will not die."

Sarevan grinned. "Vadin Uthanyas! What a ring that has. I'll have to call him that when I want to watch him lose his temper. He loses his temper wonderfully. Thunder and lightning, and the sound of kingdoms falling." He raised himself, struggling, his grin turning to a glare when Hirel laid hands on him. He was frighteningly frail. Hirel propped him with cushions and stood over him, hands on hips. His glare wavered. "Damn it, infant—"

"Thunder and lightning, and kingdoms falling." Hirel frowned. "You look appalling. What did you do to your face?"

Sarevan's hand went to it. His right hand, moving easily, and under the robe no bulk of bandages. "I've lost flesh, that's all. It will come back."

"Not that, idiot. Your beard."

Sarevan laughed so hard that Hirel thought he would break. When at last he had his breath back, he said, "I bade it a fond farewell. I'm not entirely uncivilized, you know. Only when I'm Journeying, and hot water is hard to come by, and time's not for wasting with a razor and a scrap of mirror. Besides," he added, "it made you so happy: such highly visible evidence of my barbarity."

Hirel's teeth set; but he smiled, honey-sweet. "You look," he said, "somewhat younger than you claim to be. And very . . . comely. I think we are a closer match than you would like."

The bright brows met. Hirel laughed at them. "Insolent whelp," Sarevan muttered. Hirel sat on the bed and refused to be insulted. Sarevan sighed. "I suppose you expect me to be indulgent, now that I owe you my life."

"I did nothing but accept my captivity and see that you were brought where you had promised to put an end to it. I do expect you to drop this game of yours and call me by my name."

"How cumbersome. Asuchirel inZiad Uverias, what an arrogant creature you are. Is there truly a rod of steel in that spine of yours, Asuchirel inZiad Uverias? Ah, Asuchirel inZiad Uverias, how prettily you glare at me."

"Priest," Hirel said with icy precision, "you know full well that I can be called Hirel."

"But that's merely Old Asanian for Son of the Lion. Lion's Cub. Cubling."

"At least it is *Old* Asanian." Hirel folded his arms. "Yield. Or I call you *mongrel* forever after."

"How dare you—" Sarevan stopped. Scowled. Laughed suddenly. "Cub— Hirel Uverias, you are growing into a formidable young man. How long has your voice been breaking?"

Hirel flushed scarlet, and cursed the wit that could spin a new victory out of a clear defeat. "It is not—"

It did, appallingly. His mouth snapped shut.

Sarevan lay back, highly amused. "Avaryan help me, I think I've been growing you up. Small wonder I've got so feeble. It's a task for giants."

"That, having seen the Zhil'ari, I would hardly call you." Hirel's voice held its range, for a mercy. "I am tiring you. Can you rest, now that you know your prisoner is secure?"

The lightness left the worn brilliant face. "Does it gall you so much?"

Hirel considered the question with some care. At length he answered it. "I am not an utter fool; I understand your reasons. But yes, it galls me. How can it not?"

"Do you hate me?"

"No." Hirel stood. "Rest. I will come back later. See that your guardhounds are so instructed."

No doubt Sarevan saw through it. That Hirel left because he could not bear to know the truth: that Sarevan was not yet claimed fully for the world of the living. He could still let go. He could still die.

The tall lord admitted it. He had died indeed with an assassin's spear in his heart, and he had come back at the Sunborn's call, when Mirain An-Sh'Endor was a youth barely set upon his throne and Vadin his reluctant squire. But Vadin's wound had been one of the body, with nothing sorcerous in it. This was different. Sarevan had come as far as Keruvarion's magic could bring him. The rest lay with time and the god.

Hirel lingered for a time in the chambers to which the lord had led him. They were fully in keeping with his royalty. They closed in upon him.

He fled. He sought his mare, found her more nondescript than ever among the seneldi of the high lords of Keruvarion, knew that she had few equals for spirit or for swiftness. He was not comforted, even though he rode her for a little, to her great and queenly pleasure. He left her, to wander the palace.

It was all open to him now. People stared and murmured as he went past. Rumor gave him a hundred names, a hundred tales. A few were accurate, or close to it. He found the Zhil'ari; they were content with their barracks, though not with the order that they restrict their paint to a pathetic sigil between their brows. It was indecent, all that bare skin flaunted to the world. Hirel commiserated, and throttled his impulse to laughter, and wandered on. He felt like a shadow, a thing half real, visible yet intangible.

The sun sank. Hirel climbed the long stair to the prince's door, and the strangers on guard did not try to challenge him. Sarevan was asleep with his arm about Ulan's neck. Hirel sat by him in silence as the shadows lengthened. Faintly through the open windows he heard chanting. Avaryan's priests were singing their god to his rest.

The priest on deathwatch left; another took his place, settling on the edge of Hirel's awareness. From where he sat he could see the sky flame with sunset and fade slowly. A star kindled. Behind Hirel the watcher lit a lamp, a flicker in the twilight.

Hirel straightened. He was stiff with long sitting. He rose, and stretched each muscle as he had learned to, with grace and precision. Making a dance of it, his tutor used to say. The old man was dead now. He spoke too freely to someone powerful, and one morning there was a new and much younger man waiting to instruct his imperial highness in the proper pursuits of princes.

Hirel turned. The new watcher was a woman, and patently akin to the redheaded princes of Han-Gilen. She did not appear to share her young kinsman's hatred of Hirel. Her eyes admired his figure, and certainly his unconscious display of it.

She was not a priestess, he noticed; she wore no torque, nor any ornament at all. Her gown was green, and very simple, like a servant's. Her bright hair coiled at the nape of her neck. She was well past that first bloom which the poets judged to be the perfection of a woman's beauty, but well shy of raddled age; her features were too strong for perfection, in truth would not have looked amiss on a boy, and her figure in the gown, though far from boyish, was somewhat scant of breast and hip. She was, in truth, too old and too thin, and she was far from pretty. She was the most beautiful woman Hirel had ever seen.

He blinked. She did not vanish. Her eyes had the southern tilt, but they were more round than almond-narrow, long and very dark in the honey-gold face—Asanian blood there, no doubt of it. There were shadows under them. Her cheek was scarred, thin parallel furrows, ivory on gold. The marring only made her more beautiful.

She rose. She was somewhat taller than Hirel. She bent over the sleeper, smoothing his hair with ineffable tenderness. Hirel's heart, ever a fool, throbbed with jealousy. Oh, yes, his brain mocked it. Begrudge a woman's love for her son. Fall instantly, hopelessly, and eternally in love with the Empress of Keruvarion. Why not? His father had done it before him. And been sent packing with courtesy but with great dispatch, because she preferred a fatherless upstart to the heir of the Golden Throne.

It was as well, Ziad-Ilarios had said once. The royal line had clung to its purity against a millennium of alien wives and concubines, had fought an often desperate battle to stem the sullying tide. Ziad-Ilarios had gone home alone to Kundri'j, wedded the sister whom the High Court had allotted as his mate, and begotten an heir of unimpeachable legitimacy. No wild redheaded savage to cast shame upon the dynasty.

Hirel shivered. One word from this woman's mouth, and he would never have been. Nor Sarevan. Nor this hour in Endros, full of lamplight and darkness.

She stood erect. A pin slipped free; her hair tumbled down her back. She snatched, and muttered something utterly unqueenly. Her glance crossed Hirel's, bright with temper. His lips quirked. He bit them. Hers were tight, but they wobbled. It burst forth all at once, as laughter must, even in the very midst of grief. "You look," she gasped, "you look exactly like your father."

"So I am told."

Her laughter died. He was sorry: she had a wonderful laugh, rich and full-bodied, like Sovrani wine. "He could do that, too. One look, and all my crotchets would collapse." She paused. "Is he well?"

"He was when I left him."

"I've always regretted that we were what we were. That we had to make choices." Hirel was silent. She smiled quickly. "You are very welcome in Endros."

He bowed. She touched him, a feather-brush of her hand across his cheek. It felt not at all like *lèse-majesté*.

"Yes," she said, "you are his image. He was the fairest of men, and the gentlest, and one of the strongest."

Hirel laughed a little. "I fear I fall far short of him."

"Ah, but he was older. Those shoulders, look, they've inches coming. And you'll be taller than he was." Mischief sparkled in her glance. "Come back to me in a hand of years, and I'll gladly run away with you."

"Need we wait?" asked Hirel. He took her hand and kissed it. "Come now, be my love, and let the empires fend for themselves."

"Why," she said in wonder, "you almost mean it."

"It must be in the blood." He sighed. "They breed us for beauty, for color, and for such size as we can attain; and, it seems, for conceiving mad passions for redheaded royalty."

"No," said Sarevan behind him, "that's not madness, that's taste."

They turned. Sarevan was wide awake. Perhaps he looked a little better; perhaps it was only the warmth of his smile. "Good evening, Mother," he said. "Good evening, O lion of the west. Would either of you be inclined to succor a starving man?"

When Sarevan ate, Hirel discovered that he could share it; and that it would stay quietly in its place. As if his stomach knew what his brain had not yet comprehended. The crisis was past. Sarevan was mending. He would live and be strong.

Eight

HIREL WAS NO STRANGER TO TEMPLES. ASANION'S HIGH PRINCE was high priest of a dozen gods, each with his shrine and his worship and his priesthood, each with his festivals which royalty must adorn. If Avaryan's temple in Endros had been set among the others Hirel knew, it would have been but middling large, and though extraordinarily well attended by both priests and people, not remarkably rich. Folk in Asanion would have looked on it with disfavor, muttering that the god's own son could spare so little of his fabled wealth to adorn the holy place. But here it was of a piece with the rest, simplicity shaped into high art. All that simple pillared hall of gold-veined stone looked toward its center: the altar, and above it an orb of gold suspended in the air, its heart an everlasting fire. Nothing held it up. Nothing at all.

Hirel had come here out of curiosity, and because a novice had brought a summons worded properly and courteously. He stopped to stare at the altar and the orb, and to wonder how anyone could have wrought such a prodigy.

"Magic," said the novice as if he had spoken. "It's nothing in particular, though it makes ignorant people afraid. A few of the novices stole it once and played ball with it. They say it was Prince

Sarevan who scored a goal with it, full in the prioress' fishpond, and he not even a novice yet, though he was bound for Han-Gilen's temple that High Summer. But he was mageborn; he didn't need the spells that all the others had to sing to keep the Orb in the air."

"Are you all mages here?" Hirel asked a little sourly.

The child skipped, tossing her long unruly hair. "Most of us. We're New Order here, under the Sunborn; we're priest-mages, white enchanters."

"You too?"

"I will be," she said from the promontory of her nine summers. Or did she have so many? "I was chosen. The empress says I'm mageborn; she says I'll know it when I'm a woman, and I'm lucky, because by then I'll be old enough to use my power properly."

"Unlike her son."

"Ah well, what can he do? He's not only mageborn, he's godborn; it's a fire in him. That's why he did his novitiate in Han-Gilen. They're Old Order there, no mages, but the Red Prince is the wisest mage in the world. He taught the Sunborn, and he took the Sunborn's son in hand, and tamed him nicely, everybody says." She stopped short. Her eyes filled with tears. "Is it true what they're saying? Is he like to die?"

"Not now," Hirel answered her.

The tears fell; she shook them away, scowling to make up for them. "Thank Avaryan! We've all been praying our hardest. I wanted to do my praying where he was, but no one would let me. It's because I'm still too young; I haven't come into my power. But when I do . . ."

Hirel gratified her with a very visible shiver. She was formidable enough now; she would be a woman to walk well shy of. He narrowed his eyes. "Would you be the empress' fosterling? The one whom Sarevan—"

"Yes, I'm the one who's here because he did something with his power that he shouldn't have. That's why I'm mageborn. A mage made me. When I want to make him annoyed, I call him Mother." She tilted her head, bright-eyed. "He must be very fond of you. He doesn't tell everybody. Only people he trusts."

Hirel blinked. She waited for him to gather his wits. She was another mongrel, a small wiry brown creature with hair and eyes of purest Asanian gold. When she was older she would be striking.

She was going to be very dangerous indeed.

She grinned, gap-toothed, and patted his cheek. She had to stretch to do it. "Poor child, you're shaking. What's the trouble? Is it all too much for you?"

"It is all impossible!" he burst out.

"Of course it is. We're mages." She took his hand without the least suggestion of diffidence. "Come now, we're dallying."

Hirel had not known what to expect. A priest certainly. A mage, from the child's chatter. But not precisely this. The blunt earth-colored face bespoke the Nine Cities, whence had come the Order of Mages; the greying braid, the torque, the white robe marked him a votary of Avaryan. He sat over a scroll in a bare sunlit chamber, companioned by a small bright-eyed creature that sat on his shoulder and purred.

"I had not known," said Hirel, "that a mage of the guild would endure Avaryan's yoke."

The man looked up with perfect calm. His familiar coiled its long tail about his neck and yawned in Hirel's face. The priest stroked it; it arched its supple back. "I had not known," he responded, "that an heir of the lion would endure captivity in Keruvarion."

Hirel smiled with a distinct edge. "It is given out that I am a guest here."

"Are you?"

"I bow to the inevitable."

"Of course." The familiar left its perch to stalk a shadow. Its master rolled and bound his scroll, turned to face Hirel fully. "Have you approached the Asanian ambassador?"

"Is that a concern of yours?"

The wizard-priest folded his hands. To the eye he was utterly harmless, a small aging man with tired eyes. "It concerns me that I be able to trust you."

"Why?"

The man sighed. "The heir of the Sunborn has known betrayal in one of its more appalling guises. He may yet die for it. And you are the highest lord but one, of the people who betrayed him."

"I am no stranger to treason."

"From which side of it, prince?"

Hirel drew himself up, measuring his words in ice and iron.

"Much ill can be said of me, and much has been said, by your own prince not least. But of that I am not guilty." He advanced a step; his voice quickened, heated. "What can you know of all that he has suffered? How can you begin to comprehend it?"

"Peace," said the priest, unruffled. "I but do my duty."

"They did their duty likewise, who would have left your high prince to die within call of his father."

The priest rose. His familiar wove mewing about his legs. He cradled his arms; it sprang up weightlessly and curled there, fixing Hirel with a steady golden stare. He glared back, gold for gold.

The mage's voice seemed almost to come from within the creature's eyes, a soft voice, but implacable. "If you had brought him here, there would have been no such contention."

"I brought him to his father as he desired."

"Commendable," the priest said evenly.

"Why have you summoned me?" Hirel demanded of him. "What use can I be to you? Will you make an example of me, and execute me for a traitor?"

"That is the emperor's province. Not ours."

"Why, then?"

The priest looked long at him. Certainly he used more than eyes. Hirel's nose twitched at the tang of wizardry.

At last the priest spoke. "I wished to see you. To know what you are."

"And?"

"You are not what you think you are."

"Folk seldom are."

"Your self-possession is admirable."

"I am a prince."

The priest bowed. Mocking, and not mocking. His familiar purred. "I would not doubt the truth of your birth. But do you know the fullness of it?"

"I have been instructed."

"By philosophers." The priest was above scorn. "Logicians. Men who see with their eyes, but who are blind to the vision within."

"What is there to see, save the reflection of one's own face?"

"What was it that slew your mother?"

The blow rocked Hirel to his foundations. His eyes went dark; his mind emptied. From far away he saw himself, frozen, stunned;

and watched his body spring from immobility into deadly flight. The mage fell back, raising neither hand nor power in his own defense.

With all the strength that was in him, Hirel quelled the killing stroke. He withdrew a step, two, three. He remembered who he was, and what he was, and how he had come there. He said, "She died by her own hand."

"Why?"

A prince did not give way to pain. Hirel was surely and entirely a prince, but his training was not yet perfect. He had not learned, yet, not to feel the wound. But he could speak through it with quiet that was only cross-kin to calm. "She failed of her blood. She could not learn to be a queen."

"She looked within and saw only void; looked without, and saw only a cage."

Hirel saw her more clearly now than he saw his tormentor. He was growing into his father's image; in childhood he had been his mother's. Her softness, like his own, had been only for the eye. She was steel beneath, but steel flawed, trammeled in the chains of womanhood and royalty. She had wanted too much: a life of the body as well as of the mind. She had won from her husband the training of her son. She had made him what she herself would have been, had she been born a man.

"They say that she was mad," Hirel said. She faced him in his memory as she had been the day she died: all gold and ivory, perfect in her beauty, with eyes that had forsaken hope. "My father accepted the burden of his birth. She could not. She resisted to the utmost, until she broke. She denied even the gods."

"Often," said the priest, "one denies what one most fears."

"Do not you yourself do the same?"

"I deny your thousand gods. I do not deny the One who embodies them all."

Hirel hissed. Memory was fading; impatience was rising to rule him. "What has my mother to do with you, or with me, or with your god?"

"Little," answered the priest, "and much. She could not bear to face herself; she took refuge in death. What did she see that so frightened her? Not prison bars alone. In extremity, she saw the truth. It slew her."

"Truth." Hirel's lip curled. "I have heard no truth here. Only cruelty."

The priest bowed his head. It was a most convincing semblance of humility. "Truth is cruel. Your mother raised you well, prince, but not well in all. It would have served you better to have learned somewhat from your father. Of gods; of magery."

"Prince Sarevadin has done what he may to fill the void," said Hirel.

"He has indeed. But do you believe?"

"In magic," said Hirel, "perforce. In gods, not yet. I can hope that it may be never. I have no desire to be bound by the caprices of divinity."

The temple did not quake; the priest did not rise up in wrath. "Caprice may prove to be purpose, and chance a design beyond our frail conception."

"Ah," said Hirel. "You have brought me here to convert me. A mighty coup that would be: a servant of Avaryan on the Golden Throne."

"It will yet be so."

"Not while I live."

"Swear no vows, prince, lest they betray you."

"I swear them. I swear that I will not bow to your god. Nor will I surrender my throne to him."

"Even for love?"

Pain drew Hirel's eyes downward. His nails, growing long again, had drawn blood from his palms. He had fallen out of the habit of allowing for them. With great care he unclenched his fists. "I may acknowledge that a god exists, if it can be proven to my satisfaction. It is not reasonable to demand that I love him."

"Love is not demanded. Often it is not even wished for. But it comes."

"Not to the High Prince of Asanion."

The priest looked long at him, but not with pity. "You name yourself truly. You do not know what your name signifies. But that will come. I pray my god that it will not come in pain."

Hirel escaped from that quiet wizard-priest with the bitter eyes and the oracle's tongue. He knew he trod the bare edge of courtesy; he chose not to care. The impudent novice had made herself scarce. He found his own way out of the temple—it was much simpler, he noticed, than the path by which the child had led him—and walked slowly back through the city. Anger pricked him. So many words, to so little purpose; and yet they had struck deep, at wounds which would not heal. He had been tested, he knew it surely; but for what, he did not know. He did not want to know.

His mother had fled her lineage and her duty. He would not. He had tarried long enough, both within bonds and out of them. Now he would see what place this world had left for him: if he was a prisoner here, or if he was a free guest; if Asanion was prepared to reject him or to have him back.

Sarevan was up. More, he was walking, with Ulan for a prop, and after a moment's astonishment, Hirel. He tried not to lean heavily. Hirel could feel him trying, shaking with the effort. His face was grim. "Once more," he gritted when they had struggled from bed to wall and back again. Hirel swallowed the words that came to him, and steadied the lunatic with an arm about his waist.

Sarevan fell into his bed, grinning like a skull, panting as if he had run a race. "Every hour," he said with all the strength he could muster. "Every hour I'll do it."

Hirel kept his face expressionless, spreading the coverlet over the wasted body. It shifted, restless already, though it must have been a great labor even to raise a hand, to catch Hirel's wrist. "I'm mending, infant. I'm sure of it. I'm stronger already than I was this morning. Tomorrow I'll be stronger yet. Two days, three—I'll ride."

Hirel's mouth wanted to twist. Such a creature, this was. Not only did he cherish hope; he clutched it with both hands.

He let Hirel go and shifted again, lying on his side. His grin had shrunk to a wry smile. "I bore you to tears, don't I? Why do you keep coming back?"

"I am still your prisoner."

Hirel had not wanted it to sound so flat, or so bitter. Nor had he meant to wipe the smile from Sarevan's face. Not so completely. "You are not," Sarevan said with as much heat as his weakness could muster. "I promised you. As soon as we came to Endros—"

"We have been four days in Endros."

Sarevan closed his eyes. He looked weary beyond telling. "You are free," he said just above a whisper. "You were free the moment you faced my father."

Hirel voiced no thanks. He owed none. As he turned, the thin hand caught his wrist once more. He looked down into a face that had willed itself to life. "What are you going to do?" Sarevan demanded.

"Nothing unduly treacherous," answered Hirel. The dark eyes shamed him with their steadiness; he said more reasonably, "I had in mind to speak with the Asanian ambassador."

"Is it wise?"

"That is what I intend to discover." Hirel sat on the bed. Sarevan reclaimed his hand, turning it so that the *Kasar* caught the light. Hirel slitted his eyes against the flame of it. "Will you stop me?"

"Of course not. Old Varzun is safe enough; he's impeccably loyal to his emperor, and my father says he's been mourning you with honest grief. But some of his people may not wish you well."

"I do not doubt it," said Hirel. "I would send a summons worthy of his rank. May I borrow one of your guards?"

"Avaryan! You're slipping. You actually asked." Sarevan grinned at Hirel's scowl. He raised his voice and called out with surprising strength, "Starion!"

The guard burst in with a mighty clatter, armed for war. Once again Hirel met hostile eyes over the glitter of a spearpoint.

"Cousin," said Sarevan mildly. The spear lowered a fraction; the glare abated not at all. "Cousin, if you can spare a moment from your heroics, we have a task for you."

The young Gileni flushed dark under the bronze. He did not look well in the scarlet of the emperor's squires: it clashed abominably with his hair. Yet he was a very comely young man, and he acted as if he knew it. He grounded his spear with a flourish that came close to insolence, but that was for Hirel; his eyes on Sarevan were a roil of love and grief, anger and anxiety and simple worship. "Is he troubling you? Is he sapping your strength with his nonsense?"

"Not as much as you are with yours." Sarevan's smile took some of the sting out of the rebuke. "Do you think you can bring yourself to be civil to an Asanian?"

The boy's thought was as clear as a shout: *If only it need not be this one*. Aloud he said stiffly, "Stop chaffing me, Vayan. What do you want me to do?"

Sarevan glanced at Hirel, who told him. He listened; repeated his message word for word; bowed with perfect correctness, and left.

Sarevan contemplated the emptiness where Starion had been. "Bless the boy," he said, half amused, half dismayed, "he's jealous. And he's the one who prayed for the day when I'd find someone else to play elder brother to. Or is it—" He laughed suddenly. "I have it! He's afraid you've displaced him as the beauty of the family."

"That," said Hirel, "is not possible. Not while you live to outshine both of us together."

"Ah now, I'm nothing much. This nose of mine . . ."

Hirel snorted. Sarevan wisely fell silent.

Nine

"I DUVARZUN INKERIZ ISCHYLIOS," THE SERVANT ANNOUNCED WITH proper dignity and passable accent; and shattered it with a grin and a wink which, by fate's own mercy, the ambassador did not see. Hirel set himself sternly to be as blind.

He received his father's envoy in a chamber small enough for intimacy, large enough for dignity; seated in a tall chair, not quite a throne, with attendants about him and the sun ablaze on his golden robes. Seven of them, one atop the other, and the eighth, the one which marked his rank, pouring over the chair and pooling on the floor about his bare and gilded feet. Its sleeves flowed over his hands, permitting a glimpse of gilded fingertips; its collar rose high, his face within the frame of it almost stark in its plainness: barely touched with either gilt or paint, ornamented only by a single earring, vivid against the darkened skin.

Still though he held himself, his heart thudded painfully as the man appeared upon the heels of his name. Hirel knew him. He was a kinsman, and the old blood was strong in him; age had bleached his hair to the ivory of his skin and brought out the fine proud bones beneath, but the eyes in deep sockets were keen as a falcon's, the gold of them rimmed just visibly with white. Even as he went down upon his knees, he stretched the limits of protocol. The face of a high prince was to be stared at, scrutinized, committed to memory, as an emperor's was to be hidden forever behind the golden mask; but this stare endured for an eternity, edged with doubt, and shock, and slowly dawning hope. "My lord?" Varzun whispered.

Hirel beckoned. The ambassador came forward on his knees, with much grace for one so old. At two paces' distance he halted and held up his hands. They trembled as Hirel touched fingertip to fingertip, the greeting of close and royal kinsmen. Varzun looked long at the thin brown fingers with their blunted nails, and up into the altered face. "My prince. What have they done to you?"

Hirel rose and signed a command. Varzun resisted but obeyed, rising also. He was a little the shorter. He blinked, and found a smile to brighten the sudden tears. "Little one, you have grown. But this"—his hand sketched a gesture toward Hirel's hair, toward the sharpened cheekbone—"this is unpardonable. Who has done it?"

"No one in Keruvarion," Hirel answered him. "Indeed I owe my life to the Varyani prince. He found me where my flight had cast me, and preserved me from the hounds that would have torn me, as from the men who would have sold me gelded into slavery."

With each word Varzun paled further; at the last of it he nearly toppled. "My prince. Oh, my prince!" But he mastered himself; he stood straight and spoke clearly. "Your brothers?"

"The slaves' whelps: Vuad and Sayel. And no doubt," said Hirel, "Aranos from amid his priests and his sorcerers, although he would never stoop so low as to take part openly in the plot. That might jeopardize his claim to my place."

"It is rumored that Aranos will be named high prince when the time of mourning is past. But it is also rumored that the princes are quarreling over the spoils."

"They are very certain that I am dead. What tale do they tell of that?"

Varzun lowered his eyes, reluctant. Hirel waited. Slowly the old man said, "It was sickness, they say, my prince. Something swift and virulent, that made imperative the burning of your body and your belongings. They gave you a great funeral, with many sacrifices."

"My slaves? My senel?"

"Sent to bear you company in the Ninth Heaven."

Hirel stood still under the weight of his robes. He was dimly aware of the ambassador's concern. Old fool, the High Court reckoned him, loyal enough and dimwitted enough to suffer exile of honor among the barbarians, blind enough not to perceive that, while he represented the soul of peaceful honesty to the mages of Keruvarion, his servants spied and intrigued and did what harm they might in the heart of the empire. He was much too direct in his speech to make a courtier, although what Hirel had seen of this court made him seem as subtle as any serpent in Kundri'j. And he had a glaring flaw: he dared permit himself to love his emperor and his high prince. Either of whom would calmly slay him if need demanded.

As Hirel's brothers had slain his servants, that they betray no perilous secrets. And his golden stallion, that they should not seem overeager to usurp the privileges of the high prince. Not that the creature was a great loss; for all his shimmering beauty he had been as placid as a plowbeast. The slaves were only slaves, hands that served and legs that ran. Though Hirel would miss the little singer, and the eunuch whose hands were so clever when he needed easing and had neither time nor inclination for a woman, and Sha'an who alone had ever been able to comb his hair properly and painlessly, and—

They brought it home to him. The finality of it. The Son of the Lion was dead and burned and enrolled among the immortals, with ritual regret that he had not had time to become an ancestor. Ah well, folk would be saying, poor little thing, always sick and never very strong, though he was a pretty one to look at while he lasted. He did seem to have been getting over his youngling weaknesses, but blood and the gods would always tell. Between them they had carried him off.

Hirel let his head fall back, and laughed long and loud and free. Still laughing, he flung off his damnable swaddlings and faced Varzun in the bare sufficiency of silken trousers. The old man looked ready to faint again, more at his prince's nakedness than at the scars revealed upon it. Hirel's mirth died. He rapped Varzun lightly with a finger, driving the poor man back to his knees. "Sit," Hirel commanded him, "and ease your bones. And listen."

Varzun took the chair one of the servants brought, but he took little ease in it. Doubt was creeping back into his eyes. Hirel was not conducting himself as he ought; the old man's scrutiny hardened, searching the altered face.

"Yes," Hirel said, "I am your prince, and I have changed. I wandered the roads for a Greatmoon-cycle and more, companioned only by a priest of Avaryan; I dwelt for a while among northern savages. And what brought me to it, that laid bare a new face of the world. I am not the child who rode trustingly into the claws of his dearest brothers." His raised hand forestalled Varzun's speech. "By now the couriers will be well on their way to Kundri'j with the news of my resurrection. I will follow them. Not at once and not as swiftly, but neither will I ride in imperial state. Have you a dozen of the warrior caste whom you may trust beyond death if need be?"

"My prince, you know that all I have is yours." The ambassador was not an utter fool; despite the blows it had suffered, his mind had begun to work again. "My Olenyai are not all as loyal to me as they pretend, but your dozen I can find. Must you venture abroad with so few?"

"I require speed and secrecy. I shall ride as a lordling who comes to Kundri'j with his Olenyai, to claim his place in the Middle Court. My enemies will not learn the truth of my coming until I am upon them."

Varzun was becoming inured to shock. He did not protest the unseemliness of Hirel's plotting, still less the madness of it. He said only, "Then you will be using the roads and the posthouses, and you will need a token of passage. But, my prince, the lands may not be—"

"See to it," said Hirel. "I must be in Kundri'j by Autumn Firstday." Varzun had the sense to venture no further protests; he bowed in his seat. Hirel returned to the tall chair and vouchsafed his most charming smile. "Now, honored uncle, tell me all that has passed since I left Pri'nai."

* * *

Hirel had expected to be summoned in his own turn and called to account for his machinations. He had not expected the messenger to be waiting when Varzun left. He eyed the eightfold robe which would have been proper, settled upon coat and trousers, and followed the liveried squire, holding apprehension firmly at bay. He had no apologies to make and no secrets to keep. Even before Mirain An-Sh'Endor.

But, having summoned Hirel, the Sunborn kept him waiting for a bitter while. He was comfortable enough, it was true: the antechamber was rich, furnished with cushions and carpets in the western manner, and a servant brought wine and sweets and even a book or two, none of which Hirel was minded to touch. He sat, arranging himself with care, and simmered slowly.

He had reached a fine pitch of temper when the squire called him into the emperor's presence. But he was cool to look at, composed, imperial.

The Lord An-Sh'Endor was not even attired for audience, much less set aloft in the Hall of the Throne. He had been standing for a sculptor; the man was there still, measuring living body and half-hewn marble image with cord and calipers. The statue wore the beginnings of state robes. The emperor wore only his torque and his kingship. He had no more shame than his son, and no less beauty of form. Over the sculptor's head he addressed a man in full court dress, who seemed unperturbed by the disparity. "By now even they should know what they've brought upon themselves. I am not betrayed twice."

"And their messenger, sire?" the courtier inquired.

"Give him his fee and let him go." The man bowed; his lord shifted at the sculptor's command. "One wing of cavalry should suffice. Mardian's, I think. He's not as close as some, but he's been idle lately. A short campaign should distract his men from the local beer and himself from the local matrons. Write up the order; bring it to me before the sunset bell."

The man bowed again and departed. The sculptor finished his measuring and departed likewise. At last the emperor deigned to notice who stood by the door. "High prince! I pray your pardon. As soon as I'd sent for you, half the empire decided to descend upon me."

Hirel bowed acknowledgment.

A servant brought garments for his emperor: shirt and trousers, heeled boots and richly embroidered coat, the casual dress of a lord of the Hundred Realms. "I do turn and turn about," the Sunborn said to Hirel, easily, as to a friend. "Now a Ianyn in kilt and cloak, now a trousered southerner. It keeps folk in mind that I belong to no one realm, but to all together." He beckoned. "Come, walk with me."

He did not speak as one who expected to be refused. As Hirel moved to obey, he considered his own wisdom in discarding Asanian robes for eastern trousers. The Varyani emperor had the long panther-stride of his northern kin, that Hirel had to stretch to match.

They did not go far. Only to that great hall in which Hirel had expected to be received. It was even plainer than the rest of the palace, austere in truth: a long lofty pillared expanse, its floor of white stone unadorned, its walls bare of carving or tapestry. At its farthest limit stood a dais of nine deep steps, and a broad chair that seemed carved of a single immense moonstone, its back rising and blooming into the rayed sun of Avaryan. Solid gold, all the legends said. Its rays ran from wall to wall and leaped toward the lofty vault of the ceiling. Surely any man who sat beneath that mighty flame of gold would seem a dwarf, an ant, a mote in the eye of his god.

From the hall's end, the throne seemed to glow in the gloom. An illusion: the hall was shadowed, lit only by the sun through louvers in the roof, and the gold cast its reflection upon the translucent stone of the chair. But as the Sunborn drew closer, it grew brighter. Hirel's eyes narrowed with the beginnings of discomfort. Brightmoon itself attained no such splendor, even at the full.

But the emperor did not choose to mount the dais. He stood on its lowest step and eyed the shining throne, his right hand clenching and unclenching at his side. His face was still, young and old at once, ageless as the face of a god. "Do you know," he said quietly, "when I sit there, I come as close to freedom from pain as I may ever come, save only in the arms of my empress. But only for a little while. If I linger, if I begin to grow proud, if I consider all the uses of this power I bear, the pain swells until it casts me upon the edge of darkness."

Hirel did not speak. The Sunborn faced him, eyes glittering. "Often as I sit there, I consider my power. I consider life and death, and thrones, and empires. More than once I have sought a way round our long dilemma. Your father has daughters, all wellborn and many beautiful and some legitimate. I have a son. Our empires united, war averted, peace purchased for us all. Who can find fault with such a course?"

"My father has considered the same expedient. For all I know he considers it still, but not with any great hope of fulfillment. Your empire is too young and too vigorous and too close to its god. The union would be all Keruvarion, and Asanion would fall as completely as to any war."

"Would that be so terrible?"

Hirel looked at the Emperor of the East. Remembered the tales. Upstart, fatherless, ruthless warrior and inexorable conqueror, blind, fanatic, driven by his god. His son had been born while he conquered the Nine Cities, born on the battlefield in the midst of hell's own storm; had grown to boyhood in the camps of the army as it spread north and east and south and slowly, with many pauses, west. He had only known peace as his son began to grow from boy into youth, when the empires settled into the uneasy half-amity of warriors who, finding themselves equally matched, see no profit in endless, fruitless struggle. But they maneuvered; they tested. They wielded spies and insurgents and mages, bandits and border lords, even hunters and herders who set no great store by the borders of empires.

The warlord of Keruvarion was warlord still even in the garb of a southern princeling, lean and hard and honed to a razor's edge. And Hirel had seen his people. Outside of Endros the common folk might have become complacent with peace. Within it, lords and commons alike had a look for which only now did Hirel find a name. The look of the falcon: bright, fierce, and poised for the kill.

"The god would have it so," said their lord, not entirely without regret. "Asanion is ancient and it is still strong, but its strength in great part overlies corruption. It has forgotten its gods. Its people embrace mere cowering superstition. Its great ones cleave to the cold follies of logic, or to nothing at all save their own pleasure. In the name of their gods, or of their pleasure, or of this new sophistry which they call science, they practice horrors. Life, say they, is nothing; light is illusion; darkness waits and beckons and proffers the delights of despair."

Yes, Hirel thought. A fanatic. He sounded like a madman in the bazaar. *Woe, woe unto the Golden Empire! A worm has nested in its heart. Soon shall it wither and crumble away.* Madmen had been crying thus for a thousand years. Some had raised armies; some had even claimed descent from gods. But they were gone, and Asanion remained. She had swallowed them. So would she swallow even this greatest of the bandit kings.

The Sunborn laughed. His mirth seemed genuine, if not unalloyed. He ran lightly up the dais, turned. The throne was a blaze behind him, yet he outblazed it. He shone; he flamed; he towered against the image of his father. He sat, and he was a dark slight man of no great height or handsomeness. Yet try though it would, Hirel's eye could not force itself to see aught else. The throne on which he sat, the Sun which rose behind him, seemed but a setting for his royalty.

Hirel raised his chin and set his mind against his eyes' seduction. This man had greatness, yes, he granted that. Power in many senses, and presence, and a mingling of art and instinct that put a Kundri'ji courtesan to shame. How easy to yield, to bow down, to worship the godborn king. Let his armies roll over languid world-weary Asanion, scour it, cleanse it, make it anew in the image of Avaryan. A kingdom of light, where slaves were free and free folk lived in peace and plenty, and lords ruled in wisdom and in justice, and all gods were one god, and that god had sent his own son to sit above them all.

"No," said Hirel. "War is war, even if it be holy war. And conquest is conquest. You stretch your hand toward that to which you have no right."

"I have the right which my father gives me."

"We have the right of our ancient sovereignty. When you were young and bold, you wounded us deeply; you eroded our southern borders, you seized half our northern provinces. Where we were weakest, you struck deepest, until my father's father, worn with war and with the cruel years, sued for peace. Why did you grant it?"

The Sunborn answered willingly, as one who indulges a child's attempts to be wise. "I too was weary, and my army longed to see its homelands again, and my empire had need of a lord who was not always riding to war. The old emperor's death, the masking of Ziad-Ilarios, lengthened the peace and made it stronger. As it strengthened my empire."

"And now the peace is breaking. I hear much of what my father does to threaten Keruvarion. I hear nothing of why he does it. Your armies gathered and moving. Your spies spreading disaffection even into Kundri'j itself. The revolts fomented in your name among our slaves. Your taking of yet another northern satrapy."

"That was a general grown overbold with power. He has been punished."

"Aye," said Hirel, "with the governorship of your new province."

"No." The Sunborn spoke with an edge of iron. "He was executed. The province we kept. It was no use to you save to feed your slave markets."

"It was ours."

"Was," said Mirain An-Sh'Endor. "So too were the Hundred Realms, half a thousand years ago. Now both are mine, and both are glad of me."

"Of course. They dare not confess otherwise."

"I would know."

Hirel looked up at him and thought of being afraid. "Why did you summon me? To subvert me? To forbid me to depart?"

"Neither." The emperor rose from his throne and came down. Hirel faced him steadily. The Sunborn smiled with no suggestion of strain. "I owe you a debt as deep as any man has ever owed another. I would pay it as I may, though in the end we must be enemies. What aid I can give you in your riding through my lands, I will give; I lay no restrictions upon you, and demand no conditions. I do not even ask that you dine with us before you go. Unless, of course, you wish it."

"You have no tasters here," Hirel said. "Your magic is enough, people say. Poison turns to honey in the cup." He paused. Suddenly he smiled. "I have a fondness for honeyed wine. I will dine with you."

The Sunborn laughed. "Honeyed wine it shall be, and fine company, and for yet a while, honest friendship. Whatever may come after."

PART TWO

Sarevadin Halenan Kurelian Miranion iVaryan

Ten

SAREVAN HAD NEVER RECKONED HIMSELF A SEER. THAT BURDEN was his mother's, and in lesser measure his father's. They could raise the power at will and at need, and sometimes it would yield to their mastery. He had no such gift. He had one dream only; but that dream was true. It shifted and changed, but its import was always the same. It began in peace. A green country, sunlit, quiet. Yet slowly he saw the lie beneath the serenity. The green withered. The earth shriveled, and the sun slew it, beautiful, benevolent, relentless. No cloud dared veil its face. *See,* it sang, *how fair am I, how splendid, how merciful. No night shall come to torment my people. No cold shall wither my lands.* It sang; and endless day destroyed them, and heat unceasing seared them to the root.

It haunted him, that dream. From the time he first became a man, it had beset him. It had come perilously close to driving him mad.

Time and teaching had given him, if not mastery, at least endurance. It had not blunted the edge of the vision. What was veiled came ever clearer. What began as simple nightmare kindled into the full fire of prophecy. The sun took on his father's face. The land became his own Keruvarion. He saw its cities ravaged, its

119

people slain, its dominion given over to the carrion crow. And his father sat above it and smiled, and stretched out his hand. Westward the sun sank; westward was peace, however flawed, and a man in a golden mask, aging and mortal and indomitable.

It was madness, that twisting of the world's truth. It was maddening. To look for peace to raddled harlot Asanion with its thousand lying gods; to find destruction in the hands of the Sunborn.

Even upon death's marches Sarevan had seen it. Had broken and bolted from it, and fled, and found his father's face; and recoiled in mindless horror. It was not Mirain who had won the battle for his life, nor Vadin whose name and love he bore, nor even Elian who was soul of both their souls. Han-Gilen's Red Prince had brought him back, had taught him anew to bear the pain of his foreseeing. And before Prince Orsan, another. A face beyond memory; a voice he could not name, although he struggled, waging war against forgetfulness. That will without name or face had turned him to the light, and sent him forth into Mirain's hands.

He did not remember all of it. He had fought. He had lashed his father with hatred. He had called him liar and murderer and worse. He had wielded the full force of his seeing; and he had fallen. Mirain was stronger. "It will not be so," the Sunborn said with the force of a vow. "I will not let it be so. I bring peace and plenty, and the victory of light over the ancient darkness."

And Asanion?

"Asanion will see the truth I bear. She is not blind but blinded. I will give her the clarity of my vision."

It was truth, that promise. Sarevan yearned toward it; and yearning, yielded, and plunged at last into healing sleep.

And dreamed. No horror, now; but this was kin to the black dream, and to memory. Nothing so clear as prophecy had led him to a fernbrake on the marches of Karmanlios, and shown him a wounded child: a child who by fate and birth and necessity must be his greatest enemy. And yet, foremost, a child, and sorely hurt. Hirel would never know truly how close he had been to dissolution, or how bitter had been the battle to heal his body and his mind. There was no magery in him, but there was something, a will or a power for which Sarevan had no name, and it was strong in its resistance.

It had found its way into Sarevan's own healing, and somehow made it stronger. It was like Hirel its master. Fierce, heedless, haughty, yet gentle in spite of itself. It neither knew nor cared where it dealt wounds, but it was swift enough to heal them, if only for its own peace. It shaped for Sarevan a vision, a young man's face. Hirel's, perhaps, shorn of its youth and its softness. It was a stronger face than Sarevan might have expected, and more truly royal, with all its pride pared clean. Sarevan could not like it, nor truly trust it. But love—yes, that would not be difficult. Neither did he like or truly trust his father. Mirain was above such simplicity.

The golden eyes opened; the vision raised its chin. Oh, indeed, it was Hirel. No one else had quite that spark of temper. "I am the key," he said. His voice was deep, and yet indisputably Hirel's. "For war or for peace, I am the key. Remember."

"You'll never lose your arrogance, will you?" Sarevan observed.

The dream-image frowned at his levity. "I am no man's pawn. Yet I am the crux. Remember."

Remember. Remember.

"Remember!"

Sarevan started awake. His mind roiled. He clutched desperately at clarity. At memory. Not Hirel's face. Not dreams, not prophecy that must be false or mad. Clear daylight. His own bed, his own high chamber, his own half-mended body. His power—

Nothing. Silence. Utter absence, edged with agony. In dream at least, however terrible, he was whole.

He dragged himself up. Morning flamed in the eastward window. By sheer will he won his way to it. The city spread below, his father's city, his own. Above its roofs, beyond the broad flood of Suvien, loomed the rock from which the city took its name: Endros Avaryan, Throne of the Sun, and on it the tower which the Sunborn had raised in a night with song and with power, his own and his empress' and his oathbrother's. They had faced together all the million stars, and cried to Avaryan beyond them, and made a mighty shaping of magic. All night the rock was veiled in a mist of light, and when at last the sun rose, it rose upon a wonder. The lofty hill had grown more lofty still, and its upper reach was polished like black glass, edged and chiseled into a tower of four horns, with a fifth rising high from their center, and upon this tallest spire a crystal that flamed like a sun. No window broke those sheer walls, no gate divided them. The tower might have been but a deception, an image sculpted in the stone of the hill.

But it was no simple image, nor stronghold, nor monument to imperial pride. It was a temple of its own strange kind, raised to bear witness to the power of the god. While it stood, the tales said, the city of the Sunborn would never fall, his line never fail. A potent comfort while the son of the Sunborn lay yet in his mother's womb.

Sarevan stood by his window, leaning against it, staring at the black tower. Even so early, with Avaryan barely risen, the crystal blazed bright enough to blind a man. Sarevan fixed his eyes full upon it. That much at least he had still, the power to bear the sun's light without flinching. Once he could have drunk it like wine, and fed on it, and gained life and strength enough to sustain his body for a servant-startling while.

It was only light now, bright but endurable. As the earth was only earth, lovely but muted, oddly lifeless; as the air was only simple, mortal, summer-scented air. As living creatures were only bodies, and men no more than their outward seeming: hands and voices; eyes that mirrored nothing but his own face.

Ulan leaned against him, purring. Sarevan looked down. Shadow-grey cat-shape, slitted green eyes. A mute beast that, sensing its master's trouble, strove to comfort him with its body. He watched his fingers weave their way into the thick fur. They were very thin. "Tomorrow," he said, "I call for my sword." His voice, like his eyes, had changed little. It was still—almost—his own.

He straightened. He was not strong, not yet, but he could stand and he could walk, and the rest was coming swiftly enough to make a simple man marvel. He began to walk.

"My lord called?"

Sarevan, caught between window and door, nearly fell. He braced his feet and stilled his face. He did not know this nervous young creature in his own white livery. A new one, fresh from some desert chieftain's brood from the look of him.

Sarevan did not know that he had done it until it was done: the flick of his mind, just so, the gathering of name and lineage, the skimming of thoughts unwarded by power. He had done it from instinct since before he could remember, as a simple man might judge another in a quick sharp glance. He kept doing it, from instinct; he could not school himself to forbear. When nothing came, and then the lancing agony, he almost welcomed them.

One thing he was learning. He did not fall into darkness, although the boy cried out in dismay. "My lord! Are you ill? Shall I fetch—"

"No." Sarevan drew himself up again. The pain was passing. He put on a smile and said lightly, "I must be going to live. I'm down to a single nursemaid. What are they punishing you for?"

The boy's tawny cheeks flushed beneath the patterning of scars, but his narrow black eyes had begun to dance. "My lord, it is a high honor to serve you."

"Two hundred steps high." Sarevan completed the journey he had begun. The squire moved aside, a little quickly perhaps. Sarevan looked out upon the landing and down the long spiral. He knew what had possessed him to live in a tower. High air and young muscles and power that could give him wings if he had need. He had flown straight up more than once, and not always from the inside. One of the gardeners still went about with one eye cocked upward lest he lose his hat to a swooping wizardling.

Sarevan eyed the ul-cat and the sturdy young squire, and counted the steps again. Two hundred and two.

He drew a breath. With a word and a gesture he had them moving, the cat going before, the boy beside him. He walked every step of the two hundred and two, and he did not lean once on his companion. At the bottom he had to stop. His knees struggled to give way beneath him; his lungs labored; his eyes blurred and darkened. Sternly he called them all to order.

The boy faced him directly, a head shorter than he, breathing with perfect ease. The black brows were knit. "You look unwell, my lord. Shall I carry you back up?"

"What is your name?"

The boy blinked as much at the tone as at the question, but he answered calmly enough. "Shatri, my lord. Shatri Tishri's-son.

"I know *your* name, my lord," he added, like an idiot, but his eyes had filled with mischief.

Sarevan studied the bright eyes until they went wide and veered away. Shatri was blushing again. When Sarevan touched him, he started and trembled like an unbroken colt. "Hush now, lad, I won't eat you. Which name of mine do you know?"

"Why, lord, all of them. We are required to know. But we must call you *my lord* and *my prince.*"

"Why?"

"Because, my lord. You are."

"Ah, simplicity." But Shatri was not simple at all. He would walk as Sarevan bade him, and he would offer his shoulder for Sarevan's hand, but whenever Sarevan spoke to him, he suffered a fit of shaking. It was often like that with the new ones. It had little to do with the terrors of serving mages, and much to do with the terrors of serving kings.

They stopped in the stableyard beside the largest of the stone troughs. Sarevan sat on its edge. For a long while he simply sat, and his sitting was a prayer of thanksgiving that he need not force himself forward another step. His sight swelled and dimmed, swelled and dimmed. His body would not stop trembling.

Yet he smiled at Shatri, and somewhere he found the voice to say, "My senel. Do you know him? The oddity, the blue-eyed stallion. Bring him to me."

The boy hesitated. Perhaps at last he was considering other orders than Sarevan's. But he bowed and went away. Ulan stayed. Sarevan sat on the damp grass that rimmed the trough, half lying on the warm solidity of the cat's flank. Ulan began again to purr.

People came. They remonstrated. Sarevan smiled and was immovable. Then someone shouted, and darkness burst from a stable door.

Bregalan was no simple lackwit of a senel. He was of the Mad One's line: he had the mind of a man, a brother, a kinsman born to the shape and the wisdom of a beast. He did not suffer fools, or ropes, or doors that dared to shut him off from his two-legged brother; though for once he had suffered someone to saddle him, for Sarevan's sake.

He was black, like his grandsire. He was beautiful, which he knew very well. He was, as Sarevan had said, an oddity. His eyes were not seneldi brown or silver or green, nor even the rarer ruby of the Mad One and his get. When he was at peace, they were as blue as the sky in autumn. When he was in a rage, they were the precise and searing blue that lives in the heart of a flame.

They found Sarevan. They rolled. Bregalan scattered the presumptuous few who stood in his way; one, slow to retreat, he very nearly gored.

Having cleared the stableyard, he approached Sarevan with perfect dignity marred only by a snort at Ulan. The cat responded with a lazy growl. Bregalan disdained to hear it, lowering his head to examine Sarevan with great care. Sarevan reached up, wound his fingers in the senel's mane. Bregalan sank to his knees. He had never done it before. Sarevan fought the easy tears, mustered the rags of his strength, dragged himself onto the familiar back. "Up," he whispered into the ear that cocked for him.

It was easier by far than walking. Bregalan had soft paces: they were bred into him. He softened them to silk, and he wrought a miracle. He reined in all his wild temper, although he could not forbear from dancing gently as Sarevan woke to something very like joy. He could still converse with his brother, a wordless, ceaseless colloquy, body speaking to body with nothing between. He was no cripple here, no invalid, no precious prize wrested from death. He was a man, and whole, and riding free.

"Is that an art reserved for mages?"

Sarevan looked down. Wide golden eyes, all but whiteless like a lion's or a falcon's, looked up. Alone of anyone in Endros, Asanion's lion cub was brave enough to stand on ground which Bregalan had cleared. He did not seem aware of his own great courage. That was the legacy of a thousand years of careful breeding: an arrogance as perfect as Bregalan's own. And the stallion, like Ulan before him, recognized it and approved it. Ulan had been much amused. From the glint in his eye, Bregalan was no less so. Sarevan smiled. "Riding is an art which any man can learn. Much like loving. With which, I understand, it has something in common."

Hirel was losing the sun-stain of his wandering, returning to the perfect pallor of ivory; even a slight flush was as vivid as a flag.

Odd, reflected Sarevan, how a youth of his accomplishments could blush at the merest suggestion of a coarse word. But being Hirel, he covered it with prickly hauteur. "I can ride. I am reckoned a master. But not without a bridle."

"Ah," said Sarevan, "but that's only for the Mad One's kin. This is his daughter's son."

Hirel laid a hand on Bregalan's neck. Bregalan did not warn him away. Sarevan knew an instant's piercing jealousy. An outlander, a haughty infant with no power at all; and Sarevan's horned brother not only suffered him but showed every sign of approving of him. The little fool did not even know that he was honored.

Sarevan slid from the saddle, which was half his penance for thinking like an idiot. The other half he set in words. "Do you want to learn how we do it? Bregalan will teach you, if you promise not to insult him by regarding him as a dumb beast."

The Asanian was cool, but Sarevan had seen the sudden light before he hid it. "What is he if he is not a beast?"

"He is a kinsman and a friend. And he has a thinking mind, though he has no tongue to tell you so." Sarevan gestured, princely gracious. "Will you mount?"

Bregalan was the tallest of the Mad One's line; and while that was nothing remarkable for a stallion of the Ianyn breed, it was a goodly leap for a prince of the old Asanian blood. Hirel made it with that studied, dancer's grace of his, and looked down for once into Sarevan's face. Sarevan grinned at him. "Now begin. You have no bit and no reins, but you have your whole body. Use it. Talk to him with it. Yes, gently. Listen now; he answers. Yes. Yes, so."

Sarevan ended again on the grass with Ulan, voice pitched to carry well without effort. People had gathered: grooms, stable-hands, the inevitable scattering of idlers. This was a great rarity, a stranger mounted on one of the Varyani demons; that it was an Asanian, and this Asanian to boot, made it worth a stare or six.

And, Sarevan admitted reluctantly, they had come to stare at him. For their sake he sat upright, cross-legged in his no longer pristine white robe, and leaned on Ulan more than they knew but less than he would have liked to.

Another voice slid smoothly into a pause in Sarevan's. "No, don't lean. Sit straight; guide him with your leg. Your whole leg, sir. Heels are merely an annoyance."

How dull the world had grown, that Mirain An-Sh'Endor was only a slight man, very dark, with the bearing of a king. No blaze of light; no high and singing presence in Sarevan's mind, part of it, source of it, anchored as firmly as the earth itself. Even when he came and settled his arm about his son's shoulders, he was only warm flesh; beloved, yes, but separate. Sundered.

Sarevan would not cling and cry. He had done that when he made the long terrible journey from the marches of death's country, and woke, and found himself a cripple. No power at all, only the void and the pain. He had wept like a child, until his blurred and swollen eyes, lifting, saw the anguish in his father's face. Then he had sworn. No tears. He was alive; his body would mend. That must suffice.

"He does well," Mirain said, holding Sarevan up and mercifully refraining from comment on his condition. Bregalan was showing Hirel how a battle charger fought in Keruvarion; the boy had dropped all his masks and loosed a blood-curdling whoop. They were a fine and splendid sight: the great black beast with his blue-fire eyes, his rider all gold and ivory, molded to the senel's back, singing in a voice too piercingly pure to be human.

Until it cracked, and Bregalan wearied of perfect obedience and bucked him neatly into the trough. He came up gasping, more shocked than angry, but he came up in a long leap that somersaulted him over the javelin horns and onto the back that had spurned him.

A roar went up. Laughter, cheering, even a spear smitten on a guardsman's shield. Hirel sat and dripped and grinned a wide white grin. Bregalan raised his head and belled in seneldi mirth.

Sarevan was not regretting what he had done. Not precisely. He had had no strength left to face the stair; his father had carried him up, taking not the least notice of his objections, standing by sternly while his servants stripped him and bathed him and laid him in bed. "And mind that you stay there," said Mirain; and he left Shatri on guard within the door. The squire, transparently grateful to have escaped with a mere reprimand, took his charge all too seriously. If Sarevan moved, Shatri was there, alert, scowling most formidably.

Not that Sarevan moved much. He was discovering muscles he

had not known he had. There were not enough of them, that was the trouble. The bones kept thrusting through.

He slept a little. He ate, to keep his nursemaids quiet. When they pressed wine on him, even his sluggish nose could catch the sweetness of dreamflower. He flung the cup across the room. That was petulant, unprincely, and very satisfying. And it persuaded even Shatri to let him be.

Sarevan started awake. Hirel regarded him steadily, without expression. For a moment Sarevan could not choose between waking and the memory of a dream. It was a little unreal, that face, like something carved in ivory. Perfect, without line or blemish, and poised still on the edge between child and man. In gown and veil he would have made an exquisite girl; in coat and trousers he was a strikingly beautiful boy. Sarevan always wanted to stroke him, to see if he would be as pleasing to the hand as to the eye.

Hirel's eyes flicked aside; his brows met. "You drove yourself too hard. I should have seen."

"You couldn't have stopped me."

Hirel answered that with a long look. Abruptly he said, "Roll over."

Surprised, piqued with curiosity, Sarevan obeyed. Quick hands stripped off the coverlet. He shivered a little. The corner of his eye caught Hirel's infinitesimal pause, the widening of the golden eyes. "Not pretty, am I?"

"No," Hirel murmured, hardly more than a whisper. His hands found one of the hundred screaming muscles. Sarevan gasped and tensed; Hirel did something indescribable; the pain melted and flowed and transmuted into pleasure. The boy's deepening voice spoke just above his head. "No, you are not pretty at all. You are beautiful."

Sarevan's cheeks were hot. Thank Avaryan and his Ianyn ancestors, it never showed. And his tongue always knew what to do. Lightly, carelessly, it said, "What are you trying to do, infant? Make me vain?"

"That," said Hirel, "would be salting the sea." His weight settled on the bed, kneeling astride Sarevan's hips; his hands wrought wonders up Sarevan's back and across his shoulders.

Sarevan sighed from the bottom of his lungs. It was almost sinful, this. Purest animal contentment.

What an artist the child was with those hands. What an innocent, in spite of everything. "You would have made a splendid bath-slave," Sarevan's tongue observed, incorrigible.

Hirel worked his way downward, inch by blissful inch. Then up, and with more ease than he had any right to, he turned Sarevan onto his back. A very faint flush stained his cheeks. His curls were loosening as they grew, falling over his forehead. Sarevan had no will left; he reached to stroke them.

The boy was learning. He tensed, but he held himself still. Only his hands moved. Upward.

Sarevan laughed. "I dare you," he said.

Very slowly Hirel straightened, gathered himself, sat on the bed's edge. His eyes slanted toward Sarevan's middle, and slanted away. Sarevan refused to cover it. Even and especially when Hirel observed to the air, "So very much, to so very little purpose."

"What, child! Envy?"

"Moral outrage." Hirel tucked up his feet and drew his brows together. The line between them was going to be etched there before he was very much older. "Sun-prince, there is that which I must say."

Sarevan waited.

Hirel's hands fisted upon his knees. "This should never have come to pass. You, I. You should have slain me before ever I woke by your fire. I should have taken your life while you lay helpless by the Lakes of the Moon, or held you back upon the journey until you died of your own accord. We cannot be what we are. We must not. For I have heard and I have seen, in Kundri'j and in Endros. I know that two emperors rule the two faces of the world; but when our time comes, only one of us may claim throne or power. And that time is coming soon. Your father makes no secret of it. Mine intends to move before him. Has moved already, subtly. Are you not the proof of it?"

Sarevan's throat tightened into pain. He thrust his voice through it. "I'm proof of nothing but my own stupidity."

"That too," Hirel said all too willingly. "As am I of mine. Your father declares that his god will not permit a peaceful union of our empires. Mine insists that we must not be overrun by the barbarian vigor of the east. Yet here are we. I am not going to find it easy to encompass your death."

"What ever makes you think that you should have to?"

"Bow to me, then. Bow to me now, and swear that you will serve me when I am emperor."

Sarevan sat bolt upright. The last languor of Hirel's ministrations had vanished. His branded hand had flared into agony. But he laughed, though it was half a howl. "You forget, cubling. You forget what I am. Avaryan is not only my father's god. He is mine, and he rules me. He—still—rules me."

Still. Sarevan laughed harder, freer, cradling the pain that was driving him through madness into blessed, blissful clarity. Avaryan. Burning Avaryan. No mere mage could drive him from his only son's only son. He was there. He was pain. He was—

Sarevan's cheeks stung. He rocked with the force of Hirel's blows, blinking, still grinning. "Are you mad?" Hirel all but screamed at him.

"No," said Sarevan. "No more than I ever am."

The boy hissed like a cat, thrust his hand into his coat, held it up shaking and glittering. "Do you know what this is?"

Laughter, joy, even madness forsook Sarevan utterly. The thing in Hirel's palm glowed with more than sunlight, yet its heart was a darkness that writhed and twisted like a creature in agony. Or like a slow and deadly dance. It lured Sarevan's eyes, drew them down and down, beckoned, whispered, promised. *Come, and I will make you strong again. Come, take me, wield me. I am power. I am all the magics you have lost. Take me and be healed.*

Sarevan gasped, retched. "Take it—take—"

It withdrew. Slowly, far too slowly, into the embroidered coat.

"No!" cried Sarevan. "Not there!" He snatched wildly, striking, hurling the jewel through the air. It fell like a star, whispering. He seized Hirel's wrists. "How often has it touched your skin? *How often?*"

The boy blinked like an idiot. "Just now. And when first I took it. I do not like to hold it. But—"

"Never," said Sarevan, choking on bile. "Never touch it again. It is deadly."

"It is but a jewel. The deadliness lies in what it stands for."

"It is an instrument of blackest sorcery." Sarevan dragged himself up, dragging Hirel with him until he remembered to let go. He snatched the first cloth that came to hand, and fell to his knees. The stone sang to him. *Power. Power I bear.* His sight narrowed. He groped. His right hand throbbed.

He fell forward. His hand dropped boneless to the stone. He had no will to rule it. To close. To take, or to cast away.

Gold met topaz. The song rose to a shriek. The pain mounted through anguish into agony, through agony into purest, whitest torment, and through torment into blissful nothingness.

"Vayan. Vayan!"

Sarevan groaned. Again? Would he never be allowed to die in peace?

"Sarevadin." That was his mother, in that tone of hers which brooked no opposition. "Sarevadin Halenan, if you do not open your eyes—"

His mind cursed her, but his eyes opened. He was in bed again, and they were there, she and his father, and Hirel green-pale and great-eyed beside them. "Poor cubling," said Sarevan. "We're too much for you, we madmen."

"Mad, yes," snapped Elian, "striking an Eye of Power with no weapon but your *Kasar*."

Sarevan struggled to sit up. "Is it gone? Did I do it? It wanted me to take it. It promised me—it promised—"

They all fell on him at once, bearing him down, holding him, trying to stroke him calm again. But it was his own will that stilled him, and his own wish that laid him back in his bed, somehow gripping three hands in his two. One freed itself: his mother's, strong and slender. She looked angry, as always when her pride refused to weep. "Will you never learn?" she demanded of him.

"I rather think not."

"Puppy." Her slap was half caress. "It's gone. There are aching heads from here to Han-Gilen, but the Eye is broken. As you very nearly were."

"I wish I had been!" he cried with sudden passion. "I wish I had died in Shon'ai. What use am I? Crippled, helpless, weak as a baby—what good am I to anyone?"

"At the moment," Mirain said coolly, "not remarkably much."

He won back his hand and turned to Hirel. "Prince, are you well? That was a great flare of power, and you almost upon it when it burst. If you will permit . . ."

Whether Hirel would or no, Mirain searched him with eyes and hands and power. Sarevan, numb to the last, still could know that it was there, and how it was wielded, and why.

But he was forgetting the vow which he had sworn. He willed away the unshed tears and sat up. This time no one stopped him. He set his feet on the floor, gathered all his wavering strength, rose. His knees buckled. He stiffened them. He made them bear him to the eastward window, although he asked no more of them there, but let them give way until he half sat, half lay upon the broad ledge. Night had fallen without his knowing it; the air was cool and he as bare as he was born. He shivered.

Warmth folded itself about him. One of his own cloaks, with his mother's hands on it and her arms circling him. Her swift unthinking smile was for an old jest, of mothers and of great strapping broad-shouldered sons. Her scowl was for the jut of bones in those shoulders. He kissed her cheek, quickly, before she could escape. "I'll be strong," he said as much to himself as to her. "I will be."

Eleven

"LITTLE WHORE."

The voice came from beyond the door into the Green Court. Sarevan knew it, as he knew the one which spoke after. "Yellow barbarian. You couldn't kill him cleanly, could you? You had to make him suffer."

And a third: "But we know. We see what you try to do to him now that he can't defend himself."

"Yes, catamite," sneered the first, "try it. See where it gets you."

Sarevan shot the bolt, blind for a moment in the dazzle of sunlight, forcing his eyes to see. Hirel stood at bay in a cluster of young men, some in the emperor's livery, others clad as the lordlings they were. Sarevan knew them all. Some he even loved.

Whatever Hirel had tried, he had forsaken it in favor of his imperial Asanian mask. Only his lips betrayed him; they were tight, and they were bone-white.

Starion had spoken third and most ominously. Now he spoke again. He sounded as if he had been weeping, or as if he were not far from it. "I saw him yesterday in the stableyard. I saw how he had to be carried away. Your doing, you and your devil of a father.

You lured him into the trap that almost killed him. You tricked him into bringing you here. You set your Eye of sorcery in his very hand; and yet you found a way to crawl into the emperor's good graces. But *we* know you for what you are."

"Spy and traitor," said a prince's son from Baian, his round amiable face gone grim, "set here like a worm to gnaw Keruvarion's heart. Is it fools you animals take us for?"

"What's the use of talk?" Ianyn, this great yearling bull of a boy, not quite the tallest but by far the broadest of them all. "He's Asanian; he was born with a serpent's tongue, though he's not deigning to use it on the likes of us. Not when he's got royalty to hiss in the ears of. Here, little snake, I'll tie your tongue for you."

Hirel spat in his face.

Sarevan hardly heard the snarl, or saw the lunge of several bodies at once. He was in the midst of them, striking openhanded, taking at least one blow that all but felled him, until someone cried sharply, *"Vayan!"*

The circle had widened in dismay. Sarevan almost laughed to see their faces. With great deliberation he laid his arm about Hirel's rigid shoulders and said, "So there you are, brother. I've been looking for you."

Starion broke at that. "Don't you know what he *is,* Vayan?"

"Certainly," Sarevan answered. And to Hirel: "Come with me. There's something I want you to see."

"How can you show him anything? How can you trust him? He's here to destroy us all, and you foremost."

Sarevan drew a deep breath. "He's so thin," someone whispered, too low to put a name to the voice; and Sarevan would not take his eyes from Starion. "So weak. O 'Varyan!"

Sarevan swallowed bile and spoke as evenly as he could. "Kinsmen, your concern warms me. But I would thank you to reserve your righteous passion for those who truly mean me harm. Of whom this prince is not one. Touch him again, threaten him, speak one ill word of him, and it will be I who call you to account." He drew Hirel forward. "Come."

"That was not wise," Hirel said.

Sarevan laughed lest the pain lash him into shameful tears. "What's wise? I've pulled rank on that pack of idiots before.

Though not," he admitted, "quite so viciously as that. I'm afraid
I've not done you much good with them."

"Or yourself either."

"That's nothing. They'll mutter a little, they'll cold-shoulder me
for a while, and then they'll come back as if nothing had ever
happened. They always do."

"Unless they are driven too far."

"Not yet," said Sarevan with more confidence than he felt. He
opened a locked door, passing again from dimness into the heat
and the glare of noon in full summer, and had his reward: the
catch of Hirel's breath. "This is my own garden. My father and
mother made it for me with their power. It's not as big as it looks."

"The pool seems as broad as a sea," Hirel said, sounding for
once like the boychild he was. "A sea, and a forest, and a green
plain. What mountain is that?"

"The palace wall, painted and ensorceled to look like the peak
of Zigayan as it rises over Lake Umien." Sarevan shed his kilt and
waded into the water. After a long moment Hirel followed.
Sarevan struck his shoulder lightly, challenging. "Race you to the
island."

Hirel won, but only barely. They lay on the grass, getting their
breaths back, grinning at one another and at the brazen sky.

Hirel's grin died first; his frown came back. "Sun-prince, I was in
no danger, and I was about to escape. You had no need to go to
war for me."

"No? It looked as if they were going to war for me." Something
in Hirel's face made Sarevan tense, rolling onto his stomach,
raising himself on his elbows. "What is it? What aren't you telling
me?"

"Nothing."

"Don't lie, cubling. You're no good at it."

"Very well, mongrel. I will tell you. They are indeed going to
war for you. And not they alone. It is noised abroad in your
empire: my father and I between us fomented this plot to destroy
you, and through you your father and all his realm. Your people
are crying for vengeance. Your lords and your princes are arming
for war. Your wise men are calling for calm, but no one heeds
them."

For all the sun's heat, Sarevan was cold to the bone. He had come to Endros for his father's sake, with warning of war in Asanion; with hope, however frail, that he could hold it back. And he had failed more utterly even than he had feared. Coming as he had come, on the very edge of death, he had fanned the spark which he had meant to quench. Now it was a full and raging fire; and all for his own invincible folly.

"No," he said. "Not yet. My father has a little sanity left. He will stop it."

Hirel laughed, short and bitter. "Your father could ask for nothing better. He has you, alive and well enough, and he has the war for which he has waited so long. By next High Summer, he has sworn, he will sit upon the Golden Throne."

"No." Sarevan could not stop saying it. "Not for me."

The boy's face hovered close. He looked frightened. As well he might. Sarevan was losing what little wits he had had. He lurched to his knees; his fists struck the ground. He flung himself into the water.

He must have remembered to dress. His hair had worked out of its braid, but it was drying; and for the first time since he left Shon'ai, his body had forborne to betray him. It carried him he cared not where.

To his tower, in the end. To court dress and the massive weight of his torque and a feast to which he had not been bidden.

Because someone—Shatri, damn his diligence—had made him rest a little, he was late. They were all seated. Emperor, empress, Lord of the Northern Realms, Lord Chancellor of the South, their ladies, their servants, certain of their children. And in the place of honor, still as a golden image, Hirel Uverias.

Their eyes weighed him down. Most were seeing him for the first time since he came back. He read horror in them, and dismay, and pity swiftly veiled. And anger, deep and abiding, most strongly marked in the youngest, who were his kin and his friends.

He gave them his whitest, wildest grin, and said, "Good evening, my lords and ladies. I hear you're having a war without me."

No one spoke. He did not look at his father, or at his mother, although he knew she had half risen. He sat beside Hirel and reached for a brimming cup. He raised it. "To death," he said.

* * *

He paid for that, and not cheaply. Not that Mirain dealt him a reprimand. The emperor said nothing, which was infinitely worse. And Sarevan must sit, eat, drink, prove to them all that he was still Sarevan Is'kelion.

He woke as inevitably he must, in a bed not his own. Hirel slept in a warm knot against him. "Damn them," he whispered. "Oh, damn them."

"Damn whom?"

He started up, winced, clutched his stomach, fell back, torn between anger and mirth. "Cubling! I thought you were asleep."

"Obviously not." Hirel settled more comfortably, head on folded arm. His eyes were soft still with sleep. "Damn whom?" he asked again.

"Everyone!" Hirel raised his brows. Sarevan had better fortune in his second rising. He spread his arms wide. "They've made me an object of rage and pity, a banner for their war."

"I know," said Hirel. "It amazes me that you did not. That you came as you did, when you did, in my company—how could it have ended otherwise?"

Sarevan's own thoughts, bitter to hear from a stranger's mouth. His hand flew up to strike; with all his strength he willed it down.

"You should be rejoicing," the young demon said. "You are getting a war. A chance to look splendid in armor, and brandish a sword, and win a hero's name. Is that not the heart's desire of every good barbarian?"

"Barbarian I may be," gritted Sarevan, "but I will not be the cause of this war. I will *not*."

"Is it not a little late for that?"

"It may not be." Sarevan stopped short. His teeth clicked together. "It is not. I will not have it!"

For a miracle, Hirel was silent. Sarevan's chin itched. His fingers rasped on stubble; he grimaced, rising slowly. His knees were steady. A wave of sickness passed, and it was all wine. No weakness. He stretched each muscle, and each responded, remembering at last its old suppleness. As close to rage or madness as he was, he could have sung.

He availed himself of Hirel's bath and servants, and sent for his own clothing, and ate while he waited for it, for a mighty hunger had roused in him. Which was an excellent sign, better even than the ease with which he moved. When he dressed, he dressed with care, contemplating his image in the tall bronze mirror. Clean, smooth-shaven, his hair tamed as much as it could ever be: yes. And the princely plainness of his boots and trousers, and the understated elegance of his coat, and the rich red gold of the torque at his throat: excellent. His eyes were too large and bright in the hollowed face, but that he could not help; though he had a moment's regret. If he had had all his wits about him, he would not have sacrificed the concealment of his beard.

He sighed and shrugged, and smiled at Hirel whose reflection had come to stand beside his own. Hirel looked him up and down, eyes glinting. "Are you plotting to seduce someone?"

"Keruvarion," Sarevan answered.

The boy tilted his head and vouchsafed one of his rare smiles. He looked like a cat in cream.

Sarevan swallowed. It hurt. "Hirel," he said with great care, "last night. What did I—"

"You were remarkable," said Hirel. "You were the life and soul of the gathering. You were a light and a fire, and you held each man and woman in the palm of your hand."

"Of course I did. That's what I went for. But why was I—" This was hard, and Hirel was making it no easier, going all warm and supple and melting-eyed. Playing some game of his own, and enjoying it much too much. "How did I end in your bed?"

"You do not remember?"

His astonishment was well played, but not well enough. Sarevan fixed him with a grim eye. "All right, cubling. What did I do, and what are you up to?"

Hirel dropped the mask of the courtesan for that of the spoiled princeling, a little sulky, more than a little offended. "You did nothing. Except drown yourself in wine, roister everyone into a stupor, and fall into bed. Mine. Because, you said, two hundred steps were too many, and people were talking, and you were minded to give them something to talk of. Surely you remember."

"Vaguely," Sarevan admitted. "Now answer the rest of it."

"No."

Sarevan gripped that stubborn chin, forced it up. It set against him. With a rush of temper, he bent and seized a long, thorough kiss. Thorough enough to bruise, and long enough to heat them both. He let go so swiftly that Hirel swayed. "Is that what you're angling for?"

Hirel bared his teeth. It was more grin than snarl. "It will do," he said, "for a beginning."

Sarevan's temper subsided; he took Hirel's shoulders, but gently, shaking them a little. "They're only a pack of jealous children. For all their prattle, they know the truth as well as we do."

"But," Hirel asked, "what is the truth?"

"What should it be?"

Hirel tossed his head, swift, nervous, as if he would fling back his lost splendid mane. "The truth," he snapped, "is that I am a whore and a spy, and I was your prisoner, and I contemplated your murder, and at a word, at one lone word, I would fling myself into your arms." He glared into Sarevan's craven silence. "No, I cannot help myself. No, I am not glad of it! I am the worst of all fools. I took you to wield you, and because there was no one else to take. I gave you my trust. I found that I could not hate you, even when you seemed to betray me. And now I am lost. I would be your lover, and I would do it gladly, and I would not ask even a harlot's recompense. But in the end, I remain as I was born. High Prince of Asanion. They know, your kinsmen. They see clearly. I would love you without regret, and betray you with deep regret, even to your death."

"Avaryan," Sarevan said softly. "Sweet Avaryan. I never meant—"

"What an innocent you are," said that most unchildlike child, shaking the slack hands from his shoulders. "You are plotting something, and I know what it must be, and I think that it is utterly mad."

"You can't stop me."

"I would not if I could. I will help you as I can. But I give you fair warning. I will not betray my empire, and I will think nothing of betraying the god to whom you are sworn."

Sarevan laughed suddenly. "I'll take my chances. If I win this throw, there will be no need for betrayal. If I lose it, I doubt I'll be alive to care."

"That is the heart of it, is it not? Without your power, you see little purpose in living."

"I see one, and I am pursuing it. By your leave, sir?" Sarevan asked, mocking.

Hirel bowed, mocking. With a grin and a flash of his hand, Sarevan left him.

It was flight; but it was flight from bad to worse. Sarevan's new strength could not carry him quite as far as he had to go. He paused in a side chamber of his father's antechambers, in a recess that offered a moment's curtained quiet. The press of people did not find its way here; the servants were elsewhere about their duties.

As he gathered himself to go on, he froze behind his arras. Swift feet; the snick of a bolt; laughter barely stifled. It rippled in two ranges, man-deep and woman-sweet. What accompanied it was obvious enough. A pair of lovers had found a haven.

Sarevan did not know whether to laugh or to groan aloud. There was no door but the one the lovers had barred, and no escape except past them; and he was in no state to eavesdrop on their sport. They were most merry in it. He blocked his ears as best he could, and shut his eyes to aid them. Behind the quivering lids, Hirel smiled: but Hirel become a maiden, sweet and wicked. Grimly he began the first of the Prayers of Penitence, with its nine invocations of bodily pain.

The lovers ended before the prayer. Sarevan, lowering hands from ears, heard only silence. He waited, hardly breathing. Nothing moved. No voice spoke. With great care he parted the curtain.

His breath caught. They were there still, in a nest of carpets. Her head lay on his shoulder; his hand tangled itself in her hair. Hair that, had she stood, would have tumbled to her knees, fire-bright as Sarevan's own.

He sank back in his hiding place, hands clapped over mouth. His shoulders shook with the utter and delicious absurdity of it. Lovers, indeed. The Emperor and the Empress of Keruvarion, twenty years wed, trysting like children; and their son trapped without escape, all unwilling to be their witness. Elian would be livid when she knew; he could hope that she would soften into laughter. He did not fancy another nine months' span in a woman's body.

She spoke, a murmur, drowsily tender. Sarevan, moving to uncover himself, paused.

"No one's here," Mirain said. "We have a while yet before anyone looks for me. I told them I was going to ride the Mad One."

She laughed softly. "And no one dares to trouble you then. Alas for me, I never stopped to think. They'll be combing the corridors for me."

"Let them." Properly imperial, that, but with a smile beneath it. "Were you so eager, then?"

"You hardly gave me time to begin. Hot as a boy, you are. And you more than old enough to know better."

"Come now, madam. May not even a greybeard take what pleasure he can?"

She snorted. "Even if you had a beard, which I am glad you do not, there would be scarce enough silver in it to buy a night with a camp follower."

"I found a thread," he said, "this morning."

"Where?"

"Here."

"I don't see—" She stopped. There was a flurry, with his laughter in it, and her mirthful outrage. "Ah, trickster! That's the silver in your robe."

"It's all I have. I'm not aging gracefully, my love. I keep thinking I'm a youth still."

"You are!"

His voice held a smile, for her vehemence. "And you are as wild as ever you were. But not," he added judiciously, "as beautiful."

She growled. He laughed. "O vain! You were nothing in your youth to what you are in this your womanhood. Men sighed for you then. Now they swoon over you."

"Indeed," she muttered. "Flat at my feet, mooncalves all, and blind with it. Though one or two . . . if you were not so fierce in your jealousy . . ."

"When was I ever—"

"When were you not? Vadin you never minded: the world never saw a man more thoroughly married than that one, or more perfectly a brother to his soul's sister. But let other eyes slide toward me, and you turn all to thunder."

"Only once," he said, "and that was long ago; and I had reason." He paused. His tone softened. "Elian. Do you regret it? That you chose as you did, and clove to me, and let the prince go back alone to Asanion?"

"Sometimes . . ." Her voice was softer even than his. "Sometimes I wonder. But regret, never. You are all that I ever wanted."

"Even my damnable temper? Even our battles?"

"What would life be without a good clean fight?"

"He would have given you a spat or two, I think. He was never as insipid as he looked."

"He was not insipid! He was gentle. You were never that, Mirain. Tender, with me, with Sarevan when he was small. But never gentle."

"Ziad-Ilarios was as gentle as a lion sleeping. His son is more like him than anyone might guess, though not so soft to the eye or the mind. There are scars in that child. New wounds; but old ones too, buried deep. He'll be a strong emperor, or he'll break before he comes to his throne."

"If he were going to break, he would have broken before this. Do you know what it cost him to bring Sarevan to us?"

"Not entirely of his own will," said Mirain.

"Less so than he or anyone thinks. He has his father's curse. He's honorable."

"Not all would call it honor, to bring an Eye of Power into Endros."

"He didn't know what he was doing."

"Did he not? He hid it from us. He brought it to Sarevan in his greatest weakness, and very nearly destroyed him."

"In ignorance," she persisted. "He knows nothing of magic; he knows little more of trust. But Sarevan he trusts, though not willingly. He brought a thing that frightened him, to the one person he knew who might know what to do with it."

"If I grant you that, will you grant me this? There was design in what he did. Not his own, maybe. But he found a place of black sacrifice—Asanian black sacrifice—within sight of my city. He brought what it had wrought into the heart of my palace."

"Traps within traps," she said slowly. "Wheels within wheels. It's too obvious. As if someone were trying, deliberately and all but openly, to turn you against the Golden Empire."

"Need it be so complex? Asanion is arming on all fronts. And it has the Mageguild."

"Does it also have Ulan? He set the Eye in the child's hand."

"Oh, come," said Mirain with a flicker of impatience. "You yourself saw a reason for that. He sensed the evil; he cherishes a remarkable fondness for the boy. He trusted Hirel to dispose of the thing."

"You underrate Ulan, I think. If he was ever an ordinary creature, he's one no longer. He's steeped in magery."

"And whose fault is that?"

"Vadin's, for hunting an ul-queen and bringing back her cub. Yours and mine, for letting our own cub out of sight for long enough to lose him. Sarevan's, for finding his way to the cage and witching away the lock and swearing brotherhood with the cat. How were we to know that he had that much power, at five years old? Or that he'd give his heart to the deadliest of all the world's hunters?"

"It's done," Mirain said. "I don't think it was ill done. The beast has played his part more than once in keeping the boy alive. He's part of no conspiracy. But that Asanion has declared war in its own subtle and serpentine way—that, I'm sure of. It chose my son as its target. It will pay." His voice deepened. "It will pay to the last man."

"Someone may be longing for precisely that. Any man in the world can name your weakness: Prince Sarevadin."

"He is my son. He is all that I may have."

"Mirain—" she began.

He silenced her. With a kiss, from the sound of it, a long one, ended with reluctance. When he spoke, he spoke softly, with a hint of sadness. "Of all that I am and have done, this I most regret: that I could give you no more than the one son."

"Sarevadin is enough."

"Surely. But I would have given you a daughter for yourself."

"I need no more than you gave me." Her voice was strange. Sarevan, listening in helpless fascination, could not put a name to the strangeness. It faded almost as swiftly as he noticed it. "I want no more than I have. But I would not have you destroy an empire for his sake alone."

"For what higher cause would you have me do it?"

"You may have no cause!" she cried. "This that he suffers, he did to himself. He knows it. He wants no vengeance. He wants no war."

"He will have both."

"He will die to stop it."

"He will not."

"How can you know?" Her passion rocked Sarevan in his shadow, flung him against the cold stone of the wall. "I carried him in my body. I feel him there yet. He is an open wound; he will do anything, anything at all, to put an end to the pain."

"He will not," Mirain said again, grim as stone. "I will avenge him. He will rule the world with me, and none shall live who dares to stand against us."

"Oh, you *man!*" If Sarevan had been less benumbed by all he had heard, he would have smiled at the depth of her disgust. "Can't you ever see anything but force? You'll settle it all with the sword, and set his will at naught while you do it, and expect him to be glad of it."

"How else can anyone unravel this tangle? I should have struck against Asanion when Ilarios took the throne. I listened to prudence; I had mercy. I gave them peace. Fool that I am. You see how I pay: with my only son. If he dies before this war is ended, I swear to you, I will leave not one stone standing upon its brother. I will raze Asanion to the ground."

"Not before I will." She was as grim as he. "But it will cost you more than Vayan. It will cost you me."

"It will not."

The silence stretched, as after thunder. Sarevan's hand reached of its own accord, drew back the curtain. They did not see. They stood face to face, eye to eye.

"I walk with the god," he said. "He gives me victory."

Her head tossed. All of Sarevan's protests blazed in her eyes. Her hand flew up. Mirain stood steady. She laid her palm against his cheek. "I love you," she said, soft, barely to be heard. "I love you more than anything in the world."

He turned his head to kiss her palm. Their eyes met, held, broke free. Wordless, oblivious to the one who watched, they left the chamber.

Sarevan stumbled from the alcove. The nest of carpets lay forgotten. He stood over it. He was shaking; he could not stop. He said the words with which he had meant to begin. "Father," he said. "Father, consider. What can war do, that words and wisdom cannot?"

He had his answer. Avenge one man's idiocy. End an ancient enmity. Give Mirain the dominion for which he had been born. Which he meant, in its proper time, to pass to that young idiot who was his son.

"Not," said Sarevan, "if I can help it. Not this way."

The shaking had retreated inward. He could move. Hold up his head. Put on the most rakish of his faces. Stride forth into the full and brazen light of Avaryan.

Sarevan wooed Keruvarion with his presence and his smile and a word here and there. He traversed the palace; he sat an hour in the hall of audience; he made himself a magnet for the young bloods of the court. With Bregalan under him and Ulan striding by his side, he rode about Endros. He traded jests with his father's soldiers, and took the daymeal with his own guard, and had an uproarious reunion with the Zhil'ari who had ridden with him from the Lakes of the Moon.

He sang the sun down from his own tower, and let his nursemaids put him to bed, clucking over him as they did it. He would not let them feed him, but he ate enough to quiet the loudest of them. "And now," he said, "off with you, and let me sleep in peace."

Sleep came fitfully, peace not at all. Behind Sarevan's eyes shuddered the darkness of madness, or of prophecy. Death and destruction; bitter sunlight; a new dread: his mother fallen, his father gone mad over her body. He tossed in his bed, battling, as if his hands alone could drive back the horror that haunted him.

With infinite slowness he quieted. His breathing eased. His mind cleared; his will hardened. But he did not sleep. He dared not. He watched the moons' patterns shift upon the floor. The windows were open to the wind; shadows danced, now lulling, now startling, now alluring his eyes. One was very like a human shape. When it moved, it moved with fluid grace. The rest now approached, now retreated with the wind's turning. This paused often, but never drew back.

It stilled. Its shape was human surely: slender, supple, not tall. It sat at his bed's foot, and its weight was not considerable, but weight it certainly had. It tucked up its feet and settled its rump and regarded Sarevan with wide moon-brightened eyes.

A stare, like a shadow, can have weight. Sarevan fretted under it. It did not waver.

"Cubling," said Sarevan with elaborate patience, "it's late. Haven't you noticed?"

"There are hours yet to midnight," Hirel said. He blinked, which was a small but potent mercy.

"Surely you have better things to do with those hours than sit and stare at me."

"No," Hirel said. "I do not."

Sarevan sat up. "Damn it, cubling! What's got into you?"

"You kissed me."

Sarevan scrambled himself together, cursing the mane that tumbled and knotted and tried to blind him, raking it out of his face. Hirel watched with grave intentness. For once in his life, Sarevan was aware that he was naked: and under a blanket yet, and a heavy cloak of hair. "Damn it," he said again. "Damn it, infant. That was a game I played, to stop your nonsense."

The golden eyes narrowed. "A game, prince?" Hirel asked very softly.

"A game," Sarevan repeated. "That was all. I erred, I admit it. I cry your pardon."

Hirel sat motionless. Sarevan could not read his face at all. He was all alien, inscrutable, like one of his own discredited gods.

"Cubling," said Sarevan, meaning to be gentle, sounding lame even to himself. "Hirel. Whatever you think I meant, I was only playing. Being outrageous, because you were there and being infuriating, and I couldn't help myself. I'm like that. It's the most glaring of all my flaws."

"What should I have thought you meant?"

Sarevan gritted his teeth. "You know damned well—"

Hirel tilted his head. "Would you be so angry if it truly had meant nothing?"

The silence was deafening. Hirel shifted minutely, almost smiling.

"Listen to me," Sarevan said at last. "To you I'm a horror of no small proportions: a man who's never had a woman; nor, for the matter of that, a boy. I won't say it's been easy. I won't say it's easy now. But my honor binds me, and my given word. Can you understand that?"

"It is most immoral," said Hirel. But quietly, as if he considered the matter with some shadow of care.

"What is moral? To those children in the Green Court, *you* are the outrage."

That roused a spark. "They? They would happily die to have what I have."

"You frighten them. They think you have the power to corrupt me, if not to kill me outright."

"And so I do," said Hirel, serene in his certainty. "As do you over me. We are equals. That is what they cannot bear."

"Equals." Sarevan was not sure he liked the sound of it. He, and this epicene creature?

Not so epicene, sitting there, looking at him. It was only youth. Sarevan at not quite fifteen had been pretty enough, eagle's beak and all. Was still rather too pretty for his own comfort, without a beard to mask the worst of it: as he had been amply dismayed to discover, when the razor showed him how little he had changed.

Equals, then. Sarevan lowered his eyes. He had been treating Hirel as a child, or at best as a weakling youth. And weak, Hirel certainly was not.

"So then," said Sarevan, mostly to himself. "What do we do now?"

"You do not know?"

Hirel was mocking them both. Sarevan snarled at him. He grinned back, which was always startling. "Something," said Sarevan with swelling heart. "Something outrageous."

"I will not swear priest's vows!"

"And I won't claim your harem," Sarevan said with a flicker of laughter, though he sobered swiftly. "You can be a moral man for both of us. But harken now—what can a pair of princes do when their fathers foment war?"

"Fight," Hirel said, but slowly, watching him. "What else can we do? We are born enemies. There is not even liking between us; nor, once I leave Endros, any debt of life or liberty."

"And yet there is something." Sarevan held up his hand, the left, which bore no brand. "Equality. A love for this world which one of us must rule; a deep reluctance to see it marred."

"Marring can be mended, if there is peace under a single lord."

"Not such marring as I can see." Sarevan's hand clenched into a fist. "And it is my father who will begin it. Meaning naught but good, in the god's name; seeing only the peace that will follow. Blind, stone blind, to its cost." He let his head fall back, his eyes fix upon the vaulted ceiling. "You don't believe me. No one believes me. Even my mother, who has seen what I see, has refused it: she has sold her soul for love of my father. If she won't listen, how can you? You don't even believe in prophecy."

"I believe in you."

Sarevan's head snapped forward. Hirel was grave, steady. Truthful; or playing a game which could cost him his neck.

"Mind you," the boy said, "I do not do this easily. Yet I am a logician. I who have seen magecraft cannot deny that it exists. Prophecy is part of magecraft by all accounts, yours not least. You are outrageous, and you are quite mad, but a liar you are not. If you say that you have seen war, then war you have seen. If you say that it will be terrible, so is it likely to be. I have spoken with your father. I have seen what he is like, and I can guess what he will do when the fire of his god is on him."

"I love him," whispered Sarevan. "Dear gods, I love him. But I think that he is wrong. Utterly, hopelessly, endlessly wrong."

He rocked with it, no longer seeing Hirel, no longer hearing anything but the echo of his own terrible treason.

Terrible, and treason. But true. He knew it, down to the core of him.

There was peace in it, almost. In knowing it for what it was. In ceasing his long battle to deny it. He had been no older than Hirel when it began. Maybe, when his power had gone but the dream held firm in all its terrible strength, it had broken him at last.

"I think not," he said. Hirel was staring at him. He mustered a smile. "No, brother prince, I haven't lost the last remnant of my wits. I see a way through this tangle. Will you tread it with me?"

"Is it sane?" asked Hirel.

Sarevan laughed, not too painfully. "Do you need to ask? But it may work. Listen, and decide for yourself."

Hirel waited. Sarevan drew a long steadying breath. "I'm going to Asanion with you."

Hirel's eyes widened a careful fraction. "And what," he asked, "do you hope to accomplish by that?"

"Peace. My father won't attack Asanion if I'm held hostage in Kundri'j Asan."

"Think you so? More likely he will raise heaven and hell to get you back."

"Not if it's known that I went of my own will."

"Ah," said Hirel, a long sigh. "That is blackest treason."

"It is." Sarevan was dizzy, thinking about it; bile seared his throat. "Don't you see? I have to do it. He won't yield for anything I can say. I have to show him. I have to shock him into heeding me."

"What if I will not assent to it?"

Sarevan seized his gaze and held it. "You will," he said, low and hard.

The boy tossed his head, uncowed. "And if I do—what then, Sun-prince? I am Asanian. I have no honor as you would reckon it. You are a fool to dream of trusting me."

"You won't betray me."

"No," said Hirel after a stretching pause. "You are my only equal in the world. That cannot endure; but while it does, I am yours. As you are mine."

"We ride together."

"We ride together," Hirel agreed. He stood. "The Lord Varzun has been commanded. I depart on the third day from this. I shall give thought to the manner of your concealment."

"As shall I," said Sarevan. "Good night, high prince."

"Good night," said Hirel, "high prince."

Twelve

THE ZHIL'ARI, LIKE HIREL, HEARD SAREVAN OUT. UNLIKE HIREL, they did not hesitate. They were apt for this new mischief. He told them what he would have of them; they obeyed with relish, but with astonishing circumspection. No one remarked that the nine most recent recruits of the high prince's guard had vanished from Endros. They might never have come there at all.

Sarevan's own part, for the moment, was an old one. When the new sun struck fire in the pinnacle of Avaryan's Tower, he appeared on the practice field with sword and lance. If anyone took note that the prince chose to confine himself to mounted exercises, he did not speak of it. From the field Sarevan came to his father's council, and to a wild game of club-and-ball in one of the courts, and again to a leisurely meander through the streets of Endros. At nightfall he dined with a youngish lord and a merchant prince and a glitter of courtiers.

The second night of his plotting was quiet, as if his will, having set itself on treason, was minded to let his body rest. The second day brought rain and wind and the empress' presence in the window to which Sarevan had retreated. It was a broad recess, and

150

very deep, and cushioned for ease; it lay in the lee of the wall, letting in neither wind nor rain, only cool clean air.

He started when she laid her hand on his arm; his body gathered itself, coiling to strike. The blow died unborn, but he was on his feet with no walls to hamper him, and she was braced for battle.

She relaxed all at once. He was slower. He made himself sit again, and laugh, and take her hand, and pretend that nothing had changed. "I'm well trained, aren't I?"

"Too well," she said, but she smiled. "You're a perilous man altogether. Do you know, there's a whole bower full of women yonder, and every one is passionately in love with you?"

"Was my chatter that captivating?"

"Not only your chatter."

"Oh, yes. My charming smile. My even more charming title. Who's offering daughters this season?"

"Everyone but the Emperor of Asanion."

It was an old jest. Yet Sarevan stiffened. She could not know what he was doing. No one could walk in his maimed mind. His father, finding it broken beyond all mending, had sealed it against invasion. Even Mirain's power was shut out; only the rebirth of Sarevan's own magics could lower those walls.

She did not know. She could not. Sarevan was doing nothing but what he always did. It was only what he did it for that had changed. And the intensity of it. Perhaps. Time was too short for subtlety.

She was frowning at him. She felt his brow, traced his cheek that was no longer quite so hollow. "You push too hard," she said, "and too fast."

"Not fast enough for me."

"Of course not." She sat by him. She would never admit to weariness, but surely that was the name of the shadows beneath her eyes, and the faint pallor of her honey skin, and the stiffness with which she held herself erect.

He settled his arm about her and drew her to him. "Tell me what it is," he said.

She laid her head on his shoulder and sighed. For a long while he thought she would not answer. When she did, her voice shared not at all in her body's languor. "It's always something. Generals getting out of hand. Governors maneuvering for power. Common people losing patience. Ianon crying that it was never more than a stepping-stone to Mirain's empire, when it should be the first and foremost of all his realms, the only one to which his blood entitles him; but he abandoned it to rule out of the south. As if he never spent two seasons out of every four in Han-Ianon, remote and troublesome as that can be for the ruling of an empire as wide as his. And the Hundred Realms cry now separately and now in chorus that he gives too much of his heart to the north, when it was they who made him emperor. Forgetting that it was the Prince of Han-Gilen who inveigled and threatened and flogged them into it. And the east wants more of him, and the west more yet, and the lords want war, and the commons want peace, and the merchants want their profits."

So much of an answer, and it was no answer at all. "And?" he asked.

"And everything, and nothing. I never wanted to be empress. I only wanted Mirain."

"You should have thought of that before you tricked him into marrying you. Found some well-connected lady with a strong aptitude for clerkery and none at all for the arts of the bedchamber, and tricked him into marrying her, and established yourself as his concubine."

She pulled back, her temper flaring. "Concubine! I would have been his lover and his equal."

"And therefore, empress to his emperor." She glared. Sarevan laughed, truly this time, and kissed her. "I for one am glad you married him. It makes life easier, legitimacy. Now stop evading and tell me what's got you prowling the halls when you ought to be bewitching the council."

"You."

His mind spun on, expecting subtleties, shaping counter-subtleties. The silence shocked it into immobility. She never did what one expected, did Elian of Han-Gilen, the Lady Kalirien of the Sunborn's armies.

She knew. She had come to stop him.

No. Whatever was in her eyes, it was not the horror of one who faces treason. She was blind, as they all were. She saw only her poor maimed child.

Sarevan let his mouth fall open. He knew he looked a very proper fool. "Me?" He inspected himself. He was dressed as a southerner, because the multiplicity of garments covered his bones. But he was less thin than he had been. His body, wonderful creation, wasted not one grain of all he fed it. "Don't fret yourself over me. I'm mending, and I'm mending well, and I was just going to sit in council. Shall we go together? Or would you rather do something else that needs doing? I can speak for us both if there's need."

Now it was her part to stare and pause and hunt for words. She did not look like a fool. She looked more beautiful than ever, and more tired, and more—something. Sad. Angry. Pitying. "No, Vayan," she said much too easily, "I can face it alone. If you won't rest, will you look in on our guest from Asanion? I saw him a little while ago, cursing the rain. He seemed in need of company."

Sarevan sat still. There was a darkness in him, a bitterness on his tongue. She had not used that tone with him since he was still small enough to carry. That tone which said, *Yes, yes, child, of course you may help Mother, but not now; Mother will come back when she's done, and then we'll play, yes?* Which said, *Of course you can't handle the council alone, poor innocent. You have no power to handle it with.* Which said, *You are weak and you are a cripple, and you tear my heart, because you strive so bravely to be as you were before. But you cannot. You cannot, and you must not pretend that you can.*

Sarevan was on his feet again. It could still surprise him to find her so small, no higher than his chin, who had towered over his childhood. Now he was a man, and if not the largest of her redheaded Gileni kinsmen, not the smallest, either.

Among mages, he was nothing at all. "Yes," his tongue said, acid-sweet, "I'll go and play with the heir of Asanion. He wants to teach me a new game. It's played in bed, mostly, and it's fascinating. Though I may be a little old to learn it properly. Am I too old, do you think, Mother?"

She slapped him. Not lightly. Not in play. He swayed with the blow, and met her white fury with something whiter and colder. "Don't treat me like a child, Mother. Or like a simpleton. Or like a broken creature who must be handled gently lest he shatter. I'm none of them. I still carry Avaryan's brand, and the fire that comes with it. I'm still High Prince of Keruvarion. And nowhere," he said, soft and deadly, "nowhere at all does the law ordain that the king must also be a mage."

Her rage had chilled and died. "Vayan," she said. "Vayan, I didn't mean—"

"You didn't, did you? You only believed it. That's your deepest trouble. Keruvarion's heir is no longer fit to hold his title. Keruvarion's emperor refuses to speak of it. Keruvarion's chancellor insists that there's no profit in fretting. The Lord of the Northern Realms, most reluctant of mages that he is, has no sympathy to spare for you. And I—I know that if I don't teach myself to live as a simple man, I won't be able to live at all."

"That's what I'm afraid of," she said.

"Such trust. Such faith in your strong young son."

"Don't sneer. It's unbecoming."

His lip curled further. He raised his chin. "I'll go to my lessons, Mother. Then at least, if I can't rule, I'll know how to beget a son who can."

If she tried to stop him, she did not try hard enough. His temper brought him to Hirel's door and flung him through it.

No one was there to applaud or to jeer. He stalked through the rooms in the dim rainlight. A lamp burned in the innermost chamber, shining on two twined bodies, bronze and gold. Hirel had a woman in his arms, and neither wore more than a bauble or two, and it was clear enough what they had been doing. Even as Sarevan froze upon the threshold, Hirel's hand moved, wandering over a ripe swell of breast.

Sarevan backed away. That was not jealousy, that twisting in his vitals. It was outrage. This was a lady. A baroness. The widow of a high baron. How dared she let that infidel seduce her? How dared he do it?

They saw him. She rose with aplomb. Her eyes sparkled; her cheeks were rose-bronze. She curtsied deeply. "My prince," she said. Her face had no great beauty: broad-cheeked, blunt-nosed, wide-mouthed. But her eyes were splendid, and her body . . .

She covered it, not hastily, not slowly, and took her graceful leave.

Sarevan shuddered and remembered to breathe. Hirel had risen to face him. The boy did not have the grace to look ashamed. "Is that your revenge on Keruvarion?" Sarevan asked him. "The corruption of its nobility?"

"You say it, not I."

"So." Sarevan advanced into the chamber. "Corrupt me."

"No."

"Why? Because I want you to?"

"Not at all." Hirel returned to his nest of cushions, stretching out like a cat, yawning as maidens were taught to do, with becoming delicacy. He propped himself on his elbow and looked up under level brows. "I do not corrupt. I teach, and I tame, and I set free."

Sarevan dropped to one knee, bending close. "Free? Can you set me free?" His hand closed lightly about the boy's throat. "Can you, Hirel Uverias?"

"You," said Hirel calmly, "are in a remarkable state. Are you dangerous? Should I be begging for mercy?"

Sarevan looked at the placid face. At the hand below it. At the body below that. He thought of being dangerous. Of falling upon Hirel; of disdaining to grant mercy.

His hand fell. He tasted bile. He was not made for that sort of violence.

He lay on his face among the cushions. It was that, or run howling through Endros. "I won't," he gritted. "I *won't* be shunted aside, watched over, indulged and protected like an idiot child. They'd leave me nothing that befits my breeding or my training. Only pity. Because they are all mages, and I—and I—"

"Stop it," said Hirel. "Or I swear, I will laugh, and you will try to strike me, and I am in no mood for battles."

Sarevan thought of murder. Even with power he would have gone no further than that. But his mind did not know it. It reached for what was not there, and touched something, and that something was pain.

He dragged himself up. He fought his hands that would have clutched his throbbing head. "Tonight," he said. "Tonight we ride."

"So soon? But I have told Varzun—two days—"

"Tonight." He turned with care. He set one foot before the other.

He struck an obstacle. It was well grown and strong, and subtly skilled in the use of its strength. It said, "You are being quite unreasonable."

"Be ready," Sarevan repeated. "I'll come for you."

"You are mad," Hirel said. But he let Sarevan pass.

Sarevan nursed his temper. It had to bear him up until he was well away from Endros. He nursed it well and he fed it with good food and ample, and he masked it with his best and whitest smile.

He was not smiling when his father found him. He was in his tower, bare and damp from the bath, turning a length of white silk in his fingers. It was naked yet, its mate lost in Shon'ai with its four disks of gold hammered from coins as custom commanded, pierced and sewn by the hands of the priest who bore it. No time now to make them anew. That would have to wait until this coil was all unraveled.

He heard the door open. He knew the tread, light, almost soundless. He had been expecting it. It always happened when he quarreled with his mother. His father gave him time to cool a little, and came, and sat by him, saying nothing. His mother did it, for the matter of that, when he crossed wills with his father. It was one of the world's patterns, like the dance of the moons.

He had to struggle. To turn his eyes deliberately toward the night within him, to rouse the vision which told him why he must not yield.

A hand set itself beside his own. Palm beside palm. *Kasar* and *Kasar*. Sarevan's eyes narrowed against the twofold brilliance. "While you have this," Mirain said, "you are my heir. I made that law when you were born, and I will not alter it."

"Nothing was said of altering it. Much was implied of regretting it."

"Only by you, Sarevadin."

Sarevan flung up his head, tossing the damp coppery hair out of his face. "Don't try to lie to me. I'm worth nothing as I am, except to those who would shatter Asanion in my name. For revenge. Because I was too bloody arrogant to know when I was outmatched."

"Not so much arrogant as unwise. And you're no wiser now. All your mother wanted was to keep you from killing yourself with too much strain too soon."

"She succeeded, didn't she?"

"Hardly," said Mirain. "You should have done as you threatened to. You'd have been the better for it."

"I am a sworn priest," Sarevan gritted, to keep from howling.

"So am I."

"But you are a king."

"And you are High Prince of Keruvarion."

"I wish," said Sarevan, and that was not what he had meant to say at all, "I wish he were a woman."

The silence stretched. Mirain's charity. Sarevan wound the Journey-band about his hand and clasped his knees, letting his forehead rest briefly upon them. He was not tired, it was nothing so simple. He ached, but that was more pleasant than not, the ache of muscles remembering their old strength. He shivered a little, not wanting to, unable to help himself.

A robe dangled before him. He let his father coax him into the warmth of it. "We never could keep clothes on you," Mirain said. When Sarevan looked, he was close to a smile, though he retreated all too soon. "We can't keep you here. Even if your Journey would allow it, you wouldn't stand for it."

Sarevan could not move. He hardly dared breathe.

Mirain went on calmly, as if he could not reckon Sarevan's tension to its last degree. "The Red Prince has sent a message. He wants to see you. Soon, he says, and for as long as you please. There's work and to spare for you, if you're minded to do any, and you can prove to Han-Gilen what you've tried so hard to prove to Endros: that you're none the worse for wear."

Sarevan started at that, but he bit his tongue before it could betray him.

"You'd do well to go," said Mirain, "for a while. When Greatmoon is full again, Vadin will be riding to Ianon to secure it and the north. I would like you to go with him."

In spite of himself, Sarevan whipped about. "Why? What can I do that Vadin can't?"

"Speak as my chosen successor. Prove that I haven't abandoned my first kingdom for the decadence of the south. Wield the power of your presence."

The words came flooding. *What power? What presence?* Sarevan choked them down. He had been wielding the latter in Endros without care for the cost.

This much he had won. His father would grant him a Greatmoon-month in Han-Gilen with the man he loved best of all his kin. Who had taught him the mastery of his power; who had brought him back from death. Who had no patience at all with self-pity. And after that strong medicine, a trust as great as any he had been given: to speak for his father before the princes of the north.

His eyes narrowed. His jaw set. "So Grandfather's to be my nursemaid. And when he's tired of me, Vadin will take me in hand."

"Vadin will ride under your command. He proposed it. It's past time you earned your title."

Sarevan almost laughed. "O clever! You'll bribe me with the sweetest plum of all: the promise of a princedom. No doubt I'll be allowed to rule it as I choose—and well out of the way of your war."

Mirain did not even blink. "You can't stay here. Nor can you wander free as you have until now. The lands are too unsettled; and you are much too valuable. Twice our enemies have sought to snare you. The third time may destroy you."

There was no danger now of Sarevan's temper cooling. He let it flame in him, searing his mind clean even of awe for the Sunborn. His voice was soft, almost light, deadly in its gentleness. "Ah," he said. "I see. You and Mother both—you labor to protect me. I'm your only son. For good or for black ill, I'm the only hope you have of a dynasty. You guard me and shield me and shelter me lest any danger touch me. And where your guardianship has failed, you take most dire vengeance."

"How have I sheltered you?" his father asked, quickly, but calm still. "Have I ever denied you anything you wished for? You wanted priesthood and training in magecraft. I never hindered you. You Journeyed where you chose, even into deadly danger. I never raised my power to hold you back."

"But you watched me. Your power haunted me. All through Keruvarion your guards were never far from me. They failed in Asanion; but that was not for lack of trying. I've heard how Ebraz of Shon'ai paid for the trap he laid: paid with life and sanity. I know how you searched for me and never found me, though you combed the empires for me. It drove you mad that I had escaped your watchfulnes; that I had only my own will to guide me."

"My hunters' blindness has been dealt with," said Mirain.

Sarevan raised his clenched fists, swept them down. "Damn it, Father! Am I still a child? Am I incapable even of picking myself up when I stumble? How long are you going to live my life for me?"

At long last, Mirain wavered. His face tightened as if with pain. "I let you do as you would, even when you would do what I reckoned madness or folly."

"But you were there, always, to do the letting."

Mirain stretched out his hand. Not beseeching; not quite.

Sarevan pulled back out of his reach. "Even this war—even that has begun for me. Has it never crossed your mind that I might want to win something for myself?"

"You will have it all when I am gone."

"When you are gone!" Sarevan laughed, brief and bitter. "All signed and sealed, from your hand. A gift and a burden and a curse, and none of my doing. Am I so much less than you? Do you think so little of me?"

"I think the world of you."

Sarevan was trembling. His eyes were open, and he was as full awake as he could ever be, and all his sight was lost in the blackest of his dreams. Elian Kalirien dead in the ashes of the world, and the Sunborn gone mad.

"Vayan," his father said. Had perhaps said more than once. "Vayan, forgive me."

Mirain An-Sh'Endor? Asking forgiveness?

"You are all that I am and more," he said, raw with pain. "And I love you to the point of folly. I never meant to cage you. I only wished to keep you safe, so that you may be the emperor you were born to be."

"Emperor of what?" Sarevan cried from the depths of his darkness. "Dust and ashes, and war's desolation?"

"Emperor of all that lies under Avaryan. I was born for war, for the winning of empires. Peace saps all my strength. But you—you can rule where I have won. You have the strength of will that I have not, to hold in peace what war has gained. Don't you see, Vayan?

You are not simply my son and my heir. You are the fulfillment of this creature that I am. You as much as I are the instrument of the god."

"The sword cuts," said Sarevan. "It cuts too deep for any healing."

"Save yours."

Sarevan's sight cleared, a little. He saw his father's living face. It was close, a shadow limned in light, with shining eyes. There were tears in them. He had struck harder than he knew, and deeper.

No, he warned himself. No softening. This man who grieved for his son's pain was king and conqueror; and by his own admission, born and shaped for slaughter.

"I will not haunt you," Mirain said. "No longer. When you go into the north, you go free, to rule in my name but according to your will."

"Even if that will is to oppose you?"

Mirain started, stiffening.

"If I hold the north," Sarevan said, "and forbid it to join in your war, what will you do?"

"Would you do that, Sarevadin?"

Yes, Sarevan was going to say. But he could not. To defy his father by himself—that, he could do. To take a kingdom with him, a kingdom that had been his father's . . .

"I could do it," he said.

"Would you?"

He shivered. "No," he said, slow and hard. "No. That would rouse war as surely as anything else I've done since I resisted you and went into Asanion."

Mirain smoothed Sarevan's hair with a steady hand, worrying out a tangle, stroking beneath where he was cold and shaking. Sarevan tensed but did not try to escape.

"Father," he said after a while. "Must you fight this war?"

The hand did not pause in its stroking. "You know that I have no choice. Asanion's emperor will not yield for words or for wishing. Only war can choose between us."

"If you could see what I see—would that stop you?"

"I see that the darkness has deceived you. Another trap of our enemies' laying. They know what you are; that you are more perilous even than I. They have labored long and hard to ensnare you; to destroy you, lest you become what they most fear."

"What am I, that you are not thrice over?"

"You will be lord of the world."

"I don't want—" Sarevan stopped. That, he knew in the cold heart of him, was false. He wanted it with all that he was: a wanting so deep that it seemed almost the negation of itself. But what it was, and what his father wanted it to be—there they differed. "I don't want it stained with blood and fire."

"Perhaps it need not be. But perhaps," said Mirain before hope could wake, "it must. Will you rule the north for me?"

"Will you stop the war for me?"

"No."

That was absolute. Sarevan drew back, steadying himself. His temper had died; he was, almost, at peace. He found that he could smile, though faintly, and not for pleasure. "I love you, Father. Never forget that."

"Will you rule the north?"

Sarevan let himself sink down in weariness that was not feigned. "I need time," he said. "I'm not—I can't— Give me a day. Let me think."

For an instant he knew that he had gone too far. But Mirain said, "Think as much as you like. Your princedom can wait. So," he added more softly, "can I."

Slowly Sarevan turned. Mirain's face was not soft at all. Sarevan hardened his own to match it. "A day," he said. "To set my mind in order."

"A day," Mirain granted him. "Or more, if you have need of them."

Sarevan shivered. His eyes dropped; he could not force them up again. "No," he said very low. "A day will be enough. Then," he said, lower still, "then you will know."

Thirteen

WHEN SAREVAN CAME, HIREL WAS READY. SCOWLING BUT
ready, in plain dark riding clothes, with a long knife at
his side and a scrip in his hand. "I have had the
ambassador's message," he said with no warmth at all. "You are
thorough."

"Of course." Sarevan turned. "Follow me."

They walked quietly but not stealthily. There were secret ways; a
palace was not a palace without them, as Mirain often said. But this
palace was full of mages, and they would be on guard, alert for
walkers in the dark. Walkers in the light, however dim, they might
not pause to wonder at.

Sarevan carried his coat slung over his shoulder and, as by
chance, over both their scrips. He did not hasten; he did not linger.
Above all else, he did not think of mutiny. "Think," he warned
Hirel when they began, "of a restless stomach and an hour's brisk
walking, and of deep sleep after."

Hirel had given him an odd look, but had not protested. He did
not speak at all as they went, until they met a lord with his retinue.
The voices came first; at the sound of them, Hirel slipped his arm
about Sarevan's waist and leaned, hand to middle. His face when

he lifted it was pale. "A little better," he said loudly enough to be heard, "but still not—"

The company was upon them, large, varied, and warm with wine. Sarevan almost groaned aloud at the sight of the leader: a baron from the east of Kavros, rich with pearls and with sea gold, older than he liked to be and less powerful than he hoped. He dandled a girl on each arm; he thrust them away, to bow as low as his belly would allow. "Lord prince! How splendid to see you about, and so strong too, after all I had heard, though you look thin, very thin; that is not well, you must look after yourself, we need you sorely in Keruvarion."

Sarevan's smile bared set teeth. "Good evening, Baron Faruun."

"Oh, good, yes, very good, my lord, as the lord your father said to me, just a little while ago it was, he said—"

"I think," said Hirel distinctly and rather more shrilly than he had in many days, "that, after all, I shall be ill."

Sarevan caught at him. He looked ghastly. But his eyes were lambent gold. "You can't," Sarevan said as that shimmering stare dared him to. "I won't let you. Think about keeping it down. Think about the honor of princes."

Hirel sighed, and swallowed audibly. "You are a tyrant, Vayan."

"I'm growing you up, little brother. You can't do this every time you drink a cup or three."

Hirel drooped against Sarevan. "I want to go to bed," he said plaintively. Swallowing in the middle. Nuzzling a little, working mischief with his hands where the watchers could just see.

"You'll pardon us, I'm sure," Sarevan said, flashing his teeth at them all and sweeping Hirel away.

Hirel recovered quickly enough once he had no audience to play to, although his color was slow to come back. He did not let go of Sarevan; Sarevan let him stay. Laughter kept rising and refusing to be conquered. "*You* can laugh," Hirel snarled at him.

Contrition sobered him, somewhat. "But you aren't really—"

"I always am."

Hirel's bitterness was real, and deep. Sarevan pulled him forward. "Quick now; be strong. We're almost out."

They met no one else of consequence. A servant or two; a lady's small downy pet trailing its jeweled leash and looking utterly pleased with itself. Then they had passed an unwarded postern and entered the city. The rain had ended; wind tattered the clouds, baring a glimpse of stars, a scatter of moonlight.

The main thoroughfares of Endros were lit with lamps and tended by honored guildsmen, but its side ways were dark enough for any footpad. Sarevan kept to the latter, daring now to run, dragging the other by the hand. Nothing threatened them save a cur that snarled as they passed.

The wall came sooner than Sarevan had expected. By the wan gleam of Greatmoon he groped his way along it, searching for a stone that would yield to his touch. If he had come too far, or not far enough—

It turned under his hand and sank. The wall opened into a tunnel a little higher than a man and a very little wider. Sarevan could just walk erect. Hirel followed him without trouble, gripping his belt.

Another stone, another shifting. They stood on the open plain with the wind in their faces. Sarevan drank it in great gulps. Hirel retched into the grass.

He would not let Sarevan carry him. His resistance was quiet but furious, and he gasped through it, choking, until Sarevan shook him to make him stop. "You're wasting time, damn you! Up with you."

"I am not," Hirel gasped. "I am not—I had to convince—I convinced myself. Put me down!"

He walked, though he let Sarevan hold him up. It was not remarkably far. A thousand man-lengths, perhaps more, perhaps less. There was a hill and a copse and a crumbling byre, and in the byre Shatri with Bregalan and the striped Zhil'ari mare and one more: a rawboned, ugly-headed, sand-colored creature with a bright wild eye and a laden saddle.

"No," Sarevan said. "No, Shatri."

The squire did not even lower his eyes. "He told me, my lord. Your father. Whatever you did, to stay with you."

"Are you his man or mine?"

"Yours, of course, my lord. With all my soul. But he is the emperor."

That, said Shatri's tone, was inarguable. Sarevan drew breath to argue with it.

The sand-colored mare snorted and rolled her eyes. The source
of their wildness stalked out of shadow, rumbling gently. Of the
seneldi, only Bregalan was calm; but Ulan had been there when he
was foaled. The great cat circled Shatri, who stood very still, and
came to press against Sarevan and purr. "Go back," Sarevan
commanded Shatri. "I am a priest on Journey. I may have no
squire or servant."

"But, my lord—"

"In Avaryan's name," Sarevan said, relentless, "and in the name
of his priesthood. Go."

"My lord!"

Sarevan turned his back on him and mounted.

"My lord," the boy said, pleading.

Bregalan sidled but would not advance. Sarevan would not turn.

Hirel's voice in the dark was cool and calming. "Your lord has
need of you here, to conceal his absence, to divert pursuit. He has
trusted you with this most difficult of all our tasks; will you prove
his trust misplaced?"

There was a silence, until Shatri broke it. "My lord." He gripped
Sarevan's knee. "My lord, I—you never—I wasn't thinking."

"Nor was I," Sarevan admitted, with a glance at Hirel. "If you
don't think you can do it—"

Shatri's head whipped up. "I can do it! My lord," he added after
a pause. He let go, backed away, bowed desert fashion: dropping to
one knee, setting palm against palm. Pride had struck fire in his
eyes. "Have no fear, my prince. They'll not come after you while
I'm here to stop them."

Sarevan saluted him. His smile was luminous. Then at last
Bregalan would heed the touch of leg to side. He sprang forward.
The dun mare ran swift in his wake.

Even in the dark before dawn, Bregalan knew this country as he
knew his own stable. He set a strong pace, but one the other could
match with ease, striking westward across the plain. As it rose into
wooded hills, he slowed a little, but he ran lightly still, unwearied.

Dawn rose in rain-washed clarity. Sarevan called a halt to rest
the beasts and to see that Hirel took a little bread and a sip or two
of wine. By sunrise they were in the saddle again. Their shadows
stretched long before them.

They went by paths Sarevan knew, swift enough yet hidden from spying eyes. The shifting armies did not close in upon them; if they were hunted, the hunters did not find them in the wilderness through which they rode. Hirel practiced one of his greater virtues: he was silent, neither questioning nor complaining.

They rode through the first day and well into the night, until at last Sarevan's urgency would let him rest. Hirel's mare was stumbling with exhaustion. The boy's face was ghost-pale in the moonlight. He fell from the saddle into Sarevan's arms, so limp and so still that for a moment Sarevan froze in fear. Then Hirel drew a long breath, shuddering with it. With utmost gentleness Sarevan laid him down, spreading all their blankets for him, wrapping him in them. Cursing that damnable pride which would never yield to its body's frailty.

Sarevan left the child to sleep. He ate a little, drank from the stream by which he had camped. The seneldi grazed, placid. Ulan had gone hunting. Sarevan lay back against his saddle and sighed. He did not want to sleep: the dream waited, armed and deadly. He settled more comfortably. Brightmoon gazed down. Greatmoon had set; she had the sky to herself, for a while. His eyes filled with her cool light.

The sun woke him. He lay under it, eyes closed, neither knowing nor overmuch caring where he was. He ached in sundry places, not badly, but enough to rouse curiosity, and with it memory. He started up.

He had not dreamed it. He was doing what he had resolved to do. For all the sun's warmth, he shivered.

"Don't think about it," he commanded himself. "Just do it."

Hirel stared at him, half asleep still, baffled and scowling and all bright gold. Sarevan laughed at the scowl and leaped up. "Come," he said. "Ride with me."

They rode; and still no hunter followed them. Sarevan was not easy, nor did he trust this quiet, but for a little while he accepted it; he let it think that it had mastered him. Slowly he relaxed his vigilance, letting it pass through thrumming tension to constant quiet watchfulness.

Sarevan gained strength. Hirel went brown again, and his mask slipped, and sometimes he smiled. Once or twice he even laughed.

But for the most part he was silent, somber. "This venture of ours may fail," he said, a camp or four after that first hidden haven, when they had taken to riding at night and sleeping through the burning brightness of the day. "My father can be no less intransigent than yours."

"But," Sarevan pointed out, "even mine isn't likely to attack Asanion while I stand hostage in Kundri'j Asan."

"If we come so far. Even if you are caught and returned to your father, you have less to fear than do I. No one in your empire wishes you dead. Whereas I, and mine . . ."

"We'll face that when we face it," said Sarevan. He lay on his back and laced his fingers behind his head. He was stripped in the heat, his breeches new-washed and spread where the sun could dry them. It was warm on his skin, the air still, pungent with the scent of spicefern. He yawned. His back itched; he wriggled.

Hirel was watching him. Without stopping to think, he rolled onto his stomach, resting his chin on folded arms. It pricked. He was growing his beard again; it was little enough yet to marvel at, and it would grow less lovely still before it remembered what it had been. He rubbed it where it itched, and tried not to feel the eyes on him. In a moment or an age, they granted him mercy. When he looked again, Hirel was asleep, curled on his side, childlike.

And yet he was a child no longer. The swift onset of first manhood was full upon him, working its magic from sunrise to sunrise, almost from hour to hour. He had grown a hand's width measured against Sarevan's shoulder, since he woke wounded and haughty on the marches of Karmanlios; his voice cracked seldom now, and then more often downward than upward. It was going to be deep, that voice, as already he was tall for one of his kind. His shoulders were broadening, beginning to strain his coat, and there was no softness left in him except, a little, in his face: a rounding still of cheek and chin, a fullness of the lips that recalled the girl he might have been. And he was waxing into a man where manhood most mattered.

He was still very young, and delicate in odd ways: in what he could eat, in how much he slept. "Inbred," Sarevan said as they camped in the west of Inderan. "The blood is good, but it's thin. No sister-wife for you, my lad, if you want a son who'll live to be a man."

"What!" said Hirel, and perhaps his indignation was real, and perhaps it was not. "Would you have me beget a litter of mongrels?"

"Mongrel blood is strong." Sarevan grinned. "Look at me, now. Bred of every race that walks the earth; and two nines of days ago I was a rotting corpse, and here I am. Riding all night on a diet of air and wildbuck, up half the day drinking sunlight, and sleek as a seal."

Sarevan had meant to jest. But he looked down at himself and started slightly. Why, he thought, it was true. He was as strong as he had ever been. He felt of his face, suppressing the urge to bring out his scrap of mirror. The angles were familiar angles, the hollows the old hollows, the skull returned at last to its proper place beneath the skin.

Air and wildbuck indeed, and the sun's fire, and dreams that drove him hard but were no longer a torment; and no pursuit. None at all.

Once Hirel ventured into a town, armed with his brown face and his vagabond's garb and a fistful of Sarevan's silver. He returned with both their scrips full, and even a coin left in his purse. "And news," he said, settling on his heels beside Sarevan, watching as the other fell on the sweetmeats which were his great prize. He nibbled a honeyed nut; he took his time about it, until he had Sarevan still and staring, mouth full of spice and sweetness. "No, Sun-prince, nothing of our riding, and no sign of a hunt. Rumor has it that the Prince Sarevadin is sojourning with his grandsire in Han-Gilen, preparing for a new task: the taking of Ianon's regency. For practice, it is said. To prepare him for a greater throne."

Sarevan's breath caught. Suddenly he had no taste for spicecake. He choked down the last of it. His fingers, unheeded, raked through his new beard. No hunt at all? He could not believe that. And yet he had seen it. And that the common talk should be full of what had been between himself and his father, as if he had never committed this treason, as if he had gone docilely where he was meant to go—there was no sense in it. And yet there was.

Frightening sense. If someone knew or guessed what he did, and favored it, or was not minded to stop it . . . if someone was willing to cover his trail, even to lie outright for him . . .

Shatri had promised to do just that, but he had not this measure of power. Vadin? The Lord of the North belonged to his emperor. Even for his namesake, whom he loved as a son, he would not turn against Mirain. Elian—maybe. She was capable of it. But in this he could catch no scent of her. The Prince of Han-Gilen . . .

Sarevan pulled at his beard, scowling. This was his treason, and his alone. He would not share it with some faceless power, some web of purpose and counterpurpose that dared to weave itself into his own. That would not even grant him the courtesy of naming its name or asking his leave.

"You are very well thought of," Hirel said, oblivious to his fretting. "Every idler remembers you, or claims to. Did you know that you spent three seasons in the dungeons of the evil emperor himself? You escaped in fire and magic, took his heir for a hostage, and died in battle with his mages; your body returned to Endros in no less than nine pieces, borne upon the backs of demons. Your father bound the fragments together with his power, and called your soul from Avaryan's side, and made you live again. And when he had done that, he swore a mighty oath: that the Emperor of Asanion would suffer each and every torment to which he had subjected you."

Sarevan would have liked to leap up, to bolt into the woods. To run away from it all; or to run full into it, crying anathema upon all liars and their lies.

He sat still, eyes on Bregalan who grazed unruffled by men and their wars.

"No one hunts us," Hirel said. "No one speaks of it. It is all war and weapontakes and who will remain to bring in the harvest if the war lasts so long."

The fire was rising. Sarevan let it. Words came, slow at first, pale shadows of the rage within. "I don't like this," he said. "I don't like it at all."

"It serves us," said Hirel.

"It reeks to heaven." Sarevan sprang to his feet. "Ulan! Bregalan! Quick now, up!"

*　*　*

Bregalan was swifter than any stallion had a right to be unless he were of the Mad One's line, and the mare was of Zhil'ari breeding. They thrived on long running and short commons. Like Sarevan himself; but Hirel was not so sturdy. He needed sleep and he needed feeding. Sarevan willed himself to be patient, to stop now and then, to lie quietly while the sun wheeled overhead and his companion slept the sleep of the dead. He himself slept hardly at all. All that had befallen him since he battled mages in Asanion— all he had heard and seen and dreamed—all of it was coming together. Not wholly, not yet. But he saw the first blurred glimmer of a pattern. He had stopped raging at it. He had sworn, and he would fulfill his oath: he would learn the name behind the plotting. Then he would exact its price.

The farther they rode, the quieter the land seemed. But that was only a seeming. Every town had its company of armed guards. Every castle rang with the clamor of men in training and of weapons in the forging. Travelers were few, and those rode armed and watchful. Not all the men who had gathered meant to fight for their emperor; of those who did, some few had a mind to end old feuds before they rode to war, or else to pick up the odd bit of booty while they waited. Armies took considerable maintenance; if a captain could keep his troops honed with a quick raid and fed with the proceeds, so much the better.

None of them came near to Sarevan. Perhaps he owed it to Ulan's watchfulness and his own caution. He would not have sworn to it.

He rode because he must, drawing the others with him. He did not pause to fear that he rode into a trap: his plots betrayed, the borders held against him. With the fear that rode him now, he would have welcomed so simple a snare.

At last they came to the marches of Karmanlios, and to Asan-Vian gasping in the heat of that cycle of Brightmoon called the Anvil of the Sun. Hirel's mare was close to foundering; even Bregalan showed ribs beneath a sun-scorched coat. Hirel's head was down, his body stiff, bracing at every jolt. There were blue shadows under his eyes.

Vian was the castle which ruled among others the town of Magrin. Its lord had died wifeless and childless; his fief had passed by his will into the care of the Sun's priests. Whose senior priestess in the barony was Orozia of Magrin.

She was waiting for the riders. So too were nine Zhil'ari and a dozen Asanians and a handful of closemouthed servants. Their greetings were various: Zhil'ari exuberance, Asanian reserve, and Orozia's long level gaze that warmed into welcome. "Well come at last, my lord," she said, "and in good time."

Sarevan looked hard at her. She smiled. He saw no deception in her, nor scented any. After a moment, he bowed low. "Reverend sister. All is well?"

"All is most well."

He had not known how tautly he was strung until the tension left him. He staggered. She was there, and nine Zhil'ari with her, desperately anxious. He fended them off. "Here now, don't hover. Look to the lion's cub."

His hellions were obedient. Orozia did not choose to follow them. "I have prepared everything as you would wish it."

He considered her. Her loyalty; her strength. A smile found its way through his new-raised walls. He brushed her cheek with a finger, half in mischief, half in deep affection. "You don't approve, do you?"

"Of course I do not. I am only half a fool. But that half has proven the stronger. It dares to hope that this madness of yours will bear fruit." She shook herself. "Enough now. Time is short and the borders too well watched on both sides. You will rest the night and the day. At full dark tomorrow, you must ride."

No sooner, though Sarevan burned to be gone. Hirel could not ride again that night; they could not dare the armies under the sun.

The company, at least, was excellent, and the food was passable; the wine was cool and sweet. Sarevan finished off a jar with Orozia's aid, sitting late and unattended in the room which had belonged to the old lord.

"You look well," she said when speech had waned into wine-scented silence. "As well as you ever have; as if you were taking your sustenance from the sun itself."

"That," said Sarevan, "I can't do. Not any longer."

"No?"

The wine rose strong in him. It loosened his tongue, but it

lightened the words that rolled out, leaching them of pain. "I'm a mage no longer. I've got used to it; I don't waste time in bemoaning my fate. It's even pleasant, when I stop to think. No thoughts clamoring through my shields. No fire begging to be set free."

"No?"

He peered into his cup, found it empty, filled it to the brim. When he had drunk a great gulp, he laughed. "You look exceedingly oracular, O friend of my youth. Of course, no. That part of me is dead. Gone. Burned away. I'm a man among men, no more, if never less."

"No," she said yet again, flatly. "You will never be a mere man. You are the son of the son of the Sun."

"Ah well, that's something I'll have to live down, won't I?"

She slapped him, not hard, but hard enough to sting. He gaped at her. She blazed back with rare and potent anger. "Did we labor so long in Endros and in Han-Gilen to create a fool? Is it true what the philosophers say, that great men by nature can only engender idiots? Are you *blind*, Sarevan Is'kelion? Look at yourself! No mortal man could suffer as you have suffered, ride as you have ridden, and sit as you sit now, no more weary than any man who sits late over wine."

"My father healed me. That's the miracle you see."

"It is not," she said stubbornly. "I watched you from the walls. You had the sun in your face, and it was pouring into you, filling you as wine fills yonder cup."

He drained it. "So then. The god hasn't abandoned me. Maybe he approves what I do, in spite of my father's convictions to the contrary. That doesn't make me a mage."

"What does it make you?"

"God-ridden." Sarevan yawned and stretched. "There's nothing new in that. And for once I'm glad of it. It's high treason I'm committing, Orozia. You can still escape the stain of it, if you move quickly."

She moved. To touch his hand, to meet his eyes. He shivered a little. There were not many who knew her secret: that she was a mage. There was no other power quite like hers, strong, skilled in its strength, yet strangely circumscribed. Of the lesser magics she had few; she could walk in a mind only if her hand lay upon the body of its bearer. But none could walk in hers save by her will.

None at all could walk in Sarevan's. She sighed faintly. Her eyes lowered, although her hand remained. He turned his own, clasping it. "I'll fight," he said, "but I won't blame you."

"You have no need. I too would see this war averted. Though not at the cost of your life."

"Maybe it won't come to that."

She said nothing. There was too much to say; she let it all pass unsaid. In a little while, Sarevan went to his bed. He suspected that she did not follow suit; that she sat there nightlong in the fading scent of wine, staring into a darkness which her power could not pierce.

Sarevan had not known how much he feared for Hirel, until he saw how greatly the princeling profited from a full night's sleep and a full day's idleness. He was even glad when Hirel slid eyes at him—in Orozia's presence, yet—and smiled the most wicked of all his smiles. That was proof positive: there was nothing wrong with the boy but a lifetime of pampering. He would not die of a few days' hard riding.

But those days had been only the beginning. "You can stay here," Sarevan said. "You'll be safe; you can give me a token for your father, to prove that you're alive and well."

Hirel would not dignify that with a response. When night fell, he was ready to ride, clad as a young lord of eastern Asanion who chose to affect the Olenyai fashion: the black robes, the headcloth, the two swords; but never the mask that was permitted only to the true bred-warrior. In his scrip he carried the token of carven ivory that would pass all gates in the Golden Empire and open the posthouses with their beds and board and remounts.

The twelve true Olenyai surrounded him, shadows in the dusk, masked and silent. They did not glance at Sarevan. His part was less simple than theirs, and more perilous. He was to be the young lord's slave, he and Zha'dan who was near enough to his own size to make no matter.

Hirel had taken wicked pleasure in pointing out what neither of them had wanted to remember: that slaves in Asanion kept neither

their beards nor their hair. Zha'dan howled in anguish. Sarevan
set his chin and his will, and took a firm grip on his braid. "This
belongs to the god. I will not give it up."

The boy inspected his hands with studied casualness. He had
sacrificed his barbarian claws again to look a proper warrior, as on
a time he had tried to look a proper commoner.

"That is different!" Sarevan snapped at him. "Look here,
cubling—"

"My lords." Orozia came between them, grave, but clearly
trying not to smile. "I can satisfy you all, I think, although my lord
of Keruvarion must yet pay a price."

And so he had; but it was one he could pay without undue
reluctance. The dye, she assured him, would wash out easily
enough with cleanroot and ashes. Zha'dan had assented grudging-
ly to the shortening of his beard, that the two of them might
match; in the same cause, Sarevan lost a handspan of his mane.
They put on slaves' tunics and bound their necks with collars of
iron—Sarevan's the heavier by far, and Sun-gold beneath its grey
sheathing—and stood together before the castle's silver mirror.
Sarevan gaped like an idiot. Zha'dan laughed aloud. They looked
like more than kinsmen. They looked like brothers of the same
birth.

Sarevan rubbed his arm, where no copper glinted to betray him;
ran a hand over his many oiled braids, that were as safely dark as
Zha'dan's own. "I've never looked like anyone else before."

"You're beautiful," said his image in Zha'dan's voice.

"You are vain," Sarevan said. Zha'dan laughed again, incorrigible.

Hirel's expression, when they came out together, had been
thoroughly gratifying. He looked from one to the other. Stopped.
Looked again. Blinked once, slowly, and drew a long breath.
"Very . . . convincing," he said at last, in the face of matched and
blinding grins.

Sarevan was still fingering his drying beard, wondering that it
did not feel stranger. His other hand gripped a sturdy chain, with
Ulan collared and deceptively docile at the end of it. There had
been, both Orozia and Hirel had assured him, no other way to
bring an ul-cat safely into Kundri'j Asan; and Sarevan would not

leave him, even to Orozia's care. They had not been apart since they became brothers. They did not intend to begin now.

Ulan was well content; but Sarevan had not reckoned on Bregalan. Hirel left his wicked little mare behind out of care for her life. The blue-eyed stallion would not be so forsaken. Four years of seeing his two-legged brother only when Sarevan paused for a day or two in his Journeying, or when the court's yearly progress from Endros to Ianon crossed the young priest's path, quite obviously had exhausted his patience.

He was in the courtyard as they readied to ride, trailing his broken bonds. He would not attack a mare who had done him no injury, but he saw to it that Sarevan could not approach the rawboned bay whom he had chosen.

Sarevan seized the stallion's horns. "Brother idiot, you are interfering with my insanity. Move aside." Bregalan laid back his ears and set his feet firmly on the paving. "You fool, you can't come with us. We'll be riding posthaste, with remounts at every stop. Even you can't keep the pace we'll set."

The wild eyes rolled. *Try me,* they said.

"And," said Sarevan, "moreover, O my brother, a slave is forbidden by Asanian law to bestride any stallion, still less a stallion of the Mad One's line. Would you betray me to my death?"

Bregalan snorted and stamped. He had no care for mere human laws. He would go with his brother.

Hirel was watching. Sarevan caught his eye, paused. His own eyes narrowed. "If you go," he said slowly, "you cannot carry me. You must carry the lion's cub."

Bregalan lowered his nose into Sarevan's hand and blew gently. Sarevan thrust him away in something very like anger, and called for his saddle. Bregalan was all quiet dignity, with no hint of gloating. Sarevan summoned a bridle. The stallion, who had never in his life submitted to a bit, opened his mouth for it and stood chewing gently on it, placid as a lady's mare.

Hirel approached him. He whickered a greeting. The boy was all prince tonight, but standing beside Bregalan, stroking the arched neck, he loosed a little of the delight that was singing in him. Lightly he sprang onto the stallion's back.

Sarevan glared at them both. "Mind," he said to Hirel, sharp and short. "The bit is for show. No more. You keep your hands off it. Tighten the reins one degree, raise one fleck of foam, and if he doesn't throw you off his back, I will."

Hirel's nostrils thinned. He did not speak. His hands were eloquent enough. He knotted the reins on Bregalan's neck, folded his arms, and looked haughtily down his nose.

Sarevan laughed suddenly, at both of them, but mostly at himself. He left them to one another and went to claim his nameless mare.

Eight Zhil'ari watched them go, tall as standing stones about the still form of Orozia. Sarevan looked back once, with uplifted hand. Gold flashed in the torchlight. He veiled it again and turned his face toward Asanion.

Keruvarion's wardens never saw them. By careful coincidence, as Hirel's company neared the border, a pack of young savages fell whooping and laughing upon the border wardens' very camp. One patrol, coming in, stumbled into the very midst of the melee. The other, going out, met it head-on. Asanion's prince and twelve Olenyai and two northern slaves, with an ul-cat loping among them, passed all unseen.

Asanion's guardians might have been more fortunate. There were, after all, only eight Zhil'ari, and they were thoroughly occupied in convincing the Varyani forces that they were a full tribe. But there were a round dozen Olenyai, and Halid their captain, though no greybeard, was old in cunning. While Ulan struck terror among the cavalry lines, the captain laid a false and twisting trail. By sunrise he was riding briefly eastward, to encounter a company in disarray, with lathered and wild-eyed mounts.

"Raiders," their commander said, too weary even for anger. "We lost them, but they were headed west. Keep watch for them, and have a care. There's a lion loose in the woods."

Halid spoke all the proper words, while Hirel waited near him, haughtily indifferent. Zha'dan was shaking with silent laughter. The Olenyai, masked and faceless, were unreadable; but their eyes glinted. Within the hour they rode west again openly: a young lord with his following in a country full of his like. In a little while Ulan returned to them, to suffer again the collar and the chain which his disguise demanded, loping docilely at Bregalan's heel.

Fourteen

N OW I'M SURE OF IT," ZHA'DAN SAID IN THE ANONYMITY OF A posthouse thronged to bursting. "The god is with us. Else we'd never have come so far so easily."

He spoke in Sarevan's ear, in Zhil'ari, without greater conceal-ment. Sarevan frowned at him. "The god, or someone mortal, weaving webs to trap us in." He glanced about. People were staring in Asanian fashion, sidelong. Halid was settling matters with the master of the house. Hirel had a table to wait at and his Olenyai to wall it and his great hunting cat to guard his person, and his exotic slaves to serve him wine and attract attention. The proper sort of attention, Sarevan could hope. No one would be expecting the lost high prince to appear so, neither in his own person nor in secret.

"I like this," said Zha'dan, unquenched by Sarevan's severity. "I'm not the runt of the litter here. Look: no one's taller than I. I'm a giant."

"You are also a slave," Sarevan reminded him.

He shrugged, but he had the sense not to grin. "Stars! People are ugly here. Yellow as an old wolf's fangs. And fat, like swine fed on oil. And they stink. How can they stand one another?"

Hirel spoke from between them, through motionless lips, in tradespeech. "If you are not silent, I will have you whipped."

Zha'dan started, teeth clicking together. Sarevan bent down to refill the barely emptied cup. "You wouldn't dare," he said in the same tongue, in the same fashion.

Hirel's eyes flashed at him, unreadable. His own flashed back in purest insolence.

Even in a posthouse thronged to bursting, a young lord was granted his due: a chamber for his following and a chamber for himself. The inner room had amenities. A flagon of wine; a bowl of sweets. An enormous mound of cushions which in Asanion betokened a bed, and artfully arranged among them, the specialty of the house. She was clad from head to painted toe, but her draperies were little heavier than gossamer. Her hair was butter yellow and carefully curled and, Sarevan judged, owed little more to nature's hand than his own black braids. Her body was riper than he liked but comely enough to make him wish, however fleetingly, that he were free to savor it.

Zha'dan was both repelled and fascinated. He would have hung over her, all wide-eyed wonderment, if Sarevan had not kept a firm grip on him. He almost groaned when Hirel spoke her fair and accepted a moment's intimate fondling and sent her away. Her regret had an air of ritual; her eyes on the seeming slaves were wry and much too wise.

"Did you see?" Zha'dan marveled as she betook her wares to another and more amenable patron. "No fleece at all, anywhere. Not even on her—"

Sarevan stopped listening. Hirel had cast himself among the cushions, and he was trembling, and trying visibly not to. Sarevan knelt by him. His fists clenched convulsively; he pressed them to his eyes.

Sarevan caught them. They did not resist him. Neither did they unclench. He held them to him, first to his breast, then to his cheeks. They were cold, quivering in spasms. "Cubling," he said softly, as he would to a small child or to a frightened animal. "Hirel. Little brother. You will be strong; you will conquer. You will live to be high prince again."

Hirel stilled, but it was not calmness. His fists opened, and then his eyes. "Soft," he said, wondering, like a child. His fingers moved, stroking. "It is soft."

"I'm young yet," said Sarevan, trying to be light. He had not been wise, again. He let go Hirel's hands. They did not fall. Hirel's eyes were all gold.

Very carefully Sarevan eased himself free. This child was more beautiful than the innkeeper's whore could ever be, and infinitely more perilous; and he knew it. He said, "While you are with me, I do not find it easy to endure a lesser lover."

"Then I should leave you," said Sarevan, "lest I condemn you to chastity."

Hirel pondered that, gravely intent, and all the more deadly for it. "Or lest I condemn you to worse. How ingenious, that treachery would be. I need but seduce you as I very well can, and see that your chief priests know of it, and let them put you to death."

"It's not death now," Sarevan said, low, edged with roughness. "I'd only lose my torque and my braid, and suffer a flogging, and be bathed in salt and cast out of the temple in front of all my torque-kin."

"Naked, one can presume?"

"Naked," Sarevan answered. "Body and soul."

"But alive."

"That's not life," Sarevan said.

"And yet you will commit treason, knowing what you do, knowing that you may die for it."

"Some things are worth dying for."

"And I am not?"

Sarevan's lips set. Hirel did not know how to be contrite, but his eyes lowered.

"Child," said Sarevan, vicious in his gentleness, "be wise. Cure yourself of me."

"What if I do not wish to?"

"Then you're a worse fool than I took you for."

"Both of us," said Hirel, rising, seeking the wine.

Hirel was wise. He took Zha'dan to bed with him. Sarevan, curled in a corner with Ulan for blanket and bedfellow, refused to hear

what they did; even if it were nothing. He told himself that he was
no lover of boys, which was true. He told himself that he cherished
his vows to the god, which was truer yet. He told himself most
sternly that he had nothing to fret over, and that was not true at
all.

Damn the boy for laying open what Sarevan had schooled
himself to forget. Damn himself for falling prey to it. It was hard
won, this holiness of his. His body knew what it was for; it had no
more sympathy than Hirel had with this most painful price of his
priesthood. At the very thought of a woman, it could stand up and
sing.

At the thought of Hirel, it barely quivered. But his soul, that had
never before come even close to falling—his soul was in dire
danger.

This was not friendship, this that he had with his brother prince.
Often it was very nearly the opposite. And yet, when he thought of
leaving, of never seeing that maddening child again, or worse, of
meeting him on the battlefield, he could not endure it.

When he was very young, there was one thing in his world that
he had never understood, nor known how to understand. Other
children had mothers, fathers, uncles: that was right and proper.
But no one had a mother or a father or an uncle who were like his
own. To power's eyes they were hardly separate at all, though in
the body they were most distinct. When Mirain worked great
magics, he never worked them without his empress or his Ianyn
oathbrother.

"He can't," the Lord Vadin said once, when Sarevan dared to
ask. Mirain had been too kingly proud to approach with such a
question, and Elian was not the sort of person one asked difficult
things of, unless one needed them desperately enough to be
snapped at before one was given them. Vadin always managed to
have time for a small prince with a great store of questions; and
although he was most splendid to look at, taller than anyone else in
Sarevan's world, glittering in his northern finery, and his beard
gone august silver already though he was not even thirty, he was
never either stern or lordly when he was with children.

He sat on the sweet blue grass of Anshan-i-Ormal, on a hill that
looked out over the Sunborn's camp, and smiled at Sarevan. After

a moment Sarevan decided rather to be content than to be proud; he settled himself in his uncle's lap and played with one of the many necklaces that glittered on Vadin's breast. "Your father can't work high magic without us," Vadin repeated. He had another virtue: he did not mistake Sarevan for the four summers' child he seemed to be. He talked to him as if they were equals. "We're our own selves, have no fear of that; but in power we're one creature. Horrible, some would call it; unnatural. I call it merely unheard of."

"None of you tried to do it," Sarevan said.

Vadin laughed. "We most certainly did not! If you'd told me when I first met Mirain what the two of us would turn into, I think I would have killed him and done my best to kill myself. Or run very far away and never come back."

"Why?"

"I wasn't born a mage," said Vadin. He was not looking at Sarevan now; his eyes were lifted, staring straight into the sun. Sarevan had learned that no one could do that except Vadin and Elian and Mirain, and himself. It was because they were part of the Sun's blood. He was very proud of it, but a little afraid. It turned his uncle's dark eyes to fire, and filled him as water fills a cup. He spoke through it in his soft deep voice, the way he did when he was remembering something long past but not forgotten. "I was a simple creature. I was a hill lord's heir; I knew what my lot would be. I'd do my growing up in my father's house with my brothers and my sisters. Then I'd be a man, and I'd be sent to serve the king for a year or two, to uphold the honor of my house. Then I'd come back home and learn how to be lord in Geitan, and when my father died I'd take his place, and take wives and sire sons and rule my lands exactly as all my fathers had before me. But then," he said, "but then I stood guard at a gate of Ianon Castle, and it was a fine morning of early spring, and the old king was on the battlements above me; and a stranger came to shake me out of all my placid certainties. His name was Mirain; he proclaimed himself the son of the heir of Ianon who had died far away in the south, and the king named him heir in her place, and made me his personal servant. I hated him, namesake. I hated him so perfectly that I couldn't see any revenge more apt than to force him to accept my service."

"You don't hate him now."

Vadin smiled at the sun. "Sometimes I wonder," he said. "We're beyond hate, he and I. I think we're beyond even love. Your mother knows it. She didn't want this, either. She wanted your father, that's true enough; but I wasn't supposed to be part of it. I died for him, you see. An assassin had a spear, and I stopped it, and thereby stopped myself. But he wouldn't let me go. He had his own revenge to take, and we had a wager on whether we'd ever be friends. He said I would. I said never. I'd lose, of course, in the end. He brought me back to life; and he left some of his power in me, and a part of himself. Then in his turn he almost died, waging duel arcane with a servant of the darkness, and Elian and I between us brought him back, and now we were three in one."

"I was part of that," Sarevan said. "I wasn't born yet."

"You were barely there, infant," said Vadin. "Now when we raised the Tower on Endros, that's different. By then you were big enough to kick, and you put something of yourself into the working. That's when we knew you'd be a mage."

"I've always been a mage."

"From before the beginning of time," Vadin agreed gravely, but with a touch of wickedness. "And now you see, power isn't always contained in one mage at a time. Sometimes it's two together, or three. Souls are the same, I think. Some of them aren't made to be alone. They may think so. They may live for years in blessed solitude. Then suddenly, the other half or the other third comes, and the poor soul fights with all it's got to stay alone, but it's a losing fight. Souls and power, they know what they are. It's minds and bodies that struggle to be what they think they are."

Sarevan's mind and body, grown and set on betraying all three faces of that one great shining power, had no power of their own to fight against. But soul they had, and the soul had found its match. The other did not know what it was; he called it desire, and yearned for what he could not have.

"Avaryan," Sarevan whispered. "O Avaryan. Is this how you amuse yourself? Of all the souls in the world, this is the one you've made for me. And you set it in that of all the bodies there are. We can't be man and woman together. We can't share the world's rule. We can't even be brothers, still less lovers while I wear your torque.

What do you want us to do? Suffer in silence? Tear one another apart? Kill one another?"

The god's answer was silence. Sarevan buried his face in Ulan's warm musky fur. The cat purred, soft, barely to be heard. Slowly Sarevan slid into sleep.

Zha'dan would never dream of gloating, but he was conspicuously content. "It's true what they say," he said toward the next sunset, "of Asanian arts."

"I'm sure," said Sarevan, meaning to be cool. His tongue was not so minded. "It's me he wants, you know."

Zha'dan did not flinch from the stroke. "Of course he does, my lord. But even he knows better than to stretch so high."

"He's no lower than I."

Zha'dan was polite. He did not voice the objections that glittered in his eyes.

This inn was no less crowded than the last, but its master was more difficult. He took exception, it seemed, to Ulan, or perhaps to the young lord's slaves. Hirel had expressed his will already. The cat was to be neither caged in the courtyard not penned in the stable. The slaves did not leave his presence.

Halid was making slow headway. Hirel had settled for the siege, drawing prince and savage to the heaped carpets at his feet, which he rested on Ulan's quiescent back. Zha'dan was entirely content to lean against Hirel and be stroked and fed bits of meat from the Asanian's plate. Sarevan was not content at all, but resistance here would have been too conspicuous. He yielded because he must.

Hirel smiled at his rebellious glare and fed him a beancake dipped in something dark, pungent, and hot as fire. Sarevan gasped, sputtered, nearly leaped up in his outrage. His tormentor caught him, bending close as if to kiss. "Do you see those men in yonder corner?"

Sarevan stilled abruptly. His eyes were hot still, hotter even than his throat, but his mind had remembered princely training. He knew better than to turn and stare; but the edge of his eye marked them. Two Asanians sitting together, eating and drinking as did everyone else in the common room, doing nothing that might rouse suspicion. Their hair was cut strangely, shaven from brow to crown, worn long and loose behind.

"Those," said Hirel, "are priests of Uvarra. They were in the inn last night. They watched us then as they watch us now."

"We're interesting," Sarevan said, "and we're on the straight road to Kundri'j. Why shouldn't they be on it with us?"

Hirel fed him wine in dainty sips, a lordling amusing himself with his favorite slave. "Priests of Uvarra do not wear that tonsure unless they serve in the high temple in Kundri'j Asan. Nor do they wander as your kind do, save for very great need."

"They're too conspicuous to be spies."

"Perhaps, like us, they know the virtue of hiding in plain sight."

"But why—"

"They are mages."

Sarevan's teeth clicked together. Oh, indeed that was stretching coincidence. But how could the boy know? He had no power.

Sarevan darted a glance. One's robe was light, and perhaps it was grey. The other's was dark: violet, perhaps. Guild colors. A lightmage and a dark.

"They're sorcerers," murmured Zha'dan, resting his head on Hirel's knee. Sarevan's eyes flashed to him. He would know. The wisewoman of the Zhil'ari was his grandmother. He was her pupil and her heir, and quite as mageborn as Sarevan himself, though never so free with it. Mages of the wild tribes did not wield full power until they were judged worthy of it.

A custom which Sarevan might have been wise to follow. He met Zha'dan's clear stare with the width of Hirel's knees between. "You've set wards?" he asked in Zhil'ari, just above a whisper.

Zha'dan's eyes glinted. "I hardly need to. You're guarded. The veiled ones are invisible to power—I'd pay high to know how they do that."

"They pay high for a spell; it's laid on each of them at initiation. In an amulet." Sarevan was in no mood for teaching, even in a good cause. "And the cubling?"

"Safe," said Zha'dan. "With little enough help from me. He doesn't chatter inside. He knows how to throw up walls."

"He's no mage."

"He's not. But he has shields."

Sarevan scowled blackly at nothing. Hirel had never had shields when Sarevan had power. His mind had been as open and aimless as any other man's, with walls where scars were, closing off memory that pricked him to pain; but nothing a mage could not pass if he chose.

If it puzzled Zha'dan, he did not let it vex his peace. He stroked his cheek against Hirel's thigh, catlike, smiling at Hirel's frown. In tradespeech he said, "We talk about how beautiful you are."

Hirel flushed, but he had perforce to swallow his temper. Halid had won his battle with the innkeeper. The innkeeper himself had been prevailed upon to serve the young lord's pleasure. He occupied them all with his fluttering, until at last they drove him out. By then, Hirel had forgotten Zha'dan's insolence; or simply let it pass.

They were being followed.

It was not always obvious. The roads were crowded with troops, with travelers, with traders. But Sarevan remembered faces, and even where that failed in the likeness of one plump yellow face to another, Uvarra's tonsure and the Mageguild's colors, once noticed, were hard to mistake. He did not see them every day; nor every night in inn or posthouse. Still, he saw them often enough, and perhaps they had allies: men less conspicuous yet oddly tenacious; the same faces, or faces very like them, appearing again and again.

"They're not strong in power," Zha'dan said of the mages.

"Who needs strength?" Sarevan demanded. "They only need to know where eyes have seen two black slaves together."

Zha'dan regarded his hands on the reins of his gelding. "Better black than bilious," he said.

Sarevan bit back laughter. "Oh, surely! But there's no one like us between here and the Lakes of the Moon. We're noticeable."

The Zhil'ari looked about at the Olenyai ringing them, the prince on the blue-eyed stallion in front of him, the traffic of the Golden Empire making way for their passing. "Illusion?" he suggested.

"Too late for that. They'd track us by the scent of your power." A knot of wagons blocked their path; Sarevan muscled his ironmouthed nag to a halt beside Bregalan. The stallion adamantly refused to collapse, or to go lame, or even to look tired. Maybe he had learned to drink the sun. The Mad One could; why not his daughter's son?

Sarevan straightened in the saddle and set his teeth. His head had been aching in spasms for a day or three. Not often; not in any pattern. He could have blamed it on the sun, but today there was none: the clouds were heavy, threatening rain.

This was no dull throbbing ache. This was pain as keen as a dagger's blade, stabbing deep behind his eyes. It wrung a gasp from him. "Hirel," someone said, light and bantering, "Hirel, think about last night, and Zha'dan, and the woman with the passion for two lovers at once."

The someone was himself. He was going mad.

Hirel had flushed scarlet, which made Zha'dan grin, but his eyes on Sarevan were steady. Thinking hard.

With crawling slowness the pain faded. Sarevan almost fainted with the relief of it. And with the knowledge.

Now he must suffer not only when he tried to get out of his mind, but when someone else tried to get in.

They had said it, the old masters. For him who slew with power, there was no end to expiation. Even if he had not intended to do it. Even if he had done it in the best of causes. Even . . .

"Stronger shields," Zha'dan was saying in his own tongue. "Dream-wards. I'll post them hereafter. I'll snare our hunters with false dreams."

"Even in our young master?"

Zha'dan laughed. "Even in the little stallion; though he's doing well enough by himself. Maybe when he dies he'll come back one of us."

The lion's cub would have been appalled at the prospect. Sarevan sipped wine from the flask at his saddlebow, washing away the sour aftertaste of pain. They had skirted the wagons. At the head of the line, Halid signaled a quickening of pace.

"Tell me about your brother," Sarevan said.

Asanian modesty had its uses. A young lord could purchase a room in a bathhouse, with a bolt on the door and his own slaves to wait on him. There he could lie on a bench above steaming stones with his head in Zha'dan's lap and Sarevan sitting at a judicious distance. Hirel eyed him with a flicker of amusement. Without his tunic he was an odd harlequin creature, copper-pelted on breast and belly and between his thighs, but all the rest of him safely dark.

The boy sat up suddenly, leaning toward him, and peered. "You will be needing the dye again soon."

"We only touched it up two days ago."

"Your body is not pleased. The black wishes to turn to rust. And thence, I presume, to honest copper."

"Too honest for my peace of mind. The dye is almost gone." Sarevan rubbed his chin. It itched incessantly and with waxing ferocity. He struggled to keep from clawing it. "Maybe I should shave my face and blacken my brows with charcoal and wash my hair clean, and find a hat to cover it. It would be easier. It might work. Who'd recognize me even if I lost the hat? You traveled with me for half a season without the slightest suspicion."

Hirel pulled Sarevan's beard until he hissed in pain. "I was an unconscionable fool. Our . . . friends are not."

"Why? What are they likely to know? I'm a slave. Slaves count for nothing."

Perhaps he sounded more bitter than he knew. Hirel regarded him oddly. Zha'dan said, "I'd dye my hair red for the splendor of it and for the confusion of our trackers, but my beard I'll not give up. I'm no capon."

Sarevan's eyes narrowed. "Would you, Zhaniedan? Would you go from night to fire?"

"With delight. But *not*," Zha'dan said vehemently, "from man to eunuch."

Hirel looked from one to the other of them. "Have you lost your wits?"

"I'm losing my disguise," Sarevan reminded him. "And we'll find precious little black dye here. But copper—that, I think . . ."

Zha'dan was warming to the sport. "Let's do it, my lord! Let's do it tonight."

But Sarevan had cooled a little. "Soon," he said. "Maybe. I need to think. And while I do it," he said, turning his eyes on Hirel, "you can do as I bid you. Tell me about your brother."

For a moment Hirel looked ready to upbraid his insanity. Then the boy sighed, sharp with temper, and lay down again. He took only a small revenge, but it was ample for the purpose: he set his feet in Sarevan's lap. They were very comely feet. "Surely," he said, "you mean to say my brothers. I have half a hundred."

Zha'dan was properly impressed. Sarevan did not stoop to be. "Most of them are nonentities. Even the two who trapped you—you've said yourself that they couldn't have conceived the plot alone. Tell me about the one who matters. Tell me about the Prince Aranos."

Hirel hissed at him. "Not so loudly, idiot. Ears are everywhere."

"Not here," said Sarevan. "Zha'dan's on guard. He's mageborn."

Hirel started, half rising, staring at his nights' companion. Zha'dan was grave for once, level-eyed. Hirel was surprised. That was rare; it made him angry. "Is there anyone in Keruvarion who is not?"

"It's only Zha'dan." And Orozia; but that was her own secret.

"Ah," said Hirel, unmollified. He faced Zha'dan. "That is why you fretted so before we came to Endros. Because you have power, but it was not enough to heal your prince."

Zha'dan looked down, embarrassed.

"Did you fret?" Sarevan asked him. "I'd forgotten."

Zha'dan mumbled something. Sarevan cuffed him lightly, brother-fashion. It soothed him, though he would not look up. Sarevan turned back to Hirel. "Now, cubling. Answer me."

Hirel's brows drew together. Sweat did not presume to bead and streak and stink upon that gold-and-ivory skin. It imparted a polished sheen, salt-scented, with a hint of sweetness. "Aranos," he said at last, "is the eldest of my father's sons. His mother was a prince's daughter from the far west of Asanion. They say she was a witch; I no longer deny that possibility. I do not think that Aranos is mageborn."

"Mages need not be born. They can be made. We call them mages of the book. Sorcerers. They have no native power, but they find it in books; in spells and in rituals; in summonings of demons and elementals and familiars. Does your brother have a familiar?"

Hirel lay back again, shifting until he was comfortable. "I think not. Perhaps it is only, not yet." He raised his head slightly, struck with a thought. "Is Ulan your familiar?"

Sarevan quelled a retort. The child could not know how he

insulted them both. "Ulan is my friend and my brother-in-fur. He is neither slave nor willing servant."

"Ah." Hirel's frown was different, puzzled, seeking to understand. "A familiar provides power to the powerless. It is a vessel. An instrument."

"In essence, yes. But any man can't set himself up as a sorcerer. He has to have a talent for it. A desire for power. The willingness to devote his life to the finding of it. Singlemindedness, and ruthlessness, and a certain inborn strength of will. You have it, Hirel Uverias. You have so much of it that you're almost mageborn."

The boy reared up like a startled cat. All the color had drained from his face; his eyes were wild. "I am not a mumbler of spells!"

"It's in your blood. Ulan sees it and approves of it. So does Bregalan. So most certainly does Zha'dan. It's the heart of the lion."

"Ah," said Hirel, relaxing by degrees. "It is royalty, that is all."

Sarevan did not gainsay him. Let him call it that, if it gave him comfort. "If your brother is anything like you, then he may very well be a worker of magic."

Hirel had drawn taut again. "We are not alike. We are—not—"

"He's royal, isn't he?"

"There are," said Hirel with vicious precision, "three ranks of imperial princes, and the high prince above them all. Princes of five robes are sons of slaves and commoners. Princes of six are sons of lower nobility. Princes of seven are sons of high ladies. Vuad, who is a slave's child, is a prince of seven by my father's favor, because his mother is the most favored of the concubines."

"Is? Still?"

"My father is renowned for his constancy." Hirel had recovered himself. It was frightening to see how young he was, and how cold he seemed, and how dispassionately he spoke of betrayal. "There was no perceptible sign of my eldest brother in what was done to me, and yet he must have been the master of the plot, the mind behind the bodies of Vuad and Sayel. He had the most to gain from it. They could not have hoped to seize my titles while he lived, nor to dispose of him as easily as they thought to dispose of me. That they failed, speaks very ill of their intelligence. Aranos would not have failed."

"He may not care, if it gets him what he aims for. It's fairly certain, isn't it? He'll be named high prince on Autumn Firstday. I'll wager that your father won't live long thereafter."

"No wager," Hirel said. "Even before I left Kundri'j I had heard whispers that Aranos was surrounding himself with mages. I do not need to wonder why. To protect him while he lives; to forestall opposition when he has the throne. And yet he cannot have set these mages to spy upon us. A lordling of the Middle Court is no threat to the Second Prince before the Golden Throne. If he knew what I truly am, he would have slain me long before this."

"Maybe he doesn't know. Maybe it has nothing to do with you at all. Zha'dan and I could very well be Varyani spies."

"Perhaps," murmured Hirel. "It is what we might expect of your father: outrageous, and blatant, and insolent. It is not at all like Aranos. It is too simple."

"It looks complicated enough to me."

Hirel's glance was purest Asanian arrogance. "Ah, but you are of Keruvarion. To you I am subtle, a proper golden serpent; and yet in the palace I am reckoned the purest of innocents, a sheltered child who knew no better than to trust his brothers. Aranos was weaving plots in his cradle."

"You were a child when your brothers trapped you. How were you to know that they'd turn traitor?"

"I should have known. They are my brothers. But Aranos . . . Aranos is a very prince of serpents. I shall never be more beside him than a pretty fool."

"And his emperor."

"There is that," said Hirel. He frowned, brooding. "The Golden Palace cannot but know that I live. It has not seen fit to publish the glad tidings, else there would be no mention of a new high prince."

"No," said Sarevan. "They'd be saying that you'd gone over to us, or that you were our prisoner."

"With much outrage and no little relish." Hirel smiled a little. "A banner for their war. My father would not wish that. Aranos most certainly would not. He will be making certain that he receives the title as the empire expects. Then, alive or dead, I can do nothing: I will have been superseded in law."

"Surely your father won't allow it."

"By law, if I am not present on the day of my coming of age, I forfeit my right to the title. He can do nothing to change that. Even if he would. For then I would prove myself unworthy to rule after him."

"Hard," mused Sarevan, "but fair enough. Maybe it's he who's behind it all. Testing you."

Hirel bridled. Sarevan grinned at him. He leaped up, nearly casting Sarevan upon the stones. "Into the water with you, barbarian. You reek."

"Of what?" Sarevan asked sweetly. "The truth?"

Their attendant mages, whether Aranos' hirelings or another's, seemed not to have found their way to this latest resting place. But someone had; and perhaps he had only been caught by the young lord's unusual retinue, and perhaps there was deeper purpose in it. This was, after all, Asanion.

The messenger was waiting at the door of the bathhouse. "Young lord," he said, bowing and touching his shaven brow to Hirel's foot, "my master, the Lord of the Ninth Rank Uzmeidjian y Viduganyas, begs the pleasure of your company at his humble table."

Even Sarevan, whose Asanian was hardly perfect, could detect the intonation that made the request a command. Hirel's lips thinned. Sarevan, trapped in his disguise, could say nothing. After a pause Hirel said, "Tell the Lord of the Ninth Rank that the Lord-designate of the Second Rank Insevirel y Kunziad will be pleased to accept his most august hospitality."

The Lord Uzmeidjian was likewise a traveler, but his estate was too lofty by far to suffer the indignities of the posthouse. With his small army of Olenyai and plain men-at-arms, his slaves and his servants and his veiled and secluded women, he had appropriated the house of a magnate of the town.

He himself was a man of middle years inclining toward age. His body was strong yet, for an Asanian's, but softening, growing thick about the middle. His virility, of which he was quite publicly proud, had tonsured him in youth, but he cultivated the fringe of

hair that yet lingered, cajoling it into oiled ringlets. He gilded his
eyelids, which plainly Hirel did not approve of: it was, perhaps,
above his station. Though he stood very high, at the height of the
Middle Court.

His manner toward Hirel was that of a great lord bestowing his
favor upon a being much lower than himself. Hirel did not bear it
with perfect ease.

"Of the second rank, are you, lord-designate?" the lord inquired
after the innumerable courses of an Asanian banquet had come
and gone. Only the wine was left, and a sweet or two, and a bowl of
ices. He had eaten well and drunk deep. Hirel had hardly eaten at
all, and only pretended to drink. "Coming to take your place in
court, I presume. Commendable, commendable. It is the first time,
no?"

Hirel murmured. It might have been taken for assent.

Lord Uzmeidjian took it so, expansively. "Ah, so! I am sure you
have been well taught. But the Court of the Empire is unlike
anything the provinces might dream of. Even the Lower Court: it
is preparation, certainly, but nothing equals the truth."

"Have you ever been in the High Court, my lord?"

That was malice, clad as innocence. The lord flushed. Perhaps it
was only the wine. "I have not been so privileged. It is very rare,
that dispensation. The High Court is far above us all."

"Indeed," said Hirel.

"Your accent is excellent," the lord observed, mounting again to
his eminence. "Indeed it is almost perfect: scarce a suggestion of
the provinces."

Hirel bit his lip. His eyes were smoldering. Sarevan damned
protocol and laid a hand on his shoulder, tightening it: warning,
strengthening.

And diverting the Lord Uzmeidjian most conclusively. "Ah,
young sir, such slaves you have! and matched so perfectly. Your
slavemaster must be a man of genius."

Zha'dan, who knew no Asanian but who needed to know none,
and Sarevan, who was pretending to be ignorant of it, stood
perforce in silence. The lord reached for Zha'dan who was closer,
taking the young man's arm, feeling of it. "You leave them in their
natural state, I see. But cleaner, certainly cleaner, and sweeter to
the nose. I had thought that they were all as rank as foxes."

"My overseers were careful to teach them proper cleanliness," said Hirel.

"That is clear to see. They were taken as cubs, I presume; they do not train well else. And left entire—that was courageous. Or did you wait for the beards to come before you had them gelded?"

"They are quite as nature made them," Hirel said.

"So," said the Lord Uzmeidjian, "I see." And so most certainly could he feel. Zha'dan was rigid. Not with outrage at the fondling hand; his own could be free enough, and Zhil'ari did not know that kind of shame. But the talk of gelding had frozen him where he stood.

And now, in more ways than one, his lordship came to it. "I confess, Lord Insevirel, that I am most intrigued. In the high arts I have a certain reputation, yet this I have never known: the embrace of a savage in his natural state."

"They have no art," said Hirel.

"But instinct, young lord—that surely they have. Like bulls, like stallions. So huge, so beautifully hideous: animals, yet shaped like us. Splendid parodies of humanity."

"Their beards are harsh to the hand," Hirel said.

Lord Uzmeidjian proved it to himself, shivering with delight. "O marvelous! Lord Insevirel, I should not ask, I overstep myself, and yet—and yet—"

"Ah," said Hirel, wide-eyed, regretful. "But I promised. My father made me swear on our ancestors' bones. I may not part them, nor may I sell them. I may not even let them wander apart from me. They are our slavemaster's triumph. They are to give me consequence at court."

"Indeed, young lord, they shall," said the Lord Uzmeidjian. "And yet surely, if you should merely lend them for a night . . ."

Hirel was silent. Sarevan's hand tightened on his shoulder. He seemed not to feel it. At last he said, "I promised."

The lord smiled, but his eyes were hard. "A night. And in the morning their swift return, alive and undamaged, with gold in their purses."

Hirel drew himself up sharply. "I am not a merchant!"

"Most surely you are not, young sir. No more than I. We are courtiers, both of us. The court is difficult for one new come to it; but if a high lord should deign to take a young one into his care, what might that young lord become? Your family holds the second rank, and there, alas, it is not the highest, else certainly I would know its name; but it need not remain so forever. A house may rise high under a clever lord. Or," he added, soft and smooth, "it may fall."

Hirel looked into the lord's face. Slowly he said, "Please, my lord. Pardon me. I am new to this; I do not know the proper words to say. Would one of my panthers suffice for you? Then I would break only half of my promise."

Lord Uzmeidjian laughed, all jovial again. "Surely, surely, you must not break it all! This beauty, by your leave, I shall keep; in the morning he will come back to you. You have my word on it."

"With honor?" Hirel asked, innocently precise.

"With honor," the lord answered him with only the merest shadow of hesitation.

Sarevan held his tongue by sheer force of royal will, and held it full into the posthouse, and even into Hirel's chamber. But when their door was shut and Ulan was greeting him with princely gladness and Hirel was moving calmly about the shedding of his robes, Sarevan's rage burst its bonds. He was on Hirel before the boy could have seen him move, bearing him back and down, shaking him until his neck bade fair to break. "You son of a snake! You pimp! You panderer! By all the gods in your sink of a country, how could you think—how could you *dare*—"

Hirel twisted, impossibly supple, impossibly strong. He broke Sarevan's brutal hold. He rolled to his feet. A dagger glittered in his hand.

Sarevan sat on his heels, breathing hard. The fire had left him. He was cold; his head throbbed dully. "How could you do that to Zha'dan?"

"Would you rather I had done it to you?"

Sarevan surged up. Hirel was not there; his knife was. With the swiftness of thought, Sarevan spun it out of his hand.

They stood still, wrist crossing wrist, like fencers in a match. Hirel looked up into Sarevan's burning eyes. "I had no choice. He was seven full ranks above what I pretended to be; and he was beginning to suspect trickery, else he would never have warned me that he had not heard of my house. I trod the edge in resisting him even as far as I did. He could have seized you, slain or imprisoned me on a charge of imposture or worse, and had his will of us all; and he would have been perfectly within his rights."

"That is unspeakable!"

"It is the world's way. I preserved your precious virginity, priest. Does that count for nothing?"

"Not when you bought it with Zha'dan."

Hirel lowered his arm. "Do you rate him so low? I do not. He is, you say, a mage; he is insatiable in pleasure; and he has more intelligence than he would like any of us to know. If he does not turn this night entirely to his own advantage, then he is not the man I took him for."

Sarevan tossed his aching head. Hirel had the right of it. Damn him. "That doesn't excuse your peddling him like a common whore."

"It does not," Hirel said wearily, startling him speechless. The boy sank down to the scattered cushions of the bed, half-clad as he was. His underrobe was torn. He struggled out of it and lay in his trousers, closing his eyes. "I did what I had to do. It does not matter that you hate me for it. You will hate me more deeply still before it is ended, if we come to Kundri'j, if I take back my titles."

Sarevan was silent.

"I have told you what I am," Hirel said. "Now do you begin to believe it?"

"You weren't like this in Keruvarion."

Hirel's eyes opened. There was nothing of the child in them. "I had no occasion to be. Your empire is remarkable, prince. It is young. Its emperor is a god's son, and a mage, and a very great king. He can afford to live by the truth; so likewise can his people. I never feared that he would break his word to me while I kept mine to him."

"Nor even when you didn't," muttered Sarevan. He dropped to the cushions. "We're clean in Keruvarion. We're honorable. We don't play foul even with our enemies."

"How fortunate," said Hirel with weary irony. His hand brushed Sarevan's cheek. "I lied a little. Your beard is not harsh to the hand."

"Neither is Zha'dan's."

"There is power in words; particularly in words addressed to a man already well gone in lust."

Sarevan ground his teeth. "That swine. That barrel of butter. I would have strangled him if he had touched me."

"Therefore I did not let him. I would not have liked him to see your true colors."

Sarevan's cheeks burned. He buried them in the cushions. He hated this unnatural child. He hated all this lying empire. And he had trapped himself in it. For its sake he had turned traitor to all that he had ever been.

How long he lay there, he did not know. Pain brought him up at last. The throbbing behind his eyes was mounting to agony.

"Sorcery," he whispered. Even that nearly split his skull.

Hirel was asleep, or feigning it. Ulan lay across his feet. The cat raised his head and growled softly.

Sarevan struggled to his knees. If he could think—if he could only think. Plots, counterplots. Zha'dan lured away, his magecraft taken where it could not protect his companions. The Olenyai—

Sarevan gasped, blind and retching, but thinking. Thinking hard, for all the good it could do. This posthouse had no space for a lord's meinie. They had perforce to lodge in the common barracks. The two who should have stood guard at the door had not been there when Sarevan came back. He had been too wild with rage to notice, still less to care.

Sorcery. Betrayal. Deadly danger. This was Asanion. *Asanion.*

Cool. Hands. Cool hands. Cool voice—but not so cool, calling his name, commanding him to answer.

Light broke upon him. He stared into Hirel's face. He was on his back. Hirel was holding his head, looking for once entirely human. He was stark with fear. "Sarevadin, if you die now, I shall be most displeased. Sarevadin!"

Sarevan could not help it. He laughed, though he paid for it in white pain. "I haven't died on you yet, cubling."

"That is not for lack of trying," Hirel snapped.

Sarevan sat up, reeling. All lightness drained from him. "We're in a trap. They've got Zha'dan away from us and stripped us of our Olenyai. You said Aranos hadn't tried to kill you yet. This may be the stroke." He rose, though Hirel tried to stop him. His sight had narrowed, but he could see. He could walk.

"Where are you going?" Hirel demanded of him.

"To confront a pair of sorcerers."

"You are mad! You have no power. You can barely set one foot before the other."

"What would you have me do? Lie quietly and wait for them to slaughter us?"

"They will hardly slay us with their power. I have a little skill in arms; and we have Ulan. We can give a good account of ourselves."

"If any of us kills a man here, we'll all pay in blood."

"So then," said Hirel. "Can you ride?"

"Yes, damn it!" Sarevan paused. Escape now. Yes. But with pursuit on their heels; and Zha'dan . . .

A new wave of agony crested, passed. He snatched up their belongings, flung Hirel's discarded garments at him, scrambled together what food he could find.

The inn was utterly quiet. No one walked the passages. Nothing moved there at all. It was as if it were all enspelled. Sarevan dragged Hirel through it with growing heedlessness, flinging them both from inn to open air to the dark odorous confines of the stable. Beasts thronged it. Sarevan found Bregalan almost by instinct. The shadow next to him was tall enough to carry a tall man, which was not common in Asanion. Sarevan found saddles, bridles.

Hirel waited just past the door with Ulan, who could not enter among so many seneldi lest he drive them all mad with terror. The strange senel, scenting him, snorted and danced, but under Sarevan's hand it eased to a trembling stillness.

They rode slowly from the yard, keeping to shadows. No one challenged them, not even the hound that had welcomed them with yapping and howling. The air was still. The gate was open. Trap?

They spurred through it. Nothing stopped them. The posthouse lay outside the walls of the town, hard by the road; there was no second gate to pass. They kept to the grass on the verge, which made for swift going, and silent. Town and posthouse shrank behind them.

The pain receded slowly. Sarevan's mount was smooth-gaited. In the starless night he could not guess its color, save that it was dark. It was hornless: a mare. All the better. Mares were swifter and hardier and less given to nonsense; and even yet he did not want to be caught on a stallion.

Hoofbeats behind. Sarevan clapped heels to the mare's sides. But Bregalan had broken stride, was turning. Was he mad? Had the spell caught Hirel at last?

Cursing, Sarevan wheeled his own mount. Bregalan had stopped. Sarevan snatched at his bridle; he shied away. "He will not heed me," Hirel said. He was calm, but it was a desperate calm.

The hoofs neared swiftly. It was only one senel. Sarevan, peering, could discern a swift-moving shadow. Metal hissed. Hirel had drawn one of his swords. The other flashed in sudden moonlight. Sarevan caught the hilt. Armed and defiant, they waited.

It was a lone rider, and he was all a shadow. Sarevan's heart knew him before his mind could wake. "Zha'dan!"

The Zhil'ari pounded to a halt beside them. He was breathing hard and his senel was blowing, but he grinned whitely in Brightmoon's gleam. "Thought you could creep out on me, did you?"

"We tried," said Sarevan.

"Good," he said. His grin vanished. "There's death on the wind tonight. Best we not tarry for it."

They rode until Zha'dan would let them stop. The sky greyed with dawn. The seneldi, ridden at the pace of the Long Race in the north, surpassingly swift but not meant to kill, had a little strength left; but none of the riders was minded to squander it. Posthouses would not be safe thereafter; they had no swift hope of remounts.

They found refuge at some distance from the road, in the deep cleft cut by a stream. Its banks offered grass for their seneldi; a thicket offered both shelter and concealment, and a blessed gift of thornfruit to eke out their scanty provisions.

Hirel, having eaten as much as Sarevan could bully into him, fell at once into sleep. The others lingered, crouched side by side. "Was it bad?" Sarevan asked.

Zha'dan shrugged. "He wasn't the little stallion. He was smooth all over. His yard was a bare finger's length. He kept calling me ugly." Zha'dan was indignant. "I may be small, but even Gazhin admits that I'm beautiful. I look like you, don't I? You're the most beautiful of us all."

"Not to an Asanian," said Sarevan. He gestured toward Hirel. "That's beauty here."

"He's not ill to look at. But he's white, like a bone, and his eyes are yellow. That's all very well for an honest lion, but men's eyes are black. And his nose, look. No arch. What's a nose without an arch?"

"Pitiful," Sarevan said wryly, rubbing his own royal curve. "So his lordship has a crooked passion for beautifully ugly barbarians. And then?"

"And then," said Zha'dan. "He didn't last long. He fell asleep, and I was thinking of going, and then the mages struck. They were only trying to read me, to be sure I was well occupied. I gave them something to keep their ears burning for a while. Then they turned on you. And there I was, locked in walls. I couldn't get out. By the time I found a wall to climb over, you were up and running. I borrowed one of the seneldi you left, and followed you." Zha'dan paused. Suddenly he grinned. "They won't follow us for a while, I don't think. I told the seneldi to wait a bit. Then I untied them, and I left the door open."

Sarevan laughed with him, freely, but hit him without gentleness after. "Whelp! This isn't a raiding party."

Zha'dan hit back. Sarevan lunged at him. They rolled on the grass in laughing combat. Ulan made himself a part of it, growling in high delight. At the end of it they lay all together, hiccoughing, scoured clean of aught but mirth.

Sunset brought battle again, but battle of words, without laughter. Sarevan was minded to cross Asanion as he had crossed Keruvarion, in secret, taking sustenance from land and sky. Hirel would not hear of it. "This is not your wild east. The hunting belongs to the lords and satraps, each in his own demesne. Those who hunt without leave are reckoned thieves and punished accordingly."

"Not with Ulan and Zha'dan to cover our tracks," said Sarevan.

Hirel tossed his head, impatient. "And if they do, how swiftly can we ride? How far must we wander, to be secret, to fill our bellies? How careful must we be to spare our seneldi, now that we may find no others?"

"What do you want to do? Take the open road? Invite our assassins to finish what our foolish flight interrupted?"

"Take the road, yes; outrun our enemies. If enemies we have. I saw no daggered shadows. I tasted no poison in our wine. The posthouse might have been abandoned, so easily we left it."

"It was not—" Sarevan's tongue met his mind and froze. He had been too busy running to think. He had forgotten indeed that this was not Keruvarion.

"Speculate," said Hirel, "if you can. Sorcery nearly felled you. You gave way to instinct: you fled it. What if you were meant to do just that? To run into a trap. Or more subtle yet, to abandon the swift way; to take to the shadows. And thereby most certainly to delay my coming to Kundri'j."

"And if you are delayed, Aranos becomes high prince." Sarevan liked the taste of it not at all. It was alien; it burned, like Asanian spices. He spat it out. "But if we ride openly, the enemy will know. He'll lay new traps. I don't think he'll wait long to make them deadly."

"Are you afraid?" Hirel asked.

"Yes, I'm afraid!" Sarevan shot back. "But a coward, I'm not. I don't want to arrive late, but neither do I want to arrive dead."

"That would not be comfortable," said Hirel. "We have Zha'dan and Ulan. We have you, whom sorcery cannot fail to rouse. We even have myself. I have no power and no great skill in hunting or in fighting, but I do know Asanion. If we vanish for a day or two, press on through the shadows, I think then we may return to the daylight."

"With stolen seneldi?"

"Ah," said Zha'dan, entering the fray at last, "that's easy. We find a town with a fair. We trade. We do it twice or thrice, over a day or two. Then when our path is quite comfortably confused, we go back to the inns and the highroad."

"It won't work," Sarevan said. "We may lose a pair of seneldi, but we can't lose our faces."

"You may," Hirel said slowly. "Sometimes, Olenyai go all masked. It is a rite of theirs. We cannot sustain such a deception:

the masked do not mingle with folk in inns, nor speak any tongue
but their own secret battle-language. But for a day, two, three—it
is possible."

"Where will we find the robes?" demanded Sarevan. He was
being difficult, he knew it. But someone had to be.

"I can wield a needle," said Hirel, astonishingly. "For the cloth,
we find a fair. I can be a slave for an hour if I must: a slave whose
mistress has a fancy for black."

Sarevan opened his mouth, closed it. Zha'dan was regarding
Hirel in something remarkably like admiration.

With a sharp hiss, Sarevan conceded the battle. "Very well.
Tonight we ride in the shadows. Tomorrow we find a fair."

Hirel did not gloat over his victory. It was Zha'dan who
whooped and kissed him, disconcerting him most gratifyingly, and
went to saddle the seneldi.

They found their fair: a town with a market, and a wooded hill
outside of it, thick enough with undergrowth to shelter the beasts
and the two men who could not show their faces. Hirel went down
on foot in his underrobe, cut to the brevity of a slave's tunic, with
Zha'dan's iron collar about his neck and a purse of Asanian coins
hung from his belt. The Lord Uzmeidjian had not missed them or
their golden kin, Zha'dan had assured the two princes; and
certainly Zha'dan had earned them. Hirel had looked at him and
sighed, but said nothing.

The boy was gone for a very long while. Sarevan tried to sleep
through some of it. The rest he spent on his belly in a knot of
canes, keeping watch over the road and the town. Ulan kept him
company. He had shed his damnable tunic; flies buzzed about him
in the day's heat but did not sting, and the earth was cool. He
would have been comfortable, if he had known how Hirel was
faring. The boy had done well enough in his venture into a Varyani
town, but this was Asanion. Who knew what niggling law he might
have managed to break, all in his princely ignorance? Did he even
know how to bargain in the market? Or if the mages after all had
not lost him, and had seized him—

Sarevan set his jaw and willed himself to stop fretting. His face
itched more maddeningly than ever. He had used the last of the
dye this morning. It had stung like fire; he had almost cried out, as

much with knowledge as with pain. It was the dye that so tormented his skin: eating at it, burning it, leaving it raw and angry. Even if he could find another bottle, he did not think his face would survive it.

He worked his fingers into Ulan's fur, lest they claw new weals in his cheeks. People passed on the road. Was that a boy with hot-gold hair cropped into a wild mane, coming up from the town?

Not yet.

He set himself to his vigil. The sun crawled to its zenith.

Ulan growled, the barest murmur. Sarevan shook himself awake, peered. A slave with a pack on his back trudged slowly toward the thicket. A slave with dust-drab hair.

Dust in truth, and a handsome bruise purpling his cheekbone. He started as Sarevan rose out of the thicket; his eyes widened at the bare body. He did not speak. He looked both furious and pleased with himself. He strode into the thicket's heart, tossed down his pack, greeted Zha'dan with a vanishingly brief smile.

"You've been fighting," Sarevan accused him.

He knelt to uncover his booty. Coolly, without looking up, he said, "I have been defending my honor."

Sarevan seized him by the nape and hauled him up. "What did you do, you little fool? Were you trying to get us all killed?"

Hirel twisted free, all angry now: a white heat, rigidly restrained. "I was trying to be what I seemed to be. I did not heed the taunting of the market curs. But when they seized me and sought to strip me, because they had a wager, and they wished to see what sort of eunuch I was—was I to let them see that I am no eunuch at all?" He tossed his hair out of his eyes. They were fiery gold. "I had already let it be known that I served a lady; and the law is strict. One of my adversaries had a knife, if perchance it should be needed. Should I have let him use it?"

Sarevan said nothing, quenched for once, beginning to regret his hastiness. Hirel was white and shaking. He was worse than angry. He was on the thin edge between murder and tears.

He calmed himself visibly, drawing in deep shuddering breaths. "I defended myself well enough. Better certainly than they looked for. They chose to seek meeker prey elsewhere; and I won a modicum of respect from the merchants. They did not drive as hard a bargain as they might have."

"You liked that," Sarevan said. "Maybe you should have been born a merchant."

"Better a tradesman than a worthless vagabond. Or," said Hirel, bending again to his unpacking, "a eunuch. Of any sort."

Zha'dan looked ready to ask how there could be more than one. Mercifully for all of them, he held his tongue.

Hirel had needles and thread and cutting blades. He had bolts of black linen and bolts of fine black wool. He had belts of black leather, and black gauntlets, and boots that proved not to fit too badly; and marvel of marvels, four black-hilted swords in black sheaths. They were Olenyai blades; but he would not tell how he had found them. He looked both proud and guilty.

"He stole them," Zha'dan translated, with approval.

Hirel flushed. "I appropriated them. As high prince I am overlord of all warriors. I claimed my royal right."

Zha'dan applauded him. He flushed more deeply still and attacked the somber linen.

The others found themselves pressed into service. With Hirel directing them, they transformed themselves into *shiu'oth Olenyai:* warriors under solemn vow. When they were done, the sun was westering, and Sarevan was sucking a much-stabbed finger. Hirel slapped down his hand. "Mask yourself," the boy commanded. Sarevan obeyed rather sourly.

Hirel stood back, hands on hips, head cocked. "You will do," he judged, "for a while. If no one examines you too closely."

"You comfort me," said Sarevan.

Hirel ignored the barb. For himself he had stitched a headdress to match the rest: the filleted headcloth and the mask that concealed all beneath it, even to the eyes. A panel of thinnest linen set over them was easy enough to see out of, but from the outside seemed all featureless darkness.

"We look alarming," Zha'dan said. He sounded highly amused.

Sarevan was stifling already. At least, he reflected wryly, he would not find it so easy to claw at his itching cheeks.

People had stared at a dozen Olenyai and a young lord and his two barbarian slaves. They did not stare at three *shiu'oth Olenyai.* Their eyes slid round the shadowed shapes; their voices muted; their bodies drew back, smoothly, as water parts from a stone.

It was almost ridiculously simple to exchange the stolen seneldi for a pair of black mares. The seller did not haggle at all. He almost thrust the beasts at them, his eyes rolling white, his plump face sheening with sweat. He asked no questions. When they left him, he looked ready to weep for relief.

So with the next seller, and the next. Most often it was plain fear. Sometimes it was fear poisoned with hate. Then Sarevan's back would twitch, dreading a stone or a hurled blade.

Zha'dan was swift to lose his pleasure in the game. In the night, when they camped, he was unwontedly silent. He would speak of it only once. "I've never been hated before. It hurts."

Hirel comforted him as only Hirel could. Sarevan lay apart and tried not to hear them. The trying only made it the more distinct. Whispers. A flicker of laughter. A breath caught as if in sudden pleasure. The rhythm of bodies moving together: the oldest dance in the world.

For the first time in a long while, he was aware of the weight of his torque. He took it off, straining a little, for the iron sheathing stiffened it. The night air was cold on his bared neck. He rubbed it, feeling of the scars, the circle of calluses that had grown from old galls. A bitter smile touched the corner of his mouth. An Asanian would not have known that he was not a slave, that he had not been one for long years. The first had been the worst. He had lived with numbroot salve and no little blood, and wounds that festered, and no bandages. Bandages only prolonged the agony.

He turned the blessed, brutal thing in his hands. Disguised, it looked like what it was: a badge of servitude. He held it to his breast. It was a cold lover. It granted no mortal peace.

Yet there was peace in it, bounded within its circle. Peace that came neither easily nor quickly, and yet it came. He was still Avaryan's priest. Neither murder nor treason could rob him of that.

The hunt had lost them. Sarevan marked it in the passing of pain.

"For a long while I could feel them looking for us," said Zha'dan. "They followed the seneldi we stole, I think, and when that trail proved false, cast wide for scent of us. Now there's nothing."

"They will wait ahead," Hirel said. "In Kundri'j."

He did not sound unduly cast down. The Golden City was far away yet, and they were advancing at a good pace, under a clear sky. The brilliance of autumn had begun to touch it; the land beneath was like and yet wholly unlike anything Sarevan had known in the east.

Hirel had been wise, he conceded now, to demand that they take the open road. In this the heart of Asanion, there were no shadows to hide in: no wilderness. The broad rolling plain was a pattern of walled towns joined together by roads, each town set like a jewel in a webwork of fields. The streams here ran straight and steady, wrought by men and not by gods; the trees were planted in rows that guided and guarded the wind, or in the artful disarray of the high ones' hunting grounds. And always there were the gods, the small ones and the great ones, worshipped in shrines at every milestone, and often between.

This was a tamed land. A company could not ride free over the fields, or wander from the highroad upon a path that though narrower might prove a shorter way to Kundri'j. Even the road had its laws and its divisions, its hierarchy of passers, from the slave on bare feet to the prince in his chariot. For *shiu'oth Olenyai* on swift seneldi, there was the broad smooth verge and an open way, but they might not stray into a field or onto the road itself. And even they had to stop for the passage of a personage, or slow to a crawl in traversing a town.

Now and then as they crossed Asanion, and more often as they drew near to the imperial city, they had seen caravans of slaves shuffling in chains from market to market. Hirel had seen, but he had not seen, as was the way in the Golden Empire. Zha'dan learned that custom quickly enough: his people had captives and the odd bought servant, though never whole market-droves of them. Sarevan, raised to abhor the thought of men kept like cattle, took refuge in the schooling of a prince. What one could not alter, one endured. And though it shamed him, he was glad for once of his mind's crippling, that he could not sense the misery that throbbed about the chained and plodding lines. He could look away and make himself forget.

But he had not had to ride within sight and sound of a slave market.

Sarevan did not ask the name of the town. He did not wish to know. It was large; it trumpeted prosperity. The road ran straight through it, dividing its market, so that travelers might pause to trade a wayworn senel for a fresh one, to satisfy hunger or thirst, to buy a weapon or a garment or a jewel.

Or a slave. There were, it seemed, a number of purveyors of such goods. Some did so within the privacy of walls, marked only by a sign above the door: a gilded manacle or an image carven in the likeness of a particular breed. Others set up tents, open or half open or enclosed. And here and there stood a simple platform, perhaps canopied, perhaps not, with a man crying the day's wares to a throng of buyers.

The three of them rode close together with Hirel in the middle. Even behind his mask, the boy seemed much as always. A little stiff, a little haughty, disdaining to take notice of the world about him. His mare was moving very slowly.

She stopped. Sarevan's glance strayed. When he looked back, the saddle was empty.

Bregalan spun on his haunches, breasting a current turned suddenly against him. Sarevan raged, but the stallion could advance no swifter than a walk, and for that he was jostled and cursed, even threatened by a charger with bronze-sheathed horns. He snorted and slashed; the destrier veered away. He plunged through the gap which the other had left.

Hirel's rough-coated mare stood abandoned and beginning to wander. Beyond her the road gave way to a broad shallow space filled with people, focused upon a platform and a huddle of slaves. They were all boys, the youngest perhaps nine summers old, the eldest a little older than Hirel. They were naked, collared, their hands bound behind them that they might not seek to cover their shame. Most were Asanians, slight and tawny; two were pale-skinned green-eyed Islanders; one was a tribesman of the north, haughty and sullen, and several standing close together had the faces of desert wanderers. They were all eunuchs, every one.

Sarevan found Hirel easily enough. He was taller than many, and he was the only one in Olenyai black. He stood on the edge of the crowd, straight as a carven knight. His mask was crumpled in his hand. Beneath the dusty headcloth his face was bloodless.

Sarevan followed his eyes. One of the Asanians stood a little

apart. The others were chained together, neck and ankle. This
one had his own chain and his own guard; his collar was gilded,
and from it hung a written tablet.

"A thoroughbred," said Hirel. "He will be offered last, and the
seller will accept no price unless he judges it sufficient. See, how
fair his skin, how pure a gold his hair, how flawless his face; how
perfect his age, the very flower of boyhood. I wonder that he is
sold in the open market; that is not common for slaves of his
quality. Perhaps his lord has a debt to pay."

It was too calm, that voice. His eyes were too wide and too pale.
Sarevan gripped his shoulder; it was rigid, impervious. "It's not
you, Hirel."

"A season ago," said Hirel, "it was. It would have—I would
have—"

Sarevan pulled him close. He did not resist. He was shaking; his
brow was damp. But he would not turn away from the boy who was
so much like himself: himself as he had been when Sarevan found
him, a child poised on the very brink of manhood. He had passed it
in the season since. This one never would.

"He is not you," Sarevan said again. "He is brass and painted
bone. He is soft; he is pretty; his eyes are not the eyes of the lion.
He is nothing beside you."

"He is myself," whispered Hirel.

Sarevan slapped him. He swayed, but his face did not change.
"You are beautiful," Sarevan said to him, "and very certainly a
man. No one now can make you like him. No one ever could. He is
false coin. You are true gold."

Hirel did not hear him. Something, at last, had broken him; or
something had roused that had been long and safely sleeping.

"He's gone away." Zha'dan, won through to them. Even muf-
fled in the mask, his voice was deeply worried. "I can't find him at
all."

Sarevan reached to touch Hirel, to wake him, to lift him, he
hardly knew which. The boy, who had been so limp and lifeless to
look at, turned demon under his hands. Steel slashed. Sarevan
recoiled. Hirel whipped about in a swirl of robes and bolted.

They bolted after him. He ran like a deer. The crowd parted
before him but closed behind, hindering the pursuit, jarring it
aside, even challenging it. Sarevan drew one of his swords. The
challenges stopped. The hindrances did not.

Hirel twisted and doubled and darted. His face when Sarevan glimpsed it sidelong was chalk-white. His eyes were blind.

The throngs thinned. The pursuit began to gain on its quarry. A procession swayed and chanted from a side way, full across their path: marchers innumerable, linked hand to hand, eyes closed, trancebound. All the narrow street was clogged with them. Even at his wits' end Sarevan could not bring himself to cut a path with steel.

The procession wound away. Hirel was gone. Zha'dan caught Sarevan's arm. "There!"

They sped from the narrow way down one narrower yet, walled in the stink of cities; past blind gates and blinder walls. There was no sign of Hirel. Zha'dan slowed to a stumbling trot, then to a walk. He swayed against Sarevan. He tore at his mask, rending it, flinging it away. His face was grey and sheened with sweat. "Hard," he whispered. "So many people. So many walls."

"Hirel?" Sarevan snapped at him, cruel with desperation.

His head tossed. He halted. He leaned on Sarevan and trembled. "Can't," he gasped. "Can't—"

Sarevan would have given his soul for a few breaths' worth of power. He had only pain. No Hirel, anywhere. The seneldi were lost and forgotten. Ulan had withdrawn to circle the town. Unless he too was bewitched, led astray, ensnared.

Zha'dan staggered erect. Both his swords were out. He whirled. Sarevan backed away from him, raging at heaven. Not Zha'dan too. One madman was more than enough. "Zha'dan!" Sarevan lashed out with all the power of his voice. "Zhaniedan!"

The Zhil'ari checked, turning slowly. His lips were drawn back from his teeth. "Caught," he said. "Trapped. Sorcery—it has the little stallion. I can't win him back. I have not that much power. I can't even stop them. I can't—" He broke off. The swords fell from his slackened fingers. With a low cry, of anger, of despair, he whipped about, spinning. The air filled with a thin high keening. He was drawing in his power.

Sarevan cried out, protesting. Zha'dan never heard. Light gathered to him. Lightnings cracked.

The walls were as bare and blank as cliffs of stone. The street darkened. From either end of it, men closed in. Grim men, armored, with drawn bows.

Sarevan knew an instant's bitter mirth. Whoever the enemy was, he was taking no chances. Not even Olenyai swords could stand against a whole company of archers.

An arrow sang past Sarevan's ear. It kindled. Zha'dan flung darts of power against the darts of mortal making. He laughed in the sweet madness of magery. Setting his teeth, making all his body a prayer, Sarevan flung himself at the young fool.

They went down together. Over them hissed a rain of arrows. Power spat and flared about Sarevan, but it did not touch him. Nor did it shield him. Sarevan knew the blow before it fell. It was neither spell nor weapon. It was a bubble, drifting over them. It broke. His body had gasped it in before his mind could act: gagging, cloying sweetness; and in it, irresistible, a heavy weight of sleep.

"Not sorcery," he tried to say. To instruct Zha'dan. "Not magic. This is alchemy." It was very important that Zha'dan know it. He did not know why. He only knew. "Alchemy," he repeated. *"Alchemy."*

Fifteen

ALCHEMY; BUT MAGEBORNE. THEIR HUNTERS HAD FOUND them, and were not minded to let them go.

Sarevan did not remember all of it. He saw the mages, the dark and the light. No doubt he gave them defiance. They gave him nothing. Zha'dan was there. They looked closely at both; they were not pleased. Their armed companions pried hands from sides, fingers from palms. The *Kasar* startled even the mages, although surely they had been looking for it. Perhaps they had not known how brightly it could burn.

They left Zha'dan to drugged dreams. They stripped Sarevan, though they did not take his torque; they scoured him without mercy. His body howled with the pain of cleanroot and ashes on his raw skin. They finished with something that was purest agony, and then it was blessedly cool, with a scent of herbs and healing.

They drugged him again. He fought it: the bruises lingered. Useless enough. They were too strong.

He woke at last from a black dream. He was cold and sick, and he hurt wherever a body could hurt. The earth rocked; he clutched at solidity.

Walls, closing in upon him. They rattled and shook. Cushions narrowed the narrow prison. He was naked on them, his hair loose and tangled, and for a moment he did not understand why he was startled. It was as copper-bright as it had ever been.

He was not alone in that hot and breathless space. Someone else strove with him for what air there was. Someone as bare as himself, as pale as he was dark, coiled in all apparent comfort at the utmost end of the box.

Only Hirel's face held Sarevan to sanity. It was calm to coldness; it was entirely conscious, and sane, and princely proud. It was not the face of one whose will had broken.

Sarevan struggled up. He could sit; he could kneel, if he crouched; he could not stand. Light came through intricate lattices, one on either side of him. It shifted, changing. They were moving.

He pressed his face to the lattice. Air brushed it, warm, heavy, but cooler and cleaner than what filled the box. Shadows passed. Trees, perhaps. Towers. Mounted men.

He dropped back. He wanted to claw the walls. He drew himself into a quivering knot and glared at Hirel.

The boy uncoiled, stretching. "You look like a panther at bay," he observed.

Sarevan snarled at him. "You did this. You led us into this."

Hirel's ease shattered. "I was tricked and trapped. I was"—he choked on it—"bespelled. I knew what they were doing to me. I could not stop it. Because—because I had seen what I would be, if I did not run then, run as far and as fast as I could."

"You may be a eunuch yet."

"I may die for this, but this much I have been promised: I will not die unmanned." Hirel had calmed himself again. "We are in a litter," he said, "like ladies who must travel swiftly. You see how we are prevented from escaping."

Sarevan did not. He found a door. He set his nails to the crack of it. It groaned but did not yield.

"If you succeed," said Hirel, cool and maddening, "where will you go? An armed company surrounds us. We are unarmed and unarmored. We are also," he pointed out, "unclad."

"What difference does that make?"

Hirel looked as if he could not choose between laughter and shock. "To you, perhaps, none. To me, enough. I am not a spectacle for lowborn eyes to see."

"Why? You have nothing to be ashamed of."

"I have a body," Hirel snapped.

Sarevan was mute. Hirel withdrew again, barricading himself with cushions. The silence stretched. The walls closed in. Sarevan set all his will to the task of enduring. Of keeping himself from going mad like an ul-cat in a cage.

After an eternal while Hirel spoke, low and taut. "The people must not see. That I am mortal. That I wear flesh like any man of them. That my blood is as red as theirs, and flows as freely. I am royal; every inch of me is holy. My nails were never cut save by priests, with many prayers and incantations. My hair was never cut at all. The water of my bath was preserved for the anointing of the sick."

"What did you do with nature's tribute? House it in gold and give it to the gods?"

Hirel's breath hissed. "I did not say that I believed in it! I meant to change it when I could. But until I came into my power, I was my power's slave. I served it most dutifully. I was a very proper prince, O prince of savages."

"Wise," said Sarevan. "Did anyone ever know how much of your mind was your own?"

The golden eyes hooded. "A prince's body belongs to his people. His mind does not enter into it."

"But they aren't supposed to know you have a body."

"Flesh," Hirel said. He thrust out his arm. Sunlight shattered on the lattice, turned the fine hairs to sparks of gold, found a bruise and a healing cut and an old white scar. "Blood and bone. Humanity. When I am emperor, I will be not even that. I will be pure royal image."

Sarevan shivered in the breathless heat. He felt very mortal. His throat was dry and his face itched and he ached. He said, "*When* you are emperor? Will you come to it now?"

Hirel smiled. It was not a comfortable smile. "I will come to it. I am captive; I am not dead. And I do not surrender. Nor do I ever forgive."

"I pity your enemies."

"Do that," said Hirel, still smiling.

With the sun's setting, their prison halted. Sarevan had not spoken for a very long while. He dared not, lest he howl like a beast. He had been imprisoned before; he had been shut up in close walls, for punishment, for training as mage and priest. But he had had power. He had not been trapped within himself. He had not had to fight to breathe, to think, to be himself and not mere mindless panic.

With a scraping of bolts, the door opened. He had no will left. He burst into the light. Bodies barred him. He swept them away. He struck stone. Wall. Gate—

Men closed upon him. He fought them. They were too many, and they were armored. His hands could only rock them; could not fell them. They caught him, bound him, dragged him into quiet.

Hirel sat in it, robed from throat to toe, sipping from a cup. The walls about him were blessedly far away.

Sarevan's captors flung him into the chamber and bolted the door upon him. He lay on musty carpets, gasping, beginning to be sane again. The cords were twisted cruelly tight. His arms throbbed.

Hirel knelt by him and began to worry at the knots. "Our jailers are most impressed," he said, "with the perfection of your savagery."

"It's not the cage," Sarevan said carefully. "It's that I can't get my mind out of it. I can't breathe inside; I can't breathe without."

Hirel could not possibly understand. Or perhaps, and that may have been worse, he could. "You are not a creature of sealed palaces," he said.

Sarevan shuddered. He tried to be light, to turn his mind away from the dark. "Are our captors hoping I'll maul you to death?"

"It would be convenient," Hirel said.

"To whom?"

The boy shrugged. "I asked. I was not answered."

One by one the knots yielded. The cords fell away. Sarevan lay and tried to make his numbed arms obey his will.

Hirel sat on his heels, watching. After a moment he caught one of Sarevan's arms, bringing it back to life again with those clever fingers of his. "I have not seen our mageling," he said. "Nor our grey hunter."

Captivity had weakened Sarevan's wits. He had to struggle to understand. Hope leaped; died. "Dead. Or fled."

"Perhaps." Hirel exchanged one arm for the other. "We are wanted alive. No one moved to cut you down when you broke free. They gave way rather than wound you."

"Hostages?" The irony struck Sarevan; he laughed, though it hurt. "It may be well enough for me, as long as someone in Asanion is holding me. But for you . . ."

"I think they do not know me," said Hirel. "Yet."

He stood abruptly. Sarevan sat up, opening his mouth to speak. Hirel strode to the door and spoke. He raised his voice barely enough, Sarevan would have thought, to pass the panel, but its inflection raised Sarevan's hackles. He had never heard the twelve tones of High Asanian wielded with such deadly subtlety, by one bred to the art. "O thou who guardest this door, send to thy master and tell him. The prince who is above princes would speak to him."

No sound came back from without. Hirel returned to the chamber's center, settled himself on the mound of cushions there, picked up his cup again. His free hand indicated the table beside him. "Eat," he said.

Sarevan was more than glad to obey, though warily, mistrusting Asanian sauces. He found himself yearning for good plain roast wildbuck, or fruit untainted with spices, or simple peasant cheese. Even the language in which he had always been pleased enough to address Hirel had grown to a mighty burden. He ate in silence, to quiet his stomach, tasting little. He drank sour Asanian wine. He prowled the space, which was endurable, wide but windowless. He was going to break again. Anger did not help him. Should Keruvarion's high prince go mad like an animal, simply for a few hours' confinement?

Bolts rattled. Sarevan spun, poised. The door boomed back. Armed men poured through it. They passed Hirel without a glance, spreading to surround Sarevan.

"Thou wilt not touch him," the boy said, again in that mastery of tones which came close to sorcery.

The guards paused. Sarevan did not move. They leveled their spears, but neither touched him nor threatened him. His back was to the wall. He grinned suddenly, leaned against it, folded his arms. The men were not, he noticed, staring at him. They were working very hard at it. The tallest came barely to his chin. The smallest had to look up or sidewise, or close his eyes altogether, lest they fix on what he was trying hardest not to see. "What's the matter?" Sarevan asked him. "Haven't you ever seen a man before?"

The Asanian flushed. He did not take vengeance with his spear. Sarevan admired him for that, and said so. He flushed more deeply yet, and scowled terribly.

With the chamber well and most valiantly secured, the captain of guards stepped back from the door, sword raised in salute. All of his men who were not hedging Sarevan with bronze clapped blades to shields and knelt.

Their master entered at his leisure, escorted by a pair of Uvarra's priests, one in silver grey and one in dusky violet. Sarevan almost laughed. He carried himself like an emperor, and yet he was as small as a child. He might have been taken for one, fair and smooth as his face was, all perfect ivory: a nine years' youngling of indeterminate gender, wrapped in fold on fold of midnight silk. But his eyes were never a child's. They were like Hirel's, clear gold, seeming whiteless unless they opened very wide; and they were bitterly bright.

Hirel rose. He was tall here, even young as he was; he stood a full head above that perfect miniature of a man.

Sarevan, watching, smiled. The other carried himself like an emperor. Hirel Uverias had no need to. It was beautifully played. "Brother," he said, cool, unsurprised.

Indeed. They were very like. Hirel, sun-painted, thinned and hardened with travel, looked almost the elder.

"Brother," said the silken mannikin. His voice was sweet and nearly sexless. "I rejoice to see you well."

Hirel inclined his head. Then he paused, as if he waited. His eyes were very steady.

For the merest flicker of an instant, the other lost his poise. Hirel never moved. Slowly his brother knelt. More slowly yet under those quiet relentless eyes, he prostrated himself. His mages followed him.

Hirel looked down at them all. No smile touched his lips, but Sarevan found one in the light behind his eyes.

The princeling rose with grace, the mages with relief. Hirel did not offer his hand. He sat and tucked up his feet and said, "Your bravos should be whipped. They have given insult to a prince."

"That has been remedied," his brother said. Aranos, Sarevan was prepared to name him.

"It has not," said Hirel.

Aranos followed his eyes. Sarevan smiled at them both. The lesser prince regarded him with interest and without visible embarrassment. The fine brows went up. Aranos approached. His spearmen drew back, not without reluctance. He put out a hand. It was child-small; its nails were fully as long as the fingers from which they grew, warded in jeweled sheaths. Sarevan shivered at the brush of those glittering claws, but his smile held. "Little man," he said, purring, "I give you leave to touch me."

The hand paused. Aranos had to tilt his head well back to look into Sarevan's face. He was not at all afraid. "You are splendid," he said.

He meant it; or he was far too subtle for Sarevan's outland innocence. Or was simplicity another kind of subtlety?

"Are you insulted?" asked Aranos.

Sarevan thought about it. "That," he answered in time, "is not what I would call it. But here . . . yes. It is an insult."

Aranos bowed his head. He gestured. A garment came quickly enough to interest Sarevan. It was a robe like Hirel's, of heavy raw silk. It fit, which was more interesting still. The servant who brought it brought also a comb, which, when Sarevan had been persuaded to sit beside Hirel, he plied with a master's skill.

Aranos watched and waited. He did not sit. His robes, Sarevan thought, must have been deadly heavy. There were seven of them, one atop the other, each cut to show the one beneath.

Hirel, at his ease in a single robe, leaned back upon his cushions. "You will explain the meaning of this," he said. "We are taken like criminals. We are transported in a litter like women, but set within like slaves, in robeless shame. And yet you pay me homage. Is it," he asked very gently, "that you mean to mock me?"

"Errors have been committed," said Aranos with equal gentleness. His mages were pale; their eyes had lowered. "They will not be repeated."

"We are therefore to be set free?"

"I did not say that."

"Ah," said Hirel. Only that.

"You mistake me," Aranos said. "The Olenyai who rode with you were sworn to betray you; to complete what was left undone by Vuad and Sayel. Your companion they were to treat likewise and to send back to his father with the compliments of the Golden Empire."

Calm though he willed himself to be, Sarevan shuddered. Hirel was white about the lips. "That would not have been wise of them," he said.

"Indeed not. My mages had word of the plot; they were undertaking to warn you. But matters moved too swiftly, as did you. You mistook their sending, but it saved you. When the traitors came to seize you, you were gone."

"Even should I believe that there was a conspiracy to destroy me," Hirel said, "still I would wonder. A loyal man does not drug and abduct his high prince."

"There was no time to do otherwise. Your betrayers were closing in upon you. It was most ill-advised, that disguise of yours. No true Olenyas could have been deceived by it; and word passed swiftly that three impostors had taken the road to Kundri'j, and two of them extraordinarily tall, and one on a blue-eyed stallion."

"I do not see one of them, though he was caught with us. Nor have I seen the stallion."

"You shall see them," Aranos said. "Come now, my brother and my lord. You have always suspected me of hungering after your titles: of lying and deceiving and even slaying in order to gain them. And yet the brothers whom you thought you loved, whom you went so far as to trust, turned against you. Can you alter your vision of me? Can you begin to see that I may not be your enemy?"

"You were the heir apparent until I was born."

"Apparent only," said Aranos. "It was known to me even before our father wedded your mother that I would be supplanted by a legitimate son. When our father went in pursuit of the Gileni princess, there was open fear in the High Court, and no little resistance to the prospect of a halfblood heir; but heir most certainly that child would be. When he returned alone and rejected, to drown his sorrows in his harem and thereby to sire his mighty army of sons, I knew that in the end he would surrender to necessity. As indeed he did. He took the sister-bride who was chosen for him. He sired your sisters, those who died of their frailty and the one who lived to be her mother's image. Then at last he sired you. I would have been glad; I would have been properly your brother. But your mother would not abide me. The others she feared little or not at all. I who was eldest, whose blood was high and quite as pure as your own, in her eyes was deadly. Neither of you ever sought to learn the truth of me."

Sarevan looked from one to the other of them. He did not try to speak. Hirel was white and rigid. Aranos was pure limpid verity.

Very slowly Hirel said, "I do not know whom to trust."

"You trust yon outland prince."

Hirel's eyes flashed on Sarevan, white-rimmed as a startled senel's. "He is not Asanian."

"Do you therefore mistrust yourself?"

Hirel's fists clenched upon his knees. He drew a swift sharp breath. "Prove yourself to me. Ride with me to Kundri'j. Stand behind me on Autumn Firstday. Name me living man; proclaim me high prince before our father."

Sarevan watched Aranos narrowly. The princeling seemed unshaken and unstartled. He said with perfect calm, "So I had meant to do."

"If you lie," said Hirel softly, "then you had best destroy me now. For if I live, even if I live unmanned, or slave, or cripple, I will have your life in return for your treachery."

"I do not lie," Aranos said. He went down once more, prostrating himself, kissing the floor at Hirel's feet. "You are my high prince. You will be my emperor."

Aranos kept at least one of his promises. His guards brought Zha'dan to them. The Zhil'ari was unharmed save for a goodly measure of Sarevan's own trapped terrors, and quite as bare as Sarevan had been. He had refused a robe; they had refused him a kilt. He greeted his companions with a cry of joy and a leap that brought blades leaping out of sheaths. Hirel had to fend off the

guards: Sarevan had had the breath crushed out of him. Zha'dan
had lost even tradespeech; he babbled in his own tongue, too fast
for Sarevan to follow, until Sarevan shook him into silence.

He drew back, searching Sarevan's face. "They caged you," he
said. There was no lightness in him; none of the bright reckless
temper with which he liked to mask what he was. "I heard you. I
thought they had broken you."

"Am I so fragile?" Sarevan asked him, the sharper for that he
came so close to the truth.

He frowned. "They think they know what you are. They're
fools."

"Are they treacherous?"

"They all are, here." Zha'dan looked as if his head hurt. "They
don't want to kill you. Either of you. Yet. The ivory doll—have you
seen him? He has more in that tiny head of his than anyone might
imagine. I don't like him," said Zha'dan, "but he thinks it's to his
advantage to serve the little stallion. For now."

"I wonder why," said Sarevan.

He was thinking aloud, but Hirel answered him. "Convenience.
And cleverness. If all is as he has told us, we owe him a debt for our
escape. That can be parlayed into very great power."

"But not imperial power."

"He is my heir until I sire a son."

"You'd best get about it, then, hadn't you?"

Hirel blushed, but his tongue had not lost its sting. "Can you
preach to me, O priest of the Sun?"

Sarevan grinned. "A priest can always preach. It's practice he
has to walk shy of." He shook off levity. "Are you going to trust
him?"

"I have little choice."

Sarevan bowed to that. "We can all walk warily. I'll guard your
back; will you guard mine?"

"Until it behooves me to betray you," answered Hirel, "yes."

Hirel armed himself and rode in the free air as one of Aranos'
men-at-arms. He did not even need his helmet unless he wished to
wear it: his face was pure High Asanian, but there were others like
it in the company.

Sarevan and Zha'dan had no such fortune. Sarevan refused

flatly the concealment of the litter, and shied away from Aranos' great curtained chariot with its team of blue dun mares. He was betraying his cowardice, he knew it, but he could not master himself. He insisted on his freedom and the sweet familiarity of Bregalan's back. He won it, and Zha'dan won it with him, but as always, at a price. He wore armor from head to foot, magewrought to his measure, with a great masked helm. It was ridiculously ornate and ridiculously uncomfortable, but it matched him to the small company of the princeling's personal guard; and it hid all his strangenesses.

The mages rode with their master. The forging had wearied them; they slept, perhaps, behind the swaying curtains. Sarevan did not like to think that a darkmage had had a hand in the making of his armor. It seemed perfectly earthly gilded bronze; no stink of evil clung to it. Only when he first put it on did his branded hand throb as at the touch of power; thereafter he had no pain, of hand or of head.

If a lordling of the Middle Court or a riding of *shiu'oth Olenyai* could win free passage on the roads, a prince of the High Court could empty them before him. To him all inns were open, all posthouses his own to command; if that did not please him, he had his way of the local lords. No one impeded him; no one ventured to question him.

That Hirel had not chosen to ride in comfort with his brother was a mild scandal in the guard. Sarevan and Zha'dan were endurable: they were only outlanders, however royal they might consider themselves, and they did not inflict their barbarian faces on good human men. Hirel was more than human, and they all knew it. They liked not at all to have him riding knee to knee with the least of them, cropped head bare, helmet on saddlebow in the heat, looking as mortal as any man.

He did not seem to notice, still less to care. Often he rode by Sarevan at the tail of the princeling's personal guard and the head of the company of men-at-arms. Sometimes he reached across as if he could not help it, and stroked Bregalan's neck. He did not ask to ride the stallion, nor would he let Sarevan offer it. He was turned in upon himself. He spoke, sometimes, in the beginning, but the

Asanians would not answer him. After the first morning he did not speak at all.

On the fourth night of the compact with Aranos, three days yet at swift pace from Kundri'j Asan and four days shy of Autumn Firstday, the princeling took an inn for himself. Its patrons left perforce, with no objections that they let him or his small army hear.

It was not fitting, Sarevan had been told the first night he tried it, that he bed down with the guard. He suspected that they were not pleased to bed down with a barbarian. He was given a chamber of his own; he was allowed to keep Zha'dan with him. Tonight he had been offered his choice of the house's women, an error which had not been committed before. Someone must have forgotten to warn the innkeeper. He was interested to witness Hirel's swift and scathing refusal on his behalf. It was much swifter and more scathing than his own would have been.

Everyone looked at Zha'dan and thought he understood. Some looked at Hirel, longer, and grew very wise. The boy quelled them by choosing the most comely of the women and departing for his chamber, from which neither of them returned.

Sarevan went slowly to his solitary bed. Zha'dan took station across the door, too wise to long for what he could not have, too fastidious to sample the innkeeper's culls. "Once was enough," he said as he spread his blanket. "They're not clean, these people. No wonder they shave themselves smooth. Else they'd crawl with vermin."

"They say much the same of us, I think," Sarevan said.

Zha'dan snorted. Even if he had not bathed every day, more often if he could manage it, he would not have deigned to entertain small itching guests. Vermin did not like mages, even apprentice mages of the Zhil'ari.

Some air of it must still have clung to Sarevan. He was in comfort, in that respect at least. He lay and closed his eyes and tried not to think. It was hard. Last night, after a blessed respite, he had dreamed again. The old darkness; the old fear. But at the end of it, strangeness, which he both hoped and feared was not prophecy but plain dreaming born of wish and fear and the day's living.

It was clear in him even yet, try though he would to blot it out.
After the lightning-torn blackness of foreseeing, a soft light.
Lamplight on walls of grey stone; a tapestry, rich and intricate,
alive with myriad figures: beasts, birds, blossoms, a jeweled
dragonel. He was lying on softness, languid, free for a little while
of either horror or urgency; although there was a strangeness in
him, in the way he lay, in the way his body felt, it did not trouble
him. Stranger still was the way his heart was singing.

A light finger caressed his cheek. Its touch was very distinct. It
made him shiver with pleasure. He turned his head. In his dream
he knew no surprise at all, nor any of the alarm that in waking
would have cast him into flight. It was perfectly and properly right
that Hirel should be lying there with all his masks laid aside,
smiling a warm and sated smile. Sarevan's mind had not even
troubled to transform him into a woman. He was a little older and
a great deal larger—as large, impossibly, as Sarevan himself—and
quite incontestably a man.

Perhaps he would have spoken. Sarevan never knew. Zha'dan
had awakened him, calling him to the sunrise prayer and the day's
riding.

All day, as they rode, Sarevan had caught himself shooting
glances at the boy: not a simple feat in the heavy gilded helm. Hirel
showed no signs of growing suddenly to match Sarevan's Gileni
height. Sarevan's body did not yearn toward him as it had in the
dream, although he was most comely in the plain harness of a
man-at-arms, erect and proud, sitting his mount with the easy
grace of the born rider.

It was the mind, Sarevan told himself as he lay alone. It confused
the body with the soul. He did not want Hirel for his bed.

Then why, asked a small wicked portion of his self, was he
tossing in it like a thwarted lover?

Because he was dream-maddened. Because on Autumn Firstday
he would be one-and-twenty, and his body had never known either
woman or man, but his mind—his wild mageling's mind—had
known them both very well indeed.

The Litany of Pain frayed in his head and scattered. He tried to
mock himself. It was the Asanian air. It was full of lechery. He
offended its sense of rightness; it struggled to make him like all the

rest of the Golden Empire. Would it then turn his copper to gold and bleach his skin to ivory?

He rose on his elbow, regarding himself in the nightlamp's flicker. He was quite as perfectly a mongrel as he had ever been, and rather more rampantly male than he was wont to be. He covered it, somewhat, with the robe which one was expected to wear to sleep here: odd constricting custom, but useful if one were in a state which one did not wish to proclaim to every eye.

Zha'dan did not stir when Sarevan stepped over him. Sarevan prowled softly through the passages. Movement cooled him a little. No one else was abroad. Aranos' guards eyed him warily but did not challenge him.

The kitchen's fires were banked, cooks and scullions snoring in concert. A grin of pure mischief found its way to Sarevan's face. Royal prince and man grown he might be, but he was young yet; and it took more than a year or six to forget old skills. He uncovered a trove of sweet cakes and a flask of the thin sour wine that was all they seemed to drink here. He filled a napkin, appropriated the flask.

A small door opened on starlight and coolness. He had found the kitchen garden; a breeze was keeping at bay the stink of the midden. Near the wall stood a bench overhung by a tree in full and fragrant fruit. He sat back against the bole, filling himself with cakes and fruit, drinking from the flask. His body's heat had all but faded; the ache of it was passing. He stretched to pluck another sweetapple.

His hand stopped. Someone was walking toward him among the beds of herbs. A remnant of youthful guilt made him tense to bolt. The rest of him remembered that he was a wild boy no longer; no one would dare now to thrash him for his thievery.

He finished plucking the apple. His eyes sharpened. Not one figure approached him but two. The other paced on four legs, a great graceful shadow with eyes that, turning upon him, flashed sudden green.

He forgot guilt, manhood, gluttony, even the very fruit in his hand. Ulan met him in midleap, singing his joy-song. "Brother," Sarevan sang back in a loving purr. "O brother!"

Ulan butted him full in his center. He dropped to his rump half in the path, half in pungent herbs. He clung to the great neck and laughed, breathing cat-musk and silversage, while Ulan feigned with mighty snarlings to devour him. It was love, purely. He lost himself in it.

He remembered the sweetapple first. He was still holding it. He laughed at that, using Ulan for a handhold as he pulled himself to his feet.

He was almost body to body with Ulan's erstwhile companion. It was, his skin knew utterly and instantly, a woman. He drew back swiftly, not quite recoiling, shaping a spate of apologies.

None of them passed his tongue. The stranger had become a shape he knew: plain epicene Asanian, he had thought the creature, or even a eunuch. Tonsured for Uvarra's service; robed as a mage. The darkmage.

Knowledge and starlight limned her face, transformed eunuch softness into very feminine strength. She was not beautiful. She did not need to be. She made his body sing.

And yet his heart was cold. She had come with Ulan. A black sorceress. She had seen him in naked joy. She knew, now, the most mortal of his weaknesses.

Ulan purred against him. The cat was not bewitched. Sarevan would have known. There was no mark on him; no stink of evil.

Perhaps she sensed Sarevan's thoughts. She seemed amused. "He is a great hunter, your brother," she said. "Did you know that he tracks by scent of power? He marked mine. He cast me from my bed, that I might conduct him to you."

All of Sarevan's training cried to him that she lied; that no servant of darkness ever told the truth. And yet he knew that it was so. Ulan could scent magery. It would be like him to seek out a mage, to demand an escort to his lost brother. He knew how a simple man would see him; he did not like to be shot at.

And yet, a darkmage. Sarevan glared at the cat. He felt betrayed.

Ulan sat, yawned, began to lick his paw. His nose wrinkled. He did not like the scent of silversage.

Yes, the witch was amused. "I see," she said, "that the tales are in error that give you the readiest tongue in Keruvarion. Or is it that a priest of your order may not address a woman?"

Sarevan's cheeks flamed. "What do I have to say to you? You are a slave of the dark."

"Are you any less a slave of the light?" she inquired calmly.

"Your kind should be scoured from the earth."

She sat on the bench which Sarevan had abandoned. Her robe was belted loosely; it opened as she moved. He caught a glimpse of full and lovely breasts.

His own was not belted at all. He clutched it about him.

She smiled. "One always fears most what one knows least."

"I know all I need to know."

That was feeble, and they both knew it. She took up a cake, nibbled it with visible pleasure. "Avaryan was Uvarra, long ago. She has kept her two faces. He has bound himself to one alone. That I serve the night, that my power is of the moons' dark, does not bar me from either the arts or the worship of the light."

"There, priestess, you speak false. No servant of Night can abide the Sun."

"Is it so among your people?" She sounded both shocked and sad. "Is it all so twisted? Do you know nothing of the truth?"

The hand with the apple in it whipped back. She sat still, clear-eyed, unfrightened. She looked horribly like Hirel. With a curse he spun away from her, flinging the apple with all his strength. It arced high over the wall. He never heard it fall.

"You know," she said. "In your heart, you know. If you did not, you would not have come to Asanion."

A shudder racked him. "I came to stop a war."

"Just so."

He whirled. "You came to stop me. You find I can't be ensorceled. You think I can be seduced. First with my brother; then with your body."

She laughed in pure mirth. "See what Avaryan's vows can do to a man! If I seduced you, prince, it would not be to destroy you. It would be to heal you."

Asanian cant. It sickened him. "What makes you think that I could want you?"

"In your condition," she said with sweet malice, "any female would suffice." She looked him up and down. "You will prosper in Kundri'j. The High Court will find even your rudeness delightful."

"I'm going to be allowed to get so far?"

"We have labored long to see that you do."

"Why?"

"Rude," she mused to herself, "or perhaps simply unsubtle. And young; and ill taught; and I think, though you are no coward, afraid. It is not easy to learn that all one believed in is a lie."

"Not all," he whispered.

"Most." She laced her fingers in her lap. "I am not what you expected, am I? I am almost human."

"Your power stands against all that I am."

"Does it? Have you ever encountered a true darkmage?"

"I have taken the power of one. I slew his ally; she took my power with her. She was," said Sarevan tightly, "very like you."

"They were a testing. You failed it."

He shut his eyes. His fists were clenched. He should turn and walk away, for his soul's sake. He could not. "I have faced an Eye of Power. It was evil beyond conceiving. No sane mind could endure it, still less hope to wield it."

"Not all power is either easy or pleasant. Some of it must be neither; just as the summer requires winter's cold for its fulfillment."

That was the truth of his dream. She mocked it. For if she did not, then all that he had done had been to serve the dark, and he was worse than a traitor: he had betrayed his god.

"We of the Mageguild know what is," she said, "and what must be. I tell you a secret, Sun-prince. Every mage is one of two. Every initiate is chosen by a facet of the power, dark or light; and every one finds his match in another who is his opposite."

His eyes snapped open.

"So," she said, "are we complete. No dark without light. No light without dark. Balance, always."

"Then the other priest—is—"

"My brother. My other self."

He tossed his head. His voice shook; he could not steady it. "You should not have told me that."

"You will not betray us."

He laughed. It was half a sob. "I am the blackest traitor who has ever been."

"I trust you," she said. She stood and bowed in Asanian fashion, hands to breast. "Good night, high prince. May the darkness give you rest."

Sarevan gasped, shuddered. When he had his voice again, she was gone.

Sixteen

T HEY CALLED HER QUEEN OF CITIES, HEART OF THE GOLDEN Empire, most ancient of the dwellings of mankind, sacred whore, bride of emperors, throne of the gods: Kundri'j Asan. She sprawled across the plain of Greatflood, Shahriz'uan the mighty that bore the heart's blood of Asanion, flowing from the wastes of ice to the Burning Sea. There was no greater city, none older and none more beautiful. Its walls were ninefold, sheathed each in precious stone: white marble, black marble, lapis, carnelian, jasper, malachite and ice-blue agate; and the eighth was silver, and the ninth was all gold. Within the circles of the city were a thousand temples, domes and spires crusted with jewels and with gold, and among them the mansions of princes, the hovels of paupers, the dwellings and the shops, the forges and the markets, tanneries, perfumeries, silkweavers and netweavers, stables and mews and shambles, side by side and interwoven in the ordered disorder of a living thing.

Sarevan saw little enough of it, his first day in it. Aranos entered it like a storm off the plains, cleaving its crowds, thundering up the Processional Way on which none might ride but princes or the followings of princes. They were not acclaimed as a high lord would be in Keruvarion. Silence was Asanian reverence. It was eerie to Varyani senses, to ride in that wave of stillness; to be the only clamor within their ears' reach. And as far as their eyes could stretch, only a sea of bent backs, bowed heads, bodies prostrate upon the stones.

The Golden Palace opened to embrace them. Its arms were splendid and cold. Its secrets were impenetrable.

Not for long, Sarevan promised himself. He had to leave Bregalan, who was not pleased; he had Aranos' word of honor that the stallion would be accorded the reverence due a king. Ulan and Zha'dan clung close to him, pressing against him, darting wary glances from under lowered brows.

They were led in haste to Aranos' chambers and there secluded, with picked guards at the door. Aranos left them with a warning. "Be free of these rooms," he said. "But do not wander abroad, nor eat nor drink aught but what these my slaves shall bring you."

None of them answered him. Hirel stood very still and watched him go. Then, slowly, he turned about. Sarevan very nearly forgot all his wisdom. Came perilously close to pulling the boy into his arms: stroking him, shaking him, shouting at him—anything to warm that slowly chilling face.

A great anger rose to fill Sarevan's soul. It was not his wonted, fiery temper, as swiftly calmed as provoked. It was cold; it was bitter. It found its echo and its spur in Hirel's eyes. No man should live the life these chambers spoke of. Splendid, remote, and chill. Forbidden human warmth, forbidden even the touch of a hand, because he was royal, because he was sacred, because he would be emperor, and the emperor must be more than a man.

And less. As the image of a god is more, because it stands high and apart in its perfection. As that same image is less, because it has no heart. It is only gilded stone. Lifeless and soulless, mere empty beauty, cold to the touch and comfortless.

Flesh yielded under Sarevan's fingers; blood pulsed, muscle tautened in resistance. But the eyes were jet and amber. "Let me go," said Hirel.

"I will not," said Sarevan.

The eyes measured him. He knew to the last degree what their judgment would be. Outlander; barbarian. Blatant and improbable mongrel. Mage who had been, cripple who was. And against all of that: Prince. Emperor's son. Son of the son of a god.

He was, perhaps, worthy to kiss one of those slender and surpassingly comely feet.

Sarevan laughed suddenly, opened his hands, dealt the boy a cuff that was half a caress. "Cubling, stop trying to glare down your nose at me."

Hirel's nostrils flared. "You—"

"Bastard?" Sarevan suggested helpfully. "Son of a hound? Slave's whelp? Sensible man?"

"*Sensible* man!" Hirel spat the words. Caught himself. Struggled for composure. Failed dismally. "*You?*"

"Are you? You let Aranos bring us to this place, after all. What were you hoping for? That the rest of your brothers would be here to arrange your convenient disposal?"

"Aranos may have gone to do just that." But Hirel was calming, and not into that cold and terrible stillness. He turned about again, more quickly than before. "I have never been here," he said.

"What, never?"

Sarevan won a burning glance. It comforted him. "Are yours different?" he asked.

Hirel shrugged. "Mine are white and gold. And larger, a little. He is Second Prince before the Golden Throne. I am high prince. Will be. Tomorrow."

"Tomorrow," Sarevan agreed, setting all his confidence in it.

They wandered through the rooms. They were somber in their splendor, black and silver and midnight blue. There were very many of them.

Zha'dan was round-eyed. "Ostentatious," Sarevan said to him, deprecating room on room of nothing but clothing. One whole chamber held only gloves. Gloves for dancing. Gloves for riding in one's chariot. Gloves that were all a crust of jewels, for dazzling the High Court. Gloves that were finer than gossamer, for receiving one's concubines.

"For receiving one's concubines?" Sarevan repeated, holding one up to the lamp's light. It was like a doll's glove, tiny and perfect and utterly absurd.

Hirel snatched it out of his hand and flung it against the wall. "Do not mock what you cannot understand!"

They stared at him. He seemed to have forgotten them. He

confronted a mirror. It reflected a young man in plain armor with
the dust of travel thick upon him, and his face white beneath it, and
his eyes wild. "Look at me," he said. They were mute, looking.
Hirel raised a clenched fist, bit down hard. Blood sprang, sudden
and frightening. He did not heed it. He drew breath, shuddering.
"I shall be a disgrace. They will mock me, all of them. My head
shorn, my body grown lank and awkward, my voice less sweet than
a raven's. I have dwelt among the lowborn; I have broken bread
with them. I have walked in the sun, all bare, and the sun has
stained me. And I have touched—I have touched—"

Sarevan did not stop to think. He pulled him in. Stroked him,
shook him, murmured words forgotten before they were spoken.
And Hirel suffered it. For a very little while he clung, trembling.

He stiffened. Sarevan let him go. His hand was still bleeding. He
sucked on it; saw what he was doing; thrust it down. "You see," he
said, faint and bitter. "I am not worthy."

"You're more worthy of princehood now than you ever were."
Sarevan took the wounded hand between his own. "Listen to me,
Hirel Uverias. You've changed, yes. Inevitably. You've grown. The
child I found in a fernbrake was a soft thing, plump and pretty like
a lady's lapcat. Even after his few days' suffering, he knew surely
that the world belonged to him; he was the center of it, and all the
rest existed to serve him. He was an insufferable little creature. I
had all I could do not to throw him across my knee and spank him
soundly."

Hirel flung up his head in outrage. But he did not say what once
he would have said.

Sarevan saluted him, not all in mockery. "You see? You're not a
man yet, not by a long road, but you're well started on it. You'll
certainly make a prince."

Hirel's lips thinned. He raised his chin minutely. He began to
speak; stopped. He spun on his heel and stalked toward the outer
rooms, and Aranos' slaves, and a bath and food and a bed for his
weary body.

The slaves had no little to endure. Hirel they seemed delighted
to serve, but the outlanders and the great cat both shocked and
terrified them. Sarevan began it in the bath, by stripping and
plunging into the great basin and swimming from end to end of it.

Hirel, being scoured clean on the grate beside the pool, allowed himself the shadow of a grin.

Sarevan folded his arms on the basin's rim and floated, and grinned back. Zha'dan was watching the scrubbing and the pumicing with real dismay. One or two of the slaves eyed him; one had a razor in hand. Zha'dan took refuge with Sarevan in the pool. "He hardly has any fleece yet," the Zhil'ari said of Hirel, "and look: they're taking it. How can he let them?"

"It's the custom here," said Sarevan.

"Not for us!"

"Certainly not," Sarevan said, baring his teeth at the slave with the razor. The eunuch blanched and backed away. "We're outland princes. We keep our own customs."

"If that's so," said Zha'dan, "I want a kilt. And paint. And gauds. I want to look like a man again."

Aranos' slaves were ingenious: they found all three. Sarevan did his braids for him. It was not a thing a slave could do; it were best done by a lover. A Sun-prince sufficed. Zha'dan was almost purring, at ease with himself for the first time since he came to Endros Avaryan.

His contentment coaxed a smile out of Hirel, which passed too quickly. The boy would not eat, though he would drink: too much, to Sarevan's mind. He would not hear of stopping. When Sarevan pressed, Hirel drove them all out, cursing them with acid softness.

Sarevan let himself be driven. Hirel was in no mood to accept any comfort that he could give. Perhaps wine and solitude would calm him; steel him to face what on the morrow he must face.

The bed to which Sarevan was led was a very comfortable one, a proper eastern bed hung on a frame of sweetwood and covered with scarlet silk. Sarevan buried himself in it. Ulan poured himself across the foot of it. Zha'dan set himself, as was his wont, across the door.

Sarevan worked his toes into Ulan's thick fur and sighed. Tonight, he thought, he could sleep. It made him smile, though with a touch of bitterness. They said it of his father: he always slept in perfect peace before a battle.

He did not want to think of his father, whom tomorrow he would betray before the High Court of Asanion.

He rubbed the healing skin beneath his beard, lazily, yawning. His eyelids fell of their own weight.

A supple body lay beside him. Wise fingers found the knots of tension in his back. Warm lips followed, and a nip of teeth.

Sarevan thrust himself up on his hands. "Damn it, who told them I wanted—"

Hirel slid beneath him, all gold in the nightlamp's glow. Sarevan pulled away with tight-leashed violence. "What are you doing here? Zha'dan's not here; he's over yonder. Get out of my bed!"

"Prince," said Hirel, and he sounded not at all like the boy whom Sarevan had thought he knew. This was a man, weary to exhaustion, with no strength left for temper. "Prince, forbear. Or I swear to you, I will weep, and if I weep you will see me do it, and if you see me I will hate you for it."

The tears had already begun. Sarevan wanted to groan aloud, to thrust the young demon away from him, to shout for Zha'dan. Who could give Hirel what he wanted; what he needed on this night of all nights. Who could dry those damnable tears.

Hirel buried his face in Sarevan's shoulder and clung. Sarevan's arms went round him. He was fever-warm; his skin was silken; he smelled of wine and musk and clean young body. He was slender and strong, like a warrior woman. But he was no woman at all.

He was an Asanian courtesan, and he knew precisely what he was doing.

Sarevan lifted him bodily and bore him to the door, kneeling burdened beside Zha'dan. The Zhil'ari lay motionless, wide-eyed. Sarevan pried the arms from about his neck and held them well away from him, meeting the burning golden stare. "You know I can't," he said.

Hirel tore his right arm free and struck, backhanded. Sarevan swayed with the blow. "You are no man," Hirel spat at him. "Virgin. Limpyard. Eunuch!"

"When the wine's worn off, little brother, you're going to be sorry you let it rule you." Sarevan let go the boy's left arm. It did not strike. He brushed away a tear that crept down the rigid cheek.

Hirel shivered convulsively. "Damn you," he said. "Oh, damn you."

Sarevan stood. "Zha'dan. Love him for me." He turned. It was wrenchingly hard. His torque, gold and iron both, was strangling him. He cast himself down and cursed them all.

Sarevan had seen splendor. He had seen the festivals with which the Sunborn had regaled his armies. He had seen the lords of Keruvarion riding in triumph to the Feast of the Peace that ended the great wars in the empire. He had seen the consecration of Endros Avaryan, and the games of High Summer there every year after, and his own confirmation as High Prince of the Sun.

He had seen splendor. This did not blind him, but it widened his eyes a little. The Asanians granted to the gateway of autumn that preeminence which belonged in Keruvarion to the gateway of summer. Then were all the gods worshipped. Boys became men, girls became women; marriages were made, children named and presented in the temples, heirs proclaimed and lordships allotted and princes taken into their princedoms. The emperor held full court in the great hall of his palace, the Hall of the Thousand Years with its thousand carven pillars upholding a roof of gold. So huge was that hall that an army could array itself therein; armies had, for festivals, for the pleasure of emperors: even mounted warriors whirling upon the sand that lay beneath the inlaid panels of the floor. At the hall's farthest extent the panels were lifted from a moat of glittering sand: dust of gold, and a kingdom's worth of jewels crushed and strewn beneath the armored feet of a hundred knights. These were the Golden Guard of the Golden Throne, princes of the princes of Olenyai, a living wall about their emperor.

He sat alone within the circle of his knights, raised high upon his throne. It was no eastern chair but a great bowl of gold set upon the backs of golden lions. Even its cushions were of cloth of gold. He sat erect, banked in them, a golden image, masked and crowned and robed in the ninefold robe of the highest of all kings.

His sons held the foremost rank of the court, and Aranos foremost of them, standing with his guards and his mages and his priests before the emperor's face, three spearlengths from the Golden Guard. The prince wore full court dress, almost too heavy to stand in: the robe of seven thicknesses to which his rank entitled him, with its hood woven of gold and silk laid on his shoulders, baring his artfully painted face. He was expected to stand but permitted to lean on the arms of his two most favored mages.

Sarevan, fantastically armored and viciously uncomfortable, had taken station with Aranos' personal guard. As the tallest of the line save for Zha'dan who stood beside him, he had been given the place of honor directly behind the prince. Hirel was farther down, invisible unless he turned his head in the stiff and blinkering helmet. Which he did, more than once, damning discipline. Hirel's armor was as ridiculous as his own, his visor a dragon mask with darkness in the slits of its eyes. Of Hirel there was nothing to be seen.

When the boy woke to a pale dawn, he had been quite as catastrophically sick as Sarevan had expected. Aranos' slaves had brought him a potion with which he seemed unhappily familiar. He took it with distaste, grimacing as he swallowed it, but it brought the light back to his eyes and the color to his cheeks. He even ate a bite or two, under duress. Thereafter he seemed much as he always was, facing what he had to face with admirable steadiness.

Sarevan was not sure he trusted it. Hirel had not spoken to him since the night's bitter words. He had not let Sarevan touch him in his sickness; when Sarevan tried to speak, he turned his back. He had put on his haughtiest mask, at its most insufferable angle.

Sarevan sighed and faced forward. He could not see the army of Hirel's brothers, but he could feel them behind him. Aranos had come in last and most royal; they had had to bow as he marched in slow procession before them. Sarevan had had time to number them, even to consider faces. Forty, he had counted, which could not be all of them: the rest, no doubt, were too young or too indisposed to stand in court. Boys and youths and young men of every shade from umber to ivory, clad variously according to degree in robes of five and six and seven, bull-broad and whip-thin, twitching with nervousness and motionless with hauteur, beautiful and unbeautiful and frankly ugly, but all marked with the stamp of their lineage. It might be as little as the set of the head. It might be as complete as Hirel himself, whose portrait graced the Hall of the High Princes; but that portrait was his father's before him, and his father's father's.

Sarevan had marked two princes most clearly. They stood

highest but for Aranos; like him and like no other save a handful of very young children, they wore the sevenfold robes of princes of the first degree. They were not the least comely of the emperor's sons. Indeed Vuad might have surpassed Hirel but for the misfortune that had given him hair the color of old bronze. That was reckoned a flaw here, and a tragedy; Sarevan thought it very handsome. But he was only a tarry-skinned barbarian with no eye for beauty.

Sayel he liked less, at least to look at. He was a pale creature, handsome enough if one were fond of milk and water, attired unwisely in gradations of crimson. His eyes were sharper than Vuad's, his tension less readily apparent. He was watching Aranos as a bird watches a cat: in fear, but mindful of its beak and its claws. He had noticed the prince's following. Too carefully. By the pricking of Sarevan's nape as the ceremonies crawled on, he was still noticing it.

Sarevan shifted infinitesimally. His back itched. His bladder twinged. He cursed them both, and his armor into the bargain: steaming hot, hideously heavy, and far too ornate to trust in any battle. If its weight did not fell him, its curlicues would, catching blades and hampering his arms.

He would not have to fight. Not here. Not in front of the Asanian emperor. Courtiers waged their battles more subtly, with poisoned words and poisoned wine.

It was close now. He dared a twist of his body, a sweep of his eyes within the helmet. The princes had tensed subtly. Their eyes were wide and bright.

A very young lord was being presented to the emperor with the full rite, even to the nine prostrations. He performed them with grace and composure, although his face was ashen.

He rose for the last time, said the words which he must say, backed from the presence. When he had taken his place among the ranked nobles, there was silence. Bodies shifted, eyes flickered. Only Aranos did not move.

With imperial slowness Ziad-Ilarios stood. Not dignity alone constrained him: his robes were heavy, as heavy as all his burden of empire. He rose like an image ensorceled to life, and his face was no face at all, but a mask of beaten gold.

It was custom, Hirel had told Sarevan. The mask was the mask of a god: ageless, flawless, impervious to human frailties. How simple then, Sarevan had said, to murder an emperor in secret and to take on his mask and his name and his power. Hirel had been far from amused. The common crowd was not to know when an emperor was old or ill or uncomely. Indeed the emperor who had begun the custom had been an outland invader with a terribly scarred face and the gall to have won his predecessor's confidence, wedded that emperor's only daughter, and disposed of his marriage-father by means more foul than fair. But no one in the years since had succeeded in perpetrating an imposture. Not only were the princes and the queens and certain of the High Court entitled to see their lord's face; his identity was attested at intervals by a council of priests and lords, aged and wary and incorruptible.

So had they attested at the beginning of this endless festival. Sarevan did not need to be told. His skin knew who wore that mask; the void behind his eyes was sure of it.

Save only when he spoke of matters of the highest import, the emperor did not speak even to the High Court. A Voice spoke for him, a shadow-speaker, a herald in black whose mask was black and featureless but whose voice was rich and full. "It is time," he proclaimed, "and time, and time. The throne is filled, its majesty is strong, may its bearer live forever. But even highest majesty, which makes the laws, must also obey them. So was it decreed in the days of Asutharanyas whose memory is everlasting: Every lord must name his heir. If that heir be of full years, one naming suffices. If said heir be yet in his minority, whether babe newborn or youth well grown, he must himself, upon attainment of his manhood, request and receive the name of heir from the lips of his lord. Then only may his title be affirmed." The herald paused. The silence deepened. Even the myriad sounds of a myriad people living and breathing and standing close together had sunk into stillness. "On the first day of autumn in the thirty-second year of the reign of the divine emperor, Garan-Shiraz Oluenyas, whose memory endures forever, to the High Prince Ziad inShiraz Ilarios and to the Princess Azia of pure blood and great worship, was born a son: Asuchirel inZiad Uverias, highborn, chosen heir of the chosen heir of Asanion. In the eighth year of the reign of his majesty, the great one, the Lion, the golden warrior of Asanion, Ziad inShiraz Ushallin Ilarios, came word of the death of his chosen heir. In the night it came, in the spring of the year, in grief immeasurable.

"But the law endures; it knows no grief. Every lord, even to the very lord of lords, must name his heir. It is time; it is time and time. Hear and attend."

The silence focused, stirred, began to thrum. This was the highest of moments. The emperor must speak as the law commanded; he must name a name. The princes waited, even Aranos standing erect, alert, forsaking his pretense of ennui.

It smote Sarevan then, almost felling him. How cruelly, how bitterly they had failed. The *emperor* must name the name. If Hirel had gone to him, made himself known, assured himself of the naming—but they had obeyed Aranos. They had trusted him; they had let him seclude them all. And thus, serpentinely, he mocked them. Ziad-Ilarios did not even know that his true heir was there to be chosen. Before Hirel's very face he would name Aranos the heir of Asanion.

In the mighty silence, metal chinked on metal. Sarevan glanced aside, cursed the helmet, turned half his body.

One of Aranos' guards had left his post. He stood on the glittering sand all alone. The Golden Guard lowered their spears, warning. He had discarded his own.

The emperor seemed not to see him. He was only a lone madman, a nonentity; beyond the sand, only the princes could know that he was there. The Guard would deal with him; the court need never know what had passed. The golden mask lifted.

The man on the sand moved swiftly. His hands caught at his corselet. The emperor's knights began to close in upon him. Sarevan left his place, elbowing through startled guardsmen, shrinking slaves, the odd inscrutable mage.

Within the elaborate armor, hidden clasps gave way. The whole clever shell opened at once and fell clattering to the sand. Robes gleamed beneath, white on white on white: simplicity of purely Asanian complexity. There were seven of them. And over them, a shimmer of gold. The eighth robe, the imperial robe, the robe of the high prince.

A grey shadow sprang from air, or perhaps from among the mages. It crouched before Hirel. Its snarl was soft and distinct and most deadly. The emperor's knights paused.

Sarevan won his way to Hirel's back. Zha'dan was with him. They stood, warding him.

He seemed aware of none of them. His back was straight, slender still for all the waxing breadth of his shoulders; proud and yet ineffably lonely with all the staring eyes behind him and his helmeted face turned toward his father. He set his hands to the helmet's plumed extravagance. He flung it aside with sudden and most uncourtly force, shaking out his shorn hair. He raised his chin and fixed his eyes upon the emperor.

Sarevan's mouth was dry. He would have given much to be able to see the faces of Vuad and Sayel. But more, infinitely more, to see the emperor's. The mask betrayed nothing at all of the man behind it. He had half a hundred sons. Would he even recognize this one, altered as he was, grown from child into man? And even if he did, would he name the boy his heir?

Hirel did a thing that could only be perfect courage, unless it was perfect insanity. He walked forward. Ulan walked with him. He walked straight and unwavering toward the lowered steel. Just before the first spearpoint touched his breast, he raised a hand.

The spears hesitated. Suddenly they swung up. The Olenyai stepped slowly back.

The princes could see all of it. Perhaps some of them understood it. In the hall beyond, the silence's length had begun to rouse wonder. A murmur grew.

Hirel set his foot on the first step of the dais. He went no farther. He stood, waiting, eyes lifted still to his father. People behind the princes saw him now, and the beast with him, and the two tall guards. Their voices were like a wind in the forest, swelling to a roar.

Still the emperor did not move. His mask was bent upon his son. His Voice wavered, at a loss.

Sarevan was beginning to twitch. This had gone on much too long. If the man in the mask did not soon make up his mind, if mind he had to make up, there was going to be a riot in the hall.

Sarevan tore at the catches of his armor, shook off the shell of it, kicked it out of the way. Were those gasps behind him? He had had his own splendor of folly: he had demanded, and received, full and imperial northern finery. It would seem very nakedness to these people. White sandals laced to the knee. White kilt. A great burden of gold and rubies hung wherever an ornament would hang. It left a remarkable quantity of bare skin. Zha'dan had twisted his hair into high chieftain's braids: the Zhil'ari did not know the Ianyn royal way, and there had been no time to teach him. No one here would know the difference; and it did not matter. The color of the many woven plaits was proof enough of his station.

He tossed down his helmet, shook out all his braids, looked the emperor's mask in the eye and bowed his head briefly as king to king. "Lord emperor," he said, clear and cool above the rising tumult, "I bring you back your son." That won a spreading silence. Incredulous; avid with curiosity. Hirel was whitely furious. Sarevan hoped devoutly that Aranos was the same. He smiled. "Your son, lord emperor. Your heir, I believe. Will you name him, or shall I?"

That was boldness beyond belief. It awed even Hirel. It struck the High Court dumb.

The emperor did a terrible thing, an unheard-of thing. In all his casings of silk and velvet and cloth of the sun, in his mask and his crown and his wig of pure and deathly heavy gold, he stepped away from his throne. He moved with mighty dignity, with ponderous slowness. Yet he moved. He came down. On the step above Hirel, he stopped. He raised his hand. His knights tensed to spring. His son stood unmoving, braced for the blow.

The hand fell in its glittering glove. It closed upon Hirel's shoulder. He caught his breath as if with pain, but he did not waver. His eyes met the eyes within the mask.

It came up. A voice rolled forth from it. It was a beautiful voice, rich and deep, more beautiful even than his imperial Voice. "Asuchirel," said the Emperor of Asanion. "Asuchirel inZiad Uverias."

That was not, by any means, the end of it. Hirel and Sarevan between them had seen to that. They had shattered the ritual; they had shocked the High Court to its foundations.

It was rising to a riot when the emperor's knights swept them out of it. Hirel resisted. "We are not done," he said. Loudly, above the uproar. "I must take their homage. I must—"

"They'll take your hide," Sarevan said, laying hands on him, because no one else would. He was too furious to struggle.

Silence was blessed, and abrupt. Sarevan took in the chamber to which the Olenyai had herded them. It must have been meant for the emperor to rest in between audiences, or for hidden listeners to take their ease in while peering through screens at the throne and the hall. The screens were closed and barred now; one of the Olenyai drew curtains across it. There was something familiar about him; about his eyes above the helmet's molded mask.

Sarevan clapped hands to his swordless belt. All his weapons lay lost and useless on the floor of the hall. "Halid!"

The Olenyas bowed. His glance was ironic, his right-hand sword drawn and most eloquent. His companions ringed the walls: a round dozen.

Very slowly, very carefully, Sarevan turned back to Hirel. Ulan was alert but quiet. Likewise Zha'dan who had shed his armor, who was all Zhil'ari beneath, painted with princely richness. "We seem," said Sarevan, "to have made a mistake."

"Several mistakes."

The Olenyai snapped to attention. A man had entered through the inner door. He wore a robe of stark simplicity, for Asanion. It was merely twofold, overrobe and underrobe, plain white linen beneath, amber silk above, with no jewels save the golden circlet permitted to any noble of the High Court. He was not young, but neither was he old. The years had thickened his body and furrowed his face, and the hair cropped shorter even than Hirel's was shot with white, and his skin had a waxen pallor which narrowed Sarevan's eyes; but he was handsome still, with the strength of the lion that, though aging, remains the lord of his domains. Hirel went down on his knees before him.

He laid his hands on the bowed head. Hands stiff and swollen and grievously misshapen, trembling on the edge of perception. Yet it was not his sickness that shook them. His face was carven ivory; his eyes were burning gold.

Hirel raised his head. They had the same eyes, they two. The same blazing stare in a face scoured of all expression. It could have been deadly wrath. It could have been apprehension. It could have been deep joy, bound and gagged and held grimly prisoner. "My lord," said Hirel, "call off your dogs."

"My son," said the Emperor of Asanion, "call off your panthers."

Swords hissed into sheaths. The emperor's Olenyai knelt before their lord. Zha'dan did not see fit to follow suit; and Sarevan knelt to no one but his god. He let his hand rest on Ulan's head and regarded with interest his father's rival. Ziad-Ilarios was not at all the bloated spider that legend made him, but neither was he the splendid passionate youth who had wanted to run away with a Gileni princess. Youth was long lost, and innocence, and the gentleness for which the Lady Elian had loved him. Passion . . .

For Hirel, briefly, it had flared with all its youthful heat. But the ice of age and royalty had risen to conquer it. He raised his son, and they were eye to eye, which widened the emperor's by the merest fraction. He stepped back. He said, "Sit."

Hirel sat stiff and still upon a cushion. His father sat raised above him. Sarevan stood with his cat and his Zhil'ari. He doubted very much that he was wanted here. He doubted still more that Hirel would pass that door again unscathed. The very silence was deadly. Ziad-Ilarios had said no word for an endless while. He had glanced more often at Sarevan than at his son, cool measuring glances as empty of enmity as of warmth.

When Sarevan had had enough of it, he smiled, white and insolent. "Well, old lion. Now that you have us, what are you going to do with us?"

Hirel's shoulders stiffened. Ziad-Ilarios let his gaze rest on Sarevan. For the first time in a proud count of days, Sarevan's longing for his lost power passed the borders of pain. To touch that mind behind all its veils and masks; to know truly what that silence portended.

The emperor raised a hand. "Come here," he said.

Sarevan came. He did not wait to be invited; he sat, returning stare for stare. "Well?" he asked.

Ziad-Ilarios leaned forward. His hand gripped Sarevan's chin, turning it from side to side, letting it go abruptly. He sat back. "You favor your father," he said.

"It's the nose," said Sarevan. "It conquers all the rest." He tilted his head. "If you want to play games, I'll play them. But I'd rather come to the point. Of this meeting, or of yonder sword. If you don't want to tell me what you intend to do with us, will you tell me what mistakes you think we've made?"

"I will and I can," answered the emperor directly, without visible reluctance. Perhaps he was amused. "You should not have made it so painfully clear that Keruvarion's heir is here, and that he is here by his own will, and that he must be thanked for the return and the naming of the heir of Asanion."

Sarevan leaned against the emperor's divan, cheek propped on hand. "You weren't in any great hurry to name him yourself, and there was a riot brewing. I had to do something."

"Thereby beginning a riot indeed," said Ziad-Ilarios.

"They'll see sense soon enough. You named your heir. Once the shock wears off, they'll be content with him."

"Do you think so?"

"I know so," said Sarevan. He was not as confident as he hoped he sounded.

"And you? What will they say of you?"

"The truth. I come indeed of my own will, lord emperor. I make a gift of myself to you."

Ziad-Ilarios was neither startled nor dismayed. Of course not. Halid was his man. He knew everything; had known it, most likely, from the beginning. "There are two edges to that sword, Sunprince. I can use you as a pawn in my game. I can barter your life for your father's empire."

Tension contracted to a knot in Sarevan's middle. He smiled. "Don't trouble. He won't play. Alive I can keep him from you. Dead I can give you your war. Keruvarion you'll never get, from either of us."

"And if I desire war?"

Sarevan tilted his head back, baring his throat. "I'm yours, old lion. Do as you please."

"You are young," mused Ziad-Ilarios. His tone excused nothing. "I am not a man who whips his sons. But were you mine, I would consider it."

Sarevan sat bolt upright. Ziad-Ilarios regarded him sternly, yet with a spark beneath. "Young one, your folly has placed me in a very difficult position. I have considered returning you forthwith to your father—"

"You can't!" Sarevan burst out.

The emperor's brows met. He looked more than ever like Hirel. "Do not tell me what I can and cannot do. Your father suffered my son to return to me, great though his advantage would have been had he held the boy hostage. For that, I stand in his debt. I might choose to repay in kind. Or," he said, "I might not. I do not know what use you may be, save to cause dissension in my court. You may be better dead or in chains."

"So be it," Sarevan said steadily.

Ziad-Ilarios looked long at him. For all his fixity of purpose, for all that he had had long days to firm his will, Sarevan had all he could do to sit unmoving, his face calm, his hands quiet on his thighs. His heart beat hard; his mouth was dry. A cold trickle of sweat crept down his spine.

The emperor said them, the words he dreaded. "Do you propose to betray your empire?"

"No!" cried Sarevan, too swift, too loud, too high. Grimly he mastered himself. "No, Lord of Asanion. Never. I propose to save it." He spread his hands, letting Ziad-Ilarios see them both, the one that was human-dark, the one that was burning golden. "I offer myself. Hostage. Peacebond. A shield against my father's war."

"Are you so certain that he cannot win it?"

"I know he will."

"Why, then? Surely you have no love for Asanion."

"I know what that victory will cost." The emperor raised his brows. Sarevan swallowed. His throat seemed full of sand. "I was never the seer my mother is. But I have seen what my god has given me to see. War, Lord of Asanion. Red war. Two empires laid waste, the flower of their manhood slain, the strength of their people broken." Sarevan was on his feet. "I will not have it. If I must die to prevent it, then let me die. I will not be emperor if that empire is ruin."

"That," said Ziad-Ilarios, soft after Sarevan's passionate outcry, "is the heart of the matter. You will turn traitor rather than face what you fear will come. Even in Asanion we have a name for that. We call it cowardice."

"Old lion," purred Sarevan, "I am young and I am a fool and I have no courage to speak of, but you cannot test my mettle by twisting the truth. My father let your son leave Endros because he has no intention of keeping peace and no taste for cold murder. He never dreamed that I would go as far as I have."

"Do you believe that I cannot have you put to death for my realm's sake?"

"I believe that Mirain An-Sh'Endor will hesitate to invade Asanion while you hold me hostage. I am, after all, his only son. His father has decreed that he may never have another."

"But if war is inevitable, your death may move him to act in haste, before he is well ready. Then may I claim the advantage."

"He was ready when I left Endros. I may have delayed him by escaping his vigilance, but if I die at your command, he will fall upon you at once and without mercy." Sarevan rose and stepped back, freeing Ziad-Ilarios from the weight of his shadow. "Lord emperor, I came willingly, in full knowledge of the consequences. I am yours to hold. I will serve you, whether you use me as prince or slave, guest or prisoner, if only you do not ask me to turn against my people."

"What surety have you that I will not keep you and turn against your father? He has no child of mine in his power."

"In that," Sarevan said levelly, "I trust to your honor. And to the size of my father's army."

The emperor stood. "Asuchirel," he said. "Judge. Do I keep him? Do I put him to death? Do I send him back to his father?"

Hirel was slow to answer. Not for surprise, Sarevan could see that. He looked as if he had been expecting the burden of judgment; and it was heavy. Perhaps too heavy for his shoulders, however broad they had begun to be.

At last he said, "Death would be wise, if we would consider the years to come and the enemy he must inevitably be, but he has warned us clearly against such foresight. If we send him to Endros, it must needs be in chains, or he will not go. I counsel that we keep him. We may gain time thereby, and we will certainly discomfit his father."

"And you can always kill me later," Sarevan pointed out. He bowed with a flourish. "I am your servant, my lord. What will you have of me?"

"Respect," replied Ziad-Ilarios, with a glint that might have been laughter. "And now," he said, "I would speak with my son. My captain will guide you to a place of comfort."

It was indeed very comfortable: a suite of princely chambers, with slaves for every need, and a great bath, and its own garden. Halid, having guided Sarevan there, was not disposed to linger. Sarevan did not try to detain him. There was no tactful way to ask a captain of guards if he had intended to murder his charges.

When the man had gone, Sarevan rounded on Zha'dan with such fierceness that the Zhil'ari leaped back. His hand was on the hilt of his sword; but he had not drawn it. "Truth," Sarevan spat out. *"What is the truth?"*

"I don't think there is any," Zha'dan said.

Sarevan paced, spun, paced. "That was Halid, laughing at us. If he is the emperor's man, why did he plot to kill us? If there was no plot, why did Aranos tell us there was? What is this web we're trapped in?"

"I don't know," said Zha'dan. "I can't read these people. Even when I think I can. They keep thinking around corners."

Sarevan stopped short. Suddenly he laughed. "The sword and the serpent! And what does the sword do when the serpent coils to strike?"

Zha'dan caught the spark of his laughter. "It strikes first."

"Straight and steady and clear to the heart. We'll master this empire yet, brother savage."

They grinned at one another. It was sheer bravado, but it buoyed them up.

They were still grinning when Hirel found them, the two of them and the ul-cat, all nested most comfortably in the mountain of white and golden cushions that was the state bed of Asanion's high prince. He stopped in a cloud of slaves and hangers-on, motionless amid the dropped jaws and outrage. Sarevan watched him remember with whom he was quarreling, and with whom he was not, and why. Watched the mirth swell, perilously. "Good evening," he said in his beautifully cadenced High Asanian, "my panthers. Are your chambers not to your liking?"

"Good evening," said Sarevan, "brother prince. Our chambers are very much to our liking. But we had a mind to explore. I see you have your place again."

"It was inevitable. It is my place." Hirel raised a finger. His following scattered. Not without dismay; but perhaps there was something to be said for Asanian servility. No one argued with a royal whim.

When they were well gone, Hirel dropped his robes and stood in his trousers, drawing a long breath. His shoulders straightened; his eyes sparked. He grinned. He laughed. He leaped.

It took both men to conquer him. He had not their strength, but he was supple and lethally quick, and he knew tricks they had never heard of. And some they had, and called foul. Loudly. He laughed at them. Even with Sarevan sitting on him and Zha'dan pinning his hands.

"Beard-pulling," Sarevan told him severely, "is not honorable."

Hirel sobered. Somewhat. "It is not? Groin-kneeing, surely, but that . . . it is so irresistibly *there*."

"I didn't pull your hair."

"Ah, poor prince."

Sarevan growled. Hirel lay and looked almost meek. After a moment Zha'dan let go his hands. He flexed them, sighing. Sarevan gathered to let him up.

The world whirled. Hirel sat on Sarevan's chest and laughed. His fingers were wound in Sarevan's beard. "Never," he said, "never call an Asanian conquered until he yields."

"What happens if *I* won't yield?" Sarevan demanded, not easily. His chin had too keen a memory of anguish.

Hirel bent close. "Do you wish to know?"

Sarevan twisted. Hirel clung like a leech. His fingers tightened. "I won't," gritted Sarevan.

Hirel swooped down. He did not kiss like a woman. He did not kiss, for all Sarevan knew, like a man. He was simply and blindingly Hirel.

When Sarevan could breathe again, Hirel was on his feet,

wrapping himself in a simple linen robe. It was voluminous enough, but a good handspan shorter than it should have been. Hirel looked at it, and Sarevan forgot anger, outrage, fear that was half desire. More than half. He struggled in the endless clutching cushions.

Hirel tried to pull the robe down over his feet. It yielded a bare inch. He raised his eyes to Sarevan. "I am not the same. I am—not—"

Sarevan could not touch him. Dared not.

He bent, took up the first robe of his eight. It was silk, and rather more elaborate than practical, but it fit him. He put it on slowly, discarding the other. He straightened, worked his fingers through the wild tangle of his hair. "I am not the same," he said again. "I can laugh. I can—I could—weep. I am corrupted, Sun-prince."

"And I," Sarevan said, barely to be heard.

Hirel laughed, not as he had before. Short and bitter. "You are purity itself. A kiss—" His lip curled in scorn. "That was vengeance. For what you gave me. Now do you understand? Now do you see what you did to me?"

"But it was only a kiss."

"*Only!*" Hirel jerked tight the belt of his robe. "My father warned me. It is a Gileni magic. It has nothing to do with mages, and everything to do with what you are, your redmaned kind. A fire in the blood. A madness in the brain. You do not even know what you do. You simply are."

"But you did the same to me!"

"Did I?" Hirel smiled slowly. "So, then. It can be given back in kind. Perhaps, for that, I may concede the existence of gods." He drew himself up, settled his robe and his face. "Enough. I have been remiss; I have let myself forget who I am. Go, be free. I have duties."

"What sort of duties?"

Hirel bridled. Sarevan refused to be cowed. He lay and waited and willed the boy to remember who he was.

Hirel remembered. He eased, a little. His outrage faded. "Prince," he said. It was an apology. "My father gave me a gift. A judgment. I must make it tonight."

"Your brothers?"

The faintest of smiles touched Hirel's mouth. "My brothers."

Sarevan regarded him, long and level. "I don't like what you're thinking," he said.

Hirel tilted his head. There were diamonds in his ears; they could not match the glitter of his eyes. "What do you think I am thinking?"

Sarevan stretched the aches out of his muscles and yawned. His eyes did not shift from Hirel's face. "You're contemplating revenge. Sweet, isn't it?"

"Sweeter than honey," said Hirel, standing over Sarevan. "Would you make it sweeter? Linger as you are, half naked amid my bed."

"Hirel," Sarevan said, "don't do it."

"Can you forbid me?"

"Believe me, prince. The sweetness doesn't last. It turns to gall, and then to poison."

"How wise you are tonight." Hirel's smile was bright and brittle. "But I am wiser than you think. Watch and see."

"Hirel—"

"Watch."

They came boldly enough. Only the two: Vuad and Sayel, without attendance of their own, escorted politely but ineluctably by half a dozen of the emperor's Olenyai. They were putting on it the best faces they might. Sarevan was not half-naked in Hirel's bed; he sat with Hirel, robed like the other, his hair free and his brows bound with gold, with his ul-cat and his Zhil'ari mageling at his feet. They played at draughts upon a golden board.

Zha'dan straightened, at gaze. Ulan raised his head from Sarevan's knee. Hirel pondered the board. He was losing. He was not frowning, by which Sarevan knew that his mind was not on it. Sarevan made no such pretense. He turned to regard the princes; they stared back in a fashion he was learning to name. High indignation that a dusky barbarian should presume to conduct himself as their equal. He belonged, the curl of their lips declared, in the slave-stables with the rest of his kind.

It was hard to pity them. Even when, at very long last, Hirel condescended to notice them. Their bravado shuddered and shrank. "Good evening," said Hirel, "brothers. I trust that my summons did not inconvenience you."

"We are always at your disposal," Sayel said. "My lord."

Hirel smiled. Sarevan thought of beasts of prey. "No expressions of joy, brothers? No hymns of thanksgiving that I am returned safe to my kin?"

"Hirel," said Vuad, dropping to his knees and catching at Hirel's robe. "Hirel, we never meant it."

"Of course you did not mean to let me escape. Your guardhound was fierce. Would you like to see my scars?"

Sayel sank down coolly, with grace. He even smiled. "Surely you understand, brother. We were forced to it. We did not intend to slay you."

Hirel looked at them. The one who clung to his hem and sweated. The one who smiled. "I loved you once. I admired you. I wished to be like you. Fine strong young men, never at a loss for a word or a smile, never ill or weak or afraid. You never fainted in the heat at Summer Court. You never fasted at banquets lest you lose it all at once and most precipitately. You never paid for a few days' brisk hunting in thrice a few days' sickness. You were all that I was not, and all that I longed to be."

Sayel's smile twisted. Vuad's tension eased; he raised his head. "You do understand," he said. "After all, you do. We knew you would. It was circumstance; necessity. There was no malice in it." He managed a smile. "Here, brother. Send your animals away; then we can talk."

"We are talking now." Hirel stared at Vuad's hands until they let go of his robe.

"At least," said Sayel, "dismiss the beast with the firefruit mane." He was easing, falling into a manner which must have been his wonted one with Hirel: light, familiar, very subtly contemptuous. "Rid us of it, Hirel'chai. Our council has no need of Varyani spies."

Hirel laughed, which took Sayel aback. "I am not your Hirel'chai, O Sayel'dan, my brother and my servant. Bow to the lord high prince, who is my guest and my brother-above-blood. Crave his pardon."

Sayel looked from one to the other. His brows arched. "Ah.

Now I see where your manners have gone. Is it true that his kind ride naked to war?"

"On occasion," Sarevan replied. "Our women especially are fond of it. Beautifully barbaric, no?"

"The beauty is questionable," said Sayel.

"Bow," Hirel said very softly. "Bow, Sayel."

Vuad, less clever, was relearning fear. Sayel was still rapt in his own insolence. "Come now, little brother. Am I, a prince of the blood imperial, to abase myself before a bandit's whelp?"

Hirel was on his feet. No one had seen him move. Sayel fell sprawling; Hirel's foot held him there, resting lightly on his neck. "You are not wise, Sayel'dan. The Prince of Keruvarion was inclined to intercede for you; but you have shown him the folly of it." Hirel beckoned to his guards. "Take them both. Rid them of their manes; chain them. Bid the gelders wait upon my pleasure."

"I watched," Sarevan said with banked heat. "I saw nothing wise in what you did."

"You did not speak for them," Hirel pointed out coolly.

"You never gave me time."

Hirel said nothing, only looked at him.

He rose. "Go on, then. Take your revenge. But don't expect me to condone it."

"And what does your father do with those who betray him? Embrace them? Kiss them? Thank them for their charity?"

"You keep my father out of this."

"I will keep him where I please. We do not love him here, but we fear him well; we know how he deals with his enemies."

"Mercifully," snapped Sarevan. "Justly. And promptly, with no cat-games to whet their terrors."

Hirel tossed back his hair, eyes narrow and glittering. "Is that your measure of me?"

"You are High Prince of Asanion."

"Ah," drawled Hirel. "I break my fast on the tender flesh of children, and beguile my leisure with exquisite refinements of torture. There is one, prince; it is delightful. A droplet of water upon the head of a bound prisoner: one droplet only at each turn of the sun-glass. But sometimes, for variation, no droplet falls. It drives the victim quite beautifully mad."

Sarevan's teeth ground together. "If you're going to kill them, at least kill them cleanly."

"As cleanly as the armies of the Sun took our province of Anjiv?" Hirel advanced a step. "As cleanly as that, Sun-prince? They slew all the men of fighting age. They put the women to the sword, but not before they had had their fill of rape. They made the children watch, and told them that that was the fate ordained for all worshippers of demons; and the menchildren they put to death, but the maids they took as slaves. But no," said Hirel, "I cry your pardon. There are no slaves in Keruvarion. Only bondservants and battle captives."

"They are your brothers!"

"The worse for them, that they would destroy their lord and their blood kin."

Sarevan turned his back on Hirel. "That's not justice. That's spite." He walked away. Hirel did not call him back.

Sarevan did not know where he was striding to. He did not care. Sometimes there were people; they stared. No doubt they thought him indecent: all but naked, with one thin robe and no attendants. Ulan and Zha'dan had forsaken him; had stayed with Hirel. Faithless, both of them. Traitors to their master.

He found a tower. He climbed to the top of it and sat under the stars. They were the same stars that shone on Keruvarion, in the same sky. But the air was strange, Asanian air, warm and cloying. He choked on it.

"I did it," he said to the pattern of stars that he had made his own, the one that in Ianon was the Eagle and in Han-Gilen the Sunbird. "I confess it freely. I brought it on myself. I cast away my power and my princedom. And for what? For a dream of prophecy? For peace? For the empire that will be?" He laughed without mirth. "For all of those. And for something I never looked for. For the worst of all my enemies."

He lay back, hands clasped beneath his head. His temper had passed. He was calm, empty. "I think I hate him. I'm afraid I love him. I know we quarrel like lovers.

"And what hope do we have? If he were a woman I'd marry him, if I didn't kill him first. If he were a commoner I'd make him a lord and keep him by me. Even if he were a lord . . . even an Asanian lord . . ." Sarevan surged up, crying out, "O Avaryan! Why did you do this to us?"

The god was not answering.

"No doubt," said Sarevan dryly after a starlit while, "I've solved everything with tonight's performance. If he's even civil to me hereafter, I'll count it an honest miracle."

The stars were silent. The god said nothing.

"I hate him," said Sarevan with sudden fierceness. "I hate him. Haughty, corrupt, cruel—damn him. Damn him to all twenty-seven of his own hells."

Seventeen

THE GOLDEN COURTS SETTLED SWIFTLY ENOUGH UNDER THE emperor's strong hand; and, in the way of courts, went on as if they had never risen up in near-revolt. Hirel was solely and certainly their high prince. Sarevan was neither spy nor upstart; certainly he had never presumed so far as to ordain whom they would accept as their lord. Matters of such indelicacy were not discussed.

He was their new darling. He would have been their new pet, but like Ulan, Sarevan Is'kelion was not a tame creature. He did not trouble himself with all the intricacies of protocol; he would not keep to the paths ordained for a royal hostage. He rode his blue-eyed stallion wherever he pleased. He crossed swords with guardsmen. He wrestled uproariously with the painted savage who was his shadow, and sometimes he won, but sometimes, resoundingly, he lost. He discovered that certain courtyards looked upward to the latticed windows of the harem, and that if he lingered there alone, in time soft voices would call to him. They told him of unfrequented passages, of walled gardens and of chambers where a handsome outlander might go to be stared at through hidden screens. But never suffered to stare in return.

Even if he were minded to chance the loss of his eyes for letting them rest on a royal lady, not to mention his manhood for daring to be aware of her existence, his sweet-voiced companions grew almost shrill in forbidding it. It was sin enough that he heard them speak.

Their kinsmen were enchanted with him. He frightened them, deliciously. They reckoned him a giant; they waxed incredulous at skin so dark and hair so bright and teeth so very white; they called him Sunlord, and Stormborn, and Lord of Panthers.

He was as vain as a sunbird, but he knew what the flattery of courtiers was worth. Wizard's gold. While one labored to maintain the spell, it glittered brightly. But a moment's lapse, a few breaths' pause, and it withered away.

Avaryan knew, there were wizards enough here. The charlatans were everywhere: men of little power but great flamboyance, who wrought illusions and told fortunes and found lost jewels for the credulous of the court. But they were only a diversion. While they persuaded the skeptics of Asanion that there was nothing to fear from their kind, the true mages passed unseen and unregarded. Nondescript persons, seldom noticed but always in evidence, robed in grey or in violet, often accompanied by a beast or a bird. Sarevan did not know that any of them had the emperor's ear. They did not confess it and Ziad-Ilarios did not admit to it, although he was free enough with Sarevan in other matters. When Sarevan appeared in his council and in his courts of justice, he said no word, though eyes glittered and lips tightened at the enormity of it. The emperor refused to see, refused to restrain the interloper; who had a little sense, when it came to that. He never tried to speak where he listened so avidly, though often his eyes would spark or his jaw tense, as if he yearned to burst out in a flood of outland interference.

People were calling him the emperor's favorite. Some, in a country where tongues were freer, would have called it more. Would have remembered who his mother was, and what she had been to his majesty. Would, perhaps, have spoken of bewitchment.

There was one who did not speak at all, nor in any way betray that he had had aught to do with the return of Asanion's high prince and the presence of Keruvarion's high prince in Kundri'j Asan. Aranos had made no public appearance since Autumn Firstday. That, it seemed, was perfectly usual. He was known for his strangeness. His name, when it was spoken, was spoken most often in a whisper.

It was very cleverly done. As much as Asanian courtiers could love anything, they loved their bright and haughty high prince. Aranos they feared.

"He doesn't even have to do anything," said Zha'dan. "Just hide in his walls and refuse to come out. And let people talk."

"Serpent ways," said Sarevan. He smiled at the guard who stood before Aranos' gate. It was his most charming smile. "I will speak with your lord," he said in Asanian.

The man surprised him. He bowed with every evidence of respect. He stepped back from the gate.

A mage was waiting. Sarevan was painfully glad that it was not a darkmage. The man bowed and was most courteous. He led Sarevan into the black-and-silver chambers.

Aranos did not see fit to keep Sarevan waiting, although an Asanian would have reckoned him indisposed. Perhaps it was its own kind of insult. He had bathed; he lay on sable furs as a slave rubbed sweet oil into his skin, while another combed out his hair. His mane, unbound, was longer than his body.

He was, indeed, a perfect miniature of a man. Rumor had cast doubts on it. He had begotten no children that anyone knew of; and that, in an Asanian prince some years Sarevan's elder, was frankly scandalous.

Sarevan, looking at him, knew. His eyelids lowered, raised. He almost smiled. "I, too," he said.

Sarevan glanced at the slaves. Aranos' smile came clearer. "Deaf-mutes," he said. "Most useful, and most discreet."

"But why would an Asanian choose to—"

"For the power in it."

Sarevan sat on the edge of Aranos' furs and frowned. "I've heard of that. I never found it to be true. Maybe my kind of power was different."

Aranos was gravely astonished. "It did nothing for you, and yet you suffered it?"

"For the vows and the mystery. For the god."

"Ah." The essential Asanian syllable: eloquent of volumes. "And yet you knew me."

"No one in your harem has ever told anyone?"

"They are women," said Aranos. He did not even trouble to be contemptuous. "Every one believes that another enjoys my favors. Some have even lied to claim them, to gain what can be gained. I indulge it. It serves me; it quiets my so-called concubines."

"And you? Have you gained anything?"

Aranos shrugged slightly. "I am an apprentice still. The full power, I am told, comes with full knowledge."

"You're not mageborn."

For an instant Sarevan saw the man beneath the mask. The prince cast him down. "I am not. I must learn to fly with wings of wax and wire, where you were eagle-fledged in infancy."

Sarevan quelled a shiver. In that moment of Aranos' nakedness, he had seen desolation, and hatred, and corroding envy. And yet, beside it, he had seen compassion. Even the unmasked man was Asanian. Webs within webs. Sarevan made his tongue a sword to cleave them. "I fly no longer. I walk as a man walks, and no more. But this much of power I have left: I can see the snares about my feet." Aranos was silent. Sarevan thrust, swift and straight. "You promised to stand at your brother's back; to name him heir before your father. You did not. You accused our Olenyai of treachery. They have proven to be loyal, and to your father. How do I know that you did not lie in all the rest?"

"My brother is high prince as he was born to be."

"For how long?"

The golden eyes hooded. "For as long as he can hold."

Sarevan considered seizing him; chose not to move. "You wanted us away from Halid and his men. Why?"

"I cannot tell you."

"Cannot or will not?"

"Both."

"I can beat it out of you."

"Can you?"

Sarevan measured distances, boltholes, the prince and his two silent slaves. He smiled.

Aranos smiled back. "Beautiful barbarian. How you must tempt my brother!"

Sarevan fitted his long fingers to that delicate neck. "Tell me how I tempt you. Tell me what you plot against us."

"Truly," said Aranos, undisturbed by the hand about his throat, "I cannot. I have my own designs, I admit it freely; perhaps my brother will not be emperor as long as he would like. But this that concerns you . . . I am part of it, but I do not rule it. I am not free to tell you more."

Cold walked down Sarevan's spine. "You're lying."

"As I have never known a woman, I swear to you, I am not."

Sarevan looked at him more than a little wildly. It had been so clear. So obvious. And if he lied—but he did not. It was enough to drive a man mad. "Then, if not you, who?"

"I am forbidden to tell you."

Sarevan's teeth bared. "You are the Second Prince of the Golden Empire. How can anyone presume to forbid you anything?"

"My father can."

Almost—almost—Sarevan fell into the trap. But he knew Ziad-Ilarios. Liked him. Loved him, maybe, a little. None of it was enough to blind him. Ziad-Ilarios was a strong king, a good man as far as an emperor could be in Asanion, and an intriguer of no little subtlety. And yet. "This is not his weaving. No more than it is my father's. Neither could have done what has been done in the other's empire. Even the shattering of my power—I blamed him for it once. No longer. It was too magelike a trick. Too—much—like—"

Sarevan stilled, suddenly, completely. Aranos' eyes were wide and clear as topazes. "Mage," Sarevan murmured. "Like." A sweet wildness rose in him. Under the sky, he would have let it out in a whoop. "Ah," he said tenderly. "Ah, little man, how cleverly you plan this game. Do they know it, your fellows? Do they guess how very dangerous you are?"

"Any man is dangerous."

"Don't babble." Aranos said nothing. Sarevan smiled at last and let him go. Already the bruises were rising on his ivory neck. His skin was as delicate as a woman's was supposed to be, yet almost never was. "You are dangerous. Your brother is dangerous. I—I am violent, and therefore dangerous."

"And subtler than you think, Sun-prince."

"Avaryan forbid," said Sarevan. He rose, bowed without mockery. "I thank you, prince."

"Perhaps in the end you will not."

Sarevan paused. He could not read the princeling at all. He shrugged. "That will be as it will be. Good day, little man."

The Mageguild had settled itself in an unprepossessing quarter of the city, in the fifth circle between the cloth market and the high temple of Uvarra Goldeneyes. There along a narrow twisting street that ended behind the temple were the sages and the diviners, the sorcerers, the necromancers, the thaumaturges, the enchanters. They had divided the power into the light and the dark. They had named the greater powers, which were prophecy, and healing, and ruling of men and of demons, and mastery of the earth, and walking of the road between the worlds, and raising of the dead. They had named the lesser, which were mindspeech, and beast-mastery, and firemaking, and flying, and cloudherding, and all the arts of shifting the world's substance by will alone. They had even made a craft of the naming, turning a gift of the inscrutable gods into a scholar's pursuit.

Sarevan found the guildhall by scent, as it were: by the throbbing behind his eyes. Its door was neither hidden from sight nor blazoned with the badge of the order; it was a plain wooden panel behind a bronze gate, with a porter who eyed Sarevan through a grille. Taking in the man in plain lordly garb of the Hundred Realms, with a cap on his head but his bright hair plain to see below it, and an ul-cat beside him and a painted Zhil'ari guarding him. The eye betrayed no surprise. Gate and door opened; the porter, an Asanian of no age in particular, bowed and said, "If you will follow, prince."

It seemed a house like any other. No twisting shadowed passages. No stink of potions or moaning of incantations. No shimmering sorcerous barriers. Through open doors Sarevan saw men and a few women bent over books, or deep in colloquy, or engaged in instructing apprentices. Nearly all the masters were earth-brown easterners or bone-pale islanders. Most of the apprentices were Asanians. Some glanced at him as he passed. Curious, even fascinated, but unsurprised.

Sarevan had expected to be expected. He had not expected to

be piqued by it. They could at least have pretended to be amazed that the son of the Sunborn dared to show his face among them.

He followed his guide up a stair and down a corridor. One door in it stood open. The chamber within was a library: shelves of scrolls, rolled and tagged, and a long cluttered table, and a man working at it. There was no telling his age. His hair was white but his skin was smooth; his back was bent but his eyes were bright; and the fingers that held the stylus, though thin to emaciation, were straight and fine and strong. Sarevan saw no familiar; he knew that he would see none.

He bowed his aching head. "Master," he said. No more. No name. Mages of the order gave their names only as great gifts.

The guildmaster bowed in return. "Prince," he said. "Your pardon, I pray you; I cannot rise to greet you properly. Will it please you to sit with me?"

The porter had gone. Zha'dan established himself by the door; Sarevan sat across the table from the master, with Ulan at his side, chin on the table, watching the master of mages with an unblinking emerald stare.

They all waited. Sarevan did not intend to speak first. He glanced at the scroll nearest: a treatise on the arts of the dark. His grandfather the Red Prince had made him read it. "A mage must know all the uses of his power," Prince Orsan had said.

"And its abuses," Sarevan had countered.

"The dark arts are not abuse of power. They are as native to it as the arts of the light; but where light heals, the dark destroys."

"I would never fall so low," Sarevan had declared. "My blood is Sun-blood. The dark is my sworn enemy. I will always heal; I will never destroy."

He smiled now, bitterly, remembering. He had been too proud of himself. And now he was here, traitor to Keruvarion, facing the master of that guild which had turned its back on his father.

"Because," said its master, "he would have constrained us to his will alone. We will not deny the dark; we will not ban the practice of its arts. That would be to deny the world's balance."

Sarevan held himself still. The man had read his face, that was all. His mind was barred as firmly as ever, despite all assaults upon it. "I have heard," he said, "that you will ban the arts of light and turn all to the dark."

"There are those who would do so, out of greed or out of bitterness. I am not one of them."

"And yet you suffer them."

"While they obey me, I do not cast them out."

"Even though they work abominations in the name of their magic?"

"What are abominations, prince? Refusal to deny their gods and worship Avaryan? Insistence upon their own rites and prayers? Resistance to laws which they reckon tyranny?"

"If it is tyranny to forbid the slaughter of children," answered Sarevan, "yes. I know what rites you speak of. The Midwinter sacrifice. The calling up of the dead and the feeding of the gods below. The making of Eyes of Power."

The master folded his long beautiful hands. He wore a ring, a topaz. Sarevan shivered a little. He could no longer abide topazes. Quietly the mage said, "The world is not gentle. Nor are the gods. If they must have blood, then blood they will have. It is not for us to judge them."

"We contend that they demand no blood. That that is human avarice and cruelty and grasping after power."

"Is your Avaryan pure, prince? Has he spurned the blood shed in his name? Did he spare even his bride the pain of death?"

"Human cruelty, guildmaster. Human envy and betrayal."

"The worse for those who perpetrated it, that they had no god to make their bloodshed holy."

Sarevan sat back, stroking his beard; sure sign of his tension, but he could not stop it. "Maybe we're wrong. Maybe you are. Balance could be another name for spinelessness. Avaryan has made himself known in the world; no other god has done that. No other god will. There is none but the one."

"Save, by your belief, his sister. The dark to his light. The ice to his fire. The silence to his great roar of power. The other side of his self."

"That is Asanian teaching. We say that they are separate. He has chained her, lest she plunge the world into everlasting night."

"Or lest she prevent him from tipping the balance. The sun gives life, yet also destroys it. Excess of light condemns a man to blindness."

"Not if he be pure of soul."

"Are you, prince?"

"Hardly." Sarevan smiled, little more than a grimace. "If I were, I wouldn't be here. I'd be Journeying in blissful ignorance, or kinging it in Ianon."

The master was silent. Waiting.

Sarevan let him have that victory. "Yes. Yes, I doubt my god. I wonder if my father is mad. If the Asanians, after all, worship the truth: twofold Uvarra who is above the gods."

"Have you come to me for an answer?"

Sarevan laughed sharply. "I spent an hour in Uvarra's temple. It's much like all the others. Crusted with jewels, fogged with incense, infested with priests who know no god but gold. The image of the deity would rouse blushes in a Suvieni brothel. And yet," he said, "and yet, for all of that, when I bowed down and prayed to Avaryan, a madness struck me. I thought it was Uvarra who heard. Uvarra of the light and Ivuryas of the dark, all one. And the dark was beautiful, guildmaster. It called to me. It offered me my power, the dark power which I refused and which is still within me, if only I will free it."

"There is no law which forbids the gods to lie."

"Precisely my response," said Sarevan. "But if I can taste a lie, I can also taste the truth. And there I tasted truth."

"There is always a price."

"Of course. And for this, my mother's life and my father's heart. I refused. It was too easy, mage. Much too easy." Sarevan leaned across the table. "Choices should be difficult. I think I've yet to be given one. I know you have something to do with it."

"And how do you know that?"

Sarevan frowned. It hurt. He cradled his head in his hands. "Maybe the god drives me: whichever god is the true one. Maybe I'm mad. I think I've been chosen for something. If only for a traitor's death."

"Are you asking for a foreseeing?"

"I am asking for the truth. I know what I've done and why I did it. But it's been too smooth, mage. Too simple. I think I've had help that hasn't chosen to uncover itself."

The master raised his brows. "Indeed?"

"Indeed," said Sarevan, throttling his impatience. The tactics of the sword worked wonders with Asanian courtiers, but this was a mage, in that mage's own demesne. He chose his words with care. "Consider. A trap laid in Asanion; a prince's pride caught in it, his power taken from him. A hunt through two empires by a mighty master of power, who could find nothing; but an Eye of Power found the one for whom it was meant. Chance, maybe; a god's inscrutable will. But for two princes and two seneldi and an ul-cat to pass through the very heart of Keruvarion, under the eye of the Sunborn, with treason on their minds—for them to pass so, with no whisper of their passing, no rumor of their betrayal, no sign of a hunt raised against them, that is not chance. That is magecraft."

"Or skillful deception."

"No," said Sarevan. "It takes power to lie to my father. Power, and great bravery. And someone has done it. Someone ventured to cover my going; to open my road through Keruvarion."

"We are not the only mages in the world."

"You are the only mages, aside from the Sun-priests in Endros, who gather together under a firm rule. And they would never have woven this web: it smacks too much of treason against my father. The little prince is part of it. He professes not to be the master of it; and that's unlikely enough to be true. He's no servant, he's serving himself and no one else, but at the moment it suits him to be a loyal conspirator. He'd not be loyal to anyone whom he didn't at least pretend to respect."

"You see great complexities in what may be no more than luck and chance and a prince's plotting."

"Maybe I do. I'm a prince myself; I'm an only son. I'm spoiled. Indulge me." Sarevan smiled his whitest smile. "Your people can have no love for my father. He was too inflexible with them. Either he would rule them or they would leave his empire. They chose exile. Now suppose," he said, "that some of them have seen a path of both revenge and peace. A conspiracy. To deny him his war, to rob him of his heir, and in the end, it may be, to have their own country back again. With the Sunborn safely dead and someone young, malleable, and comfortably powerless to stand in his place."

"Logical," the master said.

Sarevan bowed to the tribute. "My insanity has been a godsend. I'm not only well out of the way; I'm in debt to your plotting. Don't you think it's time for a truth or two? A man can't pay a debt if he doesn't even know to whom he owes it."

"If you knew," inquired the master, "would you be willing to pay?"

"That depends. There may be more to this web than I've been allowed to see. It may lead to a blacker infamy even than I'm willing to stomach."

"Have your deeds been as vile as that?"

"I'm here, aren't I?"

The guildmaster smiled. "I was warned, Sun-prince. Your father is called the greatest courtesan in Keruvarion, but there are many who would contest that primacy; who would give it to Sarevan Is'kelion."

"Would you?"

The smile widened a fraction. "The Sunborn does not know that he is beautiful."

"He knows that he has never betrayed a trust."

The silence sang, hurting-sweet. Slowly the master said, "He has never been forced to choose. I envy that certainty. I would that it had been granted to me."

"Neither of us is the son of a god."

The master's head bowed. "This much, high prince, I can give you. A web has been spun about you. I will not say that you are the center of it. There is more to the world and the power than a pair of warring empires. Yet what you have done has been woven into the pattern."

"And the pattern?"

"You have seen it."

Sarevan rose. He leaned on his hands, keeping temper at bay, willing a smile over his clenched teeth. "You have told me nothing that I did not already know. Do you expect me to leave and be content?"

The master looked up at him, resting cool eyes on his burning face. "You were not born for contentment. I would give you what you ask for, or as much as concerns you, yet I may not." And as Sarevan straightened, thunderous: "Not yet. I am the Master of the Guild. No more than the Prince Aranos do I command my allies. That is given to no one of us. I must speak with the rest; I must win their consent before I uncover our secrets."

Sarevan snorted in disgust. "What did you model this mummery on? The Syndics of the Nine Cities?"

"Any tribe in the north is so ruled. Keruvarion's emperor himself pays heed to his lords in council."

"But in the end he rules," said Sarevan. "So. You have to agree to make me part of what I've been part of since it began. You'll pardon me if I feel used. And ill-used, at that."

The master spread his hands. "Prince. It shall be redressed. That I promise you."

Sarevan turned his hand palm up on the table. It burned and blazed. "On this?"

The master drew a breath as if in apprehension. He touched a finger to the *Kasar*. A spark leaped; he drew back. "Upon your power," he said.

Sarevan's fist clenched. Its pain was no greater for the mage's touch, though the man looked pale and shaken, as if he had gained more than he bargained for. "I accept your promise."

"It shall be kept," the master said. "And you shall have as much of the truth as you may. I will speak with my allies. When it is done, have I your leave to summon you?"

Sarevan considered the mage, and his words, and his honor. "You have my leave," he said.

Sarevan had his honest miracle. Hirel had been not merely civil to Sarevan after their quarrel. He had been magnanimous. He had been princely. He had chosen to forgive even the most bitter of Sarevan's words.

Sarevan found it harder to forgive himself. It was not Hirel who told him what had become of Vuad and Sayel. A courtier related it, half in admiration, half in incredulity: how the princes had languished shaven-headed in a cell of the emperor's prisons, and how after a night and a day in which they went well-nigh mad with dread of the gelders' coming, Hirel himself had come with a choice. A life of ease and power as eunuchs of the Lower Court in the far reaches of the empire, or a tour of duty as officers of the imperial army, with the strong likelihood of falling in battle, but the chance also of surviving to regain their rank and their brother's favor. Vuad had found the choice ridiculously easy. Sayel, it was said, had wavered. But Sayel was not well loved in the

Golden Courts. He had gone with his brother to serve on the marches of the east; and before they left, they swore great oaths of loyalty to their high prince.

Hirel was in the harem when Sarevan looked for him, doing his duty by his twice ninescore concubines. It was just, Sarevan conceded, that he should have to wait, and for such a cause. He did not have to like it.

He prowled his own rooms. He prowled Hirel's. He drank rather more wine than he needed, and worked it off in a heated mock battle with Zha'dan, and came very close to deciding that Hirel did not deserve an apology.

The wine was stronger than Sarevan had expected. It made him see what he should do: and that was outrageous. It kept him from hanging back.

He had a little sense. He left Zha'dan in Hirel's rooms, rebellious but subdued. Ulan would be guard enough, and would be less likely to pay in blood.

They passed the empty courtyards, traversed an unfrequented passage. Today no sweet voices called through hidden lattices. Sarevan strode beyond them on ways which he had not taken before.

The Golden Palace stood in two worlds. The outer was all of men and eunuchs. The inner was all of women and eunuchs. The unmanned walked freely in both. A whole man walked within only where he was unquestioned master: only among the women who were his own.

Sarevan was alien in the outer world. In the inner, there was no word for him. The women who dwelt there had never seen sky unbounded by walls. They had never stood face to face with any man but father or brother or master. Husband, few of them could claim. Not here, where every one of fifty princes had his proper number of concubines.

Sarevan had learned what every concubine prayed for. That her lord might marry, for then by custom he might set her free. Or better far, that she might bear him a son. Then was she not only freed; she gained honor and power among the ladies of the palace.

If he had not known it was a prison, he would have found the harem no stranger than the rest of the palace. It was opulent to satiety, it was redolent of alien unguents, it was labyrinthine in its complexity. Its guards were eunuchs, but eunuchs both tall and strong, with drawn swords. Black eunuchs. Northerners all strange with their beardless faces, their shaven skulls, their eyes like the eyes of oxen: dark, stolid, and unyielding. Sarevan was nothing to them. He was a man. He could not pass.

Almost he turned away. But having come so far, he could not surrender like a meek child. "The high prince will see me," he said. "You may impede me. My furred brother may not be pleased. I cannot answer for what he will do then."

Two swords lowered most eloquently, to pause within an arm's length of Sarevan's middle.

Ulan growled deep in his throat.

The edge bronze dropped a handspan.

Sarevan essayed a smile.

Behind the eunuchs, the door opened. Asanian, this one, and flustered. He paid no heed at all to the guards. He beckoned with every evidence of impatience. "Come, come. Why do you dally? Time's wasting!"

Sarevan stared, nonplussed. The little eunuch clapped his hands in frustration. "*Will* you come? You're wanted!"

Sarevan looked down. The swords had shifted. Carefully, restraining an urge to protect his tender treasures with his hands, he edged between the guards. The Asanian hardly waited for him.

Long as his stride was, he had to stretch it to keep pace with his guide. The harem's corridors passed in a blur. No one was in those through which he was led: deliberate, perhaps.

Bemused as he was, he found himself wondering. Was he being rapt away like the wise fool in the bawdy song? Made a prisoner among the women forevermore, his manhood slave to their every whim.

He laughed, striding. Softly; but it startled him. It was so very deep.

His guide all but flung him through a door, into a chamber like any other chamber in this palace. A space neither large nor excessively small. A low table, a mound of cushions, a flutter of silken hangings. No odalisque awaited him. He was disappointed.

There was wine. He stopped short, remembering Asanion and Asanians. Sniffed it. It was thin and wretchedly sour: superb, to Asanian taste. If there was poison in it, surely the sourness had killed it. He poured a cup, drained it, prowled. Ulan, wiser, had arrayed himself royally atop the cushions.

One of the hangings concealed a latticed window. He tensed, remembering a litter and a long day's madness. Grimly he made himself forget, set eyes to the lattice. A courtyard opened below. There was something of familiarity in it. If one set a man just beneath the window, a very tall man as men went here, with wondrous bright hair; and set a woman behind the lattice, or a handful of women, taking high delight in the pastime . . .

He turned slowly. Words began, died. New words flooded to the gates. Hirel in gown and veil, eyes dancing, mocking him, driving him to madness.

Hirel was a boy of great and almost girlish beauty. But no boy had ever had so rich an abundance of breast, so wondrous a curve of hip within the clinging silk. Hirel had never walked as this creature walked, light and supple, yes, but swaying most enchantingly, smiling beneath her veil. She was all sweetness, and ah, she was wicked as she laughed at him: great outland oaf with his jaw hanging on his breastbone. Her head came barely so high. She stood and looked and laughed as a bird sings, for the pure joy of it.

He had to sit. His knees gave him no choice in the matter. He clung to Ulan and stared, grinning like the perfect idiot he was.

Her mirth rippled into silence. She stood and smiled at him.

"You look," he said, "exactly—"

"How not? He is my brother."

Her voice. He knew it. "Jania!"

She curtsied. "Prince Sarevadin. You are . . . much . . . more imposing without a lattice between."

He had not felt so large or so awkward since he grew a full head's height in a season. He was painfully aware of his long thin feet and his long thin limbs and his great eagle's beak of a nose. All of them blushing the more fiercely for that no one could know. "Jania," he said. "How did you know I was here?"

She pointed to the lattice. "I saw you. Then I heard you at the gate."

"And you had me let in." He drew his breath in sharply. "You shouldn't have. Your duennas will flay you alive."

She tossed her head, fully as haughty as Hirel. "They will not.

Even before I knew that you would come, I informed my brother that he would give me leave to speak with you. He was wise. He granted it." Her eyes sparked. "Sometimes it profits him to remember: I could have been a man. Then he would not be high prince."

Sarevan blinked stupidly. He had known her spirit, and delighted in it, even through a lattice. He had not known who she was.

Suddenly he laughed. "If my father only knew!" Now she in her turn was speechless, caught off guard. "You could have been given to me. It was thought of: to ask the Asanian emperor for his daughter."

"He has a legion of them," she said.

"But only one born to the gold."

"Do you think that you are worthy of me?"

This was princely combat. Sarevan lounged in the cushions, Sarevan Is'kelion again, with his bold black eyes and his wide white smile. "Your brother has called me his equal."

"Ah," she said. "My brother. He has always been besotted with fire."

"What, princess! You don't find me fascinating?"

"I find you conceited." She laughed at his indignation. She leaned toward him over Ulan's body, bright and fearless, and ran a finger down his beard. He had kept it when his face healed, because no one in the court had one; this morning Zha'dan had plaited it with threads of gold, taking most of an hour to do it. "And beautiful," she said.

"Truly? Have the poets changed the canons?"

"Damn the canons."

She was a little too reckless in saying it. Defiant; outrageous. Sarevan laughed. "Have a care, princess. You might make me fall in love with you."

"I should fear that?"

Fine bold words, but they were neither of them very steady. Her fingers seemed scarcely able to help themselves, weaving among the braids of his beard. No woman, not even his mother, had ever touched him so. So soon. So perfectly rightly. "Gold," he said with dreamy conviction, "is the only color for eyes."

"Black," she said. Firmly. They laughed. Her breast was full and soft and irresistibly there. Her lips were honey and fire.

His torque was light to vanishing. He was in no danger. This was only delight. His mind remembered what one did. His body was more than glad to learn it.

Her hair was free, a queen's wealth of gold, cloaking them both. She never heeded it. She was drowning in fire and copper.

He could circle her waist with his two hands. She could bring him to his knees with her two bright eyes. He laughed into them and snatched another kiss. And another. And another.

He did not know what made him pause. Ulan's growl, perhaps. The quality of the silence. Still kneeling, still veiled in gold, he turned.

He would not again mistake Jania for her brother. They were very like; but a world lay between them. The woman's world, and the man's.

His mind, spinning on, took thought for what Hirel could see. His sister, standing with her arms about a kneeling man. Her gown and his coat and trousers were decorously in place. But her veil was gone, her hair all tumbled, and his wild red mane was free of its braid. They looked, no doubt, as if they fully intended to go on.

And did they not?

Sarevan rose. Jania did not try to hold him. Her voice was cool. "Good day, younger brother."

Hirel inclined his head. He wore no expression at all. "Elder sister. High prince."

It was cold at Sarevan's height, and solitary. The wine of his recklessness lay leaden in his stomach. A dull fire smoldered beneath his cheekbones.

Hirel was clad for the harem. Eight robes of sheerest stuff, one golden belt binding them all. He looked calm, and royal, and impeccable. His duties had not even smudged the gilt on his eyelids. He said, "You will pardon me, prince. I was given to understand that I was looked for. I shall await you in my chambers."

"No," said Sarevan. "Wait. It's not—"

He had waited too long to muster his wits. Hirel was gone. Sarevan glared after him. "Damn," he said. "And damn."

"And damn," said Jania. She meant it, but there was still a

thread of laughter in it. "My eunuch will lose somewhat of his hide for this."

Sarevan looked at her, hardly hearing her. "You are meant to be his empress."

"What, my eunuch?"

He ignored her foolishness. "You shouldn't, you know. It's gone on too long. The strain is growing dangerously weak."

It was very stiff and prim, reflected in her eyes. "Are you proposing an alternative?"

His finger traced her brow, her cheek, her chin. Ebony on ivory. "Would you consider it?"

"You ask me that? I am a woman. I have no say in anything."

"I think you do, princess."

She wound her hands in his hair and drew him down. But not for dalliance. That mood was well past. She began to comb out the many tangles, to weave again the single simple plait that marked his priesthood. "They say that you know nothing of the high arts. That you are sworn to shun them. And yet you are very much a man."

"It's you," he said. Pure simple truth.

"Is it?" Her fingers paused. After a little they began again. "If my brother were a woman, would you even trouble to glance at me?"

Sarevan twisted about. Her eyes were level. Eyes of the lion. Royal eyes. "But he's not," he said, "and you are."

"And you are the most splendid creature I have ever seen." She kissed him lightly, quickly, as if she could not help it. "Go now. My brother is waiting."

He stood. He was holding her hands; he kissed them. "May I come back?"

"Not too soon," she said, "but yes. You may."

Hirel was not waiting in his chambers. He had been called away, his servants said. They did not know when he would return.

Sarevan had had enough of tracking him down. The next hunt might not end so perilously, but neither could it end in such sweetness. "If he wants an apology," Sarevan said to his cat and his mageling, "he'll have to come and get it."

He went early to his bed. Part of it was weariness. Part,

paradoxically, was restlessness. There was nothing that was allowed to him, that he wanted to do. What he wanted most immediately was a certain gold-and-ivory princess.

Now at last he comprehended the prison to which he had sentenced himself. Ample and gilded and most gracious, and yet, a prison. He could shock the councils of the empire with his exotic and insolent presence, but he was given no voice in their counsels. The intrigues of the court meant nothing to him. Keruvarion he had forsaken. He was neatly and most comfortably trapped, fenced in like a seneldi stallion of great value and uncertain temper. He could not even rage at his confinement. He had brought it on himself.

And like a seneldi stallion shut off from the free plains and the high delights of battle, he turned inevitably toward the other purpose of a stallion's existence. He had been mastering himself most admirably. He was not prevented from performing the offices of a priest on Journey, the prayers and the ninth-day fast; these had sustained him. And Hirel was coolly and mercifully distant, absorbed in his princehood. Women heard through lattices were intriguing and often delightful, but hardly a danger to his vows.

"Am I lost?" he asked Zha'dan. The Zhil'ari sat on the bed beside him, listening in fascination to his account of the harem.

"Does she look exactly like the little stallion?" Zha'dan asked.

"Exactly," Sarevan said. Paused. "No. The beauty, it's the same, white and gold. And the face. She's smaller, of course. A woman, utterly. What he would be if the god had made him a maid. But not . . . precisely. She's not Hirel. She's herself."

Zha'dan gestured assent, paused. His eyes were very dark. "He likes me; I please him, and he pleases me. We play well together. But I'm not . . . precisely. I'm not you."

Sarevan shook that off. "I've seen so many women, Zha'dan. A prince can't help it. Before he was, there was the dynasty, and it has to go on. If a woman is unwed, unmarred, and capable of bearing a child, she's cast up in front of me as the hope of my line. It doesn't even matter that I wear the torque. That only keeps me from playing while I look for my queen."

"Have you found her?"

"I don't know!" Sarevan rubbed his hands over his face. "I was full of wine and plain contrariness. But I never fell so easily before. Or with such perfect abandon. I didn't care what I did, or how I'd pay for it; and yet I wasn't in any haste at all to consummate it. It was as if . . . we were outside the world, and nothing that mattered here could trouble us there."

"Magic?"

"Not magery." Sarevan smiled wryly. "But magic, maybe. She's not only a beauty, Zha'dan. She has spirit. She's a golden falcon, and they've caged her. I could free her. I—could—free her."

He took it into sleep with him, that singing surety. She lay with him in his dream, and they were both of them free; he wore no torque and she no veil. She was all beautiful. She said, "If my brother were a woman, you would not glance at me."

Sarevan swam slowly from the depths of dreaming. Warmth stirred in his arms, murmuring. Dream above dream. This was dimmer than the last, and yet wondrous real. He stole a drowsy kiss.

It tasted strange. Strange-familiar. His hand, seeking, found no firm fullness of breast; but fullness enough below.

Sarevan's fingers had closed. He willed them open. Hirel blinked up at him, still more than half asleep, but frowning. He was most solid, and most certainly not a dream. "What are you doing here?" Sarevan demanded, sharp with startlement.

Hirel's frown deepened to a scowl. "Do you know no words but those?"

"Do you know no tricks but this?"

"Was it I who set your hand where it is now?"

It snapped back. "I was dreaming," Sarevan said.

"Ah," said Hirel. "Surely. And not of me."

Sarevan gaped. Suddenly he laughed. It was madness, but he could not help it. It was all too perfectly intolerable. "You're not jealous of me. You're jealous of her!"

Hirel struck him. It was not a strong blow; Sarevan hardly felt it. Hirel rolled away from him, drawing into a knot, spitting words to the wall. "A man who has never had a woman is an unnatural thing. A prince in that condition is an abomination. She has done her duty by you; she has made you a virtuous man. It was my duty to you as my brother and my equal, not only to allow it but to encourage it. But it is not my duty to be glad of it."

"Hirel—" Sarevan began.

"She is the jewel of the harem. I do not need to ask if she pleased you. She is a great artist of the inner chamber; she has taught me much of what I know. And all the while you lay with her, I who am royal, I who by birth must be your enemy, I who can never be aught to you but lust and guilt and in the end revulsion—I could not rest for that you lay with her and not with me." He drew his breath in sharply. It sounded like a sob. "I give her to you. It is she for whom you were born, she and all her sex."

"Asuchirel," said Sarevan. This time Hirel did not cut him off. "Hirel Uverias, I never lay with her."

"Surely not. You knelt with her. Or did you mount her stallion-wise?"

Sarevan went briefly blind. When he saw again, Hirel was under him, and the marks of his open palm were blazoned on the boy's cheeks. "Never," he gritted. *"Never."*

Hirel was not fighting him. He began to cool, to be ashamed. He drew back carefully. "I'm sorry," he said. "For all of it. Your brothers, your sister . . . all of it."

Hirel said nothing. His face was rigid, at once haughty and miserable. His skin in the lamplight was downy, a child's. It would bear bruises where Sarevan had struck it. Sarevan's hand laid itself with utmost gentleness upon the worst of them. "Hear a truth, little brother. Jania is very beautiful. I think that I would gladly give my torque and my vows into her keeping; I would rejoice to make her my queen. And yet that gladness rises not simply out of Jania who is woman and beauty and high heart. It rises out of Jania who is her brother's image." Hirel was silent. Sarevan pressed on. "I can't be your lover, Hirel. I'm not made for it. But what my soul is, what it longs for—Jania is nothing to it. Hirel is not. Hirel is most emphatically not." He swallowed. "I'm afraid I love you, little brother."

Hirel flung himself away from Sarevan's hand. His eyes were blazing; his cheeks were wet. "You must not!"

"I don't think I can help it," Sarevan said.

"You must not!" Hirel's voice cracked. "You must *not!*"

"Hirel," said Sarevan, reaching for him. "Cubling. We can be friends. We can be brothers. We can—"

Hirel was very still in his hands. Cold again, and far too calm. "We cannot." The tears ran unheeded down his face. "I have not told you the truth. While I embodied the jealous lover, word came. Your father has received my father's message. He has answered it. His armies have begun the invasion of Asanion."

Sarevan frowned. "That can't be. He wouldn't—"

"He has. And you must die, and even if I could prevent it, I would not. And it is the custom—with royal hostages, it is the custom that the high prince commands the executioners."

It was not real. Not yet. Not that Sarevan had failed more utterly even than he had feared. That the war had come; that he would die. But Hirel's pain was present and potent. He held the boy, rocking him, wordless.

Hirel allowed it: that was the depth of his pain. "Clearly your father does not believe that we will slay you. He will expect us to shrink from the threat of his vengeance; to bargain with your life. Therefore," said Hirel, "you must die."

"Tomorrow?"

Hirel began to tremble. "I do not know. By all the gods, I do not know."

"There's still the night," Sarevan said.

"You do not believe it, either!" Hirel cried. "You think we will not dare. But we will, Sarevan. As surely as I hope to sit the Golden Throne, we will."

"I know." Sarevan played with the tumbled curls, smiling at their refusal to go any way but their own. "I'm not afraid to die. I don't even have much to regret. Though I would have liked to know a woman. Just once. In my own body."

Hirel pulled back. "I shall bring her to you."

"No," said Sarevan, holding him. "I can't do it to her. Even for my line's sake—and she would conceive, Hirel. That is certain. I can't abandon her to bear a Sunborn child in the heart of Asanion."

"I would raise it as my own."

"As your heir?"

Hirel would not answer.

Sarevan sighed, smiled a little. "You see. And yet he would overcome any heir you begot, any heir you named. There would be no stopping him. We are born to rule, we Varyani princes. We suffer no rivals."

"No," said Hirel. "You conquer them. You make them love you."

Eighteen

"SAREVAN. SAREVAN IS'KELION."

They had come for him. So soon. He was up before his eyes were well open, hissing fiercely, "Don't wake him. Don't make him do it. Take me now and get it over."

"Sun-prince."

The voice was—baffled? Amused? Sarevan glared through a tangle of hair; he raked it back. Prince Aranos regarded him with great interest. He eased, and yet he tensed. "Good. You can do it. Don't tell him till it's done."

Aranos said nothing. Slowly Sarevan's mind recorded what his eyes were seeing. The silken chamber had vanished. These walls were stone, stark and unadorned, and the floor was stone spread with woven mats, and the ceiling was a grey vault from which hung a cluster of lamps. None was lit. The light that filled the room came pouring from a high round window. Sunlight, bright, with little warmth in it.

Sarevan turned completely about. The bed was intact, rich and foreign in this stark place, with Hirel coiled in it. The scars on his side and his thigh, though paling with age, were livid still. The light was cruel to them.

On the wall above him was a tapestry. Beasts, birds, a dragonel.
Sarevan had seen it. Somewhere. He could not, in the shock of the
moment, remember where.

He faced Aranos again. The prince had companions. One was a
mage clad in the violet robe of a master of the dark. The other was
a priest of Avaryan, torqued and braided, with his familiar on his
shoulder.

Sarevan stilled. He was remembering a promise made, and his
leave given, and the part which the Mageguild had played in all of
this. "I think," he said, "that I should begin again. Good morning,
my lords. Where is the guildmaster, and what is this place?"

Aranos bowed slightly, but he was not choosing to answer. The
mage said, "You will please to come with us."

The chief priest of Avaryan's temple in Endros said nothing, but
he smiled. It was a smile that reassured Sarevan, yet frightened
him. He was all a tangle.

He took refuge in vanity. "Must I go as I am?"

"Come," said the mage.

None of them would say more than that. The way seemed long;
it was dim and cold, all stone, with now and then a lofty window.
Whatever this place was, it could not be Kundri'j Asan. The air
was too icily pure.

He was entirely out of his reckoning. It made him want to laugh.
All his plotting, his betrayals, his multiple sins, and nowhere but in
a dream which he had all but forgotten, had he seen himself in this
place.

His companions would not answer his questions. They would
not speak at all. After his third failure he desisted, not entirely
gracefully. He was not used to being ignored.

This was a castle, perhaps. The stone and the steep narrow
stairways had a flavor of fortresses. The end was a hall like the
great hall of a lord, with its central fire and its stone-flagged floor
and its walls hung with faded tapestries. Yet unlike a lord's hall, it
was all but empty. The pillared bays about its edges, where men
slept and gamed and kept their belongings and often a woman or
two, were dark. There were no hounds, no hunting cats, no falcons
on perches. No singers sang by the fire; no guards stood at
attention, no servants waited on those who sat together in the
warmth.

Sarevan stopped short. There was the master of the Order of
Mages. There was the witch of the Zhil'ari with her grandson
mute and motionless at her feet. There, in a moment, were the
priest and the mage and the prince. And there was Orozia of
Magrin, and beside her the last man whom Sarevan had ever
thought to see. Orsan of Han-Gilen, his bright hair gone all ashen
in the scarce three years since Sarevan had seen him, but his body
strong still, and his eyes darkly brilliant in the black-bronze face.

A more complete conspiracy could not have gathered. Except—
"Aren't we missing someone?" Sarevan asked. "An emperor or
two, maybe?"

"We suffice," the Red Prince said. For all his training in the
necessities of princes, Sarevan almost cried his hurt. Even at his
sternest, even in the midst of just punishment of a scapegrace
grandson, Prince Orsan had never looked as he looked now. Cold.
Remote. A stranger.

Sarevan stood straight before them all. "Well? Am I going to
have my answers? Or am I on trial for my sins?"

They were going to drive him mad with their silence.

It was Aranos who spoke, as if he too were losing patience with
this mummery. "You are not on trial, prince."

"Ah now," drawled Sarevan, "I'm not a perfect idiot. I've killed
with power. I've betrayed my father and my empire. I've sold my
soul to my greatest enemy. Now I've dared to look on the faces of
your mighty and hidden alliance, for which I'll surely die. And you
plainly intend to give me no answers, and I'm not given even a
moment's grace to make myself decent. You can't tell me that you
merely want to feast yourselves on my famous beauty."

Aranos glanced at his companions. They were like stones. He
sighed just audibly. "You have committed no crimes that I know of,
prince. Unless it is a crime to wish for peace."

"The priests would argue that," Sarevan said.

"You have sinned as all men must while they dwell in living
flesh," said the priest whose name was hidden behind his
magecraft. In Endros they called him Baran, which was simply,
priest. "You will atone for it; have no fear of that. But now we
ponder other matters." He raised his hand, commanding. Orozia
came quietly, eyes lowered. She halted behind Sarevan. He felt her
hands on his hair, braiding it with much patience for its tangles.

She bound it off and returned to her place. He thought he saw tears on her cheeks; but that was not likely. She had never been able to weep stone-faced as she wept now.

He swept his eyes around the circle. "You grant me my priesthood. Now grant me your courtesy. Tell me what I see here. Have I guessed rightly? You are a conspiracy?"

"Just so," answered Aranos. "A conspiracy of mages. Of the guild, and of those outside the guild. Of the light and of the dark. Of all those who foresee only ruin in the Sunborn's war."

"Even you?" Sarevan demanded of his grandfather.

"Even I." Orsan had warmed not at all. "I who began it by snatching a priestess from the Sun-death and by fostering the child she carried. I saw even then that in him lay the seeds of the world's salvation; yet also those of its destruction. He is truly the son of the god. Of the true god, who is both life and death."

Sarevan was not astounded. He had heard it before, if never so explicitly. But he set his chin and his mind and said coldly, "You and all your line made Avaryan supreme long years before my father was born. Are you repudiating your own doctrines?"

"I am not. No more than are you."

"I don't have any doctrines. I'm merely selfish. I don't want to be lord of a desert."

"And you love him."

"Yes!" cried Sarevan with sudden heat. "I love him, and I think he's trapped himself, and he knows what he has to do, and he knows what will come of it, and he has no escape. But at least he can die in a blaze of glory, with Asanion in ruins under his heel."

"It need not be so."

"Of course it need not. But now it must. Even for me, he wouldn't stop it." Sarevan tugged viciously at his braid. "Maybe we're all fools. If I'd succeeded, what would I have done except to postpone the inevitable? I love the heir of Asanion; I love him as a brother. But he would no more bow to my rule than I would to his. The world simply will not support two such emperors as we would be."

"Granted," said the Red Prince. "Be patient for a moment now. Believe that we shall return to your dilemma; but first, hear a tale." He paused. The young Zhil'ari rose. Like Orozia, he would not let Sarevan catch his gaze. He brought a warm soft robe which

Sarevan was glad of even so close to the fire, and set a chair for him. Sarevan sat as much at his ease as he might and waited with conspicuous patience. Something flickered in Orsan's eyes, too swift to be sure of, but perhaps a smile. After a moment he said, "As you see and as my lord prince has affirmed, we are a conspiracy. A reluctant one, truth to tell. I cannot say who began it. It seems that we came independently to the same conclusion: that both Keruvarion and Asanion were advancing toward an inevitable conflict, and that that conflict would be one not only of weapons but of wizardry. Many wielders of power would welcome that: a final battle for the mastery, light against dark, with the god's own son on the side of the light, and arrayed against him all the cult of the goddess and of the gods below.

"But a very few of us have seen past the names and the divisions. The true masters of mages, and with them the shamans of the tribes, have always known that it is not a war of opposing powers, but a balance. I have learned it slowly and against my will, for it flies in the face of much that I thought I knew.

"Some few years past, I had a sending. It was you who brought it, Sarevadin, with your dream of destruction repeated night after night until we feared for your sanity. For you were and are no prophet, and it is your mother who is the Seer of Han-Gilen; and if she has had such a foreseeing, she has not seen fit to reveal it to any of us."

"She has," said Sarevan. "She refuses it."

"So," said Orsan steadily. "I know that I wished your dream to be a nightmare only, the midnight fancies of a boy on the brink of manhood. But the truth came surely, if slowly. I saw what you have come to see. I knew that I must do all in my power to avert the destruction. First I spoke with trusted priests. Then I spoke to Baran of Endros, who sent me where I would never have gone of my own accord. He sent me to his shadow in the guild: to the one who was matched with him at his initiation, darkness to his light, black sorcerer to his white enchanter. We spoke, and it was slow, for there was no trust on either side. But at last we agreed. We would fight together to keep Avaryan within the bounds ordained for him. Which he ordained for himself before the world was made."

"Why?" cried Sarevan. "Why can't my father see it?"

"He can. He denies it. My fault, my grievous fault. I raised him all in the light. I never taught him to comprehend the dark. Nor did he ever learn it from all the wizards whom he vanquished. They turned to the dark, and they did it without wisdom, and he laid them low. When the guild would have taught him, he called it falsehood and drove them from his empire."

Sarevan's throat ached with tension. "They say," he said, low and rough, "that Avaryan is not his father at all. That you came to his mother in your magic. That you begot him upon her."

"Look at your hand, Sarevadin. Look into your heart. What do you see there?"

"Gold," grated Sarevan, "and doubt. My father is wrong in one thing. Why not in all the rest?"

"A man may err once, even if he be half a god. If he is a great man, he may commit a great error. It does not negate either his lineage or his greatness."

Sarevan let his eyes fall. His fingers flexed about the anguish of the *Kasar*. "What do we do, then? What can we do?"

"We have you," Orsan answered, "and we have the heir of Asanion. By now that is known. One hostage was not enough; two may well be."

"For a while," said the guildmaster. "This is the Heart of the World, the hidden place which only our masters may know. I will not tell you where it is. It may not be in the world at all. Certainly neither your father nor his loyal mages, nor the sorcerers whom the Asanian emperor has sworn to him, can find you and so snatch you free."

Comprehension dawned, late but still almost comforting. Sarevan's head came up. "He was going to do it. My father. Take me before they killed me."

"But we came before him."

"I would have refused. I would have killed myself to stop him."

"You would have. It would have been a great waste and a very great folly. Now that danger is averted. The Asanian prince will sleep until we wake him. For you we have a choice."

Sarevan sat very still. They had all tensed. He remembered what he had said to the guildmaster. Chance? A remnant of foresight beyond even dreaming?

It would be hard. They were not all in accord over it. The

younger mages were losing their composure, and beneath lay a fire of protest. It might be hard enough even to suit Sarevan's madness.

He smiled with remarkably little strain. "So now we come to it. You've plotted this from the beginning, haven't you? Aimed my every stroke; guided my every move. To bring me here before you." None of them denied it. He sat back. He almost easy now. Almost comfortable, here at the heart of things, with the truth within his grasp. "Tell me now, O bold conspirators. How shall we escape our dilemma? Is there any escape? I can die. That will leave my father without an heir. You can protect Hirel, and when it's over, produce him to rule the ruins."

"Or," said the Zhil'ari witch, "we may slay him and leave you alone to live. But we will not."

Sarevan shivered. He did not want to die. Yet he was ready for it. He had been ready, perhaps, since he left Endros. "So, then. Hirel lives. I die. May I ask you to kill me quickly?"

"You may not," Prince Orsan said.

Sarevan had no words to say. The Red Prince looked long at him. He stared back. He could read nothing in those hooded eyes. He was beginning to be afraid.

"There can be but one emperor," Orsan said. Steady, quiet. "Another emperor may not share his throne. But," he said, "an empress may."

Sarevan stared at him, incredulous, almost laughing. "*That* is the summit of all your plotting? Even I know it's not worth thinking of. I could marry every princess in Asanion, but the emperor would still have sons. Unless you mean to kill all forty-odd of them."

"Fifty-one," murmured Aranos. "There was no mention of their murder, and no intention thereof. Nor any, of your marriage to my royal sister."

That was a shrewd blow. Sarevan hardly felt it. If there had ever been any logic in this council, it had fled. He sat back under the force of their stares. He was quick-witted. Too quick, many would say. He had never felt as slow as he felt now. He should know what they were telling him. He could not begin to guess.

Zha'dan sprang up. "Tell him, damn you. Stop torturing him. Tell him what you want to do to him!" No one would. He smote his hands together. Lightnings cracked; he started. Sarevan would have smiled if he had had time. Zha'dan gave him none. "It's you, you fool. It's you who'd be the empress."

Sarevan laughed, sudden and full and free.

No one else laughed with him. The silence was thunderous. His mirth shrank and fled. "That's preposterous," he said. "I know shapeshifting is possible, though it's not supposed to be. But you can't—"

"We know we can," the guildmaster said. "It has been done. It has been done to me."

This was not illogic. It was madness. Sarevan could only think to ask numbly, "Why?"

"It was one of the tests of my mastery. Not the greatest and not the most perilous, but great enough and perilous enough, and not easy for the mind to endure."

Sarevan closed his eyes. When he opened them again, nothing had changed. He thought of the woman whom the master must have been. Of the girl whom Hirel could have been, to no purpose; not with fifty brothers. Of himself. Great, gangling, eagle-nosed mongrel of a creature: comely enough as a man, but as a woman—

He gripped the arms of his chair until the wood groaned in pain. He could not take his eyes from the master. He dared not; for that would slay all his courage.

"It is not easy," the master said. "There is pain. Great pain in the working and great pain after. But the foreseeings have shown us. If you do it, if you wed Hirel Uverias, if you bear him a child . . ."

He went on and on. Sarevan stopped listening. This was worse than death. Worse even than death of power.

"It is not so terrible to be a woman," said the Zhil'ari witch. Her eyes glittered, perhaps with anger, perhaps with mockery. "Less terrible than to be a man. To be a man, and to rule over ruin."

"At least I would be—" Sarevan throttled his tongue. He had never been like Asanians, who were said to thank their gods on each day's rising that they had not been born women. He knew that they were not lesser beings, or weaker vessels, or pretty idiots to be pampered and protected. He had known his mother; he had spent long hours with her warrior women. He had been one. Almost. When in Liavi's mind he had shared the bearing and the birthing of her daughter.

But to be one in truth. To face his father, his mother, his kin. To face his empire. A eunuch could not rule. And that, very broadly and very brutally, was what they would call him.

"That will be a lie," the witch said, reading him with almost contemptuous ease. "You will be a woman whole and entire, in all respects. You will unite the empires; you will lessen the destruction."

"But not stop it."

"Not what has already begun. More than ruin will remain." She folded her arms over her breasts. "No one will be astonished if you refuse. You will live, whatever befalls. You need not live maimed."

Sarevan's own frequent thought, mercilessly twisted. He flashed out against them. "I'm maimed already. A woman is anything but that. But I was never made to be one."

"We can see to that," Orsan said.

Sarevan surged up. "You. Even you would consent to this?"

"I proposed it," said the Red Prince.

Sarevan sank down, all strength gone. He had thought his world was broken when he woke without power. He had not known that it could break again. And again. And again. Or that his mother's father, his master and his teacher, his blood kin, could grind the shards beneath his heel.

"Would it be so terrible?" asked Aranos. "You longed for a solution. This one is simple. It gives you your empire and your peace. It gives you my brother whom you love."

"Will he have me?" Sarevan demanded. "Will he want me?"

"How will you know unless you do it?"

"I can ask him."

"No," Aranos said. "That is not part of the bargain. You and you alone must choose. No other may make your choice for you."

Sarevan laughed in pain. "It comes to that, doesn't it? Myself, alone. Courage or cowardice. Peace or war. Life or death. You think you know what you ask of me. Do you? Even you, master—do you?"

"Yes," the master answered levelly. "We do not compel you. It is not a simple magic, and the pain of it is terrible. All your body will be rent asunder and made anew; so too your mind and your soul. You will pass through the sun's fires, slowly, infinitely slowly, with no mercy of unconsciousness."

Sarevan shivered in spite of himself. But he said, "Hirel will survive, you say."

"And your father," said the mage who had been silent for so long.

Sarevan spun to face him. It was truth he spoke. He spoke it without joy, as one who knows he must, for the truth's sake. But he was a servant of the dark. His stare raised Sarevan's hackles. Strangeness roiled in it. Darkness. Warmthless, sunless cold. And yet, woven into it, something which Sarevan had never expected to see: acceptance. He could endure the survival of the Sunborn, if the balance was kept.

"You're lying," Sarevan said to him, a soft snarl.

"Not in this," said Baran, the light of his shadow, who never lied.

Mirain alive. Hirel alive. The war ended.

For a price.

Such a price.

Sarevan gathered his body together. His beautiful proud body, just now awakened to the delights of a woman's embrace: one woman, who might have been, who might still be his lady and his queen. He had been more vain of it than of anything but his power. He had lost the one. Now must he lose the other? Would he have nothing left?

Mirain. Hirel. Two empires made one. Peace. A child. They had all but promised that. An heir of his body.

Even if it must be a woman's body. He was not afraid of that. He had birthed a child already.

They waited. He could read them. Even Orsan. Even the darkmage. They would not scorn him if he shrank from the choice. Orsan could not have made it. None of them could. The master, who had, had begun as a woman. Had passed in the world's eyes from lesser to greater.

Sarevan stood again. His knees melted; he froze them with his terror. They asked too much. He could not do this. He was royal; he was a warrior trained. He could die for his empire. He could even betray it for its own salvation. But he was no great selfless saint, to give up all that he was and to live on after. Death was frightening, but it was final. This . . .

"I suppose," his tongue said, hardly stumbling, "that you'll do it now, before we all have time to turn craven."

Damn his tongue. *Damn* it.

No one smiled. No one looked triumphant. Orsan rose as Sarevan had never seen him rise, as an old man, stiff and palsied. "We will do it now," he said.

They brought Sarevan to a high bare chamber. Its many tall windows were open to the wind; its center was a table of stone. Dawnstone slab on nightstone base, stones of the light and the dark brought together in balance. They took his robe; they freed his hair from its braid and combed it carefully; they took the gold from his beard and the emeralds from his ears and the torque from about his neck. With no knot or weaving on him, bare as he had come into the world, he lay upon the table. And started a little. His skin, braced for cold stone, recoiled from a warmth as of the sun in summer. The dawnstone knew his lineage; it kindled for him although it was full day and not rising dawn, flushing with the splendor of the morning sky.

Blessed numbness had brought him so far; now it was forsaking him. His brain screamed and struggled, battling for escape. His body lay meekly where it was bidden. He could not even move to bid it farewell.

The mages stood about him, a circle of shadows against the windows' brightness. One bent. His grandfather kissed him very gently upon the forehead. No word passed between them. *Make me stop,* he tried to plead. *Don't let me do this.*

The Red Prince straightened. His hands rose. Power gathered in them.

Sarevan closed his eyes, breathing deep. He could still see. Witch-sight. They had given it to him: thinking to have mercy, perhaps. But they had forgotten how bitterly clear it could be.

Slowly his breath left him, and with it fear. He had chosen. Not his tongue, not his madness. His deepest self. There had never been such a choosing, for such a cause; nor would there ever be again.

Avaryan, he prayed in the center of the power, *take me. Hold me fast.*

Light wove with dark. Chanting fused with silence. Mage and sorcerer wrought together.

And there was beauty in it. There was rightness. Balance. Perfection. A strength that, wielded, could alter worlds.

He would remember. He swore it, even as the power took him. He would remember the truth.

Then there was no memory. Only pain.

PART THREE

Hirel Uverias

Nineteen

HIREL COULD BELIEVE THAT SORCERERS HAD SNATCHED HIM away from Kundri'j. He could easily believe that he was a hostage. He could even find it credible that his captors were a conspiracy of the world's mages.

But this.

At first they would not tell him what they had done with Sarevan. Then he heard them: the cries of a man in mortal agony. His jailers, a pair of young mages, one in violet and one in grey, insisted that they heard nothing; that all was silent. No force of his could shake them. When he lunged for the door, their power caught him and bound him.

The cries went on unabated. They tore at his heart; they rent his sanity. They came from everywhere and from nowhere. They echoed in his brain.

Night came. The guard changed. A man and a woman, these, older and considerably stronger. They brought silence. They forced sleep upon him, from which he woke to a cold and relentless fury. And, with crawling slowness, to what they called the truth.

They broke it gently. Too gently. At first Hirel heard only that

they had wrought some unspeakable sorcery upon Sarevan. That
they hoped by it to end the war. That they had slain him.

"No," said the woman. "He is not dead."

He was worse than dead. Hirel commanded; for a wonder they
obeyed. They took him to a chamber almost princely in this barren
fortress. They set him before the bed and left him to stare. A dark
lithe body; a flood of molten-copper hair.

A body. Hirel's mind struggled against the impossibility of it.
Liars, they were liars. This was a stranger. A stranger who was a
woman.

"It is Sarevadin," said the mage in grey, unmoved by Hirel's
rage.

She was as splendid as Sarevan had ever been. She was fire and
ebony, strength and delicacy melded together, the eagle's profile
smoothed and fined into a stunning, high-nosed beauty.

Hirel rounded on his jailers. The guard had changed again.
High ones indeed now: Han-Gilen's prince and the Mageguild's
master. He addressed them almost gently. "Undo your magic."

"We cannot," the prince said.

"You must," said Hirel, still without force, still with the semblance of reason.

"It cannot be done." The master leaned heavily on a staff; nor
was it only the twisting of his legs which so weakened him. "This
magecraft is perilous to endure even once. Twice is deadly."

"Undo it," Hirel repeated, obstinate. "Change him back. I
command you."

"No."

It did not matter who said it. Even now Hirel could recognize
finality. And hate. Hate as pure as that profile. "You will pay for
this," he whispered. He turned face and mind away from them.
"Get out," he said.

In time they obeyed. Hirel sat, cold and still, waiting with the
patience of princes. He waited long and long. The changed one
slept. Sometimes she stirred. Once she murmured. Her voice was
low, but it was most certainly a woman's.

Hirel knew when she woke; knew it beneath his skin. Carefully
he drew back.

For a long while she neither moved nor opened her eyes. Her
face betrayed nothing. When the lids lifted, the eyes were dim,

clouded. Slowly they cleared. Her hands wandered amid the coverlets. One crept up. She stared at it, turned it. Gold flamed in the palm. She flexed slender fingers, eyes wandering along the fine-boned rounded arm. She touched her thigh. Raised her knee. Frowned at it. Turned it, peering at her foot. Not a remarkably small foot, but narrow and shapely.

She was long in coming to her middle. Hesitant. Perhaps afraid. She felt of her face; of her neck. Ran fingers through her hair. Brushed a breast as if by accident, and recoiled, creeping back, trembling. Her frown deepened. Her lips set. She sat up, glaring down at the altered lines of her body: breasts high and round and firm above the narrow waist; hips a gentle flare; and where her thighs met, the worst of it. She touched it. No miracle transformed it. It was a miracle itself, frightening in its perfection; and no memory in it of the man who had been. That was all within.

She rose, awkward-graceful, feeling out the balance of this new shape. Flexing narrowed shoulders, swaying on broadened hips, essaying an uncertain step. Little by little her gait eased, though it was taut still, wary.

A shield hung on the wall, polished for a mirror; she faced it with an air of great and hard-won courage. She turned slowly, twisting about, knotting her hair about her hand, peering over her shoulder at her mirrored back. She touched her shoulder where the deep pitted scar should have been. It was gone. She was all new, whole and smooth and unmarred.

She confronted herself, face to reflected face. Her hand rose to her cheek. "I'm not ugly," she said in wonder. Starting at the sound of her voice, speaking again with an air of defiance. "I'm . . . not . . . ugly."

Hirel's body moved of itself. She spun, quick as a cat. Hirel gasped under the force of those eyes. They had changed not at all; they were black-brilliant as ever, sweeping over him, flashing to his face. "You," she said. "You look different."

His jaw was hanging. He retrieved it. Laughter burst from him: hysteria certainly, and incredulity, and something astonishingly like relief. For a moment she only stared. Then she echoed him, a great ringing peal, tribute to perfect absurdity.

They hiccoughed into silence. They were holding one another up, eye to streaming eye. She was a hair's breadth the taller.

She stiffened all at once, going cold in his hands. He let her go. She drew back. Her back met the mirror; she whirled upon it, tearing at it, flinging it wide. It rang as it fell. She sank down shivering, veiled in the bright cloud of her hair.

Hirel stood over her. Touched her.

She did not erupt as he had half expected. He sat by her, wordless. When she did not heed him, he stroked her hair. Her ear beneath it was exquisite. He kissed it.

She pulled away with the swiftness of rage. "Stop pitying me!"

"That," said Hirel, "I had not begun to do."

His flatness gave her pause. For a moment. She flung back her hair. "Not yet. Oh, no. Not yet. I merely disgust you. I did the unspeakable. I who was a lord of creation, I who was nature's darling, I let myself be twisted into *this.*"

"A woman of great valor and beauty."

"Don't lie to me, cubling. I can taste your anger. You think I was tricked, or forced. I was neither. No one made me do it. I chose it for myself." She scrambled to her feet. "Look at me, Hirel. Look at me!"

Hirel had learned to measure beauty by Sarevan Is'kelion. This that he had become was fairer still. Fair and wild, with the recklessness of despair. "I am angry," he said. "They had no right to demand such a thing of you. None even to conceive of it."

"They demanded nothing. They tried to dissuade me."

"Surely," said Hirel with a curl of his lip. "They warned you of the dangers, and spoke of the faces of courage, and named all the lesser choices. It was cleverly done. I applaud them."

"It was the only choice with hope in it." She clenched her fists. "It's no matter to you. You can wed me, bed me, get the child who will bring the peace, and go back to your twice ninescore concubines."

Hirel regarded her. She looked very young. As indeed she was: scarce a full day old. But Sarevan Is'kelion lived yet in her. It was in her eyes, and in her bearing, and in the tenor of her words. "Am I to wed you?" he asked. "I was not consulted."

"Did you need to be? It should be easy enough for a man of your attainments. You're not asked to love me. Only to beget a son on me."

Hirel frowned. She stiffened; he frowned the more blackly at himself, cursing his wayward face. This was going all awry. He tried to choose his words with care. "You are too certain of my thoughts, Sunchild. Must I be revolted by you? Might I not find you as beautiful now as you ever were? Perhaps I even find endurable the prospect of contracting a marriage with you. After all, it is logical."

"Of course it is. Else I'd never have done this."

"But," said Hirel, "I would that you had spoken to me before you submitted yourself to the mages."

She heard none of his regret. She heard only the rebuke which he had not intended. The glitter of her eyes warned him; he faced her, pulling her to him, holding her too close for struggle. She was no soft pliant woman. She was strong in her slenderness, like a panther, like a steel blade. In the instant of her surprise, he kissed her hard and deep. She tasted much the same. A little sweeter, even in resistance.

For a long moment she was rigid. With suddenness that startled them both, she kindled. Her arms locked about him. Her body arched. Her sweetness turned all to fire.

He laughed, breathless. She did not laugh with him. Her eyes were wild and soft at once, and more than a little mad. "Lady," he said. "Lady, I have wanted this, I have dreamed of this, so long, so long . . . Bright lady, I think I love you."

The softness fled; the wildness filled her. "Damn them," she whispered. "Damn their meddling magic."

He drew breath to speak. To protest, perhaps. But she was gone.

Hirel started after her, stopped. She was all raw, looking for pain wherever she turned. Pain had brought her to the choosing; pain had made the choice, and pain had wrought the woman where a man had been. Time would heal her; he could only hinder it.

He left the room slowly, letting his feet bear him where they would. He was not surprised to gain a companion, nor, at all, to recognize the man who walked beside him.

Aranos was as coolly wise as ever, and as full of serpent's sympathy. "She is a woman, brother," he said with the suggestion of a smile. "These moods will beset her."

Hirel kept his anger at bay. Saving it. Hoarding it for when he should have the power to wield it. "You have made a woman. You have not unmade the Sunborn's heir."

"Indeed we have not," said Aranos. "But we have assured that you will live to rule not Asanion alone, but with it Keruvarion."

"Do you believe that?" asked Hirel.

"It will require tact, of course. She was born a man and raised to rule. She will not accept meekly the woman's portion: the harem and the bearing of children. But her body will aid you. It will guide her on the path of her chosen sex; it will yield to your mastery. Get her with child and keep her with child, and she will be glad to surrender her power into your hands."

Hirel knew that he should be calm. Aranos spoke simple wisdom. The philosophers proclaimed it. Women were begotten of a lesser nature, of flawed seed, with no purpose but to nourish the children which their lords set in them. And of course, the sages averred, to give pleasure in the seed's sowing. Beasts might do as much. Beasts did, some believed; for what was the female but a blurred and bestial image of the male?

"No," Hirel said. "Lies and folly, all of it."

Aranos looked long at him. "Ah, Asuchirel. You have fallen in love."

"So I have. But I have not lost my ability to see what lies before my face."

"The better for you both," Aranos said undaunted, "if you are besotted with her, if only you remember who you are. And what this marriage can gain you."

"I am not likely to forget," said Hirel.

Aranos was too well trained to lay hand on a high prince, but he raised that hand athwart Hirel's advance. "See that you do not. Yon conspirators dream that they have won great victories: the Varyani that Asanion is theirs in the person of a malleable child, the mages that they have found a way to lessen Avaryan's power and to increase their own. I know that you are not the pretty fool which you so often choose to seem; I believe that the victor can be Asanion. If you press your advantage. If, having lost your heart, you do not lose your head."

Hirel smiled, honey-sweet. "My head is entirely safe. You might do well to be concerned for your own." He stepped around his brother's hand and stretched his stride. Aranos, in robes and dignity, did not see fit to follow.

They had a fine nest of mages here. One or another was always within sight, although none accosted Hirel once he had rid himself of Aranos. He paced off the limits of the fortress; much of it was carved into living rock, the rest built upon the summit of a mountain. Beyond it was all a wilderness of stone and cloud and sky. Some of the thronging peaks were higher, clad in snow. Many marched below in jagged ranks, black and red and grey and blinding white. No green. No sign of human habitation.

Water rose bitter cold from a spring within the mountain. Food came by the will of mages: solid enough for all of that, and plentiful if not rich. The cooks knew no art but the art of spiceless stews and boiled grain. The wine was little better.

But there were compensations. The purity of the air. The splendor of the heights, and at nightfall the stars, great flaming flowers in the perfect blackness of the sky.

Mages found Hirel at a high window, set a robe on him, and led him to the hall. After the vault of heaven, the chamber of stone was dim and cramped. Hirel struggled to breathe its heavy air.

The conspirators had gathered. They had a haggard look; the Red Prince was not among them, nor had they left a place for him. The Varyani sat a little apart from the mages, and Aranos stood with his brace of sorcerers. They were saying little.

The Sunchild stood alone by the fire. Her hair was loose down her back; her robe was plain to starkness, white girdled with white. She was not wearing Avaryan's torque. The Sun-priests' glances deplored it, but her shoulder was turned firmly away from them. She played with the flames as if they had been water, letting them lick at her fingers.

Hirel sprang toward her. Her glance halted him. It was a stranger's stare, cool and composed, with no spark of recognition. Hirel stiffened against it. The fire had done her no harm. Of course; she was born of it. He had tasted the anguish of the birthing.

She did not even choose to know him.

Hirel stood beside her. He knew that the mages watched. He

was past caring. He spoke quietly but not furtively, and reasonably enough when all was considered. "Lady, whether we will or we nill, we are bound together. We can make of that bond a misery, or we can transform it into a triumph."

"Such a triumph," she said. The words were bitter; the tone was remote and cold. "You with all your women. I in the harem's chains."

Aranos' satisfaction was distinct, like a hand on Hirel's shoulder, a voice murmuring complacencies in his ear. He twitched them away. "You would be a fool to choose that, lady."

"I have already."

He looked at her then. At the bowed bright head; at the suggestion of her body within the robe. At the hand half hidden in her skirt, knotted into a fist, trembling with repressed violence. "Yes," Hirel said, "it is a great pity that the spell's weaving did not slay you as you wished it to. And that, having condemned yourself to life in a woman's body, you should have waked to find yourself fair. And greatest of all, that I cannot find it in me to shrink from you. That I find you beautiful; that I desire you."

"Of course you desire me. I'm female. I'm dowered with an empire."

Hirel paused. "Perhaps," he said, "I am at fault. To your eyes I would be no great marvel of a man. I shall never be more than small as your people reckon it; I am pallid away from the sun and sallow in his presence; and I am years too young for you."

"Now who's talking like a fool?"

Hirel spread his hands. "Is it folly? You insist that you repel me. Since you do not, then surely it is I who repel you. Did they fail, your meddling mages? Did they make you a woman who can love none but women?"

Her head flew up. Her eyes were wild.

"Look at me," he said. "Touch me. What does your body say of me?"

She would look. For a long moment he feared that she would not touch. Her hand trembled as she reached, as it traced his cheek. "It sings," she whispered. "It sings of you."

"Of me? Not merely of men?"

She drew a breath fierce-edged with temper. "Of you, damn

you. It never—it didn't—I still don't want just any man. Or—or any woman. But you, I want. I want you with all that is in me."

"So always," murmured Hirel, "have I wanted you." His voice rose a little, clear and calm. "It is not the shape of you from which I recoil. It is that it was done to you. That, I can never forgive. Since it is done and is not to be undone, I bide my time; I wait upon my vengeance. And while I wait for it, I am minded to love you. I will share the world with you."

"If I am minded to share it."

"Half of it is mine, my lady."

"But half of it is not." She smiled. Hirel was comforted, a little. He hoped that Aranos was not. It was a white wild smile, with no softness in it. "You'll free your concubines, prince. You'll swear solemnly to take no other woman as bedmate or queen. Else you'll not have me."

"The concubines," said Hirel, "I can agree to. But the rest—"

"Swear."

Hirel struggled to master his temper. "You must be reasonable, my lady. There will be times when you do not want me. Would you have me force you?"

"So then. We compromise. When you don't want me, I'll find another bedmate."

Hirel flung up his head. "You will not!"

"Why not?"

"It is unthinkable. It is forbidden. It is a breach of the marriage contract."

"Exactly."

"I do not understand you," Hirel said with heroic restraint. "You suffered all of this for one sole end: to contract an alliance with me. Now you demand of me a concession which you know I cannot grant."

"Can't you?"

"I have no need of you. You need me, or your sacrifice is worthless."

"Without me, you die and your empire falls, and I live to rule."

"Who will follow you?" demanded Hirel, the more cruel for that his cruelty seemed to wound her not at all. "Who will accept the rule of a woman?"

"Who will be left to claim the power? I have the *Kasar* still; Keruvarion's law binds the empire to the bearer of the brand. Asanion will be harder, I grant you. But I can rule it, and I will. With you or without you."

"You will have to slay me with your own hand."

"Or marry you. On my terms. I'll not be your veiled and big-bellied slave, Hirel Uverias. Nor will I wait my turn with all your other slaves, contending with them for a night of your favor. Unless you agree to do the same for me."

It was to be expected. She still thought like a man. She did not know how to be a woman.

She would not lower those bold black eyes. The same eyes that had transfixed Hirel on the first night of their meeting, refusing to accede to the laws of nature: of race then and of caste, as now of gender.

She spoke almost gently. "It's hard, I know. But it's not unheard of. My mother bound my father to the same."

"Your father had been a priest; and he was never an Asanian high prince."

"So? Can you do any less than a bandit king?"

"I would not stoop to it."

She laughed. It was cruel, because there was no malice in it. It turned all Hirel's resistance into the petulance of a spoiled child.

She was glorious when she laughed. She had no shame of this that she had chosen; she had nothing resembling a maiden's modesty. In front of all the staring mages, she took Hirel's face in her hands and kissed him.

Hirel's heart thudded; his head reeled. Sarevan, mage and priest though he was, wild and half mad and as near a giant as made no matter, had never frightened Hirel more than a little. A prince could match a prince, though one be descended from a god.

This was still Sarevan, little changed once one grew accustomed to the single great change. Yet her touch woke Hirel to something very like panic. A prince could match a prince. But what of a Sunborn princess?

She drew back slightly, searching his face. It flamed under her gaze. She smiled. "I think I love you too, youngling. Don't ask me why."

"If there are gods," Hirel muttered, "they laugh to hear you."

"They do." She reclaimed her hands. Her smile took on an edge of iron. "But I am not marrying a man who refuses to grant me the full freedom which he grants himself."

Hirel's breath escaped him in a rush. "I never said that I would bind you. You need not take the veil, nor shall I imprison you in the harem. You may even," he said, and that was far from easy, "you may even bear arms, although for that we must change the law in Asanion."

"And?" she asked, unmollified.

"Is that not enough?" He knew it was not. Her brows had lowered. He glared back. "I cannot bind myself to you alone. My nature forbids it. I am a man; I am made to beget many sons. My desires are strong, and they are urgent, and they are not to be denied. Whereas a woman is made to bear a few strong children; her lusts are less potent, her needs gentler, her spirit shaped for the loving of a single man."

She laughed again, and now she mocked him. "Hear the wisdom of a child! I almost hate to disillusion you. But alas, it is illusion, and I will not be swayed by it. Bind yourself, Hirel, or set me free."

"And raise another man's son as my own?"

"Only if you demand the same of me."

He tossed his aching head. "You will drive me mad."

She would not even pretend to regret it. She only waited, unshakable. She was very beautiful. She was not the only beautiful woman in the world. She was certainly the most obstinate, and the most unreasonable, and the most maddening. And she brought with her the greatest of all dowries.

It was not worth the price she set on it.

And what price had she paid to offer it?

"Be free, then," he snapped at her. "But do not expect me to acknowledge your get."

"Even when it is yours?"

"How can I ever be sure of it?"

"You will," she said, "I promise you."

She held out her hand with its flame of gold. He stared at it until it began to fall. Then he caught it. Raised it. Kissed it. "Lady," he said, "whatever comes of this venture, certainly I shall not perish of boredom."

Now she looked as a maiden ought, eyes downcast, demure and shy. Struggling, no doubt, to keep at bay a grin of triumph. Hirel could not even be indignant. Aranos' expression was too intriguing a study.

Twenty

THE MAGES HAD WROUGHT WELL. HIREL GRANTED THEM THAT. The hall blazed with magelight: sparks of white and gold, blue and green, red and yellow, set like jewels in the roof. Flowers bloomed on the grey stone and wound up the pillars; hangings shimmered behind, light and shadow interwoven, shaping images that shifted and changed whenever he glanced at them.

He stood by the undying fire in a circle of mages, clad as a prince who went to his wedding, in an eightfold robe of gold and diamond. The mages of the guild stood two and two, each servant of the light with his dark companion. Zha'dan loomed over them, painted and jeweled and braided, outblazing the fire itself with his splendor. He flashed Hirel a white smile, which Hirel returned with the faintest of flickers.

He glanced at his companion. Aranos held the place of the honored kinsman, attended by his priests with the scroll of the contract. Han-Gilen's prince faced them with Orozia and the guildmaster. They had words to say: ritual challenges, ritual concessions. They called the lady Sarevadin. Odd to hear it as a woman's name. One might have thought that the empress had known, to choose a name which would serve for a daughter as for a son.

He marshaled his wandering wits. It was a very long contract, and very complex. But its heart was simple. The heir of Asanion took to wife the heir of Keruvarion. He granted her full freedom, as in turn she granted him. When he came into his inheritance, he must share his throne with her; so too must she share the throne of Keruvarion. The first child of their bodies would stand heir to both empires.

He set his name where he was bidden. When he straightened, he went rigid.

An Asanian bride did not show herself at the exchange of legalities that was the wedding proper. When her kinsmen had sold her with due ceremony, slaves bore her in a closed litter to her husband's house. There she would feast among the women until he had done feasting with the men. Then, and only then, would he see her: swathed and veiled and weighted with jewels, enthroned amid the riches of her dowry.

She wore a veil, a shimmer of royal white upon her bright hair. Her gown was of a northern fashion, shocking to Asanian eyes: a skirt of many tiers, white and gold, broad-belted with gold about her narrow waist, and a vest of gold-embroidered white, and a kingdom's worth of gold and emeralds about her arms and her neck and her brows, suspended from her ears and woven into her hair. None of it sufficed to cover her breasts. Her nipples, like her lips and her eyelids, bore a dusting of gilt.

She took the pen from Hirel's stiff fingers and signed her name next to his, in the characters of the Hundred Realms and again in those of Asanion. Hirel bit his lip lest he disgrace himself with laughter. Aranos was appalled. Even Prince Orsan seemed mildly startled by her coming, if not by her presumption.

Having sealed the alliance under Asanian law, they faced the prince and the priestess in the rites of Keruvarion. Orozia demanded Sarevadin's torque of priesthood, held it up in her hands, raised a long chant in a tongue which Hirel did not know. She ended on a high throbbing note. Her hands lowered. She set the torque again about Sarevadin's throat, with much solemnity and no little resistance from the Sunchild. But the prince quelled her with a stern word. "You may not repudiate your calling. You are High Princess of Keruvarion; you will continue in Avaryan's priesthood. As your father has done. As many another ruling queen has done." She bent her head then, submitting without humility.

Hirel spoke the words which he had been instructed to speak, but as soon as he had spoken, he had forgotten them. They were only words. This was reality. The hand he held, no warmer or steadier than his own; the voice that murmured in his silences; the eyes both bold and frightened, and once the glimmer of a smile. He was rapt. Bewitched. He the prince, the logician, the master of his royal will.

He hardly tasted the wedding feast. Some he must eat, and some he must drink: it was the rite. They drank from the same cup, ate from the same bowl. She ate and drank for them both.

She kindled under all the eyes. She had even cold Aranos falling into her hand, hanging on her every word, dwindling when she turned her eyes away from him. Sevayin, they called her. Sevayin Is'kirien, the Twiceborn, the Sun's child.

Then it was past, and they were alone, locked in a chamber with a hearth and a winetable and a bed broad enough for a battlefield. Hirel did not know where to go. She—Sevayin, he must resolve to call her—had lost a little of her brittle brilliance. She filled a cup with wine and held it out. Hirel declined it. She toyed with it; sipped; hesitated; set it down. "It's not done, you know," she said. "There's still the crux of it. I hope you haven't lost your courage. Because," she said, and her voice shook, "I don't think I ever had any."

She looked most valiant, standing there in all her beauty, trying not to tremble. Hirel let his body act for him. It went to her; it held her, or she held it. They clung together like children.

It was she who broke the silence. "I dreamed this," she said. "And you."

"And you call yourself no seer?"

"I'm not. I'm merely mad." She laughed as she said it, unsteadily. "And to crown it all, now I can't escape. Now I have to begin my lessons in the high arts."

"I shall take delight in teaching you." Hirel held her at arm's length. She smiled shakily. He smiled back. "I confess, I have somewhat more skill as a lover of women than as a lover of men. And rather more inclination for it."

"I . . . incline . . . very much toward you." She swayed forward, brushing his lips with hers. Her hands sought the fastenings of his robes. They were wedding robes; they parted, slipping away of their own accord. He wore no trousers beneath. Her breath caught. "You've grown again, cubling."

"How fortunate you are," he said. "No one can know when you wake to desire."

She lowered her eyes. "I can," she said very low.

He touched her. She quivered. It was not wholly true, what Hirel had said. Her breasts were taut. He freed them of encumbrances: the vest, the necklaces, the golden pectoral. He loosed the clasp of her belt. It sprang free. Her skirts fell one by one. There were nine. He appreciated the irony.

She cast off the ornaments which he had left her, and the drift of veil. Only the torque remained, and a single jewel: a chain of gold about her hips, thin as a thread, clasped with an emerald. He set his hand to it.

"Not yet," she said, her laughter half a gasp. Her heart was beating hard. "That's the maiden-chain. It has to wait until you've made a woman of me."

She was. Entirely. A maiden, and then a woman. As he breached the gate, she cried aloud. For pain. For exultation. They sang in him. They wrought a great and wondrous harmony, a symphony of bodies joined together. He soared upon it. He made himself one with it.

They descended together, he and she. He laid his head upon her breast. She wove her fingers into his hair. Slowly their hearts quieted. Her cheeks were wet, but the tears were none of grief.

He let his hand wander down her belly and her hips to the clasp of the chain. It parted. His fingers found their way between her thighs. She kindled, but she shifted slightly, away from him. He yielded to her will; his hand came to rest again upon her hip.

"Hirel," she said after a few tens of heartbeats. He turned his head to kiss her breast. "Hirel, where were you when the mages loosed their power on me?"

He raised his head, frowning that she should speak of it now of all times. But he answered her readily enough. "I was locked in a chamber, and no one would let me go to you."

She met his eyes. "Where were you, Hirel?"

"I told you, I—" He broke off. She knew what he had said. She wanted more. "I was locked away, but I heard your cries. They all denied that there was aught to hear."

"There was nothing. I was silent, Hirel."

"I heard you," he insisted.

"You did." She scowled. Damn these witches and their paradoxes. A smile flickered; she bit it back. "You were in my mind. You and the mages. You've been in and out of it ever since."

"That is preposterous."

"Have you ever had a better night's loving? Or a stranger?"

"You have a gift for it. And I am besotted with you."

Her smile escaped. "And I love you, my proud prince. But something is happening with my power. I should have suspected it long ago. I began to when I found you amid the pain, and your presence eased it a little. It's been growing stronger since; it's strongest when you touch me. I've been afraid to believe in it. Afraid I only dreamed it. But now I know. We're mages, Hirel. Both of us."

He thrust himself to his knees. "*You* are a mage. I am glad for you. It was bitter, your power's loss. But I have no part in it."

"You are the heart of it," said Sevayin, relentless. "You were there when I lost my power. You were with me when I almost died; it was you who turned me back to the light. You found the Eye of Power. You were almost on top of it when I destroyed it. We came to love one another; we faced death together, as we faced life. Somehow, in the midst of it, my magery bound itself to you. It's part of you now."

"No," Hirel said. "I can believe the improbable, but not the impossible."

She seized his hands. He could never accustom himself to her strength, even though he knew what she had been and what she would always be: born of warriors, trained for war. He glared into her eyes, and lost his battle thereby.

It was a sharpening of all the senses. He could see through stone; he could hear across worlds. His skin knew every nuance of the air. He tasted love and fear and gladness. He scented wonders.

Power, she whispered. Her lips never moved. *This is power. I thought that I had lost it. I wanted to die for lack of it.*

"I am not made for it!"

She drew back. Hirel reeled, blind, deaf, all but bodiless. By slow degrees his senses grew again, but dimmed and dulled, mere earthly senses. The only brightness was Sevayin lying beneath him, her face a vision of lamplight and shadow, crowned with fire. With great care he touched her cheek. The power roared and flamed about him.

Her smile was sad and joyous at once: warmth and coolness mingled, scented with flowers. Flameflowers, burning-sweet. "Oh, yes, my love," she said, "you are made for it. It flames in your blood. It takes its strength from you."

"Ah," he said, wry, not yet angry. "I am your familiar."

Her eyes glittered. "You are much more than that!"

"Certainly. I am your lord and husband."

"And my lover." She stroked him until he quivered with pleasure. Her joy made his heart sing. She was whole again and growing wild with it, leaping up, sweeping him with her, spinning like a mad thing. She reached for the fire that was in her; she set her will upon it.

Hirel groped through the blinding pain. He found her huddled on the floor, too stunned even for temper. "Crippled," she said. "Still—after all—"

"You are not!" Hirel cried.

She barely heard him. "I was so sure. I *knew*. My power has come back. It has been coming back ever since the change; and you are its focus. But the pain is still there. The walls are as high as ever." She raised her head. Her lips drew back from her teeth. "I will break them down. By Avaryan, Hirel, I will."

The Red Prince was gone again. So too was Aranos. The mages would not tell Hirel where. The how he could guess. Even a little of the why, if he set his mind to it. There was trouble. The war did not go well. But for which side—that, they refused to say.

He could not find Sevayin. She was present in his mind, an awareness as of his own body, a glimmer of night and fire; in time, she had promised him, he would learn to follow the presence to its source. But he had not yet learned, and she had hidden herself well. He spared a moment for temper. A wife should hold herself at her husband's disposal.

This one did as she pleased. Which was nothing but what she had always done, insofar as she could in this wintry eyrie.

Hirel could do nothing that befit a prince. There were no servants but the mages, and they performed none but the most essential of services. He must bathe and dress and amuse himself. There were books, a whole great vault of them. None could tell him what passed between the empires. One of the mages condescended to a match or two of weaponless combat; he would speak of naught but holds and throws and falls.

At length, driven by his mighty restlessness, Hirel came to the heart of the castle, to the chamber of power denuded of its wedding splendor. Its fire burned unabated. If it failed, Sevayin said, the fortress would fall; for the fire was the power that held stone upon stone.

Hirel sat on the floor in front of it. It looked like a simple mortal fire. Its warmth caressed him; its dancing soothed his temper. He closed his eyes. The flames flickered in the darkness. "If you are power," he said to them, "serve me. Tell me what my jailers will not have me know."

"Are you strong enough to endure the telling?"

Hirel glanced over his shoulder, unstartled. The fire's doing, perhaps. The guildmaster leaned on twin staffs. His robe, which had never seemed to be of any color in particular, in that light seemed woven of silver and violet together, shimmering like imperial silk. "I must know," Hirel answered him. "Has Asanion fallen?"

"No."

"Is my father dead?"

"Indeed not."

"Have I been stripped of my titles?"

"You know that you have not."

"Then," said Hirel, "I have nothing to fear."

The mage sat by him. Why, thought Hirel, the man was young. It was the twisting of his body, and the pain of the twisting, that had aged him so terribly.

It was no less than he deserved.

"Indeed," he said calmly. "It was my payment for the power I wield. I had great beauty once, and great strength, and grace such

as few of mortal race are given. I was a dancer in the temple of
Shavaan in Esharan of the Nine Cities."

"But they are—"

"Yes. They are all women. What I did to your beloved, I did to
myself. And more. All that I had been, I surrendered, to be the
master of mages."

Hirel considered that broken body, those clear eyes. "What
price will you demand of me?"

"Not I, prince. The power. It will do with you as it chooses."

"I do the choosing, guildmaster."

The master smiled. "Perhaps you do. Perhaps you have. Are you
not inextricably bound to the Sunchild? Do you not accept the
reality of magic?"

"Perforce," said Hirel, "yes." He narrowed his eyes. "Tell me."

The master bowed his head, raised it. "Perhaps, after all, it is not
so terrible. It is merely a wielding of power. We are out of your
world, prince, and out of your time. It is still autumn there; the war
has barely begun. Mirain An-Sh'Endor has taken Kovruen. Ziad-
Ilarios has announced that he will lead the Asanian armies in his
own sacred person, as he led them before he took the throne."

Hirel bared his teeth in a smile. "Scandalous."

"Is it not? But that is nothing to the greater scandal which now
rocks Asanion. The emperor your father will not only command
his own forces in the field. He has sent an embassy to the Sunborn,
proposing an alliance."

Hirel stiffened, incredulous.

"Truly, prince. An alliance against us who dare to hold you
hostage."

Hirel laughed suddenly. "Thus is the biter bit!"

"If either of them can find us."

"They will," said Hirel. "You are not the master of all mages."

"I am not," the guildmaster conceded. "The Sunborn is greater
than I. But if he accepts your father's embassy, he will have fulfilled
our purpose. They may find our gate; they may besiege it; they
may even conquer it. It does not matter. You are here, with your
lady who bears the heir of the empires."

"And they fight together." Hirel frowned. "If all is turning to
your advantage, why are your mages so reluctant to boast of it?"

"It is too early yet for certainty. The Sunborn may refuse the alliance. The Golden Courts may turn against your father. Ziad-Ilarios himself may choose to act alone in despite of his ambassadors."

"And," said Hirel, seeing clearly now, "we their children may manage to escape you. What will the Sunborn do when he discovers that he is father to a daughter?"

"He will discover it. In good time. When it will best serve us all."

"How long, guildmaster? How long will you imprison us here?"

"As long as we must."

"As long as you can." Hirel stood. "I should be compassionate. Your order will bear the brunt of the emperor's wrath. Does it trouble you that even as your people suffer, certain princes will enjoy the full trust of their lords?"

"That trust serves us well," the master said.

"Trust us, magelord. Let us share in your counsels. We are your great weapon; should we not have a voice in our wielding?"

"What sword is given such grace?"

"What sword has a will to oppose its bearer?"

"Your lady will not. She has foreseen what will be. She will not betray her prophecy."

Hirel heard the echo behind the words. "You fear her even more than you fear me. You struck a bargain of desperation with a prince bereft of his power. A mageborn princess is a new and frightening thing; for she may choose to disregard the fears and follies of her elder self. Is it you who give her such pain with each new flexing of her power? Is it you who would strengthen each wall as she casts it down?" Hirel stood over the mage, wielding his presence with all his royal skill. "Trust, we meet with trust; and there may be much that we can do to aid you. But if you persist in treating us as captives, we will do all that we can to set ourselves free."

The guildmaster sat silent, uncowed. Hirel refused to let the silence diminish him. At last the mage said, "Perhaps we have erred. We meant but to spare you anxiety."

Hirel folded his arms and bulked a little larger.

"Would you rather have heard rumors and half-truths from the mouths of our apprentices?"

"There are no apprentices here."

The guildmaster shifted his body, sighing. "Prince Orsan

warned us. My fault that I would not listen. I am not greatly skilled in dealing with princes."

"Young princes. Children who refuse to be children. Apprentices with the arrogance of masters."

The mage smiled. "Just so, high prince. Will you pardon me?"

"If you will trust me."

"I can try."

"I will know if you do not." Hirel stepped back. "Good day, sir."

It struck Hirel as he left the hall behind. A lady who bore the heir of empires.

Already.

How could they know?

Of course they must. They were mages.

He began to run. Stopped short, mindful of dignity. Damned it all and bolted toward the whisper of her presence.

It was not hard, with necessity to drive him. She was on the mountain, perched on the tip of its fang, calling to eagles. Hirel dropped gasping at her feet. Heights had never troubled him overmuch, but this was loftiest lunacy. For a long while he could only struggle to breathe. Then he looked down and nearly lost his senses. He clutched at unheeding stone and forced his eyes to open. She filled them. In the bitter cold she wore torque and trousers and an armlet or three. Her feet were bare. Her mantle she wrapped about Hirel, wrapping herself about that, firing him with kisses. "I can talk to them," she said, exultant. "The eagles. They're bronze, have you seen? They know no white kin."

Hirel glared at her. "Are you going to face the courts of the empires as you face yonder eagles?"

She followed his glance downward to her breasts. "They don't like coverings."

"Have you paused to wonder why?"

It was Hirel who blushed. She shrugged. "It's common, I suppose. I may be more sensitive than most. Or maybe I'm simply not used to it. Other women grow into it gradually."

"Yes," said Hirel, "it is gradual. Twice nine Brightmoon-cycles, more or less."

There was a very long silence. She drew back, sitting on her heels, staring down at her body. She weighed her breasts in her hands. She spanned the faint curve of her belly. She reached inward, a quiver of Hirel's newborn senses. Her head came up. Her face was blank, shocked. "I am," she said. "I . . . actually . . . am." She still did not believe it. Even though she knew. Even though she had wedded him for this very purpose.

She had begun to shiver. Hirel spread her cloak over them both, holding her in silence. Her mind was walled and barred. How far he had come in so little time: he floundered in its absence, like a man struck blind. It was easier when he was apart from her; then he could endure to be alone. But to be body to body and shut away . . .

Anger flared, warming him in the wind. Was that how he must live? Crippled when he walked alone, whole only when he lay in her embrace. Living for the touch of her hand. Pining for the lack of it.

Suddenly she flung him away from her. "I don't want it," she said. Her voice rose. "I don't *want* it! I want my body back. I want to be what I was born to be!"

Hirel's temper collapsed into terror. He hardly dared breathe. One step and she would tumble from the precipice. He watched her ponder it, poised on the edge, hands clawed as if to rend this flesh which had imprisoned her.

She whipped about. She laughed, and that was frightening. "Not me alone, my husband. That's the heart of it. Now I know why so many men try so hard to keep their women locked in cages. We're weak. We're fragile. We're strangers to reason. And we have this mighty power. Without us, none of you would be. Without our consent, granted freely or by force, none of you would have a son to brag of."

"So too must we consent," Hirel said, treading with care.

She swayed backward. His heart stopped. She bared her teeth. "Such consent! A few moments' pleasure and you can walk away. It's the woman who faces twice nine cycles of steadily worsening pain, with agony at the end of it, and all too often death."

"Not always. Far more often there is great joy."

"Maybe." She tossed her wild bright hair. "I endured this once, Hirel; and even then I could take refuge in my own body. I can't endure it again with no such escape. I'll break. I was made to hunt, to fight, to face death edged or fanged: for man's courage. Not for this."

"I never marked you for a coward."

"Of course I'm a coward. I'm a woman." She leaned toward him. "You are a bold brave prince. You carry this child."

"I cannot."

"No; you can't. You shrink from the very thought of it."

"Sevayin—"

"Sevayin!" she mocked him. "Sevayin! Sarevadin who ever was, with all the bloom worn off, and grim reality staring her in the face. It was a splendid game when it was new. A body my old self would have lusted after; freedom at last to be your lover; my power born again all unlooked for. Wouldn't you think I'd paid enough for all of that? Couldn't I stop now and go back to what I was before? I can even face the war. Nothing I've done seems even to have delayed it, let alone put a stop to it."

"Would you give me up, Vayin?"

She left the brink. She swooped upon Hirel. He tumbled backward. She raged; she laughed; she dropped beside him, hands fisted over her eyes, tears escaping beneath them. "You must despise me."

Gently he drew her hands down, holding them against his breast. "I love you."

"The god alone knows why."

"Yes." He kissed her. She tasted of salt.

Her head twisted away from him. "You like me better this way. You're freer with me."

"Because you are freer with me."

"That's not I. That's this body I'm trapped in."

"But surely your body is as much your own as is your mind."

"You don't understand, do you?" She faced him. "You love me because the mages have bound you to it. I desire you because they set the same spell on my body."

"No mage alive," said Hirel, "can compel a man to love. My body has desired you since first it saw you, all exotic insolence beside a gangrel's fire. My heart was yours soon enough thereafter." She curled her lip. He fixed her with a cold stare. "Yes, what heart I have. Do not belittle it. It belongs to you."

"You are beyond hope." She freed her hands, to clasp them behind him. "We both have matters to settle with the mages."

"We do indeed," said Hirel. "Promise me, Vayin. You will not begin without me."

She hesitated. Hirel firmed his will. Slowly she said, "If I can."

"You will."

She set her lips and would not speak. Hirel drew her to her feet. "Come back to prison with me."

"We do keep meeting in chains, don't we?" She led him down from the pinnacle, surefooted as a mountain cat, fearless as any madwoman born. It was her good fortune that Hirel loved her to distraction. Else he would have hated her cordially for daring so to best him.

Twenty-One

THE WALLS OF THE HALL OF FIRE WERE SOMETIMES STONE, sometimes tapestry, sometimes windows on alien worlds. Worlds utterly strange or strangely familiar; worlds that were hells and worlds that were paradises; worlds held motionless in time, worlds plunging headlong into the glittering dark. None was Hirel's, no more than this one with its brilliant moonless sky.

Sevayin was learning to shift the worlds, to call up new visions and to bring back the old. It passed the time; it honed her power. It diverted her from wilder pursuits: scaling peaks, herding clouds, challenging mages to combat with swords or staves or bare hands.

Hirel found her there on a day like every other day, white-sunned and bitter cold. She sat staring at one of the gentle places: green, with flowers and bright birds and falling water. Her eyes upon them were anything but gentle.

He sat on his heels beside her. She had had to forsake her breeches; it would have been like her to go naked. But she had wrapped herself in a robe the color of the sky at sunrise. It glowed against the midnight of her skin; it showed clearly the shape of her body. She insisted that she was ungainly. She had lost none of her

316

grace. It was merely changed, deepened: not the hunting panther now but the ul-queen growing great with her cubs.

Hirel's hand found its way to the waxing curve of her belly. Heels drummed a greeting; he laughed, struck with wonder. "He knows his father, that one."

"If it's a she, what will you do? Disown her?"

"Spoil her to ruin." Hirel set a kiss in the corner of Sevayin's mouth. She did not pull away, but her mood was not to be lightened by either joy or desire.

"They'll bind us here," she said, "for the full twice nine cycles, if they can. And keep our child for their own purposes."

"So they dream," said Hirel, calm because he must be. Refusing to consider that a little more than half of that span had driven him perilously close to breaking. They must not break, either of them.

Her eyes burned upon him. "You haven't heard, have you? You know my father has been up to his old bandit's tricks: running like a fire through the whole of eastern Asanion, driving the satraps' armies before him; or pretending to retreat and leading his pursuers into the full might of his army; or simply conquering with the fear of his name. And always managing by sheerest chance to escape engagement with your father's forces.

"Ziad-Ilarios' ambassadors had a bitter chase, but at last they found the Sunborn. He kept them about for days while he took a baron's surrender, rested his men, raided a fortress which had threatened resistance. But when he deigned to receive his guests, he barely heard them out. He refused the alliance. 'My son is safe,' he said, 'where none will dare to touch him. I will give him the world to rule.'"

Hirel was silent. He was not surprised. But the pain robbed him of words. Her pain.

She had honed it into anger. "And then," she said, choking on the words, "and then he began the conquest of Asanion. All the rest was merely prelude. The armies of the north have swept over the mountains. The armies of the south have flooded the plains of Ansavaar. Ziad-Ilarios is beset, driven back and back, battling for the heart of his empire."

"But surely it is winter now, even there. The rains—"

"They have not come. Avaryan rules the sky. The mages say that

that in part is my father's doing. His weathermasters are stronger than Ziad-Ilarios'; and the earth is his ally." She thrust herself to her feet. "And we sit here. Moldering."

"Growing an heir."

"An heir of what? My father has been wise in one respect: he's made little use of power beyond the encouraging of a cloud or two to shed its rain outside of Asanion. His armies have been enough; and his generalship that can leap from mind to mind across a battlefield or across an empire. But your father has unleashed his mages. Black mages, most of them, vicious with hatred of the Sun's son. Even now their master is hard put to restrain them. The city of Imuryaz is gone, and every living thing within its walls; Avaryan's banner rules the emptiness. And that is only the beginning."

Hirel had known Imuryaz. It was called the City of Spices, for there where Greatflood divided into Oroz'uan of the mountains and Anz'uan of the desert, the three great southward roads came together. Its market was the gateway to the spicelands of the south and west. It had been a city of the Compact: no wars could be waged in or about it, and within its boundaries all enmities were void. It was frighteningly close to Kundri'j Asan.

"Gone," said Sevayin, "shattered in the clashing of power. I can wish that a mage or two shared in the shattering."

Hirel was up, circling the hall, striding swifter and swifter. Trapped. Trapped and helpless, while cities fell, while barbarians destroyed the labors of a thousand years. Barbarians of both sides, and mages, always mages. Even his father had cast off the shackles of his rank to defend his realm: to take the place which should have been Hirel's. Because Hirel could not take it; because a foregathering of traitors had walled him in their prison. "How long?" he cried in a flare of passion. "How low must Asanion fall? How close must I come to madness before they let me go?"

He spun to a halt in front of Sevayin. Her face was a blur of darkness. This he had wedded, this he had bedded, this creature of sorcery. His hand was white against the shadow of her. The child that swelled her body would be like her: outland, alien, barely human. In older days they would have drowned it lest it defile the purity of the dynasty.

His head tossed. He was breaking. To think such thoughts: to shrink from Sevayin; to dream of slaying his own child. The heir of the empires, the seal of the peace.

"Peace!" Laughter ripped itself from him. "There is no peace. There is no hope of it."

"There may be," she said.

She spoke quietly, yet she shook him from his despair. He tasted blood. He had bitten his fist. The pain was only beginning.

She was calm, eyes narrowed, thinking deep within the walls of her mind. Hirel eyed her with growing wariness.

"Plots within plots," she said. "Magics within magics. Our jailers have not told us all that they know or intend. But of this we can be certain. They will do all they may to set themselves at the center of their balance."

"Whoever falls in the doing of it." Their hands met and clasped. Hirel contemplated them, hers long and slender, his own shorter, broader, with the blood drying on it. "It would serve them well were we dead and our heir newborn, raw clay to be shaped as they would have it. It would be logical. We are all set firm in our gods and our enmities, and none of us has ever yielded to any will but his own."

"What makes you think our offspring will be any different?"

Hirel's free hand rested again on her belly. Her own covered it. Her smile echoed his, slow to bloom, edged with wickedness. "The guildmaster," said Hirel, "has little knowledge of princes."

"You could never have been the hellion I was."

"I was worse. I was civilized."

Her mirth deepened and brightened. "He's mageborn, Hirel. Mageborn and twice imperial."

"He?" Hirel asked.

"Can't you tell?"

He could. He had called the little one *he,* because an Asanian did not consider the possibility of daughters, and because it irked Sevayin. But it was *he,* that body stirring beneath his hand. Mageborn and twice imperial. "He will be a terror to his nurses."

"He will," she said, and she said it as a vow.

"And it shall be we who raise him." Which was his own vow, sworn to any gods who were.

* * *

Sevayin had found it. Their own world, surely, incontestably. Twin moons looked down upon it. The winter stars filled the sky. And on the broad bare plain, replete with the flesh of plainsbuck, drowsed a green-eyed shadow.

"Ulan," whispered Sevayin.

The slitted eyes opened wide. The great head came up, ears pricked. Ulan growled softly.

"Brother," she said. "Heart's brother."

He flowed to his feet. The tip of his tail twitched. His eyes burned.

He shattered. Sevayin cried out in pain. Hirel was all but blind with it. She stumbled against him; he sank down beneath her.

"That was unwise," said the mage who was the Sun-priest's shadow. He stood over them in a dark sheen of power. Sevayin bristled at it, her own power rallying, rising, sparking red-golden.

He damped it with a single soft word. She shrank in Hirel's arms. The mage regarded her coolly. "It was clever to think to forge a gate through your brother-in-fur. But it was blindest folly. Has no one ever taught you what the wielding of the greater powers can do to an unborn child?"

"No doubt it would please you to teach me." Her voice was faint but far from subdued.

"I do not take pleasure in the destruction of a soul."

"But you would do it, if it served your purposes."

"At the moment, it does not. We need you, and we need your heir. We will not let harm come to either of you." She bared her teeth. He blinked once, slowly. "You may look upon the worlds to your heart's content. You will not attempt to meddle in them."

"Or?"

"Need I say it?"

"I hope," she said, shaping each word precisely, "that your manhood dies of the rotting disease."

He said nothing, with great care. When he had said it, he walked away.

Sevayin began to laugh. Softly at first. Sanely. But she did not stop. Nor would she, even for the mages, even for the Red Prince's coming. Her laughter turned to a torrent of curses in every language Hirel knew and several he did not. It was Orozia who dosed her at last with wine and dreamflower and saw her laid in her bed. Even under the drug she tossed, muttering, clinging desperately to Hirel's hand. One of the mages had tried to separate them; he did not try twice.

What price the darkmage paid for his mischief, Hirel did not ask. It was enough that he saw no more of the man. He had done Sevayin no lasting harm; when she woke from her drugged sleep she was as close to sane as she ever was. But she was slow to return to her hunting of worlds.

"I still have it," she said.

Hirel's mind was empty of aught but pleasure. Her skill had begun to approach art; and that art was all her own, at once wild and gentle, shot through with sudden fire.

She traced her words in kisses round his center; they sank through his skin, trickling slowly to his brain. She followed them, nibbling, stroking, teasing. Her eyes dawned on his horizon. They were wide and wickedly bright.

His breath shuddered as he loosed it. "What do you have? My heart? My hand? My—"

She tugged it; he gasped and snatched, rising, rolling. She lay under him and laughed. "O perfect! There is no world but you."

He glared. "You rob me of my wits, and then you ask me to use them?"

"Ah," she said. "I had forgotten. You strong wise men have to choose: the brain or the body. Whereas we who are women, however that came about—"

He silenced her with a kiss and a long, lingering caress. "Now," he said sternly, "what have you done?"

"Hoodwinked the mages."

He widened his eyes.

"You believed it, didn't you? That one black sorcerer could threaten my sanity."

"You gave me no reason to doubt it."

"It was my grandfather. The others don't know me; they see the body and forget what is in it. But I had to make the Red Prince forget. I had to convince even you."

"He has been gone for a hand of days."

She pulled Hirel's head down. "Don't sulk, child. Do you want to escape from here?"

"There is no escape."

"There is," she said. "And it's not insanity. I've held the link with Ulan. It's still there; it's been growing stronger. I think it's strong enough to ride on, if you give me your strength."

"You are mad." She grinned. He shook her. "You cannot do it. I am not the idiot you take me for—I know how great a magic is the building of gates from world to world. Your power is still remembering its old mastery; and the child saps it as he grows within you. This that you contemplate will slay you both."

"How wise a mage his father is." She kissed Hirel long and deep. Her mind flowed burning into his own. *They're going to kill us, Hirel. I saw it in the necromancer's mind when he thought I was too well conquered to see. But first, our fathers will die. It's all prepared. They only needed my grandfather's consent.*

Hirel's body was rousing to her touch. It had no interest in words. He made it shape them. "Why do they need—"

Because he has the power to stop them. She turned, drawing him with her until they lay side by side. Her lips withdrew; her power plunged deeper. *He won't help, but he's been persuaded not to hinder. They'll kill him with all of this, and regret it sincerely enough, and sigh that a man so old should have been caught in a war so bitter. But we are far from old, and we have power, and no one has persuaded us with logic or with threats. We will stop them.*

"We will die," Hirel said.

They've overcome you without a blow struck. They had only to hint at harm to your son.

Her scorn was like a lash of sleet. He hardened himself against it. "Very well. Work the magic. But I will pass the gate alone."

You can't. It's I whom they need to see, and I who can make my father see the danger in time to stop it.

"But—"

Would you rather die now or later? Me they'll keep alive; I'm valuable. Until I whelp their royal puppet.

Hirel let the silence swell. She played with his hair, unraveling its many tangles. He glared at the ceiling. "Power," he said. "It is all power. My brothers began this dance with their lusting after the name of high prince. Our fathers contest the rule of the world. Our jailers conspire to rule the world's ruler. And we play at magecraft and dream of thrones, and fancy that we have a right to either."

She was in his mind, mute, listening within and without.

"I would curse the day I met you, Sarevadin. If I were the child I was. If you were even a shade less purely yourself." He raised himself on his elbow. She lay all bare, tousled, swollen, glorious. "We will die together. Lead me; I follow."

He was a reed in the wind of the gods. He was a leaf in the tossing of the sea. He was the sword and she the swordsman; he was power, she power and mastery. Through him and in him she raised the shields. She laid bare the bond like a thread of fire. She sang it into a road, fire and silver, with a glitter of emerald.

They stood upon it hand in hand. He felt most solid. His heart beat; his palms were cold, his mouth dry. If he was not careful, his stomach would forget that it belonged to a man grown. A very young one. A youth. A boy.

A bark of laughter escaped him. Sevayin tugged him forward. He followed. He had begun naked; somewhere in the working of witchery he had gained boots and breeches, coat and cap, even a scrip: all his old traveling gear. But she was clad as any free Asanian woman must be who presumed to walk abroad, in the grey tent of the *dinaz* that veiled even the eyes. She passed as a shadow, laden with power.

And the worlds passed them by. The mages had wrought a new number in the reckoning of them: a thousand thousand; a million worlds. The road pierced them, or they swept over it, or perhaps somewhat of both. She did not vary her pace. Faceless, voiceless, all but shapeless, she might have been a dream, save for her hand in his. It was hot to burning.

They walked, not swiftly, not slowly. They did not pause. Not even for the strangest of the worlds: for creatures of fire swirling heatless about them; for creatures of ice with no power to chill them; for a battle of dragons in a sky of brass, and a dance of birds about a singing jewel, and once even a single human figure. He could almost have been Asanian, fair as he was, reddened by the sun of his world which could almost have been Hirel's own; but his eyes were as blue as the sea which lapped his feet. They lifted, narrowed against the glare. They met Hirel's. The man drew breath as if to speak, stretched out his hand. Before he could touch, Sevayin had drawn Hirel away.

Hirel looked back. The stranger was gone with all his world. The road stretched into bright obscurity. Uneasiness knotted Hirel's shoulders.

The bright way quivered, rippling like water. It fascinated him.

He stumbled and almost fell. Sevayin held him up by main force, flinging him forward. Her strides stretched. Her hand had gone cold.

He resisted. She was too strong, and ruthless with it. She cursed, low and steady. He twisted out of her grip.

The road was mist and water. The world was dust and ashes. The air caught at his throat.

Iron hands gripped him. He gasped, coughing, eyes streaming. "Fool!" she gritted. "Idiot child. Let go again and you die."

They were on the road again. They breathed clean air, neither hot nor cold, characterless, safe. About them lay a desert of black sand, black glass, black sky with stars like shards of glass. Behind them was mist. Shapes coiled in it.

"The mages," said Sevayin. "Damn them. Damn them to all the hells." She began again to walk, swift now, dragging him until he found his stride. He had neither time nor breath for anger. The road was narrowing, weakening. It yielded underfoot, like grass, like sand, like mire. It dragged at his feet. The mist had drawn closer. The worlds had dimmed about them.

Sevayin faltered. Her shape blurred beneath the robe. She was a shadow edged with fire, and fire in the center of her. For an instant she was not she at all, and the fire struggled, dimming, dying. Hirel clutched it in a surge of terror. The mist billowed forward. Sarevan shrank into Sevayin, doubled in Hirel's arms, arms wrapped about her burden. She flung defiance into the dimness. "Will you kill him, then? Will you shatter all your machinations at a stroke?"

Hirel did not pause to think. He gathered her up. He staggered: she was a solid weight, she and their son. He pressed on.

A voice boomed behind them, mighty with power. "It is you who slay him. Who already may have slain him in your madness."

Hirel could not listen. The road was a twisting track, treacherous, now solid underfoot, now falling away into a seething void. A wind had risen. It plucked at him. He tightened his grip, set his head down, and persevered.

The worlds went mad.

There were dragons. There were eagles. There were ul-cats and direwolves and seneldi stallions. And every one a mage; every one in grim pursuit. Some were hideously close. Some had begun to circle, to cut off the advance. *Capture.* The word rang in Hirel's mind. *Capture, not kill.*

Even the boy? A whisper, the hint of a serpent's hiss.

We may need him, the great voice said: a master's voice, calm in the immensity of its power. *If the child is damaged or dead. To beget another.*

Hirel laughed in the midst of his struggle. There was the simple truth. A prince served but one purpose: to engender his successor. Perhaps the empires should dispense with the charade of ruling dynasties: put all their lords out to stud and let the lesser folk fend for themselves.

"Yes," breathed Sevayin. "Go on."

He faltered. Was the road a shade broader? The wolves were closing in. But they had slowed. They cast as hounds will who have lost the scent. Yet Hirel could see them with perfect clarity.

Sevayin had won her feet again. "Don't stop. Nonsense distracts them. Do you know any bawdy songs?"

Hirel stopped short, mortally and preposterously affronted.

She laughed. Their pursuers had tangled in confusion. "Levity," she said. "It's a shield. It scatters their power. Did you ever hear of the Sun-priest and the whoremaster's wife?"

It was outrageous. It was scurrilous. It widened and firmed the road and quickened their pace.

Dragonwings boomed. Dragonfire seared their shrinking flesh. Dragons' claws snatched at them. *"Run!"* cried Sevayin.

Hirel took wing and flew. Worlds whirled away. Sevayin, linked hand to hand, was singing. Even in wind-whipped snatches, the song set Hirel's ears afire.

A blow rocked him. The pain came after, runnels of white agony tracing his back. His will found a minute, impossible fraction of strength. The next stroke fell a hair too short. The third wrapped claws about his trailing foot.

His training was all a tatter. He had forsaken sacred modesty, and he had learned to believe in magecraft, and his careful princely manners had gone barbarian. But he could still meet agony with royal silence, and with royal rage. He turned on his tormentor.

He flung Sevayin off. She gripped his wrist. She was as strong as the dragonmage. Stronger. He was the link and the center, and they were rending him asunder. He twisted, desperate.

His desperation had substance. It was dark, round, heavy. It lay cold in his lone free hand. Without thought, he flung it.

The dragon howled and fell away. Hirel whirled through madness. The road was lost. He was lost. He was not afraid; he was intrigued. So this was damnation. Now he had proof beyond doubting: the logicians were ignorant fools.

A few moments more and he would be worshipping Uvarra.

Something tore. Sevayin cried out, sharp and high. Hirel fell headlong into darkness.

He did not know why this dream should be pleasant. It had all the trappings of a nightmare. His back and his foot were afire; his wrist throbbed. His every bone cried for mercy. And yet he lay on that tortured back, and he saw the blue vault of the sky with the sun pitiless in it, and he knew without seeing, that the solidity under him was earth, a barren fell, bitterly cold. The wind keened over him.

It was the sweetest song he had ever heard. And the shadows that rose above him, the most beautiful he had ever seen. Sevayin's faceless, shapeless shape; Ulan's dagger-fanged grin. He flung arms about them both.

Together they drew him up. He could stand, with cat and Sunchild to hold him. He glanced once at his foot. Only once. The boot was a charred remnant. The flesh . . .

He did not want to know what the mage had done to his back. "I was beautiful once," he heard himself say.

Sevayin tugged. He swayed. Ulan crouched. He understood. He

was inordinately proud of that. He bestrode the supple back; the cat rose. His legs dangled. His foot screamed in a voice of fire.

"Vayin," he said quite calmly. "Vayin, I do not think I can—"

"Be quiet," she said, and she was not calm at all. Ulan began to move, and she with him, swift and smooth. But never smooth enough for his pain.

The sun shifted. The fell had grown a wall. Hirel heard water falling; and, sudden and sweet and improbable, a trill of birdsong. He did not wonder at it. Worlds changed. That was his new wisdom.

The wall spawned a gate. It swallowed them.

There were always voices when one dreamed. These were fascinating. One was Sevayin's, cold and quiet. "I did not escape one prison simply to cast myself into another."

"I could not let you die as you intended." Hirel knew this deep voice with its whisper of roughness. The name would not come. Merely a memory of power, a vision of fire dying to ash.

"I have no intention of dying," Sevayin said. "How can I? You made me a woman; and I have two children to think of."

"Do you believe that, Sunchild?"

"*I* do not!" Hirel would have cried, had his body been his own. Sevayin said, still calmly, "I know that if I die, they both die. And I love them. Whatever magnitude of idiot that makes me."

Hirel's eyes dragged themselves open. Sevayin confronted the Prince of Han-Gilen: old and young, man and woman, he drawn thin with age, she ripened and rounded with the child; yet, for all of that, blood kin. Redmaned Gileni mages with tempers tight-reined behind the rigid faces. Hirel was the foreigner here, half the bone of their contention. The lesser half, he suspected. He saw that she cradled her belly as if to guard it. "Let us go," she said.

"Your prince can go no farther without healing."

"Then give it to him. It was your servant who wounded him."

"It was not."

She bared her teeth. "Don't quibble, Grandfather. So it was your ally. Who bore firmly in mind that a man needs very little of his body to beget sons. And who did all he could to leave very little else."

"Sevayin," said the Red Prince, "I had nothing to do with it."

"Are we deluded? Is this not your summer palace? Did we not come to it from the heart of the Golden Empire?"

"I knew when you made your gate. I knew where you would come if you were not taken; I feared that you would be in sore straits. Thank Avaryan, you are unscathed and he is but little hurt."

"You call that little?"

"Flesh wounds," the prince said, "as you would see, were you less blind with fear for him." He bent over Hirel, meeting the boy's level stare, unsmiling. To Sevayin he said, "I will heal him."

"And then?"

"We will speak together."

Hirel struggled to rise. He came as far as his knees; he held himself there. He was naked. He had not noticed. He had no time to notice now. "We will speak before you touch me. You will tell us why we should trust you. A man who would sacrifice his own grandchild in the name of a god."

Prince Orsan's eyes considered Hirel. Reckoned the count of his forefathers. Widened at the sacrifices some had made, in the name of a god, or a throne, or their own pleasure. The Red Prince said, "You have no choice but to trust me. The mages could not keep you: they did not know your true measure. I know it, and I know that while I may not be the stronger, I have the greater skill. You will not escape me."

"We can try," said Sevayin.

"And then?" Her own words, set coolly before her. "What do you fancy that you can do?"

"Stop the war."

"No," the Red Prince said. "Tell me the truth, priestess."

She stiffened at the title. Her nostrils thinned; she would not speak.

"I will tell you," he said. "You foresee what I foresaw; what sent me from the Heart of the World. The circle of deaths which must encompass the peace."

Still she was silent.

Not so Hirel. It was all bitterly, brutally clear. "It will be soon. Within days. If it has not already befallen."

"Not yet." The Red Prince looked very old. He lowered himself stiffly into a chair, bowing his head with infinite weariness. "I was to keep you here if you came so far. I thought I had the strength. I thought that I could countenance it all, for the world that will be. Even the murder of my heart's son."

"Why not? Your body's son is safe enough. He'll have the regency when the birthing kills me." Sevayin tossed the fire of her mane, fierce with despair. "Let be, old man. You'll heal my prince, because you know you'll get no peace until you do. We'll do our utmost to get out of your clutches. Meanwhile our fathers will die, and the war will end, and the mages will have their victory. What use to say more?"

"Yes," said Orsan, sharp enough to startle her. "What use? Your heart is set on hating me. I am the one you loved most, who betrayed you most bitterly."

"Just so."

Hirel let himself fall. Let a cry escape him. At once they were beside him. The fear in Sevayin's eyes was little more than that in the Red Prince's. He quelled a smile. So then: he was worth a moment's anxiety. He lay on his face, masked in pain, and let them fret over him. The heat of their anger abated, and with it the fire of his wounds. It was fascinating. It was pleasant, like the first movements of the high art. Very like.

Sevayin's hands stroked where the prince's had passed. Her kiss brushed his nape; her whisper sighed in his ear. "You were too clever, cubling. You tried the merest shade too hard."

He yawned. His foot itched; he rubbed it. It was all healed. So too his back. It could be convenient, this magic. "I shall remember," he said drowsily to Sevayin, "when next you quarrel."

She nipped him. He only laughed, and that for but a moment. Her kinsman was watching. Hirel said, "I do not trust you, Red Prince. I do believe that you will let us go. My lady is in no danger while she carries the child; and she may work a miracle: end the war without ending the lives of its principals."

"You are clever," Orsan said, "and cold, and wise. If you did not have the grace to love my grandchild, I would crush you as I crush a scorpion."

Hirel smiled. "And I detest you, old serpent. I do not make the error of despising you."

They understood one another, as true enemies must. The Red Prince vouchsafed the glimmer of a smile. Hirel saluted him as a warrior will who grants his opponent due respect. But no quarter. Not now, not ever.

PART FOUR

Sevayin Is'kirien

Twenty-Two

NO ONE WOULD EVER KNOW HOW MUCH SHE HATED THIS BODY. Hated it and loved it. Its softness. Its roundness. Its downy skin. Its heavy swaying breasts; its grotesquerie of belly; its limbs like a spider's, thin and strengthless. It knew what it was made for. To receive a man's seed. To carry his children.

To carry this child, this alien, this stranger growing and dancing and dreaming within her. She hated him as she hated the body that had conceived him. She loved him with an intensity that made the *Kasar*'s fire seem a dim and warmthless thing. When on the road she had nearly lost the bonds of her being, and her son with it, she had known surely that if he died, she could not bear to live. She still reached often for him with hand or mind, assuring herself that he was well; that he had not suffered, that he was prospering. She loved only Hirel more. She loved her body but little less. Because one of them loved it, and one of them waxed within it, and she had chosen it in full awareness of what she did.

As full as it could be, when she was he. She did not know the whole of it yet. She was too new to it.

But the heart of the matter was purest simplicity. The shape had changed; the self remained the same. She laughed in the darkness,

333

knowing it. There was no escape from the tangle of loves and hates and fears and joys and flaws and perfections that were Sarevadin.

She hated it. She loved it. She was beginning, slowly, to accept it.

She lay beside Hirel, that last night before they faced their fathers, and watched him sleep. There was no sleep in her. She had done all her shaking; she had caged her myriad terrors. She was calm, resting her eyes on his face. He looked like a child.

She could go. Leave him there, safe and hidden, and soothe his anger after. She did not need him. It was not his father who would accept no end but his own and utter victory. She only needed herself as she was now, carrying the heir of the empires.

He stirred, seeking her warmth. His hand found her middle. Even in his sleep he smiled. His dream saw a bright-headed manchild, night-skinned, with startling golden eyes.

She buried her face in his hair. No. She was lying to herself. She could not leave him. She needed him. Her dream had seen it long since. He was the key to her power. She could not even hate him for it: there was too much else to hate.

Prince Orsan would not ride with them. He had turned his coat too often; this last turning had broken him. The man who faced them in the dark before dawn was become a stranger, ill and old, leaning heavily on a staff. He was their servant in spite of their resistance. He fed them. He led them to bathe. He offered them clothing: garments fit for princes who must face their people, splendid to garishness but practical enough under the crusts of gold and gems. The eightfold complexity of Hirel's robe went on all together, like his wedding garment; this was divided for riding, its folds as supple as good armor. Its diamonds adorned his every point of vulnerability; a great collar of gold and diamond warded his throat, and his coronet was of an ancient style, shaped as a crowned helmet. He smiled when he put it on, an edged smile.

Sevayin's own finery was less warlike, if no less antique. Men and women both had worn it a hundred years ago in Han-Gilen. Its ornateness bespoke the Asanian fashion. Its simplicity was of the east. Boots heeled with gold, their soft leather dyed deep Gileni green. Trousers cut full, cloth of gold with Asanian velvet within. A breastband, which she was wise enough to put on in silence. A shirt of fine linen. A tunic, knee-long, stiff with embroidery. A great glittering overrobe, half coat, half cloak, which would pour beautifully over a senel's back, and ward off arrows with all its gemmed embroideries, and merely in passing disguise both her sex and her condition. Her torque guarded her throat; for crown she had her hair, woven with strings of emeralds and coiled about her head in the helmet braids of the Ianyn kings. Hirel helped her: she would not let Orsan touch her. She almost pitied him, such pain she gave him, and he grown too feeble to conceal it. But she could not stop herself.

Mounts awaited them in the court of the green silences. At sight of the smaller, Hirel nearly forgot his princely hauteur. Time had done little for her beauty and less for her temper, but the Zhil'ari mare had gained back all her strength. She greeted Hirel with the air of one who has waited much too long for a dawdling child; her nostrils trembled with the love-cries which she would not utter. He greeted her with a tug of the girth and, under lowered lids, a shining eye. They were made for one another, they two.

Sevayin forced herself to walk forward. Ulan was waiting, soul's kin, and no foolish man to care whether she was one who bore children or one who begot them. Bregalan stood prick-eared beside him. For all the splendor of his caparisons, the stallion wore no bridle; his saddle was a tooled and gilded offspring of the flat training saddle, no high pommel to mock her ungainliness. His gladness sang in her. Come, his eyes called to her; come and ride, run, be free and together, soul and soul and soul, beast of prey and beast of the field and mage of the bright god's line.

He was a poet, was Bregalan, although he scorned mere rattling words. She smiled and thought warmth at him, but her heart was cold. For he stood in the center of a guard of honor. Nine Zhil'ari in the full panoply of their people. Nine proud young men who had known the Prince of Keruvarion. Their eyes glittered in their fiercely painted faces. Fixed on her. Level, bitter-bright, relentless.

"We are yours," said Gazhin. Great Gazhin-ox who never lied, because he never saw the need; who never bowed, because a true king knew who revered him and who did not. "You are the great one. The Twiceborn, the dweller in the two houses, the mystery and the sacrifice. We are yours. We would die for you."

Sevayin laughed like blades clashing. "Don't. I'm not worth it."
Nine pairs of eyes refused belief. Zha'dan said, "We belong to
you."

She looked at him. He was wearing his best air of innocence, the
one with the wide liquid stare. "And what does your grandmother
say to that?" she demanded.

The mageling's eyes held fast. They had laid aside their
innocence. "Sometimes," he said, "one has to make choices."

She paused a breath, two. She bowed to that, to all of them.

Bregalan pawed the turf lightly, barely scarring its mown
perfection. Before she could think, she was on his back. No one
troubled to marvel at her feat. She was not maimed, or ill, or too
old to master her body. She was simply with child.

Self-pity was a curse. Her grandfather had taught her that. She
would not look at him as she rode past him, or bid him farewell. It
was Hirel who did both, rebuking her with his graciousness.

At the gate she turned back. Or Bregalan turned. Orsan stood
alone on the trampled grass, bent and frail but mantled even yet in
his power. It held open the mage-way into Asanion. It asked
nothing of her. Not understanding, not acceptance, and certainly
not forgiveness.

"Not now," he said. "Now is not the time for that choosing. Go
with the god, Sarevadin."

She could not answer him, either to bless or to curse him. She
raised her burning hand. Bregalan spun away.

The Army of the Sun and the Ranks of the Lion stood face to face
across a field of desolation. It had been a city once: Induverran, the
City of Gold, which guarded the gate of Asanion's heart. Mages
had cast it down, warring over it: a blast of fire; a wind out of the
dark. Its towers were fallen, its walls laid low. The shrines of its
gods were smoking ruins. Its men were slain; its children were
dead, or wandering, or wailing in the emptiness. Its women lay in
the ashes and wept.

Sevayin paused at the summit of a low hill, drawing a cloak of
power about her company. The air was heavy with the reek of
death. Death, and magery. They had loosed the power; it had
tasted blood. It roamed now like a living thing, hungering.

This was worse than dream. The sounds of it. The carrion

stench. The beast that walked the ruins, neither shadow nor substance, fed by the hatred of warring mages.

They had ceased their open battling. The emperors who wielded them had reined them in. The bonds of royal will strained sorely: the beast snarled as it stalked the domain it had made.

Sevayin saw them all with eyes and power. She saw the armies arrayed upon the smoldering field. Asanian gold, Varyani gold and scarlet, brave and splendid. They stood ranked and ready, poised on the edge of battle: that moment when all rituals were done; when the heralds had withdrawn from the game of threat and parry, and the companies taken their places, alert, braced for the signal. The generals played at patience. Even the beasts—seneldi ridden or yoked to chariots, warhounds, fighting cats, eagles of battle—even they were still, waiting.

It was like a game upon a board. Perfect, frozen, comprehensible. Ziad-Ilarios had chosen the classic opening of the west: the Three Waves of the Great Sea. First his infantry, serfs and slaves and half-trained, half-armed peasants, driven like cattle before scythed chariots. They would die to hinder the enemy's knights, while the chariots mowed down friend and foe alike, and the archers in the second wave sent down a hail of arrows. Third and last and irresistible would ride his princes: cataphracts in massive armor on stallions as huge as bulls, and the swifter, lighter Olenyai lancers on racing mares, and a wall of the terrible chariots.

Before that formidable precision, Mirain's army seemed scattered, each company setting itself where it pleased. Sevayin, who had been born and raised in his wars, saw the order in the careful disorder. Three wings of manifold talents, three armies trained to fight as one, taking their shape from the necessities of the battle. Against the Three Waves they offered a shieldwall, and a wall of mounted bowmen, and a shifting fringe of foot and knights and chariotry. The center beckoned, its line a shade thinner, with a flame of scarlet waiting in it. His crowned helmet caught the sun; his black stallion fretted, goring the air. Green glowed beside him, green knight on red-gold mare: his empress riding as ever at his right hand, and behind her, her warrior women.

Sevayin's eyes were burning dry. The Lord of the Northern Realms commanded the right under Geitan's crimson lion; the left looked to the flame and green of the Prince-Heir of Han-Gilen.

How brave they looked, those mighty princes, with their knights about them and their panoply glittering and their armies straining to run free.

Brave fools. Children gone mad in the wreck of worlds.

Hirel sat his senel knee to knee with her. His hand closed about hers. He was half a child who pleads for comfort, half a man who comforts his woman. She could not find a smile for him. He kissed her fingertips. "Consider," he said with royal Asanian steadiness. "We are not—quite—too late."

Not quite. She glanced at the Zhil'ari. They waited, patient. On the field below, a horn rang.

"Now," she said. Bregalan plunged down the hillside.

Hirel rode still at her knee, his mare defending valiantly the honor of her sex. The Zhil'ari fanned behind. Ulan wove through them, settling at last on Sevayin's right hand. He laughed his feline laughter, drunk on the sweet exhilaration of danger.

Her own fear had burned away. The child was quiet within her, but his soul was a white fire, exulting, exalted. She looked about her and knew that the battle had begun. A sound escaped her, half laughter, half curse. She cast aside all concealments.

The armies surged toward one another. Arrows fell in a sparse rain. Horns blared, drums rattled. Men sang or shouted or howled like beasts. Where the air had bred nine Zhil'ari and two princes, the battle eddied. But like the storm and the sea, once it had risen, it knew no mortal master.

She was no mortal woman. They were hers, all her barbarians. She drew their wills together. She set her power above them, burning through the glass that was her prince. She forged a weapon like a blade of fire. It clove the armies, flung them back. It swelled, billowed, grew. Arrows fell in a shower of ash. Beasts veered and screamed and fled. Men struck the wall and could not pass. Could not pierce it, though Varyani pressed face to face and all but sword to sword with Asanian warriors.

The melee ground to a halt. On both sides seethed the chaos of a rout. Men had died, were dying still, crushed in the confusion.

But most, having barely begun the charge, or having waited in reserve for the second assault, had fallen back in good order. These were the cream of their empires: seasoned fighters who knew how to face the unexpected, and who knew when to wait.

There were mages among them. Sevayin felt the pricks of their power, testing this working of hers, measuring her strength; goading the beast that haunted the field, deepening the shadow of it. It crouched, catlike. Its eyes were madness visible. It began a slow and sinuous stalk.

It was not even a tool, that creature. No mage had willed to make it. It was pure raw power. Neither dark nor light; neither good nor evil. Death was its sustenance.

Power only fed it. Lightnings only swelled it. The wall was nothing to it. It had never lived, therefore it could not die.

She gave it flat denial. It was not. It had never been. It had no power to touch her.

It stretched forth a limb like the shadow of a claw.

She refused its existence.

It closed its claws about her.

She felt nothing. She saw nothing. There was nothing.

The sky was clear. A shadow passed: a bird, a cloud, an eyelid's flicker. Sevayin wound her fingers in Bregalan's mane. Night and raven, woven. The stallion danced gently. "Yes," she said. He gathered his body, held for a singing moment, loosed it.

She rode headlong between the armies, flaming in the sun. One bold bowman loosed an arrow. She caught it, laughing, and flung it skyward. It kindled as it flew, flared and burned and fell.

Now they knew her. The roar went up behind her, followed her, rolled ahead of her. "*Sarevadin!*" And in the army of Asanion, someone had counted robes and marked a crown and raised the cry: "*Asuchirel!*"

Army faced army once again across the no-man's-land, the broad expanse of ash and ruin made terrible with power. In its center, Sevayin halted. Her Zhil'ari spread in a broad circle. Hirel set his mare side by side with Bregalan, facing his people as she faced her own. The thunder of their names rose to a crescendo and died.

Gazhin circled the circle, his stallion dancing, snorting at shadows. He halted a little apart and raised his great bull's voice. The clamor sank into silence. "The heirs of the empires have come before you. They command you to lay down your arms. They bid you lay aside your enmity. They say to you: 'We must rule when the war is ended. We will not rule a realm made desolate. If you will not give us peace of your own will, then we will compel it, as we compelled the sundering of the armies.' "

Never had such words been spoken on any field of battle. Never had the heirs of two great kings not only refused to fight, but put an end to the fighting by sheer force of wizardry. It was presumptuous. It was preposterous. It was highest treason.

Sevayin was well past caring. She could not sustain the wall. The Zhil'ari were flagging. Hirel had begun to waver. Healed though he had been, he was but newly come from a bitter wounding. Already the power was escaping his control, sending darts of fire through brain and body.

With infinite care she loosed the bonds. Too swift, and the power would run wild and destroy them all. Too slow, and Hirel would break and burn and die. He knew, because she knew. His fear, rising, sapped her strength. It fed the power. He struggled in vain to quell it. She could not touch him; dared not. He was a shell of glass about a rioting fire. A breath would shatter him.

The last bond melted. Sevayin nearly fell. Hirel snatched. Sparks leaped, startling them both. He recoiled in horror; but it was only power's fierce farewell. Sevayin gripped his hands and laughed. He scowled. "I am a disgrace to my lineage."

"You are indeed. Practicing high sorcery, interfering in imperial wars—"

"Turning coward at the crux and nearly destroying my consort."

"You'd be worse than a disgrace if you hadn't, cubling. You'd be truly, heroically stupid."

He glared at her. She remembered the lesser world, and turned to it. It had gone mad. Much of it was howling for blood. Some was roaring for the emperors' destruction and the enthronement of their heirs. A vanishing fragment was striving for sanity. The battle looked fair to begin again, true chaos now, man against man, mage against mage, and no commander but the beast-mind of the mob.

She raised a cry with more than voice, a great roar and flame that cowed, that quelled, that fixed every eye and mind and power upon her alone. She made of them all a summoning. *You who would rule this waste, come forth. Answer to me.*

She could not see the emperors. They were lost, walled and buried in furious princes. Asanian, Varyani, they thought for once with one mind. They cried treachery. They dreaded a trap. And in it the bait: the heirs of the empires. Prisoners still, or illusions of magery, set to lure even greater hostages than themselves. Or set to lure the emperors to their deaths.

She shifted infinitesimally. Her bones ached with the passage of power. It took most of her strength to sit unmoving, to keep her head up and her mind shielded. Mages sought to pierce it; their touch was pain. With each swift stabbing probe it mounted higher, with no blessed gift of numbness to grant her ease.

The end of it came all at once. In white flame among the Varyani; in a scattering of Asanian princes. The Mad One burst from the lines. Ziad-Ilarios' chariot rolled past the last of his attendants, his twin golden mares matching stride and stride.

Sevayin's lips stretched in a grim smile. They were alone, both of them, without attendance: Mirain with only his Mad One, Ziad-Ilarios with only his charioteer. Yet neither came without defense. Mirain needed none but his power. A thousand archers stood in the forefront of the Asanian army, bows strung, arrows nocked, aimed, waiting.

The emperors advanced without haste, moving slowly, yet all too swiftly. The Zhil'ari drew back before them.

They halted. Mirain was not quite close enough to touch.

Sevayin held herself rigidly still. His anger was hot enough to feel on the skin. Too hot to let him see aught beyond a dark face, a bright mane, a defiance the more bitter for that it was his own child who defied him. He flung it back in her face. "What have you done? You young fool, what have—you—"

She watched it strike him. Watched him refuse it. Watched him struggle to see the truth. His truth. His son who was young enough still to change remarkably from season to season; who had gained flesh, but who had needed it desperately, and who even gaunt to a shadow had looked much younger than his years. It was not impossible that in full health he should look more like a beardless boy than a man grown. A very beautiful boy. A boy as lovely as a girl.

She sensed rather than saw Hirel's moving away from her, dismounting, advancing to help his father from the chariot. She knew when Ziad-Ilarios laid aside his mask: Hirel's pain was sharp within her. The emperor had aged terribly. He walked because he must, but his every step was anguish, his every joint swollen and all but rigid; his face had lost the last of its beauty, his hair gone white. But he embraced his son and let himself weep.

Mirain had not changed at all. He was a little leaner, perhaps; a little harder. He looked as he had when his heir was a child, when he waged his wars in the outlands of the world. Although Sevayin knew with mage's certainty that he was mortal, she could comprehend the tale men told of him, that he was a god incarnate; that he would never age or die.

Good bones and good fortune, and hair that was slow to go grey. He dismounted slowly, calm now: a quivering calm. His eyes never left Sevayin's face. He took off his helmet, hung it from the pommel, shook down his simple braid. Their minds could not meet while hers was barred.

She touched Bregalan's neck. He knelt; she left the saddle. Her knees buckled briefly. The child kicked hard, protesting; her breath caught. She drew herself up.

He could not deny it now. It was as obvious as the shape of her under the archaic robe.

He stepped toward her. She stiffened, willing herself to stand fast. She was not as tall as he. His army saw it; they were slow to understand it. His hand brushed her hair, her cheek. "What have you done?" he whispered. *"What have you done?"*

"Given us hope."

He flinched at the sound of her voice. He touched her again. Set hands on her shoulders, gripping cruelly tight. Tears of pain and weakness flooded to her eyes; she would not let them fall. "Why?" he cried out to her in pain at least the match of hers.

"It was possible," her tongue said for her. "It seemed logical. Should I simply have killed myself?"

"You should have killed the lion's whelp."

"I love him."

"You—" He stopped. His eyes were wild. "You fool. You bloody *fool.*" He shook her until she gasped. "You have betrayed us all."

"I have saved us." She tore his hand from her shoulder, pressed it to her middle. "This is our hope, Father. This is our peace."

He tensed to break free. The child kicked. He froze.

"Our son," she said. "Mine; the young lion's. He shall be mageborn, Father. Mageborn and doubly royal."

He said nothing. He seemed transfixed.

She laughed, sharp and high. "Yes, go, disown me. It's your right. I'm an attainted traitor. I've sinned against you; I've sinned against nature itself. But you can't deny your grandson his inheritance."

"Do you think that I can deny you?"

She started, swayed. He held her up. There was no gentleness in him; his wrath had diminished not at all. He said, "I do not revoke the laws which I have made. Nor do I call you to account for this latest of many madnesses. Not yet. But if I come within reach of those who laid it upon you . . ."

"There," Hirel said, "I am your ally." He stood with his father, the emperor's hand on his shoulder, two pairs of burning golden eyes. Hirel moved slightly. Warning, as a cat will, or a wolf: *This is my mate. Touch her at your peril.*

Mirain regarded them steadily. "You have gained much," he said to Hirel. "Are you regretting it?"

"Never," Hirel answered. "Nor shall I forgive those who wrought it."

Sevayin set herself in the cold space between them, filling it with the heat of her temper. "You'll both have to wait until I'm done with them." All three would have spoken. She overrode them. "Have you forgotten where we are? Or why?" She spread her hands across her swollen middle. "Here lies the end of this war. Will you leave him a world to rule?"

The emperors did not move, and yet they had drawn away. "It is not so simple," said Ziad-Ilarios. And Mirain said, "You cannot buy peace with love alone."

"Why not?" she demanded. "Why ever not?"

"Child," said Mirain. "Lady," said Ziad-Ilarios.

She flung up her fists, swept them wide, taking in the ruin about them. "I will not hear you! One of you must rule. You hardly care which. You care not at all what price the land pays for your rivalry."

"I care what price Asanion pays," Ziad-Ilarios said. "And it has paid high. Our most grievous fault. We are men of reason. We have little defense against the fanatics of the east."

"And what is reason," Mirain countered, "but blindness of soul? You deny your own gods. You refuse aught but what your eyes can see, your hands touch. You call us fanatics who are merely believers in the truth."

"Are you?" They both rounded on Hirel. He folded his arms and regarded them coolly. "There are times and places for the settling of old grievances. I do not believe that this is one. You have seen us; you know that we come of our own will, and that we have made our own peace. Will you accept it? Will you agree at least to consider it?"

The emperors eyed one another. Sevayin saw no hate in either, nor even dislike. In another world they might have been brothers. In this one, neither could yield. Too much divided them. Too many wars. Too many deaths. The world was not wide enough for them both.

She came to Hirel's side, even as he came to hers. They stood shoulder to shoulder. "You can kill one another," she said. "We will live, and we will do what you refuse to do. Now or later, Father, Father-in-love. Choose."

There was a long silence. Hirel, so calm to look on, was trembling just perceptibly. She shifted, leaning lightly against him; his arm circled her waist. She tasted the emperors' bitter joy. Every man rejoiced to see his line's continuance. But that it must continue thus—that was not easy to endure.

Slowly Mirain said, "I can consider what you have done. I cannot promise to accept it."

"And I," said Ziad-Ilarios. "My people must know, and I must think. You will come with me, Asuchirel. You will tell me, at length and before our princes, why I should yield to your presumption."

Hirel drew his breath in sharply. "How do I know that I can trust you? I have seen enough of betrayals, and more than enough of prisons."

Anger sparked in Ilarios' eye. He spoke with deadly softness. "You are my son and my heir. Neither title is irrevocable. Remember that."

Hirel started as if struck. Sevayin held him tightly. "Trust him," she said. "He may try to lure you into his war, but he won't compel you. He knows there's no profit in turning you against him."

"I will not go without you," Hirel gritted. "I will not."

"You must." The Sunborn's voice was velvet and steel. "Someone must face my army. Someone must tell them what has become of their high prince. I am not minded to lie to them, and I am even less inclined to give my enemies a hostage."

Sevayin had been expecting it. She did not have to be eager for it. "I must go, Hirel," she said as steadily as she could.

His face set in imperial obstinacy. "I will not hand you over to our enemies."

"They are my people," she shot back. "And no one hands me over to anyone. I go where I choose to go."

"You are my wife."

"I am not your property!" She wrenched away from him before she struck him. "Damn it, cubling, now's no time to get unreasonable. Go with your father. Beat some sense into his head. And be sure of this: I don't intend to do my own arguing from a cage."

He was stiff and haughty, lest he break down and cry; angry, lest he blurt out the truth: that he could not bear to be apart from her. He would never know what it cost her to kiss him lightly, flash him her whitest grin, and turn her back on him. She was on Bregalan's back before anyone could be solicitous, dispatching her Zhil'ari to guard Hirel. On that, she was adamant. She had Ulan, who was worth a dozen men, even men of the White Stallion. She did not watch them ride away. Her eyes and her mind were on the army. Her father's army. Her own by right of birth.

If they did not rise up to a man and cast her out.

Twenty-Three

THE TRUTH CRESTED SLOWLY, LIKE A WAVE: RISING, GATHERING, poising long and long at its summit. It crashed with deadly and inexorable force.

The Sunborn's tent was an island in the torrent. The empress' women guarded it with their full strength, which was potent, but which was sore beset. They could not abate the roar that overlay and underlay all that passed in the cramped and crowded space.

Sevayin stood against the central pole with Ulan for wall and guard, facing her father's princes. She had expected revulsion. She had been braced for bitter recrimination. She had known that a precious few would begin to accept her, and that all too many would reject her out of hand. But her foresight had failed her. That their high prince should sacrifice his manhood for his empire, that, they could endure. It was the act of a hero, of a saint; it had a certain tragic splendor. And she was very beautiful, they said, seeing her there, glittering, growing desperate.

They could endure a woman's rule. They would not contemplate an Asanian consort. "I carry his son!" she had raged at them while she still had strength to rage.

"You carry a Sunborn prince," said the Chancellor of the

346

Southlands. His Gileni temper was well in hand; he was struggling to be reasonable. "Sarevadin"—he said it gingerly as they all did, not wanting to slip and wound her with her old usename, not ready yet to call her by her new one—"Sarevadin, we cannot grant Asanion so much power. We are too young and too raw; it will overwhelm us with the strength of its thousand years. Keruvarion will shrink to a satrapy, a dependency of the Golden Empire."

It was not the first time he had said it. It was not the last. They all said it, singly and in chorus. They spoke of Asanion. Of the Golden Empire. Of *it* and *they*. Never of Hirel Uverias, or of Sarevadin who had no intention of dwindling into a mere and ornamental queen. When she cast the truth in their faces, they took no notice of it. She was a woman. Of course she would yield, or she would die. Asanion would make certain of it.

"No," the chancellor said at length, as weary as she. "It is not that you are a woman. It is that you are Varyani and their high prince's mate. They will not suffer equals. They will assure that their prince holds all the power."

"Are you any different?" she demanded of him.

He smiled wryly. "Of course not. We wish you to rule; we cannot let you share your throne."

"What will you do, then? Poison my husband? Strangle our son at birth?"

"We do not murder children," he said.

"Hirel is hardly more than that."

"He is old enough to father a child. He is more than old enough to rule an empire."

"He'll never be old enough to rule me."

"His empire—" the chancellor began.

"Uncle," she said. "Halenan. If he dies, I die. You call yourself a mage. Look within and see. We are soul-bound. There is no sundering us."

He looked within. He was gentle and he was skilled, but she was a tissue of half-healed wounds; and he had not his father's mastery. He all but blinded her with pain. "You fool," he said. "Oh, you lovestruck fool."

"It was not her doing." The empress had been silent throughout that bitter hour. The princes had all but forgotten her. Sevayin had not. Elian had said nothing, done nothing, revealed nothing behind the walls of her mind. She had scarcely glanced at the child she had borne. She did not raise her eyes now, but gazed into her folded hands, her voice cool and remote as when she spoke in prophecy. "Brothers, you accomplish nothing. The lady is weary; and she has another to think of. Let her be."

"But—" said Halenan.

"Let her be."

In time they left, all of them. Mirain was the last. He paused to kiss Sevayin lightly, without ceremony. Accepting her. It nearly broke her. But she was his child. She stood firm and watched him go.

When he was gone, she let her body have its way. It crumpled to the threadbare carpet.

"They're right, you know." She started, glared. Vadin had done what he did all too often: effaced himself to invisibility, and so escaped both notice and dismissal. It was one of his more insidious magics.

He paid no heed at all to her temper. He knelt beside her, easing off the gaudy robe, tugging gently but persistently until she lay back against Ulan's flank. "Stop fighting, infant. Do you want to lose the baby?"

Sevayin drew up her knees and sighed. Vadin watched, studying her. "You knew," she said.

"I guessed. A mage, even as reluctant a mage as I am, can always tell whether a woman is carrying a manchild or a maid. With you we never could. We were afraid you'd be a monster: both and neither."

"I am," she muttered.

"Stop it, namesake." He was stern but not angry. Calmly, deft as any good servant, he began to unbind her braids. "Your mother knew, I think. She wasn't as glad as we were when you proved to be as fine a little man as ever sprang out yelling from his mother's womb. She insisted on bringing you up with both men and women. She made you live in Liavi's mind while she carried her little hellion."

"She did her best to beat the arrogance out of me." Sevayin laughed thinly. "Though in that at least, she failed. I'm still intolerably proud."

"Royal," said Vadin.

Sevayin fixed her eyes on the tent wall. "Father is taking it well."

"What else can he do? He can't disown you. You're all he has."

She flinched. Anger flared. "That's why it was even possible. Because I'm the only one. The only heir he could ever beget, the sole and splendid jewel in the throne of Keruvarion. Do you think it's been easy for me? Do you think I welcome all the stares and gasps and cries of outrage? Do you think I don't know what battles I'll have to fight all my life long, because I gave up my very self for love of an Asanian tyrant?"

"Not your self," said Vadin. "But there is a little truth in the rest of it. Your uncle sees it. Keruvarion will never accept a western emperor. Too much of it has fought too long to avoid just that."

"Hirel would never—"

"Your young lion is as charming as his father ever was, and as honorable, and as perfect an epitome of Asanian royalty. He was bred to be an emperor."

"But not a monster."

"Maybe not." Vadin combed Sevayin's hair in long strokes, intent on it. "Old hatreds die hard. Asanion is Asanion: the dragon of the west, the vast devouring beast with its insatiable lust for gold and souls. The only defense against it, most people would tell you, is its destruction."

Sevayin bared her teeth. "They say much the same of us. It's the same hate and the same fear. But they reckon without me and without my princeling."

"I was young once," said Vadin.

Sevayin thrust herself up; Vadin reached for another plait. She shook him off. "*Damn* it, Vadin! Stop treating me like a child."

"That," he said, "you're not. But you're carrying one."

She was mute, simmering. He reached again. Sevayin suffered him, holding to Ulan for comfort, drinking calm through the cat's drowsing consciousness.

"You are going to rest," Vadin said firmly. "Then you are going to face your people."

"Naked, I presume. So that they can be properly outraged."

"Why? Are you hiding something?"

"Only an unborn lion cub."

He looked hard at her. Her heart stilled. She had told them that the Mageguild had held her prisoner; that the master had wrought the change with the aid of Baran of Endros. She had not cried Prince Orsan's treason before the army. She did not know why. Certainly not because he was her mother's father, her father's more-than-father. Nor had he set a binding on her.

But she could not say the words that would condemn him. She strengthened her mind's shields; she put on a tired smile. The tiredness was not feigned. "I've told you all I can. Except . . ."

"Except?"

Sevayin drew a breath. Vadin looked ready to seize and shake her. She straightened with an effort. "There was more to the mages' conspiracy than a plot to unite two royal houses. When our son was born, Hirel and I were to be killed." Vadin said nothing, only waited. "But first, our fathers were to die. Are still to die. It will be soon, within days. I have hopes that our presence here, close by the emperors, will hold them back. They dare not lose me now, and they know that if Hirel dies, I die."

"Assassins are no rarity," said Vadin, "and we've met sorcerous assassins before."

"But never a full circle of mages, led by the Master of the Guild himself." Sevayin's body levered itself up, driving itself round the tent, evading cot and clothing chest, skirting the low table with its maps and its plans of battle. Abruptly she stopped, turned. "Uncle. I know the way to the Heart of the World."

Vadin rose. "Are you as mad as that?"

Sevayin grinned at him. "Do you need to ask?"

"It will be guarded."

"With Father's loyal mages, and with Ziad-Ilarios'; with you, with Mother, with Father himself, we could conquer worlds."

"Clever," said Vadin. "This world may not be wide enough for two emperors, but if there are many . . ."

Sevayin hissed her impatience. "One world or a thousand thousand, what use to a dead man? You yourself taught me that it seldom profits a commander to wait for the enemy to attack. Better to strike the first blow, hard and fast, before he can gather his forces."

"What makes you think the mages aren't armed and waiting?"

"They may be." Sevayin took up a stylus, turned it in her fingers. In Ianon they jested that a pen was a waste of a good dart. She almost smiled. "But I don't think they know what I'm capable of."

"By now they do."

She tossed her freed hair, sweeping her body with her hand. "Look at me, uncle. This is all of me that most of them have ever seen. They know why I ran away from my prison. I was afraid to die; I had my prince to be my courage and my son to make me desperate. That I succeeded—ah then, I'm a god's grandchild, and luck is his servant."

Vadin's grin was wry. "And you are quite astonishingly beautiful, and when has beauty ever needed brains?"

"Avaryan knows, I never have."

"And here I was, thinking what a marvel you were, to have learned so quickly how to play the princess."

"It's not so different to play the prince. It was much harder to teach myself to walk. I kept wanting to make my body balance like a man's."

Vadin laughed freely then, pulling her in. She let her arms close the embrace. The child kicked hard; Vadin started. For a moment all merriment dropped away. But not for grief. For wonder; even for awe. "He's strong," the Ianyn said. "And much too pretty for comfort." His laughter rang out anew. "I think your father's nose is immortal."

"And his darkness," said Sevayin, "and my mother's hair. You know this should be a brown child, or amber. So for that matter should I."

"They knew what they wanted you to be."

"This?" asked Sevayin, braced for pain.

"This," said Vadin. He smiled with a touch of wickedness. "Here's a secret, namesake. Men want sons; how can they help it? But every one of us, in his heart of hearts, prays for a daughter."

"However he gets one?"

"However he gets one." Vadin stood back, stern. "Now, namesake. Lie down and let your baby rest."

She obeyed meekly enough, lying on the cot which was barely wider than a soldier's. Vadin left to be a lord commander again. Sevayin breathed slowly, swallowing past the ache in her throat. Here in solitude, with the army's roar as steady as the sea, her sight was bitterly clear. She had solved nothing yet. She might have slain them all.

She met Ulan's green stare. The cat blinked, yawned. He did not like all this crowding and shouting; he needed the free air. But if she was about to go to lair with her cubs . . .

"One cub," she said, "and not quite yet, brother nursemaid."

Ah, then. He would go. She laid her golden hand on his head; it bowed beneath the weight of the god. With a last green-fire glance, he slipped from the tent.

Sevayin lay for a few breaths' span. Abruptly she rose. There was wine where it had always been, in the chest at the bed's foot. She filled a cup, stared at it. Her stomach did not want it. "My courage needs it," she said, downing it. It was proper Varyani wine: sweet and heady, sharpened with spices. It steadied her.

She turned to face the one who stood in front of the tent's flap. It had been a goodly time since they stood eye to eye. She had never seen in those eyes what she saw now. In Prince Orsan's, yes. When he offered her the choice which even yet might be the end of her. But not in the eyes of his daughter.

It went beyond pain. "Mother," she said, calm and quiet.

Elian came, took the cup from her fingers, filled it and drained it herself. Choking on it, but forcing it down. Sevayin stared at her.

She stared back. The cold distances were heating, closing in. "I hope you're pleased with yourself."

Sevayin snapped erect. Here was all that she had expected. From the one in whom alone she had thought to find understanding. In her mother, who had foreseen this. Who had trained her for it.

And would not, could not accept its fulfillment.

"You've set the army on its ear," said Elian. "You've shown them what in fact they've shed their blood for. You've shaken your father and all that he has made, to their very foundations. Are you content?"

"Are *you?*" Sevayin shot back. "You saw all that I saw. What did you do to stop it? What did you do that even slowed its advance?"

"I did not strangle you in your cradle."

Sevayin began to tremble. "The others are finding that they can bear what they have no power to change. You can't. Why? Does it matter so much to you whether I walk as a man or as a woman? Are you afraid I'll be a rival?"

Elian slapped her. She did not evade the blow, nor did she strike back. "Oh, splendid, Mother! You always hit what you can't answer. I've betrayed you, haven't I?"

"You have betrayed your father."

"That," said Sevayin, "is not for you to judge. I've betrayed *you*. You loved the shape I used to wear. You hate me for giving it up."

"I could never hate you."

"Scorn, then. Contempt. Outrage."

"Grief." Elian was weeping. It was bitter to see. Her face was rigid; the tears ran down it unregarded. "That you should have hurt so much. That you should have given up—all—"

"Whatever I gave up, I have gained back. I have my prince, Mother. I have my son. I have my power, and it grows stronger than it ever was before."

"But the price," said Elian. "The pain."

Sevayin was quite thoroughly a woman, and almost a mother. But she could not understand this woman who was her mother.

Elian laughed, still weeping. "That's a great secret, child. Women don't understand women, either. I was so sure that I could face this. When it came. If it came. And then I saw you, and I couldn't bear it." She laid her hands flat upon her middle. "I was very ill, not so long ago. I lost a child. It would have been your sister."

Sevayin staggered with the pain of it. Reached, to heal her, to grieve with her.

Elian eluded her hands. "She should never have been. We knew it, your father and I. And yet we dared to know joy. To hope that maybe, somehow, we could have it all: that we could be victorious, that you could be healed, that we could live in peace with our daughter as with our son. Then," said Elian, "then the pains came. Nothing that we did could stop them. They were more terrible than anything I had ever known. As if my very substance were being rent from me."

Sevayin sank down, cradling her own substance, her child who would be, must be, born alive.

"The god took her," Elian said. "And mages. I knew, Sarevadin. I knew that they were birthing you. Wielding my power. Taking my child that would be, to transform my child that had been. It was godly cold, that taking. It was divinely unspeakable."

Sevayin rocked, shivering. If she had died in the working, her sister would have lived. Would have grown to womanhood. Hirel would have survived the war; would have had to wait, in grief, perhaps in captivity. But would, in the end, have had his Sunborn queen.

"Avaryan," she said. "There is no Avaryan. There is only Uvarra." She raised her head. Her mother regarded her without pity. Pitiless. "No wonder you hate me."

"I told you, I do not." Elian sat beside her, but out of her reach. "You didn't know what you were doing; you wanted to save us all. You paid higher even than I did, and in greater pain. I never stopped loving you. I'm trying to forgive you."

Sevayin drew a sharp and hurting breath. "I don't want your forgiveness. I want your acceptance. I want you to stand with me when I face Keruvarion."

She looked at Elian and knew that she had asked too much. It had taken all the empress' strength to come here, to face her alone, to tell her the truth. More than that, Elian could not give.

Sevayin bowed her head, hating defeat, knowing nothing that would alter it.

"I do not know that I can accept you," said Elian. "But I will stand with you."

Sevayin started, half rising. Elian held her down. It hurt, that light touch. It hurt bitterly, as a touch can, when it bears healing in it.

The empress drew her into a swift embrace. They were trembling, both of them, with all that roiled in them. "Come," said Elian. "Your people are waiting."

Sevayin did not face her people naked, but she faced them as a woman, and a priestess, and a queen. She needed all her pride. She could have done without her temper.

It was not the common folk who tried her sorely. They had needed most to see her, to know that she was well and strong and triumphant in her sacrifice. She knew how to make them her own.

But no lord yet born had sense enough to listen and let be. It was the same fruitless battle. Keruvarion's lords and captains would not ally themselves with Asanion. They would not suffer an Asanian prince. They would not acknowledge the legitimacy of the union: not without contract or witnesses.

That broke her. She did not fling herself at the idiot who had

said it. She dared not; she would have killed him. But she rose from
her seat in front of her father's tent. She smiled a clenched-teeth
smile. She inquired very softly, "Are you calling my child a
bastard?"

She did not heed the scramble of denials. Commoners had
sense. They understood logic; when they hated, they hated with
reason. Lords were like seneldi stallions. They bred and they
fought; they snorted and they gored the air, and they raised their
voices at every whisper of a threat.

They had fallen silent, staring. Some looked frightened. And
well they might be. "I have heard you," she said. "I have heard all I
need to hear. It changes nothing. I have taken as consort the High
Prince of Asanion. Refuse him and you refuse me." She faced her
father. "Now the beast has danced for all your people. Has it
danced well? Has it pleased you? Must it return to its cage, or may it
go back to its mate?"

Mirain was not angry. He seemed more proud of her than not;
and he had never been one to meddle where his heir was faring
well enough alone. He sat back, arms folded, and said, "We have
matters to consider, you and I. They need a night's pondering.
Will you tarry for it?"

She could refuse. He offered that, to her who had betrayed his
trust. But Mirain An-Sh'Endor always granted a second accounting. Then he had no mercy.

"I will stay," she said, "until morning."

He bowed his head. She moved without thinking, knelt, kissed
his hand. Her eyes rose. His own were clear, steady, and filled to
bursting with his power. She shivered. He was king and emperor,
great general, mage and priest: death had always ridden at his
right hand. But now when she looked at him, it lay upon him like
his own dark-sheened skin.

"Sarevadin."

She stood on the edge of the cavalry lines, gazing over the
shattered city, watching the sun set behind the Asanian camp.
Hirel lived; she knew that. But no more. A shield of power lay
between them. She ached with trying not to batter it down.

When her father's voice spoke behind her, she was perilously close to mounting Bregalan and damning all promises and storming to her prince's rescue. She whirled, as fierce with guilt as with startlement.

Mirain's gaze rested where hers had been. There was no one with him; he could have been a hired soldier in his plain kilt, his cloak of leather lined with fleece against the chill, his hair in its plait behind him. He stroked Bregalan's shoulder, and the stallion raised his head from cropping the winter grass, snorting gently in greeting. Mirain was rare in his world: a two-legged brother. Like Sevayin herself. Like Hirel.

She shivered a little. The wind was rising as the sun sank, and her robe was less warm than it was splendid.

Mirain spread his cloak over her. She thought of resistance, sighed, submitted. It was warmer within than without, and she had nothing in truth to hate her father for. He was only doing what he must.

She closed her eyes. He was doing it to her. Again. Being the Sunborn. Luring her mind into acceptance of his madnesses. It was he who had begun this war; it was his intransigence which had brought her here, and which was all too likely to be his death.

"Why?" she demanded of him. "Why are you doing this?"

He was slow to answer. "Because," he said, "I am my father's son. I was born for this: to subdue the Golden Empire. To turn the world to the worship of Avaryan. To bring light where none has ever been."

"By invading a country in the face of its ruler's pleas for peace?"

"I gave him peace. I gave him a decade of it. And watched him strengthen his armies, and rouse my outland tribes to revolt, and free his slavetakers to raid within my borders. He lured the Mageguild into Kundri'j; he sent his sorcerers as far as Endros, to whisper in the ears of my people, to rouse them to their old dark rites, to slay as many as they might in the name of gods long and well forgotten."

"While you did almost exactly the same in Avaryan's name."

He sighed at her back, folding his arms a little more tightly about her. "There were no slaves taken and no children sacrificed at my command."

"No. Only cities leveled with sword and power, and their children slaughtered to sate your armies."

"War is ugly, Sarevadin. But I bring justice where none but princes have ever had it, and one god where a thousand had stripped bare the land and its people."

She twisted to face him, hands knotted on his chest, trembling with the effort of keeping them still. "It would have come without your war. Don't you see? Don't you understand? We did it, Father. While you great emperors glowered and threatened and called up your armies, Hirel and I forged our own peace."

"I see," he said levelly. "I understand that the Mageguild seized upon a potent and mutual infatuation, and wielded that infatuation entirely for its own ends." She would have cried a protest; he silenced her. "I have no objection to a love match. I made one myself; I swore long ago that if the god granted you the same, I would not stand against it. Nor do I object to the one you have chosen. Under other circumstances I would have urged you to take him. But we have gone well past either logic or simplicity. We were past it before you submitted yourself to the mages."

Her throat had swelled shut. She forced words through it. "You don't want a bloodless end. You want to set your foot on Ziad-Ilarios' neck; you want to see his people die. Because they pray to the wrong gods. Because they dare to call your father a lie."

He touched her torque. "Your god also, Sarevadin."

She struck his hand, flinging it from her, breaking his grip and his spell. "My god is not your god. My vision is not your vision. You call my hope simplicity, as if I were a child who would put an end to death with a garland and a song. But it is you who are the child. You strive to shape the world in an image as false as the desolation of the black sorcerers. You blind yourself to any enemy but the one who would choose to be your ally."

"Asanian friendship is the friendship of the serpent. Jeweled beauty without, poison within."

She breathed deep, willing herself to be calm, to think. To remember that men had died for words less bitter than these which she had cast in his face. Which he was suffering with almost frightening forbearance.

"Father," she said. "Suppose that you let us try our way. It can't harm you. If it succeeds, you become the begetter of the great peace. If it fails, we children forced it on you with magery and with sheer youthful heedlessness; and you can go back to war again. You know you'll win. You have a god to fight for you."

"So do I now," he said.

"But you have no son."

He stepped back. His face was very still in the dying light; his eyes were like the eyes of one of his images, obsidian in ivory in ebony.

"I can't go back, Father. Not only because the trying would kill me. I have too much pride."

"You always did."

"And whose fault is that?"

"Mine," he said, "for begetting you." He did not smile. "If my death is ordained, Sarevadin, what right have you to hinder it?"

"Every right in the world." She raised the white agony of her hand. It cast its own light, sparks of gold in his shadowed face. "This is how I endured the change. I had a pain to match it, and years to learn how to bear it. It is not the same with my dream of your death. Yours and my mother's, Father. I saw her die before you. And though the years stretch long and the pain never falters, it never numbs me. It only grows more terrible. Therefore I chose this path. It offered a grain of hope: a chance that you would live."

"And yet," he said, "if I die, I assure your peace. Living, I can only stand against you."

"Not if I can persuade you to stand with me."

"Why? Why prolong the agony, when I can be lord of the world by tomorrow's sunset?"

"Lord of the world, perhaps. But Elian Kalirien will be dead."

He tossed his haughty stubborn head. "You are no prophet, Sunchild."

"In this," she said, "I am."

There was a silence. She fixed her stinging eyes upon Bregalan, who had raised his head, drinking the night wind. Her father was a shadow on the edge of her perception.

After a long while she said, "Tomorrow you may renew your war. I shall not be here to see it."

"Indeed you will not. A bearing woman has no place on the battlefield."

"Not in armor, no. There's none that would fit me and no time to forge it. I have another battle to fight. I shall go back to the

Heart of the World and stand against the mages who have plotted
to take you."

She heard his swift intake of breath, but his voice was quiet.
"You know you cannot do it."

"With power enough, I can. The Asanian mages may be willing
to ally with me to preserve their emperor. Some of your own may
choose the same. You give them little enough to do while you wield
your armies."

"On the contrary. They hold back the Asanian sorcerers; they
ward my army against attacks from behind."

"No need for that if there is truce; if all of us are joined to break
the conspiracy."

"Light and dark together?"

"Why not?"

"You cannot do it."

"I can try."

"You must not. Your child—"

She laughed, but not in mirth. "How you all do fret! And yet I
don't think any of you knows what power can do to an unborn
child."

"We know all too well. It destroys the waxing soul. If the body is
fortunate, it too dies."

"Human soul. Human body. What of the mageborn? What of a
bearer of the *Kasar*?"

"You would be more than mad if you sought an answer."

"What choice do I have? They will kill you otherwise, and
Mother with you. I would free you at least to find your own deaths
in battle."

He seized her. "You will not!"

"You can't stop me."

"No?"

She met his glittering eyes. "I will do it, Father. You can't bend
all your power on me, and keep your army in hand, and wage your
war against Ziad-Ilarios. He has a message from me: if I fail to
appear here by sunrise tomorrow, he is to disregard any word you
speak, even of peace, and fall on you with all his conjoined forces.
He has more than you think, Father. His sorcerers aren't holding
back out of weakness, still less out of fear of your mages' shields.
They're grateful for the favor: it frees them from the need to

maintain protections while they set about opening gates.
Worldgates, Father. The dragons of hell will be the least of what
comes forth to face you."

His hands were iron, his face lost in night. She had no fear left.
She had given her second accounting. Now she would see the face
which he turned toward treason.

His fingers tightened. She set her teeth against the pain.
Abruptly his grip was gone. The pain lingered, throbbing.

"What," he demanded roughly, "if you are here and I am not?"

She hardly dared breathe. She could not have won. Mirain did
not lose battles.

He could, on occasion, retreat. To muster his forces. To mount a
new attack.

He could indeed. "I will face these traitorous mages. I will end
their plotting."

"Alone?"

"My enchanters will follow me."

"Not without me. Alone of anyone outside of the guild or the
conspiracy, I know the way."

He was silent for so long that she wondered if he had heard; or if
she had at last gone too far. Then, startlingly, he laughed. "Oh,
you are mine indeed! You have me dancing to your music; now will
you command that I dance with the Asanians?"

"Can you bear to do that?"

He pondered it. "For this cause . . . perhaps. But it can only be a
truce, Sarevadin. I will not end this war until Asanion bows to me
as its overlord."

"But now you need Asanion's strength. Without it you can't face
the full power of the Heart of the World. With it, you may be able
not only to face that power. You may be able to overcome it."

"No certainty, princess?"

"What is certain?" She wanted to hit him. He was yielding, but
in his own way. Meaning to rule even where he was vanquished.
"I'll lead you to the Heart of the World. I'll stand with you there
against all our enemies."

"With half of our enemies fighting at our side." He took her
hands, held her gaze. "You will guide us. You will not join in the
battle."

She freed her eyes from their bondage, cast them down. "If I can."

"You must."

"I'll go," she said. "I'll fight if I have to. I'll fight you as hard as any of the mages, if you try to stop me. That is my solemn oath, by the god who begot you."

His anger seared her within and without. She stood firm against it. Not fighting unless he forced her to it. Simply refusing to yield.

And he drew back. She held, lest it be a trap. He said, " On your head be it, O child of my body. May this mere and humble emperor request, at the least, that you take thought for the child of your own?"

"Always," she promised him.

It was hardly enough. But he let it suffice.

Twenty-Four

SEVAYIN DROWSED, ALONE AND LONELY IN A TENT SET WALL TO wall with her father's. Through the tanned hide she could hear the voices of mages and captains. She had banished herself from their colloquy: they could accomplish little while she was there to cloud their wits. And she was deathly tired. Alone, she could admit it. She was too tired to play the royal heir; too tired to think, too tired even to sleep.

Shatri had mounted guard outside her door. He had been appalled to see her, until he had decided to worship her. It was bearable, that worship; it demanded nothing but her presence and, on occasion, her smile. Later she would teach him that she was neither saint nor goddess. Tonight she had no strength for it.

She lay on her side, shivering under the heaped furs, and tried to shut out the murmur of voices. The child was restless; young though he was, he kicked like a senel. Her hand calmed him a little, the power of the *Kasar* over the spark that was his presence.

A familiar weight poured itself over her feet. Familiar warmth fitted itself to her body, hand slipping to cup her breast, kisses circling her nape to the point of her jaw. The child leaped no higher than her heart.

362

She turned carefully. Hirel scowled at her. She scowled back. "Couldn't you live without me for a night?"

"No." His hand was gentler by far than his voice, tracing the line of her cheek, smoothing back her tumbled hair. "Have they been cruel to you?"

"My people," she said, "are still my people. And yours?"

"I remain High Prince of Asanion."

"In spite of your unspeakable consort."

"By edict of my father, you are a princess of the first rank. Who dares speak ill of you, dies."

"How absolute." She looked at him in the lamplight. He wore Olenyai black, the headcloth looped under his chin, stark against the ivory of his skin. His eyelids were gilded. She brushed them with a fingertip. "You shouldn't be here."

"I cannot be elsewhere." He was angry, but suddenly he laughed. "One fool berated me for falling prey to a succubus. Ah, said I, but there is no sweeter enslavement."

"I hope he lived to hear you."

"My father had not yet spoken." Hirel kissed her, drew back. "Vayin," he said, "I must speak with your father."

"That's dangerous."

"What is not?" He rose, drawing her with him. She drew breath, considered, swallowed the words. In silence she took up the robe of fur and velvet which her mother had given her, and wrapped it about her. Hirel's impatience mounted, dancing in his eyes. She took his hand and led him out of the tent.

They had ample escort. Ulan leaving his warm nest at the foot of her bed, and Zha'dan with a great black cloak and a wide white smile, and Shatri. The boy bowed to Hirel with deep and revealing respect. Sevayin loved him for it.

Mirain's council had shouted itself into stillness. The princes took refuge in their winecups, the priest-mages in lowered eyes and folded hands and carefully expressionless faces. Sevayin's coming brought them all about, staring. It had always been so, she told herself. Gileni mane atop a Ianyn face, and the sheer awe of what she was: heir of the Sunborn. She showed them her most outrageous semblance, white teeth flashing, black eyes dancing, red mane tumbling over the somber robe. "How goes it, my lords? Trippingly?"

Mirain met her with a bright ironic eye and a grin as fierce as a direwolf's. He bowed his head to Hirel who had come from behind to stand at Sevayin's shoulder.

The rest, mages or no, were slow to know him. They marked the Asanian face and bristled at it, but even Prince Halenan at first did not see more than the barbarian warrior. Hirel played for them; he braced his feet and set his face and gripped the hilts of the twin swords belted crosswise over his robes. Sevayin tasted the wickedness of his pleasure. "I bear a message from my emperor," he said, speaking Gileni, which was courtesy bordering on insult. "Will the Lord of Keruvarion deign to hear it?"

"The Lord of Keruvarion," said Mirain, "would gladly hear new counsel."

It was dawning on the rest of them. Vadin was amused. One or two of the priests were appalled: the more for that they could see how the power ran between Sevayin and her prince. A simple man could have seen it, strong as it was, growing stronger in the face of all their magecraft. Hirel's eyes were molten gold. She could not resist and did not wish to; she poured herself into them, and out again, effortless as water.

"This is an abomination!"

No matter who said it. It burst from a Sun-priest's torque, child of a mind grown narrow, blinded by the light. Sevayin remembered the fire's heart and the darkness which dwelt there. She spread her hands, black and burning gold, and spoke as sweetly as she had ever spoken. "We are your peace. We who were born for undying hatred; we who without power could never have been. The god has willed it. He is in us. See, my lords. Open your eyes and see."

"I see it," Mirain said, and he did not say it easily. "Speak, high prince. What brings you here?"

"Your daughter." Some of them grinned at that. Hirel grinned back. "And of course, Lord An-Sh'Endor, my father. He proposes a two days' truce, a pause while his mages settle a certain matter. He bids me assure you that the matter is nothing of your making, and that your people will not be harmed in the resolving of it."

"There is truce until morning," Mirain pointed out.

"And a pair of cold beds." Vadin said it lightly, but his eyes were level upon Hirel. "Why, prince? What do they need to do that will take the night and two days after?"

"It may not take so long." Hirel met a captain's eyes until the man slid out of his seat. Coolly Hirel set Sevayin in it. She let him, mainly out of curiosity, to see what he would do next. Little enough, for a breath or ten. He sat at her feet, considering those whom he faced, letting them wait upon his pleasure. At last he said, "While I spoke with my father's princes, my eldest brother appeared with little escort and no fanfare. He was not astonished to see me. In part indeed he had come for my sake, with news of great and urgent import. The mages know not only of my escape with my lady but of our coming to this field and of our actions thereon. They are far from pleased. Peace they profess to seek, but it must be peace as they alone would have it."

"Aranos told you this?" asked Sevayin. She could easily believe it; she wanted to be certain of it.

"None other," Hirel answered her. "He has, he said, grown weary of that particular conspiracy. It serves Asanion no longer; it threatens to destroy us all. The time and the place are set, the mages prepared. Both emperors are to be slain at their meeting; you are to be taken, I to be held in sorcerous confinement lest you seek again to win free."

A snarl rose, wordless and deadly. Sevayin spoke above it. "I don't trust that little snake," she said.

"Who does?" said Zha'dan, coming into the light. "But it's truth he's telling."

"How much of it, I wonder?"

"Enough." Mirain met all their stares. The rumble of anger quieted. "So then, prince. You would seek out the mages, end their plotting, leave us free to choose our own peace." He leaned forward. "Why is it only truce for which you ask?"

"I," said Hirel, "do not ask it. My father has no hope of more and no will to suffer your refusal. If you will not grant the truce, he asks at least that you restrain your mages while his own are engaged in preserving your life."

Mirain laughed across the mutter of outrage. "What if I offer him my mages? Will he take them?"

"Can he trust them?"

"My presence will keep them honest."

Hirel rose to one knee. "So I told my father. I vowed that I would bring you back with me."

"And you say you are no mage." Mirain stood over him, drawing him up and embracing him with ceremony. "I will keep your vow for you."

They rode into the Asanian camp in the deep hours of the night: four priest-mages who bore within them the gathered power of their order, and Mirain, and Elian and Vadin and Zha'dan, and Prince Halenan with Starion who was the strongest in power of all his children; and Hirel leading them with Sevayin. She had lost her weariness in the exhilaration of danger, the light keen madness which comes before a battle. They all had it. Hirel thrummed with it, vaulting from his mare's back, swinging Sevayin to the ground. She snatched a kiss. He drank deep of it before he pulled free.

Ziad-Ilarios was waiting for them. He sat like a golden image within his golden pavilion, in its center where the roof lay open to the stars: a court of fire and darkness. His mages stood about him, nine men and women garbed variously as priests, as courtiers, as guildsfolk, but all mantled in power. It rose like a wall before the Varyani. They halted, drawing together. Their power gathered, flexed. Ulan growled softly despite Sevayin's calming hand.

The air breathed enmity. Sevayin thrust herself into it. Made herself face that shadow of her own power and see it as it saw itself. Born of the god as was her own. Necessary; inevitable. Her body did not want to accept it. Her mind wanted to fling it away in revulsion. Only her raw will drove her forward. Opened her mind. Embraced the darkness and the fire in its heart.

She stood before Ziad-Ilarios. Ulan was with her, and Hirel standing at her right hand. She bowed as queen to king.

The emperor took off his mask, met Sevayin's eyes. "Help me up," he said, "daughter."

She was as gentle as she could be, and yet she caused him pain. He had worsened even since the morning. Death had lodged deep within him. "No," she whispered. "Not you too."

He smiled, touched her cheek with a swollen finger. "Present me to your escort," he bade her.

She named them one by one. They bowed low, even Starion

under Mirain's stern eye. Elian did not bow. She came to the emperor, her shock well hidden, her smile warm and no more than a little unsteady. He took her hands, raised them to his lips. Neither spoke. There was too much to say, and too little. Sevayin, watching, swallowed hard. She knew what they had been once. The songs were full of it. She had known that he still loved this one whom he had lost. She had not known that her mother loved him a little still. Perhaps more than a little.

Elian drew back. Her smile died; she averted her face so that he might not see her brimming eyes. Sevayin saw and held her peace; but she reached for her mother's hand. It was thin and cold. It did not pull away, but closed tightly about Sevayin's fingers, drawing from them a glimmer of comfort.

Mirain faced his rival. He was all that Ziad-Ilarios was not: hale, strong, young in body and great in power. But they were both imperial. Mirain acknowledged it. He bent his head, sketched a gesture of respect. "It seems that we are allies after all," he said.

"And kinsmen," Ziad-Ilarios responded, "after all. I find that I am not displeased."

"My daughter has chosen well, if not entirely wisely."

"My son has chosen as he could not but choose. So too must we."

"And your eldest son? I do not see him. How has he chosen?"

"For himself." Ziad-Ilarios' irony had no bitterness in it. "He has returned to his old allies, lest they suspect that he has betrayed them. He will aid us as he can."

"He might have been better dead."

Ziad-Ilarios smiled with terrible gentleness. "Perhaps. But he has yet to betray me openly. Even were he not my son, I would not condemn him to death for simple suspicion." He raised his hand, ending the matter, inviting Mirain to his side. "The gate waits upon our opening. Will you begin, son of Avaryan?"

Mirain bowed to his courtesy. The mages of the Sun went where their lord's will bade them, weaving into the Asanian circle. It strained, resisting. Eyes glittered; tempers sparked.

It was Starion, wild Starion, who broke the wall. His mate in power was young and comely and very much a woman, and by good fortune, a lightmage, a priestess of Uvarra. His body drew him toward her; his hair caught her eye and his face held it, and won from her a blush and a smile. They had met before they knew it, clasped hands and power, and laughed both at once, both alike, for the wonder of the meeting.

The rest moved then. Light met dark, thrust, parried, struggled and twisted and locked. Their very hostility was strength, their sundering a bond as firm as forged iron, holding them ever joined and ever apart.

Out of the weaving rose wonder, and a flare of joy that was half terror. They were strong. They were *strong*.

The terror was Sevayin's. Body and power shaped the center of the circle, her body clinging fiercely to Hirel's, her power drawing its potency from his presence. And they were the strongest. Mirain himself, great flaming splendor, was less than they.

It was the two of them, and the child they had made. Because she was what she was and had been, and because Hirel was what he was: the Sun and the Lion mated before all gods who were. The third made them greater than any three apart.

The circle was in her hands. Had fallen into them. She could not even feign raw strength without skill. She wielded that skill to gather it all. Tensed to thrust it into her father's hands. Paused.

He had no part in the weaving with the dark, although he rested within it, accepting it as grim necessity. There was a sickness in him that he must do even so much. He could not raise the gate. He could not will himself to hold the dark together with the light.

Her love for him touched the borders of pain. From that pain she drew strength to hold the circle. To make it her own. To call on its manifold potencies, and from them to build the gate of the worlds.

Stone by stone she built it, each stone a mage's soul, mortared with power. Such magic had wrought the unfading gate at the Heart of the World, the highest of high magics, the blackest of black sorceries: sacrifice of souls for the gate's sake. This need not endure so long. Only long enough to shatter a conspiracy. The lesser powers that were her stones would know no more than weariness and an ache or two, and perhaps a little more. Starion was very much taken with his companion of the lintel. They met with force like love, and held with joyful tenacity.

She smiled in the working, even through the beginnings of weariness. Only the capstone remained. She chose him with care, knowing that he would resist. He was part of Mirain. He would not be condemned to helplessness while his foster brother cast dice with death.

Halenan. Her voice rang within the circle. *Halenan of Han-Gilen, you must permit it. No one else has the strength. No one else can hold the gate against the full force of the mages.*

With the eyes of the body she saw his head come up, his body stiffen, his eyes burn with the fire of his resistance. But he submitted. He bowed that high head. He yielded his power into her hands.

She accepted it as the great gift it was, and set it at the summit of the gate. The power flowed full and free. She brought her hands together; she bent her will. What she had wrought with bare power took shape in the living world: a gate indeed, because she saw it so, white stones set on black, and the capstone of its high arch all burning gold.

The mages of its making lay in a circle, linked hand to hand, seeming to sleep. One tawny head lay pillowed on Starion's breast. Power shimmered over them.

Twelve stood within them, four who were royal and four who owed allegiance to the Asanian emperor, and Vadin and Zha'dan and Ulan, and Ziad-Ilarios himself. He had no power, but he had his firm will. He would go. He would witness this great working and see it to its end.

Hirel was his prop, set against all protests. Sevayin had no strength to spare for them. Ulan's mind touched hers, with no power to offer, but the full and potent strength of his kind. It bore her up. She turned her back on fate and her face to the void and cast them all into it.

Void, Prince Orsan had taught her long ago, *seeks ever for form, as form seeks ever to return to void.* She heard him say it now, clear as if he stood beside her, cool and dispassionate, and yet, somehow, loving her. She thrust the love away. She wrought sanity from his words: knowledge; comprehension. Suspended in nothingness, nexus of power, she focused her will. They were mighty, these mages of her circle. They acknowledged no fear. She touched each briefly, imparting strength even as she drew it forth.

The road was simple and sparing of power, and she knew with

soul's certainty that it was guarded. But there was another way. A shorter way by far, but harder, and if she took it, perhaps she would spend all their strength before ever they came to the battle.

Take it. Mirain, and Elian with him, fire and prophecy, and the weft on which they were woven: the Lord of the Northern Realms in the full and quiet surety of his power.

The echo rang sevenfold, with a touch of desperation, private, Hirel-scented: *Father cannot endure the long road. Go swift, Vayin. Go now, and damn the cost.*

Formless, she willed assent. Shaping. Forming. Compelling. The void, gaining substance, gained will to shape itself. She raised the full force of her power. Chaos roared rebellion. She smote it down.

Cold stone. Air cold to bitterness. The warmth of fire. She could not see. She could not hear. All her power was draining away. She clutched at it. Not again. By all the gods, not again.

"Vayin." Hirel, tight with urgency, yet calming her. He was in her mind; she had not lost him. Light grew, limning his face. She always forgot how beautiful he was. She smiled. He scowled, lest he weaken and smile back. "Vayin, it is done. We stand in the Heart of the World. But—"

"But?"

"It is empty," a stranger said, an Asanian, a priestess in black-bordered scarlet. Sevayin wondered fleetingly which deity she served. It mattered little here.

Sevayin struggled to her feet. She had fallen by the fire, which burned as it had always burned, unwearied. Between the fire and the circle shimmered their gate; most of them stood near it, close together, taut and wary. Mirain roved the hall like a cat in a strange lair, and Ulan walked as his shadow, growling softly at the shifting world-walls.

"It is an ambush," said Ziad-Ilarios. He took the seat which Prince Orsan had so often favored. His voice and his face startled Sevayin, for they were strong, as if the power in its working had given him sustenance. His eyes were clear, bright, fascinated. They flicked round the chamber, taking it in. "Mark you," he said. "They tempt us with emptiness. They wait for us to betray ourselves; to become complacent; to let our guard fall."

Mirain halted, spun on his heel. "Yes. Yes, I sense them." He returned to the fire. It bent toward him. He laughed, spread his arms wide. "Come my enemies. Come and face me."

"Enemies not by our choice." The Master of the Guild stood in the hall, leaning on his staffs. Behind him a worldgate shimmered, changing. So with each: thrice nine gates, thrice nine mages, light joining with dark as the circle closed. Sevayin knew Baran of Endros, and the witch of the Zhil'ari, and Orozia refusing to meet her eyes. The rest were familiar strangers, faces from her captivity, silent and nameless. Some smiled. Some were only implacable.

Last of them came Aranos in his princely finery. He neither smiled nor was implacable. He wore no expression at all.

Mirain set fists on hips and tilted his head. He looked like a boy: a young cockerel with no wits to spare for honest fear. "What, guildmaster! Were you compelled to plot my death?"

"You have compelled us," the master said.

"Because I would not abandon my truth for your fabric of lies?"

"Because you will destroy all that is not of your truth."

Mirain laughed, light and easy. "Such destruction! A little matter of war and conquest; a city or two fallen. I have preserved life where it has consented to be preserved, and bidden my mages to heal when they have done with destroying. If I have been ruthless, I have been so only where mercy has failed. That is a king's fate, guildmaster, and his grim duty."

"Granted," the master said willingly. "You have ruled well, little corrupted by the immensity of your power: which alone would prove to me that you are the son of a god. Yet still you are our enemy. You have destroyed all worship but that of Avaryan; you have slain or driven out all mages but those of the light. And not only of the light, but of your light, which bows to your god and names you sole and highest master. Your Avaryan suffers no god before him; your magecraft suffers no power beside it."

"All others are corruptions of the truth."

"Corruptions? Or true faces? You thunder denunciations of Uveryen's sacrifices. What of all her temples sought out and destroyed, her priesthood slaughtered to the last novice, her rites and her holy things ground into the dust? For every temple, one man would die, perhaps, in a year; or if the observance were strict, one in each dark of Greatmoon. Abominable; horrible; and no matter that few of these sacrifices were aught but willing. And how many died in your purgings? Hundreds? Thousands? How many went to the fire, how many to the torture, for the mere invoking of the goddess' name? And all to save one life in every Greatmoon-cycle."

Mirain's lightness had gone all dark. He straightened; his face hardened. The boy was gone. The king stood in his majesty, his masks forsaken. "I cast down darkness wherever it rises."

"But what is darkness?" the mage demanded. "Can it be no more than that which dares to oppose you? You are a just king; you temper your justice with mercy. You even suffer your people to contest your judgments. Save in one thing only. Avaryan must be worshipped as you worship him. Power must be wielded as you wield it."

Mirain's voice came softer still, scarcely more than a whisper. "And for that I must die? That I do not wield power as you wield it?"

The mage smiled sadly. "To your eyes, no doubt, it would seem so. You have shown yourself incapable of comprehending the truth which lies behind all magics. Light is mighty, and it is beautiful, and it is most congenial to the human spirit. But no man can live forever under the sun. It burns him; it withers him; at last it consumes him. Remember the Sun-death of your order."

"It was swifter by far than the cold-death of the goddess."

"Extremes, both. And necessary. The day must have its night. The light must have its dark. The worlds hang in the balance; it is delicate, and its laws are ineluctable. For every flame there is a spear of night. For every good an evil; for every day of grief a day of gladness. One cannot be without the other."

"Sophistry," said Mirain, cold with contempt. "The goddess slips her chains. I would bind her fast for all of time."

"Do that, and you destroy us all. It is the law. If the light rules, so in its turn must the dark. Win us a thousand years under your god and you gain a thousand more under your goddess. We can live in the light, though in the end it burns us. In the dark we would wither away."

Mirain closed face and mind against that vision. "I will chain her. From the world's throne I will do it, and none shall stand against me."

"First," said the master, "you must come to it." He advanced slowly, and his circle advanced with him, closing upon the allies and the shimmer of their gate.

Mirain drew back into the circle. He was calm, alert, unfrightened. His power gathered to his center. Elian and Vadin, lent theirs to it. And after a moment, Sevayin, drawing in the others. Ulan set himself on guard by her side, Hirel by his father's. Wise child. She sat on her heels to ease her body's burden, and let herself be power purely, hilt and guard of the sword in her father's hand.

The mages struck hard and swiftly, and full upon Mirain. He staggered. His hands caught at the two who stood with him, Ianyn lord, Gileni lady. The mages took no notice of them, recked nothing of the unity which they made. The power struck at their center. Again. Again. It left no time to parry, no breathing space, no hope of subtlety. No need. They were many, the mages; they were strong; they willed Mirain's destruction. They did not care how they wrought it, if only he was destroyed.

Sevayin could not even cry protest. A great blow sundered her from the weaving, cast her into the living world. She crouched, struggling to breathe. All her mages were fallen, her father and her mother and her name's kin stricken to their knees in a whirlwind of power. With a mighty effort they brought up their hands. Fires leaped from them. The wind shrieked, buffeting them, beating them down.

Laboriously Sevayin straightened her back. Ulan sprawled beside her. His mind was dark, his flanks unmoving. Men hemmed her in. Mages. Strangers.

One came to face her, and she understood. Aranos was not smiling. Not quite.

Her eyes flashed beyond the circle. There was another. Ziad-Ilarios sat in it. Hirel struggled in strong hands. She lashed out with her power.

The blow recoiled upon her. It laid her low. Sundered from her kin. Sundered from her brother-in-fur. Sundered from her prince. Sundered, all sundered.

Hands stroked her. Meant to soothe; drove her all but mad.

Mages held her. They were strong. She spat in Aranos' face.

He regarded her coolly, still smiling. "I chose," he said, "long ago. My brother has served his purpose; he has begotten the child who will rule our twofold empires. You may keep him if it pleases you, though we must draw his claws. Excise his power; render him fit for service in the harem."

"Only if you suffer it first."

He was amused and slightly scandalized. "I shall have to keep you in lovers, I see. And keep you with child, until it tames you."

"You'll kill me before you tame me."

"I will not. I require you alive and obedient. Have you no gratitude? My erstwhile allies would have slain you. I not only let you live; I grant you your beloved. I will cherish you, Sunlady, and raise your children as my own."

He was pleased with himself. He thought that he was generous. He expected her defiance; he did not let it prick him. That a great war of magery roared and flamed without him, concerned him not at all.

"Come," he said, "be wise. Your father must fall, as you yourself have endeavored to make certain. Mine is dead already. My brother dies unless you accept the inevitable."

She stared at him, loathing that miniature mockery of Hirel's face. "You did it for me," she said.

"I did it for a twofold throne. But also," he conceded, "once I had seen you, for your own sake. I will not taint you with fleshly desire. I wish only to possess you. To feast, on occasion, upon your beauty."

She lunged. Her captors were caught off guard. She fell upon Aranos. He was a serpent indeed, stronger by far than he looked, and fanged. Steel flashed past her eyes. She snatched, caught a wrist as slender as the blade. She wrested it from his grasp. Thrust herself up, graceless, whirling. Men fell back. She laughed. She slashed through the second circle.

Hirel spat a curse. He was—almost—free. Blades flashed. Sevayin darted toward him.

A knife's edge lay across his throat. She halted, gasping. The blade eased a fraction. Its bearer smiled, approving her prudence.

She hardly knew. She saw only the bead of blood swelling on Hirel's neck.

She turned slowly. No one touched her. Ziad-Ilarios had fallen from his seat onto his face. He lay unmoving. There was blood on his hands, pooling from beneath him.

Aranos had regained his feet. He was amused no longer. "You have a man's spirit," he said. "Still. Be sure of this, my lady: I will break it."

He approached her. The circles parted for him. He cradled his hand. Perhaps she had broken it. He paused to regard his brother, coolly, without either hatred or pleasure; paused longer over his father. "I regret this," he said. "He deserved a better death."

"Better? How better? In bed, of poison?"

"In bed, in his palace, of the sickness which had all but taken him."

"Which, no doubt, he owed to you."

"No," said Aranos. "I would never have slain him so slowly, or in so much pain." He held out his unwounded hand. "Come."

He set power in the simple word; and compulsion; and unshakable will. She knew the shape and the taste of it. The mystery and the sacrifice. And no god to make it splendid; to give back warmth where warmth was forsaken. Cold heart, cold purity. Cold self turned inward upon itself, forgetting joy, abandoning desire.

She was light to him. Light and fire. He recoiled from her. He yearned toward her. He bent all his strength upon her.

It crushed her down and down. Alone, sundered from her power's center, she could not stand against him. He stretched out his hands. His power wrought chains to bind her. His fingers curved to close upon her arms; to claim her. He smiled, tasting the sweetness of his victory.

She struck with steel. He recoiled. Too slow. The blade bit flesh: brow, temple, cheek. Blood sprang.

The mage with the knife cried out, abandoning his prisoner. The weapon flew from his hand. Slow, slow. They were all crawling-slow. It keened past her neck, cleaving air where her throat had been.

Aranos made no sound. He leaped; he bore her back, down. Her arm struck first, brutally. The knife fell from shocked and senseless fingers. His power took its edge from pain, its strength from blood. It closed jaws upon her mind.

Beauty without will was beauty still. Beauty without mind, without spirit, without resistance. "I will have you," he said. "I will own you utterly."

She raked nails across his bleeding face.

He gasped, but he laughed. She had barely raised a welt: her nails were cut warrior-short, the better to wield dagger and sword. He raised a single jeweled claw and set it gently, gently, just below her eye. "Will you yield after I have blinded these lovely eyes? Or will you yield now, while you have all of your senses?"

She closed teeth on his arm. Her power rallied, reared up.

Shadow loomed behind him. She throttled despair.

He stiffened: pain of body, pain of mind. Shock. Incredulity. He arched backward, tearing his arm from her teeth. She gagged on blood. He twisted, clawing.

Ulan squalled in rage and pain, and tossed his wounded head. He snapped; caught the slender throat; tore.

Aranos' eyes were wide, astonished. His hands closed uselessly on shadows. He fell broken, a fragile thing of bones and blood and tattered skin.

And yet he smiled, as if it were a mighty jest: that he of all men living should die as a beast dies, and for this. An outland beauty; an outland fire.

Hirel was there. Love that she could understand; desire without taint of corruption. He dragged her up, or she dragged herself. She had no strength to waste in caring which it was. Aranos' servants were scattered: lost, wavering, waking to fear. Some already had fled. None of them tried to recapture their prey.

Sevayin first, Hirel after, fell upon Ulan. He was bleeding, yet he was grimly content, as ever at a kill well made.

He gave them strength. They linked hands over his back. Hirel's grief struck her, wrought of fire, edged in royal ice. Not only for his father. For the one who, after all, had been his brother.

It was a weapon. She sheathed it in her power. Grief, wrath—there was no time. Aranos had reft Mirain of all her strength; and through it of the bond, the union of mages. They were all fallen, their power taken or held prisoner. He was alone, he and the two who shared his soul.

He held. Battered, beaten, he held. Mages had fallen before him. Their power had gone to swell his own.

But it was ebbing fast. They were too many and too strong; too ruthless. Neither hatred nor vengeance drove them. They were cold and they were steady, implacable, willing him to fall.

Sevayin's teeth bared. She hated. She hated with crystal purity. She raised her power through the burning glass that was her lover. She loosed it in the fire of her hand. She joined it to Mirain's. The pain was terrible; unbearable. But she had borne greater in the fires of the change. She remembered. She firmed her will with the memory.

And the mages wavered. Their blows fell awry. One toppled, keening: a youth in violet, seared by the Sun's fire.

Sevayin left Hirel half lying on Ulan's back, rapt in the perfection of power. She inched toward Mirain. The mages dared not strike her. Her child was too precious. They raised their power like a hand, closing about her wrist, forcing it down, driving her back and back. She let them quench the *Kasar*. She twisted round their hindrance, flung herself toward her father. The floor caught her; she cried out, short and sharp, more in surprise than in pain. But her hand gripped his. She drew herself to him, wrapped her arms about him, held fast.

The silence was thunderous, in mind as in body. Sevayin lifted her head, met the guildmaster's stare. "Now," she said, "kill him."

"Let him go," said the master.

She set her body the more firmly between them. Mirain knelt motionless, his eyes closed. His branded hand lay half curled on his thigh, trembling a very little. Its pain was the twin to hers.

For a long while no one moved. One by one, Elian and Vadin stumbled to their feet. Hirel came dreamwalking toward them, yet clear-eyed within it, smiling, being power purely. They linked hands like children in a dance, and were still.

"Sarevadin," the guildmaster said, "you swore a vow. Have you forgotten it?"

"I have sworn nothing," she said.

"You have," he said. "In accepting the change. In shaping yourself for peace. Now you see that the balance cannot endure while he lives, nor can the war be ended. Will you honor the compact? Or will you be forsworn?"

Her body was leaden heavy; Mirain had turned to stone in her arms. "I never agreed to watch you slaughter my father."

"We are sworn to peace. We cannot gain it while he lives."

"You will not—"

Mirain's hands closed upon her wrists, prying her free, thrusting her back. His eyes tore her soul. "You have sworn," he said. "Honor your oath."

She struggled uselessly. "I have not! They promised me. You would live."

"You gave yourself into their hands. You surrendered your manhood for peace. Their peace. Which is only assured if I am dead."

"You are all mad!" She broke his grip, wheeled. "I will have *my* peace. Two emperors upon two thrones; myself wedded to Asanion's heir; our son heir of the empires. No war. No killing. No constant, relentless, implacable resistance. Will you be sane or must I raise my power?"

"It is too late for sanity," the guildmaster said.

"Far too late," said Mirain, lifting his hand.

The mages whirled to the attack. Daggers glittered; Hirel cried out. Blood fountained over his hands. Vadin sagged in them.

Sevayin cried out in rage and despair. They had come for a clash of power, not for a battle of bronze and grey iron. Only Ulan was glad. He roared and sprang. Mages fell. Blood stained the stones.

She clutched at the rags of her magery. Hirel left Vadin lying, sprang to ward her with his body. He had his two swords, Olenyai weapons, lean and wicked as cats' claws. She snatched one, won it from his startlement.

No one would touch her. Ulan crouched at bay on the very brink of the fire. Mirain stood back to back with Elian, blades in their hands.

Vadin was up. Bleeding, staggering, blessedly alive. Smiling at the mages, a bared-teeth smile. "So," he said. "This is the honor of your guild. Sword-honor. Traitors' honor." He laughed and swept out his blades, sword and long wicked knife. "Look you! I can fight as foul as any mage."

He whirled still laughing, leaped, cut down the Zhil'ari witch. A mage, death-driven, sprang full upon him. Elian's knife caught the man in the air. He fell sprawling, clutching at her. She stumbled, swayed. He dragged her with him as he died.

She struggled wildly in his deathgrip. Broke it. Surged up.

She was forgotten. They were all forgotten. Knives closed in upon Mirain. Power sang in discord, pitched for his mind's ears, dulling them, sapping his strength. Alone, he could not match them. There were too many. He crouched, eyes glittering, lips drawn back in a fierce panther-smile. He had always loved a battle.

Elian caught a blade as it licked toward Mirain's back, turned it, closed with its bearer.

"No," whispered Sevayin. She had dreamed it. Just so. The hall of stone, the figured walls, the fire. The guildmaster standing apart, dispassionate. The Asanian emperor sprawled before a wooden throne. Mirain beset, battling for his life. Vadin Uthanyas down once more, wounded unto death; and in his lord no strength to bring him back, no time to begin. Hirel flung out of the battle, wavering against the great grey cat, stunned in the shattering of power's bonds.

And first and last and most terrible, Elian Kalirien locked body to body with a black sorcerer, a man tall and strong and skilled, fierce in his hatred of all that she was.

"No," Sevayin said, louder. She shifted her grip on the swordhilt. It balanced well. She could not say the same for herself. The combatants twisted, twined. Elian's hair had escaped its net; she whipped it across the mage's face. He recoiled. Sevayin tensed to spring. A strong body thrust her aside, wrenched the blade from her hand. She stood gaping. She had seen Ziad-Ilarios fall. She had seen him die.

He should be dead. His wound was mortal. He moved on will alone, and on something very like a seer's certainty. He had come for this. He had lived for it. He sprang, blade shortened, stabbing. The mage bellowed, spun, slashed. Elian lunged for the hand, Ilarios for the heart. Their eyes met across the straining body of their enemy. They smiled the same swift smile. Bright, wild, daring death itself to touch them.

The fine Asanian steel plunged through flesh and bone, drinking deep. The mage gasped, astonished; and toppled.

Ziad-Ilarios sank down. His golden robe was scarlet. His life ebbed with the tide of his blood. His smile had died, his last sweet madness faded. But he was content. "She lives," he said distinctly. "I have died in her place. I could not have died a better death."

Sevayin swayed. Her heart thudded. The child was too still, in a stabbing of small pains. She quelled them with stiffened hands and stiffened mind. She could not see her mother.

Under the cloaked and lifeless bulk, a body stirred. Sevayin heaved the carrion away. Beginning to understand; crying out against the understanding.

Elian lay on her back, pooled in blood. But the man had hardly bled: the blade was still in him. Sevayin dropped to her knees. Elian looked up at her and smiled. She was all scarlet.

Her throat.

Sevayin's mind was very clear. For a timeless moment, she thanked all the gods that Ziad-Ilarios had died before he knew that he had failed. For even as the mage fell dying, he had remembered his weapon. Perhaps Elian had aided him: snatching at his hand, casting it awry as his weight bore her down, averting it from eyes or heart to the undefended throat. It had cut deep. Her life poured out of her, driven by her frantic heart. Sevayin could not stop it.

Mirain. Mirain was a greater healer than Sevayin would ever be. If she could only slow the torrent. If he could—

A wolf was howling.

It was Mirain. Battling to break free, trapped, hedged in bronze and in power. Going mad, beast-mad.

"Father!" cried Sevayin. Her power lashed through the white agony of magewalls. Struck his, seized Hirel's, sucked in the magegate itself.

Blades flared molten, dropped. The gate could not endure the force of it. Not her power flaming through it, and the mages rising against her, and the magefire itself roaring to meet them. Its stones writhed in agony. They were not strong enough. They could not give as she demanded.

For Mirain they would give it. She wielded them without mercy. They writhed in her grasp. One rose above them, separate, yet binding himself to them. *Vadin,* her mind whispered, protesting. He was dying. He could not. He must not.

He fitted himself to her hand. He was strong in this his second death; he had no fear of it. He wielded her as she wielded him, to set his oathbrother free.

The gate wavered. A little more, she begged it. Only a little. She fed the fires with her own substance.

No. Vadin, clear in her mind. *Will you kill your son? Back, now; this fight is mine.*

She struggled. He had not her strength, even now, but he had learned his skill from Mirain himself. He eased her out and away. He poised, paused. He made himself a spear, and plunged full into the mages' wall.

It burst in a shower of fire; the spear burst with it, exulting.

Mirain bestrode his lady's body and cried aloud. The gate was gone. Vadin was gone. Elian died even as Mirain bent to heal her.

But he who had raised the dead had no awe of death. Her soul eluded him; he pursued it. He was the Son of the Sun. He would not let her die.

You must. Hers was no witless flitting soul, befuddled with its freedom. She barred the way to him, even to him who was half a god. Perhaps she grieved that she must do it. She was stern before him and before all the silent helpless mages. *The gods are not mocked. Go, Mirain An-Sh'Endor. Leave me to my peace.*

He fought the truth of it. All death's ways had closed against him, save only his own. He contemplated it. He yearned for it.

But he was the Sunborn. He had been that before ever wife or brother came to share his soul. He was the high god's son, the Sword of Avaryan, the lord of the eastern world. The lord of the west was dead. He had a world to claim.

In the looming silence, he turned. No madness marred his face. He looked quiet and sane and worn to the bone. His hands opened and closed. No hilt came to fill them. Sevayin had destroyed them all.

He sank to one knee. With utmost gentleness he lifted his empress, his brother. He cradled them. He murmured a word, two. Sevayin did not try to understand. Gently again he laid them down, straightening their limbs, smoothing their hair, closing their eyes. He kissed them both, brow, lips, lingering.

He rose. Sevayin shivered. He was utterly, terribly calm. He raised his hand.

Twice nine mages yet remained. Most were wounded. But they had no fear of him. They had robbed him of the greater part of his soul.

Limping, halting, they came together. They raised their shields. They waited for the lightning to fall.

PART FIVE

Hirel Uverias

Twenty-Five

THE WORLD WAS ENDING. HIREL WAS NOT UNCOMFORTABLE, contemplating it. His neck stung where the knife had cut, but the bladesman was gone, felled or fled. No one else had touched him. He was the merest shadow of nothing: the Sunchild's familiar. He had no power in himself; his steel they would not face. He could not make them face it.

He had been angry, a moment or an age ago. It did not matter now. Nothing mattered but that his death was waiting. It was strangely beautiful. It had Uvarra's face.

If he lived, he would grieve: for his father, for the Lord Vadin, for the Lady Kalirien. But if he must die, he preferred to do it by his lady's side. His empress' now. He smiled a little at the irony of it, setting his hands upon her shoulders. She scarcely knew that he was there, but her body let him draw it back against him. Tremors racked it: exhaustion, fear, more pain than Hirel could easily bear. He caught his breath, set his teeth, held fast.

And the lightning fell.

There was splendor in it. Like mountains falling; like a storm upon the sea. The castle rocked beneath their feet. Whips of levin-fire lashed above their heads. The magefire roared to the roof; the world-walls writhed with visions of madness.

Mirain was a white flame in the heart of it. They had erred, the mages, in their lofty wisdom. They had slain the two who shared his self: thinking so to weaken him, to bring him into their power. So had they done with that part of him which was mortal man, that part which had seemed the whole of him. Which had been but the veil over the truth: the bonds that bound the light.

The son of the Ianyn priestess was gone. Avaryan's son stood forth in all his terrible splendor. He was pure power and pure wrath, bodiless, blinding. He would destroy those who had destroyed his empress and his brother; in the doing he might well destroy himself; and he would not care. No more than does a god when he has risen in his rage.

"Father," Sevayin said, soft yet clear. "Father." She kept saying it. Her own power had touched his once, seeking to calm him; much of her pain was the payment. He heeded her voice no more than he had her mind-cry. Mere human need, mere human strength. Not even for the light of the god in her would he turn from his course.

"Mirain." His name rang like a gong. "Mirain An-Sh'Endor."

The flame of him flickered, turning, bending toward the magefire. He spat power. The fire drank it like wine. Again the deep voice spoke. "Mirain An-Sh'Endor."

Amid the terrible brightness that had been the Sunborn, a face flickered. Eyes, dark and almost soft, entranced. The lips smiled. The power caught a handful of lightnings and cast them into the fire.

A man walked out of it as out of a gate. A young sunbird in Zhil'ari finery. His name hovered on Hirel's tongue. Zha'dan. Hirel had thought him dead. He limped: he bore a wound. But he was still bright irrepressible Zhaniedan, giving way with deep respect to the one whom he had brought. An old man, bent and grey, cloaked in black.

The old man straightened. He was tall, broad of shoulder even in his age, and perhaps stronger than he seemed.

The Prince of Han-Gilen let fall his cloak, which was not black but deepest green, and faced the pillar of fire. His hand brushed the peak of it, lightly. A breath escaped him: his only tribute to that awful strength.

Hirel reeled in sudden darkness. The flame was snuffed out. Shadow filled its place. Mirain on his knees in his black kilt, the gold of belt and armlets, torque and earrings and braids, a pallid gleam after the splendor that had been. He raised his head. His face was a skull, stripped of youth and of hope, but never of strength.

The Red Prince passed him, dropped to the floor beside Elian's body. "Daughter," he said with all the sadness in the worlds. "Ah, daughter, if you could but have waited, this would never have been." His voice died of its own weight. He kissed her brow and rose, laboring. They watched him. Hirel wondered why the mages had not struck him down.

"Because," Sevayin said, clear and bitter, "he is one of them." She dragged herself up. "Go on, Grandfather. Kill him before he gets his senses back."

The old man did not look at her. He faced Mirain, who frowned like a man in the throes of bafflement. Trying to remember. Trying to remember why he should remember.

"He led them!" Sevayin cried in a passion of despair. "He began it all. Now he ends it. Now it is all ended."

Mirain studied his foster father's face. He bowed his head a fraction. "Of course it would be you." He smiled faintly. "It has always been you. I saw your mark upon my daughter's soul. I thought only that it was her love for you, and the teaching which you gave her when she was my son. Who but you could have wrought the change?"

"No one," Prince Orsan said. "It was all mine, all this making. Now, as my lady says, I must end it."

"Or I." Mirain stood, light and swift and deadly. "Thrice nine mages could not fell me. Would you venture it, O prince of traitors?"

"I have no need. The Asanian emperor is dead. His successor stands at your daughter's back, soul-woven with her. Will you slay them? Or will you grant them the peace for which they have fought?"

"There is no peace but death."

"For you," said the prince, "there is not."

Mirain laughed bitterly. "How you all must hate me!"

"No." The prince was almost gentle. "No, Mirain. Will you not bow to defeat? In truth, it is a victory."

"My lady always told me that I had no grace in defeat. And truly I have none. I do not lose battles, prince. I do not know how."

"Perhaps it is time you learned."

"No," said Mirain. "I would have made our world a citadel of the light. You have condemned it forever to the outlands of the dark."

"So be it," Prince Orsan said.

Mirain sighed, drooping, as if weariness had mastered him. The Red Prince stretched out a hand. Perhaps in compassion; perhaps in warning. Mirain reared up like a serpent striking.

Sevayin tore herself from Hirel's hands. She sprang between her father and her mother's father. Her power roared through Hirel's brain.

The choice consumed but the flicker of a moment. It endured for an eternity. Father, grandfather. Light, light and dark together. Love, love turned to hate. Grief and grief, and no joy in any of it, no comfort and no hope.

She struck. It nearly slew her. But Mirain's power wavered the merest degree. In that weakened instant, Prince Orsan pierced his shields. Plunged deep and deep, and seized his heart, and closed.

His eyes opened wide, fixed upon his death. He knew it. He comprehended it. All of it: betrayal, and necessity, and bitter choosing. With his last desperate strength he lunged, seized the prince, seized his daughter, cast them all into the fire.

Someone howled. Hirel's throat was raw. He was blind, deaf, stunned. She was gone. He had nothing left.

Only death.

He laughed in the emptiness. For if she saw truth, he would have her back; if his was the way of the worlds, and death was mere oblivion, it would not matter.

No reasonable man would love a woman so much.

No reasonable man would have given his soul to Sevayin Is'kirien.

He was still laughing as he fell into the fire's arms.

It hurt. By all the nonexistent gods, it hurt. But it did not burn.

It was bitter cold, fiery cold, and it struck him a millionfold: each atom of his being tormented separately and exquisitely, in endless variety. And yet his scattered being laughed. What a splendid irony it would be, if the end of this pain found him in woman's semblance. Then it would all begin again, the whole mad comedy.

Pain did not like to be laughed at. It flung his body together with claws of ice, thrust his mind all battered into the midst of it, cast him down in stillness.

He was all a great bruise. Did the dead know such petty pain? He counted his bones; he had them all, etched in aches. The head was his own, the hands, the body blessedly his own. Even dead, he was the beginning of a man.

"If this is hell," he said to the silent dark, "it is a poor thing. Where are the mighty torments? Where are the agonies of the damned?"

"Perhaps," a deep voice responded with a touch of irony, "we are in paradise." A body moved; a hand groped along Hirel's arm, tightening on it. Hirel's mind quivered at a sudden mothwing touch. Slow light grew. "Ah," said Prince Orsan with a scholar's cool pleasure. "You are stronger than I thought."

Hirel spat the shortest curse he knew. It was also the most appalling. "What am I? A candle for any mage's lighting?"

"Hardly," said the prince. "I am your lady's master. Her power is woven with mine. As, therefore, is yours."

"We are not dead." Hirel's voice was flat. He rose, letting his body protest itself into speechlessness, and glanced about. It was a little disconcerting: he was the center of the light, a sheen of gold that waxed as his strength grew.

If one stood in the heart of a diamond. If that diamond's center were a flaw, black without light, a shape as simple as an altar. If two stood frozen, face to face across the altar, man and woman both in black, and a grey shadow-cat crouched at its foot. If any of it were possible, it would be this place.

"*Andal'ar 'Varyan*," Prince Orsan said. "The Tower of the Sun atop Avaryan's Throne in Endros of the Sunborn." He spoke the names with a certain somber grandeur, and a suggestion of despair. "We stand in the very heart's center of the Sunborn's power."

Mirain turned. The man and the god had come together. Once

before, Hirel had seen him so, standing in front of the Throne of the Sun. His grief had not diminished him. His loss had not cast him down. He remained Mirain An-Sh'Endor, the mighty one, the unconquerable king.

Hirel's soul knit with a quivering sigh. Sevayin was beside him. He had not seen her come. He looked at her, and she was all that her father was. And more. Because her mortality bound her; because she was she, Sarevadin.

He laid himself open to her, for the battle which now must come.

"No," Prince Orsan said. "The great wars are ended. The reign of the Sunborn is past."

He had come to the center of the light. He was no stronger here, no younger, and no less powerful.

"Tell me now," said Mirain, soft and calm. "Here at the end of things. Who is my father?"

"You are Avaryan's son," the Red Prince answered him.

Mirain held out his burning hand. "Swear on this, O weaver of webs. Swear that you had no part in my begetting."

"I cannot."

Mirain laughed. It was light, free. "You dare not. I think that you created me as has so often been proclaimed. The Hundred Realms had need of a king to rule them all; therefore you wrought me, setting me in the womb of an outland mother, casting upon her a spell of lies and dreams. But your spell succeeded beyond your wildest hopes, beyond your blackest fears. The god himself came to fill you. Thus indeed he begot me, but through your flesh and your seed."

"I summoned him," the Red Prince said. "It was the rite, as well you know: the calling of the god to his bride. My foresight brought me to it; the god named his chosen through my power. Beyond that, I do not remember. Perhaps indeed he wielded me. Perhaps he had no need. I do not seek to define the limits of divinity."

"Your working," said Mirain. "Your working still, for all that you deny it. The world has shaped itself as you would have it. Now dare you dream that I will do the same?"

"What is left in the light for you? Your lady is dead. Your soul's brother has gone back to the night from which you called him."

"Before they were part of me, I was Mirain."

"You can live without them? You can endure the emptiness in heart and power?"

Mirain stiffened. His eyes closed; his jaw set. A spasm of grief twisted his face. It passed before the strength of his will. "My armies wait for me. My war is not yet ended."

"I think," said the Red Prince, "that it is." His hand took in the two who stood in silence: Hirel because he had no part in it, Sevayin because she could not find the words to speak. Her hands were locked in his, braced above the child in her belly. "There is the end of it. You have refused it. Be wise at last, son of my heart. Accept this that you yourself have yearned for."

"And I?" Mirain demanded. "Am I to fall upon my sword?"

Sevayin started forward, breaking away from Hirel. "No, Father. You can rule as you have ruled, until the god comes to take you. Keruvarion is yours. Asanion is mine to share with my emperor. Our son will hold them both."

He could see it. It was in his eyes. Almost, they smiled.

But the prince said, "How long will you be content? How long before it begins to rankle in you? You have struck deep into the heart of Asanion. Will you insist that all you have won is yours?"

"He has won nothing yet," said Hirel.

Sevayin spun upon him. And back, furious, upon her father.

"Yes," Prince Orsan said. "There is no peace while you live, Mirain An-Sh'Endor."

"You will have to kill me with your own hands," said Mirain.

And Sevayin said very softly, "You will have to slay me if you hope to touch him."

The Red Prince looked at them all. His eyes sparked at last with Gileni temper. "Was ever a man beset by such a brood of royal intransigents?" In three swift strides he was before Mirain. He was very much the taller, and he was not to be towered over, even by the Sunborn. He did what Hirel would not have done for worlds: set hands on Mirain's shoulders and held them, looking down into the Sun-bright eyes. "I will slay you if I must. I pray that I may have no need."

He could do it. Mirain smiled. Knowing surely, as did they all, that he himself could take that life which beat so close, end it before the prince could set hand to weapon. And yet, loving him, this master of the masters of kingmakers, this weaver of plots which could dazzle even Asanian wits. Loving him and hating him. "Foster-father." His voice was almost gentle. "Tell me."

Prince Orsan met his smile with one fully as wise and fully as implacable. "There is another way."

"Of course," said Mirain.

"An enchantment." The prince paused. "The Great Spell. The long sleep which lies upon the borders of death."

"But not full within its country." Mirain tilted his head back, the better to meet the prince's gaze. "What profit is there in that? Better and easier that I die. Then at least my soul will be whole again."

"For you, perhaps, there may be no profit. For this world which you have ruled, which you may yet destroy . . . Your daughter has waked to wisdom. She sees that light and dark are one; she knows in truth what power is. To that truth you may come. And if the years pass as I forebode they will pass, a time will come when again the balance is threatened: when Avaryan shall need the Sword which he has forged."

"Thrifty," said Mirain. "And hard. Have you ever laid an easy task on anyone?"

He asked it of Prince Orsan, but he asked it also of one who could not be seen. He did not sound either awed or frightened. Hirel could admire that.

"If I won't do it," he asked, and now he spoke only to the prince, "what will you do?"

"I will do my best to kill you."

"You could fail."

"I could," the prince agreed calmly.

Mirain laughed, sudden and wonderfully light. "And if I do it—a wonder. A splendor of legend; a deed beyond any that I have ever done. But the cost . . ." He sobered. "The cost is very high."

"The great choices do not come cheaply."

Mirain's eyes flashed beyond the prince to Sevayin. They softened a very little. "No," he said. "They do not."

There was a silence. No one moved. Mirain stared wide-eyed into the dark. His mind was as clear to Hirel as if he spoke aloud, its vision shimmering behind Hirel's own eyes. Sleep that was like death, but was not death. Long ages passing. Dreams, perhaps. Awareness trapped in unending night. And at the end of it, a hope too frail to bear the name of prophecy. A foreseeing that might prove founded on falsehood. A waking into utter solitude, utter abandonment, in a world beyond any seer's perceiving.

Better the simple way. A battle of weapons and power. Death if he fell, life and empire if he won. The prince was strong, but he was old; he had never been Mirain's match in combat. Nor even yet could he equal the Sunborn's power.

Mirain drew a long shuddering breath. He looked at his daughter and his daughter's lover. Their hands had met again without their willing it, their bodies touched. Pain swayed him. His hands reached as if to seek the ones who were gone; his power wailed in its solitude. Alone, all alone.

But to die—

He had no fear of it. He knew wholly and truly what it was. And yet . . . "I'm young," he said. "I'm strong. There are years of living left in me."

None of them spoke. Years indeed, Hirel thought. Years of war.

Mirain flung back his head. It burst from him in pain and rage and royal resistance. "I am not called!"

"You are not," Prince Orsan said. "The god will accept you if you go. But he does not summon you into his presence."

Mirain closed his eyes, opened his hands. Hirel's eyes could not bear the brilliance of the *Kasar.* "I am summoned," the emperor said softly. "But not to that.

"Father," he said. "Father, you are not merciful."

"But just," said Orsan, to whom he had not been speaking, "he has always been."

Mirain smiled as a strong man can, even in great pain. He held out his hands, the one that was night, the one that was fire. "And now you see. To the will of a god, even the Sunborn can submit." He bowed his head. "I am yours, O instrument of my father. Do with me as you will."

The Red Prince bowed low. "Not for myself, my lord and my emperor. For the god who is above us all."

Mirain lay upon that table that could have been either bier or altar. Prince Orsan did nothing for an endless while, gazing into darkness. He gathered power, yet not as Hirel had known it, in light and fire. This was quiet, inexorable, immeasurable. Mirain did not move under it, save for his fist, that clenched once, and slowly unclenched.

The Red Prince stood over him. His eyes sparked. Rebellion. Repentance of his choice.

Sevayin trembled under Hirel's hands. Remembering. Living again the terror of great magic chosen and not yet begun. Seeing once more that stern dark face bent above her, pitiless as the face of a god. Hirel tried to think calm into her; to give her strength.

Prince Orsan laid a hand on Mirain's brow and a hand on his breast. Mirain drew a shuddering breath. "Now," he said, low and rough. "Do it now."

The prince bowed his head. "Sleep, my son," he said. "Sleep until the god calls you to your waking."

Mirain smiled. The air was full of power. Throbbing, singing. It filled Hirel. It poured through him. It reft him of will and wit and waking.

He caught at solidity: dark, fire-crowned. She brought back the world.

They bent over the man upon the stone. He woke still, though dimly; he saw them. He smiled. "Children," he murmured. "Children who loved beyond hope and beyond help. I see—I am glad—after all—" His voice faded. "Love one another. Be joyful. Joyful . . . joy . . ."

Sevayin broke down and wept. He never knew. He was kingly in his sleep, and young, and at peace; and on his face the shadow of a smile. Even as she wept she straightened his kilt so that it was seemly, folded his hands upon his breast, laid his braid with care upon his shoulder. She shook off the hands that would have helped her.

Slowly she straightened. Her eyes burned, emptied of their tears. "There has never been anyone like him. There shall never be his like again."

"He was a strong king," Hirel said, "and a true king, and an emperor."

"He was Mirain An-Sh'Endor," the Red Prince said.

Sevayin kissed him. One last tear fell to glitter on his cheek. "Sleep well," she said softly. "Dream long. And when you wake, may you have learned to be wise. To face the dark. To know it; to transcend it."

"Or may you never wake." Prince Orsan signed the still brow. Where his hand passed, light glimmered, shaping words of blessing and of binding. "Remember, O my soul's son. Remember that I loved you."

He turned slowly. He wept like a king, strongly, out of a face of stone. "He has gone beyond us now. His end I cannot see. Perhaps for him there shall be none.

"But for us," he said, "the world is waiting." He bowed low and low. "Empress. My soul is yours, my body, my power, my heart. Do with me as you will."

Sevayin shuddered at the title. At his oath, she raised her clenched fists. He waited, mute. His life was hers for the taking. His title, his power, all that he had been, hers. She could slay him, she could exile him, she could leave him here to go mad and die. For this was the crag of Endros Avaryan, and he was a mortal man, and the curse was strong about them all.

Her hands fell; she breathed deep, trembling. She stepped toward him. He did not move. "I chose you," she said, "in the end. It will be a very long while before I can forgive you. I may never trust you fully. But love . . . love has no logic in it." Her voice cleared, sharpened. "Get up, Grandfather. Since when have you ever bowed to me?"

"Since you became my empress."

"You never bowed to Mother. Or to Father, either. Stop your nonsense now and help me. I don't have the strength for a magegate, and there is no other way out of this place."

"There is one," he said, rising. He took her hand. It stiffened against him, eased slowly, opened. He turned the palm up. The *Kasar* flared and flamed. "Here is that which opens all doors."

"But there are no doors," she said.

"Save this." He met her eyes. "The way is simple. Inward through the *Kasar*. Outward through the Heart of the World."

She frowned. She was very close to the end of her strength. Hirel lent her what he had, hardly caring how he did it. Little by

little her mind cleared. "Inward," she said, fitting her will about
the word. "In." Gathering their threefold awareness. "Ward."
The *Kasar* swelled and bloomed and closed about them, a torrent
of fiery gold. The worlds whirled away.

PART SIX

Sevayin Is'kirien

Twenty-Six

THERE WERE NO ENDINGS. THAT WAS THE TRUTH WHICH RULED the gods. Sevayin would have been a great sage, if she had cared a jot for wisdom.

Inward through the *Kasar*. Outward through the Heart of the World. Simple; inevitable. When she came out of the darkness, it was all changed. The mages laid themselves at her feet and called her empress. She looked down at them and saw no sweetness in revenge. She glanced at her consort. "Hirel?"

He eyed his Olenyai blades, measured the bowed and humble necks. Remembered all the hatred he had borne them.

He raised his empty hands to her, angry, yet bitterly amused. "It is gone," he said. "All of it. I cannot even despise them."

"Nor I. But," she said, "this we can do. We can rule them."

"That has been all our intent," said the guildmaster.

She did not believe him; she did not trust him. But he was hers, he and his mages, while she had strength to bind him. She made them swear fealty to Hirel as to herself; she won from them an oath, that they would do no harm to herself or to her consort, or to the child which she bore.

They made her sleep, all of them together, there outside of the world's time. She wanted to fight them. Her body refused. It was fordone, and it had a child to think of. A living child, dreaming in his warm dark womb, his flame of power burning diamond-bright. The mages had been afraid for him; they would learn to be afraid of him. If he had ever been a simple mortal infant, this night's working had put an end to it.

He would be something new, this heir of Sun and Lion. Something wonderful.

"But of course," said Hirel with his inimitable certainty. "He is our child."

She was not ready to laugh again, not quite yet. But she smiled; she kissed him and said, "I do think I love you, Hirel Uverias."

She slept in her old chamber, cradling her son as Hirel cradled her; and if she dreamed, she remembered nothing of it. When she woke, she ate because she must, but her mind had leaped far ahead. She hardly saw who followed her from the chamber to the hall of fire.

Her worldgate had fallen. She had felled it herself. Vadin, Starion, her poor mages—

Inward through the *Kasar*. Outward through the Heart of the World.

Avaryan was rising. His light lay gentle on the dead. Vadin Uthanyas who had died at last, died fearlessly and joyfully so that the rest might live. His body lay in royal company: Asanian emperor, Varyani empress. Sevayin would mourn. Later. She would reckon up her guilt, when there was time for reckoning. Two armies waited, hating one another. Two herds of princes hot for war. Two empires, two royal cities, two palaces with all their flutter of courtiers. Two lifetimes' worth of battles to make them all one.

She laughed, standing over her dead, because she wanted most to howl. They were all staring. All her mages now, those who would have slain the emperors and those who would have defended them. Each had half succeeded. One alive as wicked fate had promised her, one dead as he had wished to be, both gone where no harm could reach them; where they themselves could do no harm.

So much to do. She opened her arms. "See," she said. "The

morning has come. The war is won. We have a throne to claim, my prince and I. Who dares to gainsay me?"

"I."

She spun upon Hirel in shock and sudden rage.

He stood before her, gold-maned in the morning, his robes in tatters and his eyes black-shadowed and his will indomitable. The mask of his father was in his hand. He raised it; he held it before his face. His voice came forth from it, a stranger's voice, cold and quiet. "I," he repeated. "I am the Emperor of Asanion. I yield my power to no man."

She stalked him, cat-soft. "No man," she said, "certainly. But a woman, Hirel Uverias? A woman of the bright god's line. Mage and queen and bearer of your son."

The golden face was still, inhuman, imperial. It granted nothing. It yielded nothing.

It lowered slowly. She saw his eyes over it, and then his living face, more beautiful than any mask. "And my lover? Are you that, madam?"

"That," she said, "always and ever. But before all else, I am Empress of Keruvarion."

"So." He looked her up and down. His brows met. He bent his eyes upon the mask, turning it in his hands, pondering long and deep within the walls of his mind.

She held herself still. Not even for love of him would she surrender her half of the throne.

"Only half?" he asked her.

"No more," she answered, "and no less."

He raised his hand. She raised her own. His eyes narrowed against the flame of it. He set palm to burning palm. His face was still, but his eyes were all gold. "So be it," said the Emperor of Asanion.